Advance praise for

THE FLIGHT OF SWANS

"Taking one of the loveliest of the Grimm canon, tale #49, 'The Six Swans' (one of my favorites), Sarah McGuire has grounded it with not just one strong young woman but three against a verago who could best Malificent at her evil games. McGuire has the right balance of heroics, poetics, and pratfalls. But it is the long center of the tale, where Ryn—sister to the swans—has to be silent for six long years else her brothers will die—that is simply a *tour de force* where in other, less sure hands, it would certainly have been a *tour de farce*. Brava performance!"

—Jane Yolen

"*The Flight of Swans* whisked me into a medieval world where magic seeps from forests and evil lurks in the most unexpected places. As a fanatic of all things Grimm, I loved how this story wove a fresh take on the classic tale of 'The Six Swans,' showing the power that a determined and courageous girl can have. McGuire's spellbinding writing will embark you on a grand adventure through enchanted forests, far-away lakes, dark caves, and ruined fortresses. (Just be wary of nettles, and keep a stash of cloves close at hand.)"

—Christina Farley, author of the Gilded series and *The Princess and the Page*

The Flight of Swans

Sarah McGuire

Carolrhoda Books
Minneapolis

Carolrhoda Books
A division of Lerner Publishing Group, Inc.
241 First Avenue North
Minneapolis, MN 55401 USA

For reading levels and more information, look up this title at www.lernerbooks.com.

Jacket illustration by Junyi Wu.
Moon illustration by Natalia Petukhova/Shutterstock.com.

Main body text set in Bembo Std regular 12/16.5.
Typeface provided by Monotype Typography.

Library of Congress Cataloging-in-Publication Data

Names: McGuire, Sarah, 1976– author. | Adaptation of (work): Andersen, H. C. (Hans Christian), 1805–1875. Vilde svaner. English.
Title: The flight of swans / Sarah McGuire.
Description: Minneapolis : Carolrhoda, [2018] | Summary: Elaborates on the tale of young princess Ryn, who must be silent for six years to save her brothers after they are turned into swans by their evil stepmother.
Identifiers: LCCN 2017038715 (print) | LCCN 2018007837 (ebook) | ISBN 9781512498516 (eb pdf) | ISBN 9781512440270 (th : alk. paper)
Subjects: | CYAC: Fairy tales. | Princesses—Fiction. | Brothers and sisters—Fiction. | Swans—Fiction. | Blessing and cursing—Fiction.
Classification: LCC PZ8.M17625 (ebook) | LCC PZ8.M17625 Fl 2018 (print) | DDC [Fic]—dc23

LC record available at https://lccn.loc.gov/2017038715

Manufactured in the United States of America
1-42297-26146-5/15/2018

TO THE QUIET ONES

Chapter 1

The exile of the princes of Lacharra didn't begin with swords or spells.

It began inside the castle kitchen with a quest for cloves.

It began with me.

Cooks mistrust anyone with empty hands, so I darted to the nearest table and snatched up a bowl of chopped leeks. Then I shouldered between scullery maids and undercooks as I moved toward the spice pantry.

Perhaps I was foolish. Maybe Father was just sick after being lost so many weeks in the forest. Maybe it was normal for a man newly married to hardly speak to the daughter he'd loved—

Then I remembered last night: Rees, the stable master, and the stable boy being beaten while Father looked on with empty eyes.

Something *had* happened to Father in the forest. He never would have allowed a beating for violating such a small edict, even if the woman he'd married had issued it.

Whatever she banned must be important—even if it was something as simple as cloves.

After last night, Bronwen, the cook, had probably burned them all, but she didn't know about the little bag I'd stashed under the planking.

Clutching the bowl of leeks, I wove past rows of tables covered with baskets of vegetables, poultry being plucked . . .

. . . and right into the path of a white-swathed undercook and her pot of steaming broth.

The undercook screeched and sloshed scalding broth over the floor.

I leaped back, just in time.

And Bronwen—where had she *come* from?—laid her wooden spoon across my shoulders with a sound like thunder.

I dropped my bowl with a yelp and darted away. But I stepped in the leeks I'd just spilled and my feet flew out from under me.

I jolted upright like a puppet whose strings have been yanked.

Bronwen wrenched me back to face her. I scrabbled to free myself but couldn't gain purchase in the mess I'd made.

I saw her raise the spoon to deliver another blow, raised my arm to shield my face, and—

"Ahhh!!! Princess Andaryn!" Bronwen hid the spoon behind her back and released me so quickly I fell at her feet.

Two maids dashed forward. One helped me up—the other began to clean the mess I'd made.

"Your *Highness*!" said Bron. "I didn't know it was you! We're all on edge since the Queen—" She stopped, panicked. "*Not* that we don't think she's a lovely woman and wish every blessing on her for bringing your father out of that accursed forest."

"*I* don't wish any blessing on her." It was out before I could catch myself.

Bron's ruddy cheeks paled, and she peered over her shoulder as if Father's witch-wife herself might appear. She turned back to me with a horribly cheerful expression. "What do you want, Princess? I'll fetch it for you myself."

I'd have preferred the beating with that awful spoon of hers. I hadn't been protecting myself earlier—I didn't want her to recognize me. Just as I feared, the kitchen fell silent as everyone stared at me. I could've cried, and not because my shoulders ached like fire. There'd be no sneaking to the spice pantry now.

And then, bless him, the second of my six older brothers, the one who made every girl in the castle blush, walked into the kitchen.

Mael scowled at me as he put a hand on Bron's shoulder. "I'll take her off your hands, dear woman."

When Bron saw Mael and his dark, curling hair and blue eyes, she dropped her spoon. She had a husband who worked in the forge and four children last count, yet she giggled like a girl when she saw Mael.

Mael might be handsome, but he was my brother, which mostly meant that he was annoying. Except for this one shining moment when every woman's eye was on him.

This was my chance.

I slipped into the spice pantry and pulled up the loose plank in the corner, sighing in relief when I found the bag of cloves. I'd hidden it only because Father and I liked to chew them when we read, and I'd wanted to be sure we never ran out.

Cloves were a valuable spice, of course, but they were still just dried bits of brown twig and bud. Why would Father's new wife have banned them from the castle?

The poor stable boy who'd been discovered with cloves yesterday had been dragged to the throne room. Rees, the stable master who'd always gentled horses for the House of Cynwrig, arrived minutes later. He explained that the boy hadn't heard the Queen's edict, that he'd merely gathered the cloves to make a poultice for an ailing horse.

The Queen had listened gravely . . . then had them both thrashed with a horse whip.

Father—my kind, brave father—hadn't even blinked.

I dropped the plank back into place, then slipped the bag of cloves into a pocket in my under-tunic. I smoothed my skirts as I stood, hands sliding over the dark fabric. My outer gown was loose enough that no one would notice I'd hidden anything under it.

A moment later, I joined Mael and Bron.

Bron was trying to arrange her headscarf, but Mael glared at me. "Where did you go?"

Every eye was on me once again. I looked around the kitchen, searching for an excuse among the vegetables and plucked birds and bowls.

He raised an eyebrow. "Well?"

I didn't speak, just sheepishly pointed at the table of pastries beside the spice pantry.

Bron shook her head and fetched an apple tart for me, my favorite. "Just for you, Princess."

"You're far too kind," said Mael. "We need her to help us present a gift to Father's new bride. And what does she do?"

"Tries to steal a tart," Bron chuckled. She shook a finger at me. "You're growing too old for such antics, Princess."

I wanted to tell her that I'd spent twelve full summers on this earth and was old enough to know that many things were more important than apple tarts.

Instead, I ducked my head.

"Let's go, Ryn." Mael took me by the arm and marched me out of the kitchen and into the cobbled courtyard.

I scurried to keep up with him but kept a hand over the cloves, even though my gown covered them. I couldn't let him guess what I'd done . . . what I planned to do.

I flinched when Mael reached toward me, worried he knew. Instead, he plucked the apple tart from my hand and took a bite.

"That's for making me scour the castle to find you," he said around the tart.

I sagged with relief. He wasn't suspicious. Just annoying.

As always.

He took another bite and pointed out my other five brothers standing impatiently in the center of the courtyard. "I can't believe you sneaked a tart! If I didn't know better, I'd—"

I let loose a well-aimed kick, raking the heel of my shoe down the length of his shin, channeling all my fear into that one movement. Just as I hoped, he forgot the kitchen completely—and dropped the tart he'd stolen from me in the process.

While he bent to rub his shin, I darted away to join the rest of my brothers.

Aiden, the eldest, waited for me, arms folded. "Ryn! Why did you kick him?"

"He deserved it," I answered.

Aiden raised an eyebrow, but he still put an arm around me.

I smiled. Mael wouldn't dare retaliate now that I was under Aiden's protection.

Mael limped up, cursing under his breath. All my brothers stood around me, then—a wall of dark-haired princes in the afternoon sun: Aiden; Mael; the triples, Cadan, Declan, and Gavyn; and my twin, Owain. They'd stood around me all my life, often poking or teasing while they did it. But they were a wall nonetheless, solid and reliable.

I'd just stolen forbidden cloves from the kitchen so I could free Father from a spell his new wife had cast over him. I desperately wanted to tell them everything, but—

"Who taught you to kick like that, Ryn?" Mael demanded

I crossed my arms. Who did he think?

Mael turned to Cadan, the oldest of the triples, and punched his shoulder.

Cadan grabbed his hurt arm. "What was *that* for?"

"You taught her!" said Mael.

Cadan laughed. "Are you mad she knows how to kick or that she kicked *you*? Did you leave a bruise, Ryn?"

I glared at Mael. "I certainly hope so."

Cadan nodded approval. He was the most cynical of the triples, with a cutting wit that he rarely sharpened on me. Then there was Declan, the kindest brother in all the kingdom of Lacharra, who knew the songs and stories that told the history of our people. And Gavyn? Gavyn the scholar observed the world around him: animals and plants, sky and stars. He was happy to tell anyone who listened and even those who didn't.

"Enough kicking," said Aiden.

He never had to raise his voice. He'd been commanding the troop of us since . . . since there had been the seven of us. He had the strength and heart for the task, and he had proven it while Father was missing. He'd been the crown prince bearing the weight of Lacharra all those weeks. "We need to give the Queen the gift now, before tonight's feast with the Danavirian ambassador."

The ambassador had arrived only days after Father and the woman he married returned from the forest. The weak-chinned ambassador had never been a favorite of ours. It was even worse to host him while we tried to figure out what happened to Father during the weeks he'd been lost.

I looked up at my brothers.

Perhaps they weren't trying to find out anymore.

"Why would you give her a gift after what she did to Rees last night?" I asked. "Tanwen wouldn't agree."

Aiden raised an eyebrow. "You only say that when you hope she'd agree with you."

"I can't help it that you married a woman more sensible than you are! If she were here she'd tell you that . . . *woman* . . . doesn't deserve a gift!"

Aiden, like all the crown princes of recent times, had been living at Fortress Roden, the original stronghold of the House of Cynwrig. Tanwen had remained at Roden when Aiden came to the castle in Father's absence.

"Tanwen is sick at Fortress Roden and will come greet the Queen as soon as she's well. I am sure she would do everything in her power to make Father's new wife feel welcome."

I snorted.

"Don't be a child, Ryn," said Owain. He was my twin, but lately he acted like he'd outgrown me. "Rees disobeyed her."

"Only a child would take her side!" I shot back. "Rees could barely walk to the stable afterward—and they had to carry the boy! She had soldiers use a whip on them—and Rees doesn't even use one on the horses!"

I waited for Mael to shake his head, for Cadan to swear a string of oaths so sharp that even Aiden would wince.

Nothing.

My brothers had the same empty look I'd seen in Father's eyes ever since he returned with the Queen from the forest a week ago.

No. Not them too.

"It was on his head, Ryn," said normally gentle-hearted Declan, stepping away from me. "He should have known better."

"Would you say the same if I had been discovered with cloves?" I asked.

Mael looked worried. "You don't have any, do you? Is that why you were in the kitchen?"

"No!" I lied. "I wanted a tart. And I'm sure Bron burned them, anyway."

"Good."

"But that's not the question," I pressed. "Surely you wouldn't think *I* deserved a beating if I had some?"

Aiden held out his hands in a helpless gesture. "The law applies to all of us."

"It wasn't a law! It was something she said—after she appeared with Father *a week ago*!"

"She's queen of Lacharra," said Gavyn, as if that settled the issue.

"We don't know where she came from." I forced myself to speak slowly. Deliberately. "We don't even know her *name*!"

Aiden folded his arms and narrowed his eyes. "She came from the forest. She found Father there and she saved him."

I folded my arms, even though it didn't look nearly as impressive as Aiden. "She found him there and she *enchanted* him. And she's enchanted you too."

Cadan didn't ridicule me—he just shook his head as if I'd learn wisdom soon enough. That scared me more than anything: only an enchantment would leave Cadan acting as kind as Declan.

"Call it what you want," said Mael. "It's the sort of enchantment every man hopes for, Ryn-girl. It's like falling in love just to stand beside her."

"More like the night sky, I'd say," said Gavyn. "She's the fire of every star."

"You're too young to understand," added Owain.

"You're only three minutes older than I am!"

"But clearly more mature!" He rubbed his chin the way Aiden did when he was thinking. Except that Aiden had a beard and Owain just hoped for one.

They thought they felt love and admiration, but I knew better. I also knew nothing I said would make a difference.

I should have guessed how powerful the Queen was after she'd changed Father so much. I should have been afraid of someone who influenced my brothers so quickly.

But I was too angry to fear her. How dare she do this? My family was no one's plaything.

In that moment, I vowed to free them all.

I, Andaryn of the House of Cynwrig, would not lose my family to a woman who'd found my father in the darkest corner of the forest.

I vowed it on my life.

Chapter 2

"She asked about you," said Aiden.

I pressed my palm against the hidden cloves. "What did she want?"

Gavyn shrugged. "You haven't visited her since the wedding. It's been nearly a week."

"Don't be a ninny," said Mael. "Help us give her the gift. You'll like her when you know her."

I didn't want to see Father's wife in Mama's old chambers. I didn't want to deliver *anything*, unless it was a scoop of horse dung from the stables.

I sighed. "What are you giving her?"

Aiden opened his hand to reveal a small silk bag. "The Cynwrig Brooch."

I could barely breathe. "How *could* you—?" The Cynwrig Brooch, shaped like the entwined necks of three swans, had belonged to the three original Cynwrig brothers and their sister, Hafwen. It was supposed to be mine when I married.

And yet, when they gave it to the Queen, Father might be alone. He normally read in the library this time of the day. I pushed aside my hurt and changed my attack. "How *could* you give her the brooch without its box?"

Gavyn shook his head. "There's no box to hold the brooch, Ryn. It would have been mentioned in the *Annals*."

Trust Gavyn to reference a book. I shot him a withering look. "It doesn't *have* to be a box mentioned in the *Annals*. It just has to be better than the water-stained silk you wrapped it in."

Aiden peered at the silk, worried.

I backed away from them. "You go to her! I'm going to find a proper box and then I'll join you."

Aiden nodded.

I started to run away, calling over my shoulder, "It might take a little while, but don't worry! I'll be there soon!"

Then I ran for the east wing, hurrying up the three flights. I'd done it! I'd have an hour with Father in the library before my brothers missed me.

Yet as I stepped onto the corridor's lush carpet, I felt a prick of fear like a finger pressed between my shoulder blades.

The Queen was coming.

The feeling was so strong that I looked back down the tight curve of the stone staircase. I could only see a half-turn's worth of stairs in either direction, but everything was silent.

I held my breath, straining to hear footfalls. A voice.

Nothing.

Of course there was nothing.

Think of cloves. Think of Father. Think of the world made right again.

My steps didn't falter as I walked down the corridor to the library doors. My fingers brushed the crest carved into the wood: three swans, wings outstretched in flight, one for each of the valiant Cynwrig brothers who established Lacharra over two centuries ago.

Father used to say there were spaces between heartbeats and breaths, between the smallest moments of time. That those were the places we did most of our living.

I thought I could feel the moment open before me. If I could just see clearly enough, if I could find the right words, I'd be able to save my family.

Help me be brave.

Help me be smart.

Help me free my father.

I pushed open the library door.

⁂

The normal murmur of voices was hushed, the clerks darting like frightened cats from shelf to shelf. I peered at the raised alcove at the far end of the library where Father always read.

Father sat there unmoving, his head half-bent over his folded hands. He reminded me of a stone monument placed on a tomb.

He was still, but he wasn't silent. He hummed a lurching, distorted tune with the devotion of a priest.

This *wasn't* my father. This wasn't the man who had nicknames for the different tomes . . . who could recite entire passages by memory . . . who chewed cloves while he read because it was a low habit for a king and this was the only place where no one would notice.

Something was horribly, horribly wrong.

I slipped my hand through the pocket slit in my gown and felt for the bag of cloves. They were a pitifully small weapon. Hardly anything against what the Queen had done.

Help me!

Then I strode across the room and stepped up into the alcove beside Father's table, a table piled with untouched books.

Father didn't move, didn't stop humming.

I looked down at the table and the bent heads of the swans that formed the table legs. Their arched wooden necks were glossy from years of me petting them as Father read. I stroked the nearest one once for luck.

"Father?" I whispered. "It's me, your Ryn."

"Andaryn?" He looked up, squinting in the light that streamed through the broad windows. "Oh. How nice. I was just reading." He gestured toward the tower of books on the table behind me. Then his head dropped down again, chin nearly on his chest.

"You look too tired to read. You've been tired ever since you've been back."

Father nodded. "It was awful. I can't forget how dark it was beneath those trees."

I tried to speak gently, though I could feel my pulse in my throat, I was so frightened. "I haven't seen much of you since you returned. You're always with—"

"Don't speak against my wife, Andaryn!" he barked out. "I won't have it."

It knocked the breath from me. Father had been angry at me before—and for good reason, most times—but he'd never flashed out like that before.

I didn't know what to do. So I set *The Annals of Lacharra* in his lap.

"I'll read to *you*, then," I said quietly and opened the book.

The scent of cloves rose from its pages. Small surprise, for Father read the *Annals* often. I paused, hand on the pages, and breathed in the scent, trying to remember the times Father and I had read this book together.

I quickly flipped past the sedate parts of the book: the drawing of the Cynwrig family tree and the chapter describing how, over two centuries ago, the Cynwrig brothers had served as chiefs to the old king of Brisson.

I stopped when I reached the war. This would do. Perhaps Father would remember some of his own valor as he read about the valor of our ancestors.

"Cloves," he murmured.

"What did you say?"

"Cloves," he repeated, in a voice like the one I remembered.

Out of the corner of my eye, I saw the clerks stand straighter. They'd heard Father. Then they scurried to the far side of the room as if even hearing the word *cloves* discussed might earn them a beating.

"I missed them while I was lost. Once, when . . ."

He shook his head. "I don't remember. It was dark. I thought if I could only have cloves I'd be able to find my way back here to you. But I was still so sick and needed rest. She sang me back to sleep and said we'd return to the castle soon. Sometimes I still hum that song just to make the darkness go away."

The tune I'd heard him humming.

Could she have forbidden cloves simply because they'd help Father remember who he was? "If you want them so much, why were they banned—"

"There are none left, she says."

I risked another question. "What about Rees and his stable boy last night?"

Father shook his head, puzzled. "I was too tired to tend to them, but my beloved did all that was needed."

They needed a flogging?

But it would be useless to argue while Father was still enchanted.

One last glance around the library. The clerks must have left, slipping silently out the door.

Help me be brave.

Help me be smart.

Help me free my father.

I slipped my hand through my pocket slit, fingering the bag of cloves.

"Father?"

He turned to me, his face his own again.

"I used to keep cloves just for when we read together. Would you like one?"

"I should have known my Ryn would have the solution! Yes, let me have one. The forest dark still presses in sometimes."

Fingers trembling, I opened the bag and pulled out a clove. Such a small brown bud!

Slowly, he opened his hand, and I placed it in his palm.

He pulled the scent inside him, eyes already brightening, then popped the clove in his mouth, closing his eyes as he savored it.

He smiled.

Cloves *were* a potent reminder of some of my best times with Father. Was it really as simple as helping Father remember? Very well, then.

If the Queen wanted Father to forget everything but her, I'd do all I could to remind him.

Beginning with Father's favorite story. I swept my hand over the open book before us.

"Will you read to me, Father?" I asked. "I've missed that as much as you have missed your cloves."

He cleared his throat, looked at the page I'd opened to, and grinned up at me.

"This is a good part. You always knew how to find the exciting passages." He cleared his throat and read in a clear, steady voice:

> *The king of Brisson called the Cynwrig brothers his game of swans, for they were fierce but beautiful in the battles they fought for him. But the king became corrupt and demanded Hafwen, their sister, as his concubine.*

When she refused, he gathered his forces to take her from her brothers' manor by force.

The Cynwrig brothers would not fight their king, but they would not abandon their sister. They refused to act as his chiefs and fled the land he'd given them before he could claim Hafwen.

And so a game of swans, bearing swords, flew up from the south.

The House of Cynwrig settled among the lakes of the north and all the lands in between, establishing their fortress at Roden and naming the land Lacharra. Then the King of Brisson gathered his allies, lords from the east and west and princes of the River Cities. They brought their might against the brothers Cynwrig.

I sat on the arm of his chair and leaned close so I could read over Father's shoulder, just as I'd always done.

And the scattered fragments of my world began to knit back together.

Father looked up at me, his face inches from mine. "Do you know why the Cynwrig brothers were called a 'game of swans,' Ryn?"

I did. He asked it every time he read this to me. And every time, I had told him to keep reading and not stop in the middle of the good part.

But not this time. "Tell me."

He kissed the tip of my nose, and I smiled at the scent of cloves. "By calling them his 'game of swans,' the King of Brisson made them no different from the other game on his lands: the deer, the fish, the quail. The phrase transformed them into creatures that lived only by his goodwill."

It was a golden moment—whole and shining—but I didn't know how to keep it from shattering.

"Would you like another clove?" I asked.

He put his finger on the place where he'd been reading and nodded.

I handed him another, keeping a few in my hand so I wouldn't have to open the bag every time he wanted one.

He took it with a smile. "Now attend to what the brothers are called now as they challenge the king who has brought war to them. Not a game of swans—"

"—but a flight," I finished for him. "So they no longer belonged to the king, but to themselves."

"That's my girl! Now we read on:

> *The flight of swans, bearing swords, met the King of Brisson and his allies in combat. When the battle was at its thickest, when the dust from the warriors smeared the sky brown and red, Emrys ap Cynwrig looked up and saw white against the dark: swans soaring over the battle, untouched by the arrows that flew as thick as gadflies.*
>
> *Emrys gathered his brothers . . .*

"What is *this*?" The Queen stood before us, dark eyes watching Father and me.

Oh, she was beautiful, with moonlight-pale hair braided and twisted into a crown on her head. Her face was as smooth as a girl's, but her dark eyes were as old as memory.

I'd never seen her so angry. Not even last night as she ordered Rees away.

I stood, but I kept my arm around Father's neck. I felt the strength and purpose drain out of him the moment he saw her.

"I thought you were finding me the box for the lovely brooch your brothers gave me, Ryn. And yet you are here with your father, when he is still not recovered from his ordeal in the forest."

I glanced at Father. He hadn't seemed weak until she said that he was.

"He's reading to me," I answered. "It's the story about the House of Cynwrig settling here in Lacharra. Why we have three swans on our family crest."

"Your father is too tired for such things."

Father faltered, hands moving to close the book.

I put my hand, palm down, on the pages to keep him from doing it. "He didn't seem tired to me."

She didn't reply, just studied us, taking in every detail before her: me standing beside Father, the still-open book. She stiffened when she saw a stray clove that had fallen into the crease between the pages.

"Ah, little cygnet," she murmured. "You have no idea what you've begun. I cannot let this go unchallenged."

I glanced at Father, half-fearful that he'd send me off for a beating. But he smiled gently up at his wife. "She found some cloves and brought them to me. Imagine that, when we thought they'd all been used!" He pinched the stray clove between his fingers and held it up as proof.

I turned to her, triumphant. What would she say now?

She didn't say anything, just stepped forward and traced a gentle finger along Father's jaw.

"My dear, dear husband. You poor, silly man. Cloves make you sick. Your stomach twists. The bile rises . . ."

I could feel my own stomach turn.

I closed my eyes till I could clearly remember Father and me reading and eating cloves.

My stomach calmed.

But Father was looking ill.

"You just ate some, Father!" I whispered. "You told me you missed them."

"He missed the *idea* of them. He talked about cloves while he recovered, but he gagged while he did so."

The base of Father's throat worked, as if the sickness was already rising.

The Queen's gaze danced between the two of us. Fast as lightning, she plucked the clove from Father's fingers. I grabbed for it but wasn't quick enough.

But she didn't snatch it away. She pressed it into Father's mouth, holding her palm against his lips until he retched.

It was the work of a moment, and in that moment between heartbeats, I lost Father.

By the time I grabbed her wrist, she'd pulled her hand away from Father's face and he spat the clove out, mouth twisted with disgust.

She straightened, staring at my hand still wrapped around her wrist as if she couldn't believe I'd dare touch her.

But I didn't release her.

I squeezed tighter, hating her beautiful face and her pale-as-moonlight hair and her too-dark eyes with nothing shining in them.

"Go away," I said. "Go away, and leave us alone!"

Her eyes widened, and I saw her fury rise. But there was fear too.

I stepped closer. "Go *away*! You're not wanted—"

"Silence! How *dare* you speak to me so?"

She wrenched her hand free and slapped me so hard my vision danced.

I staggered back but regained my footing, blinking away tears of rage and surprise. "Father!"

Surely he'd do something. Say something.

He simply stared, his eyes dull and sightless.

But she wasn't finished.

"A child as insolent as you ought to be punished." She stepped closer and slapped me again. I threw the cloves I'd been holding in her face, hoping they had some power to stop her.

There was no broken spell, no diminishing of her power.

The cloves might have reminded Father of me, but they only infuriated the Queen.

She backhanded me so hard that I fell. "You can't really believe that your father would choose *you* over me."

I realized then that she meant to beat me.

And Father would watch. Only watch.

I scrabbled away, but the Queen planted a slippered foot on my skirt, pinning me in place. She blocked the alcove so that I couldn't see the window, couldn't see Father. All I saw was her—a dark pillar against a flood of light—and the Cynwrig crest on the ceiling above her: three white swans flying to freedom while I cringed at her feet.

She pulled her pale hand back for another blow. Fear gave me strength. I yanked my skirt free, sending her stumbling backward.

I didn't wait to see if she fell.

I had to get away. I had to tell Aiden.

I leaped to my feet and ran.

Chapter 3

"Ryn!" Aiden exclaimed when I burst into his privy chambers. "What happened? She was dismayed when you didn't come—"

I stood before him, trembling and breathless from my run. He needed to see the Queen's handiwork.

Disheveled hair.

Bloody lip.

Torn skirt.

"Did Owain do that?" he thundered. "He can't just tussle with you anymore—he doesn't know his own strength."

I shook my head. "The *Queen* found me, Aiden. She found me in the library with Father."

Aiden recoiled. "What did you do?"

"What did *I* do? Can't you see what *she's* done?"

"I can't believe you'd provoke her—"

"*Look at me*!" I stomped my foot like a child, but it made Aiden stop. I knew somehow it was important that he truly see me, remember what he knew. "What do you see when you look at me?"

"I see . . ." He folded his arms. ". . . a silly girl who won't accept that her father can marry whomever he chooses."

I thought of Father in the library with the Queen and redoubled my attack. "What color are my eyes?"

He rolled his eyes in response, but I could see something change the longer Aiden looked at me. "Your eyes are hazel. Your hair is black, just like Father's. Just like Mother's." He winced then, as if remembering the mother who'd died birthing Owain and me. "Just like mine."

"And do I have Father or Mother's mouth?"

"Mother's." He focused on my mouth, eyes widening when he saw the blood. "Good heavens, Ryn! What happened?"

And this time, he meant it.

"She found me with Father and she hit me." I spoke slowly, afraid he'd blame me again.

"Let me see." Aiden tipped my chin so that the light from the window shone on my throbbing cheek and bloody mouth.

He pulled a kerchief from inside his tunic, poured water on it from a pitcher, and handed it to me. "Tell me everything."

I did, my words sometimes muffled by the kerchief. Aiden's eyes didn't leave my face as I told him about Father sitting like a stone and humming the tune the Queen had sung to him. He didn't blink when I told him I'd brought Father cloves, and that I thought the Queen had forbidden them because they made Father remember us.

"You're not angry about the cloves?"

"Oh, I'm furious," he said. "What were you thinking, endangering yourself with that sorceress? What would have happened if you hadn't been able to run?"

"You told me an hour ago that Rees deserved his beating!"

"Perhaps she really did enchant us." He shook his head. "But I'm back, Ryn-girl. What happened next?"

I threw myself at him and hugged him so tightly that I embarrassed myself. I made sure to scrub my cheek against his tunic so there wasn't any trace of tears on my face when I stepped back.

I didn't have time to tell him more. One of the captains had come to Aiden's door.

I heard Aiden murmur something in response. "—my brothers meet me in the courtyard."

"A band of men is approaching," he told me when he returned. "I need to be there, and I want you with me. I'm not leaving you alone again."

"Visitors for the Ambassador from Danavir?" I asked.

"I don't think so. The watchman reports he's never seen anything like the approaching band. That's why they called me." Aiden swiped at the dampness on his tunic. "Are you well enough to come with me?"

"Never better." I hadn't broken Father's enchantment and I was still trembling, but Aiden was himself again. I wiped the blood from my lip and followed him to the courtyard.

⁂

The cobbled courtyard, like every other part of the castle, was quieter than it had ever been before. I could still hear the ring of the blacksmith's hammer. The hunting dogs bayed from their kennels.

But the men and women working in it were subdued, and the undercooks scurrying to and from the pantry that supplied the kitchen didn't look up. Rees walked with a horse to the post where it would be saddled, and I couldn't tell if he led the horse or leaned upon it.

My home had changed that much in only seven days.

I watched as Aiden scanned the courtyard. He noticed it too. His jaw clenched, his eyes narrowed, and he smiled just a little. Those who didn't know him paid attention to the smile. I knew it meant he didn't want his opponents to know he was about to attack.

He strode to the gatehouse, and I trotted to keep up with him. The constable and the Captain of the Guard waited for him.

The Captain silently handed Aiden a looking glass, and he peered out to the approaching band.

"Drop the portcullis. Now." Aiden handed the looking glass back to the Captain. "I don't know who they are, but they don't enter the courtyard until they swear peace and surrender their weapons."

"That bad?" I asked as Aiden escorted me back across the courtyard, toward the well by the kitchen and pantry—as far from the gatehouse as possible.

"Perhaps. Perhaps not. But I won't risk it."

"Aiden!"

Mael and Cadan were jogging to meet us. Declan, Gavyn, and Owain weren't far behind.

Declan noticed my face first. "What happened, Ryn?"

I glanced at Aiden, unsure how much to tell.

"She angered Father's new wife," he spat out.

Cadan cocked his head, as if he didn't believe his ears.

"What did you do?" Mael asked me.

Cadan's gaze lingered on my swollen lip. "She did that to you, Ryn? With her own hands?"

I nodded, willing him to see all that had happened.

"She's a gentle soul!" protested Mael, and Declan nodded agreement.

Cadan blinked, and I saw her hold on him evaporate. "Maybe she isn't a gentle soul, Mael."

Gavyn nodded. "A gentle soul wouldn't resort to violence."

"Don't speak against her!" blurted Owain.

Three brothers believed me. Three remained enchanted.

The standoff was broken as a horn from beyond the gatehouse rang out. It had a fierce center to it: music made from an animal roar.

The mysterious band had arrived.

The Captain of the Guard called out that they announce themselves, surrender their weapons, and swear peace.

Silence from beyond the portcullis. Finally, a gravelly voice that we could barely hear from across the courtyard answered, ". . . the white lady."

The Captain looked at Aiden from the gatehouse and shook his head.

Aiden cursed under his breath. "Cadan, stay with Ryn. Don't leave her side."

Then he strode over to the gatehouse.

Cadan tugged me to stand by him. "Here, Ryn. Stay close and protect me from these mighty warriors."

He tickled me—just enough to keep me distracted—while Aiden joined the Captain. We stood nearly fifty paces from the gatehouse, but we all saw Aiden stiffen at the sight of the band.

"I don't think—" I began.

"Raise the portcullis!" The Queen's voice rang out like a bell.

She stood at the library balcony, only a little to the right of the gatehouse.

Aiden bowed. "My Queen, they have not—"

"You must not have heard me, young Aiden: Let them in. They serve *me*."

"That's little comfort," murmured Cadan.

After a dreadful pause, Aiden motioned to the gatehouse soldiers. The *clang, clang, clang* of the portcullis being raised echoed off the stone walls.

No one else dared speak.

A moment later, the men entered the courtyard. They looked wild, with unkempt hair and eyes that flashed warily in dirty, bearded faces. None of them possessed metal armor. Instead, they wore battle-scarred leather breastplates.

Cadan pulled in a hissing breath. "They are *not* from Danavir. Gavyn?"

Gavyn knew the crests and flags of all the lords and chiefs of neighboring lands. He was almost as good as a book, but even he shook his head. "I've not read or heard of anyone like them."

The men didn't even nod to Aiden or the Captain of the Guard. Instead, they looked around insolently, chins raised, eyes roving, like they'd caught scent of something. They reminded me of the blacksmith's dog that prowled around the bellows looking for something to make him snarl.

"I greet you, men of the forest!" the Queen called out.

"Our Queen!" called a tall man near the front of the pack.

"How did they know she was here?" whispered Gavyn. "Or that she is queen? It's been only a week."

The wild men arranged themselves into rows and drew their swords. Then they held their black weapons over their hearts and saluted the new Queen of Lacharra.

"Captain!" called the Queen. "You will make sure that my guard is given room in the barracks."

The Captain glanced at Aiden, who nodded reluctantly. Then the Captain motioned that the wild men should follow him.

"Obsidian blades," murmured Gavyn as we watched the men sheath their dark, glossy swords and disperse to the barracks. "I know of no warriors who carry them."

"Warriors in the old songs did," offered Declan, smiling as if hearing the ancient melodies. "The ancient ones abhorred metal, so they carried obsidian weapons. But I never thought I'd see black blades in *this* world."

Mael didn't share Aiden's worry or Declan's fascination. "In *this* world, obsidian shatters. One blow from a regular sword would ruin these. Don't let the blades frighten you. They're good for only one cut."

"One may be enough," muttered Aiden as he joined us. "I don't like this."

"But they're with her," reassured Mael. "We're safe—you can trust that."

"Are you *that* foolish, Mael?" snapped Cadan. "Wild men with blades out of the ancient tales stroll in and you don't wonder if perhaps something is amiss?"

"I'm no fool," Mael shot back. "I trust the woman who saved Father from the forest! Don't you?"

"I did until I saw what she did to Ryn."

But Mael wouldn't even look at me. Declan shook his head sadly as if the bruises were merely a misunderstanding. Owain glared.

They turned and walked away.

"Never mind them, Ryn. I'll take you to your rooms." Aiden turned toward the nearest entrance to the living quarters. He stopped at the sight of the wild men standing in the way.

"This way." He moved toward the other entrance near the gatehouse, the one near the balcony where the Queen stood. "Don't look at her. Just walk."

I could feel the Queen's eyes on me, bright and burning as the summer sun.

Just before I followed Aiden into the passage, a small, dark object flashed before me and landed at my feet.

A single clove lay on the narrow cobbles.

I looked up.

The Queen smiled down at me. "You forgot this, cygnet."

I wished I had a grand and cutting reply that would wipe the smile from her face. I wished I was powerful enough to banish her for all the evil she'd wrought.

Instead I stood silent and still, ashamed at how my rabbit-heart raced at the memory of her attack.

"I will not forget your defiance in the library," continued the Queen.

And still I had no reply, except the anger rising up in me. I glared up at her and slowly—deliberately—ground the clove to dust beneath my foot before following Aiden.

Somehow, that was reply enough.

Chapter 4

Aiden walked me straight to my rooms and didn't relax until Cadan and Gavyn joined us.

He shuffled through the mess that covered my writing desk, then pulled parchment and ink forward. "Tell Father you don't feel well and that you'll miss the ambassador's feast tonight. I don't want you anywhere near that woman." He pointed to Cadan and Gavyn. "You two stay with Ryn until the feast begins and lock the door behind you. No one visits in the meantime. No maids. No guards. No one."

"Not even Mael or—?" I couldn't finish the question.

Aiden shook his head. "They'll come around."

That's what I thought about Father.

I felt like I should argue with Aiden about going to the feast, but I was relieved. I wanted to pull the walls of my chambers closer, like a blanket around me, until my heart stopped racing.

Until I felt certain we could defeat the woman who had so completely invaded our lives.

I wrote the note to Father under my brothers' watchful

eyes. Before Aiden left, I pulled a sleek, pale feather from one of the drawers and laid it on the desk.

"I found this four days ago," I told them.

"The Queen attacked you, her wild men have entered the castle without surrendering their weapons, . . . and you're showing us a feather," said Cadan.

Aiden elbowed him, but Gavyn picked up the feather and examined it. "Where did you find it?"

"Just inside my open window."

Cadan rolled his eyes. "So a swan flew near Ryn's window and a feather dropped in."

"It isn't from a swan," said Gavyn. "I've never seen a feather like this before."

The long drooping feather looked like the mother-of-pearl that traders brought to court. It glistened with pinks and yellows, greens and purples, and every shade in between.

"It was inside your window?" asked Aiden.

I nodded. "The window was open. But that's not all."

Cadan half-shrugged: *Go on!*

"I dreamed I heard singing that night. Or maybe I fell asleep to it. It was just *there*."

"That's not very sinister," said Cadan.

"The singing wanted something from me—wanted me to fall into it, I think." I glared at Cadan. "Like when Cadan wants me to believe one of his wild stories. Except this was more. It reminded me of the Queen, wanting me to surrender to it. So I didn't."

"Because you are stubborn and irritating *even in your dreams*." Cadan grinned.

"Then what?" Aiden wasn't smiling.

I paused. This was why I hadn't told them about it days ago.

"Ryn?"

"The castle burned. Sheets of fire covering everything. It felt like a threat. Or a warning. And then it was just the Queen and me. And I told her something. Just one word, I think. Or maybe two. And she disappeared."

Aiden put an arm around me. "I was a fool not to see who she was, Ryn. I left you unprotected."

I shook my head. "That's not—"

"We would have had nightmares if we'd recognized how evil the Queen was," said Gavyn.

"But that doesn't explain the feather!" I protested.

They just stared at me.

"I don't think it was a dream," I said slowly, hoping they'd believe me. "I think she was trying to enchant me too."

"With a *feather*?" asked Cadan.

"No! What if she sent the bird?"

"She sent a bird to enchant you?"

"Gavyn said he's never seen anything like this feather! And when I wouldn't be enchanted"—I faltered—"what I saw became a threat."

I felt like an idiot the moment I said it aloud. My brothers—even Cadan—were kind enough not to say they thought the same thing.

"Ah," said Gavyn, using a tone like he was talking to a child. "Except that if she was threatening you, she wouldn't end it with you defeating her, would she?"

He was right.

And then Aiden was hugging me as he slipped out to prepare for the feast, and I was standing in my rooms, feeling like a little fool.

"Come sit beside me, Ryn." Cadan patted the spot on the bench by the fire. "We'll sort this out."

"Will we?"

"Of course we will!" He pointed to the new purple- and crimson-edged tapestry on the wall. "Little wonder you feel morbid with the Lady Rhiannon staring down at you!"

He was trying to distract me, and I was grateful for it. I tucked my feet under my gown and leaned against him.

"She used to scare me when I was little. I always tiptoed past her when I went to Mother's chambers."

The Lady Rhiannon in the tapestry *was* beautiful—and fierce. She stood at a lake's bank, her ankles in the water, her gold and green skirts floating around her, as if she'd just stepped into this world. Three birds gathered around her. Gold threads twisted with other colors etched their wings and the long plumage that trailed behind them. According to Declan, she was the Queen of the Otherworld. She ruled a realm with colors deeper than sight and music that echoed in bone and blood. Her birds, the *adar rhiannon* in the old tongue, could sing the heart's deepest desire so that the souls of men would step away from death—or toward it, if she commanded her birds to sing so.

"What sort of girl is scared by a tapestry?" teased Cadan. "And then hangs that tapestry in her room?"

"You'll think I'm silly."

"I already do. So tell me."

"I thought she'd step out of the tapestry and kidnap me."

Cadan snorted.

"But I also liked her because she was in Mother's room."

He sat quiet for a moment, the way he did when he didn't want someone to guess how he felt.

Then he studied the tapestry, eyes narrowed, before looking at me. "Please tell me you don't think that your feather came from Lady Rhiannon."

"She doesn't have feathers," I said, trying to dodge the question.

"That isn't what I meant, and you know it. *Do you think the Queen is Lady Rhiannon?*"

I'd have said *no* just to make Cadan stop. But as I looked at the tapestry, I realized I didn't believe it either. The Lady was fierce and grand and the *adar rhiannon* could sing songs that wrapped human hearts around them, but . . .

. . . the Queen was too small inside, somehow. Too hungry.

"No," I said. "I don't think she's the Queen."

Cadan looked relieved. "Very well, then. So why did you bring this tapestry of a purely-mythical-figure-who-is-*not*-the-Queen into your room?"

I rolled my eyes. Cadan could never be subtle.

"It made Mother seem so grand to have the tapestry in her quarters. And I decided years ago I'd be brave enough to hang frightening tapestries in my room when I was a lady. So when *she*"—I hated calling her *the Queen* out loud—"stripped the tapestries from Mother's quarters, I asked the servants for it."

"Even with the tear?"

The tapestry had been damaged in the move: an ugly tear crossed the Lady's neck and the bodice of her dress.

"Even with the tear."

Cadan chuckled. "You're a funny thing, Ryn-girl. But Mother would be proud of you."

"Truly?"

"Yes." And then, because Cadan could never *stay* serious: "She'd have her doubts about Owain, though. We all do."

A knock at the door made all of us jump. Gavyn opened it cautiously, then returned with a note bearing Father's seal.

"It's for you, Ryn."

Chapter 5

The note *was* from Father, written in his own hand, pressing me to attend the feast. He wanted to see me.

Maybe the cloves had helped him remember more than I thought.

"I'm going," I told Cadan and Gavyn.

That evening, I wore my favorite gown, an undertunic of fine white linen with an over-tunic of blue velvet: blue like the background of the Cynwrig crest, blue like the sky the white swans flew through. I cinched it with a belt of finely wrought gold that had been Mother's.

Aiden was worried, despite Father's request, and insisted that Gavyn and Cadan escort me to the Great Hall. But no danger lurked in the corridors—we didn't even see any of the Queen's wild men.

And then we stood at the entrance to the Great Hall, my brothers on either side of me.

Cadan paused at the doorway. "Are you ready, Ryn?"

I thought of Father's note and smiled. "Lead on!"

"That's my girl." He nodded at Gavyn, and they each looped my hands through their arms like proper escorts.

A moment later, we were in the Hall itself. Father sat at our table at the far end, on the raised dais. The walls were hung with the shields of long-dead warriors who had fought alongside the House of Cynwrig. Nobles sat at two long rows of tables positioned against the walls, and just near the dais, the great fireplace roared, sending shadows streaming and dancing.

I felt a surge of pride as we walked to our table. We were all part of a great and grand kinship: *a flight of swans bearing swords.*

Not even Father could forget *that.* He'd invited me here, despite all his wife had tried to do.

Finally, we stopped before the dais and the table where my family and the ambassador would dine. When I looked up, Father was smiling down at me.

"Andaryn, my dear." He motioned us up. "Come! Sit."

I smiled back at him, not even glancing at the Queen. It was going to be a perfect evening. The only shadow was the Queen's wild men, who stood in a ragged line along the back wall, just a few strides from the table itself. I could feel them behind me as I sat.

Troubadours and magicians stepped into the Hall, filling it with song and laughter. There was a flourish of trumpets, and servants arrived in a grand train, piling the tables with stuffed quail, platters of fruits that glistened in the candlelight, and pastries formed into swans as big as the ones that lived outside the castle.

I was reaching for my goblet when I saw it: a single clove just beside my plate.

The world slowed around me as I looked at the Queen.

She smiled.

The clove wasn't just a warning. It was a promise of punishment for defying her. Father's invitation hadn't meant her power was weakening.

It was bait for a trap.

I wanted to run, but Father was already standing.

He gestured to the ambassador seated beside him. "Welcome to the heart of Lacharra, seat of the House of Cynwrig! May the Swans of Cynwrig ever fight beside Danavir—and never have reason to oppose it."

Even in my haze, I saw the puzzled look on the ambassador's face at the warning in Father's voice. We'd always been allies with Danavir. We had no reason to fight them, nothing to gain.

The Queen, however, watched the ambassador with narrowed eyes. *Nothing except a larger kingdom.*

Father continued. "This is not only a feast for allies—it is a celebration of the bright flame who found me in the forest and rescued me." He held a hand out to the Queen, who stood beside him.

Father kissed her hand and motioned to the archway nearest the dais. Two men inched out of the shadows, their backs bent under the weight of what they carried between them. They deposited their burden before the dais, turning the massive stone so that the swan carved on it faced our guests.

The Kingstone.

The entire Hall fell silent.

As a child, I'd played with Father's crown. I'd whacked Owain once with the scepter of Lacharra. But even I gasped to see the Kingstone pulled from its proper place in the Abbey and dragged into the Hall. It felt like someone had yanked the moon from the sky and hung it from the ceiling like any other bauble.

To the confused Danavirian ambassador, it must have looked like an ordinary building stone, pulled from some forgotten ruins.

But to any citizen of Lacharra, it represented the root of the king's authority. The Kingstone was the only thing the Cynwrig brothers brought from their manor when they fled the King of Brisson. When the first Cynwrig brother was crowned King of Lacharra, he'd stood upon *that* stone, which was engraved with a swan wearing a collar around its neck—a sign of their former bondage to the Brisson king.

From that first coronation, every Cynwrig king received the crown while standing on the Kingstone. It became part of the king's authority, a way of saying: This is where we came from, collared to another king. This is what we will *never* be again.

And Father had dragged it into the Hall.

"People of Lacharra!" he announced. "You know that I have been restored to you through the good graces of my wife, the Queen of Lacharra. It did not seem enough thanks to merely crown her Queen."

Father turned to two men by the Kingstone. One of them drew a mallet and chisel from his leather apron.

"No . . . ," I murmured.

Cadan grabbed my hand and squeezed a command: *Hush!*

He was right. The Queen looked around the Hall to see if anyone challenged her right to the Kingstone. To Lacharra itself.

We all knew that anyone who challenged her would lose.

Aiden spoke anyway, his voice carrying across the now-quiet hall. "Father."

For a moment, I thought I saw Father falter.

The Queen laid a pale hand on his arm, and the Father I'd known disappeared once again. "I *will* do this. Do not stand in my way, boy," he said.

The mason shuffled up to the Kingstone, holding the mallet and chisel in shaking hands, while his head swiveled from Father to Aiden and then back again.

Father raised his chin. "Bring me a piece of the Kingstone. Bring me a piece from the swan itself!"

He pointed to a portion of the swan that showed the collar low around its neck and a portion of its wing. "There!"

Horrified, the mason looked around the Hall one last time, a plea that someone—*anyone*—stop him.

The room was silent.

He brought the mallet down, and it struck the Kingstone with a sound like a broken bell.

A small fragment clattered to the Hall floor.

He'd done it. Father had actually done it. I think every soul in the Hall would have been less astonished if he put his own crown on the Queen's head.

The mason picked the fragment up and gently set it on the defaced Kingstone before hurriedly backing out of the Hall. How I envied him! I wanted nothing more than to escape that awful moment.

Father's voice echoed in the breathless hall. "Bring it to my wife . . . Andaryn."

I touched the clove the Queen had left for me.

What a little fool I'd been! Here was the Queen's trap: defy Father or give the Queen something that represented the heart of Lacharra.

I saw Cadan's shoulders bunch, his brows lower. Gavyn stirred. They were going to do something. And Father would punish them in front of all Lacharra.

I shot to my feet and left the table before they could stop me. Then slowly, I stepped off the dais.

It was like moving through water, approaching the Kingstone while every soul in the Hall watched. Sounds were muted too—even the roar of the fire seemed to come from a distance.

There was only me and the Kingstone—the poor, ruined Kingstone.

I ran a hand along the still-intact neck of the carved swan, fingers trailing over what remained of the collar. Then I picked up the fragment, feeling the sharp edges where it had just been chipped free.

What do I do, Mother?

I turned to Father, desperate for time. "Tell me the story, Father. Tell me about the House of Cynwrig and the Kingstone."

He smiled the way he had in the library, when he explained why "game of swans" was an insult. "Ah, Andaryn. Tell us yourself!"

It was more than I'd hoped for. Time to think. Time to speak. And the opportunity to use my family's story as a weapon.

I began to recite the portion from *The Annals of Lacharra*. And when I had told of the battle, I recited all that had happened with the Kingstone, how Emrys ap Cynwrig had stood on it when he was given the crown of Lacharra.

And as I spoke, I knew I could never give the Queen any part of the Kingstone.

I held Father's gaze as I finished. "That is the story of the House of Cynwrig, the flight of swans. This is the story of the Kingstone, the story of how we will never be collared to another king."

I drew a deep breath. "Or to another Queen."

And I threw the fragment of the Kingstone over the heads of the nobles nearest me and into the great fireplace.

The next moments were a blur.

The great hearth's flames enveloped the Kingstone fragment.

The murmur in the Hall swelled to a roar as my brothers—all of them—leaped up and raced toward me.

The Queen shouted something, and one of her wild men ran to the fire.

Father's shout rose above the clamor: "Seize her! Seize her, I say!"

Father's guards at the dais reached me before my

brothers did. The moment they took hold of me, the Hall silenced. My brothers slid to a stop.

"Bring her closer," demanded Father.

Aiden went to Father and whispered something.

"No. I will *not* overlook this!" Father bellowed. "She has defied the crown and will suffer the consequences."

Suffer the consequences? I wasn't a knight. I was his only daughter!

I'd never seen Aiden or my brothers so shocked. Even the ambassador looked frightened. My family was unraveling before me.

"Father," I stammered, "please . . . don't be angry with me. Look at me. I'm just your Ryn."

The hard-as-iron fury in his eyes softened.

"Please, Father!"

Then the Queen touched Father's shoulder.

"Kneel," he said.

I stared at him, unbelieving.

"*Kneel*, Andaryn, or my guards will make you kneel."

I slowly gathered my skirts. I'd spent my life curtsying, but not kneeling. And never to my father. I faltered and fell the last few inches to the flagstones.

An awful, ugly stench filled the room as one of the wild men approached. He knelt before the Queen, extended a horribly burned hand, and placed the fragment of the Kingstone at her feet.

I gasped. He'd pulled it from the fire.

"For your continued, public defiance of the crown, for the disrespect shown to the Queen of Lacharra . . ."

Father's words buzzed in my ears.

Mael shook his head, horrified.

". . . for these crimes, you will be banished from Lacharra. You are no longer a daughter of this house. You are no longer part of this court. You will spend this last night alone in your rooms. In the morning, you will be taken beyond the borders of Lacharra and delivered to your fate. You will be punished by death if I ever suffer your presence again."

I fell forward, both hands braced against the floor. I couldn't breathe. I crouched on hands and knees, staring at the cracked flagstone beneath me, while my breath came too fast and my heart beat too slow.

"Remove her." I could hardly hear Father over the roaring in my ears. "The Queen's guard will see her to the border tomorrow."

The guards pulled me to my feet. Some small part of me knew I'd never survive the trip to the border if the Queen's men escorted me.

But I couldn't think past *banished.*

Banished.

Everything after that was unclear, images half-drawn and blurred around the edges: my brothers standing near, whispering that they'd do something, as the guards led me away . . . my chambers without a single maid waiting for me . . . the scrape of the key as I was locked in.

I slowly sat with my back to the locked door, hands covering my face.

The trap had been sprung.

Chapter 6

Get up.

The words were so strong, so real, that I raised my head to see who'd spoken them.

My chambers were still empty. Shafts of moonlight fell across the floor, bleaching all color from the rich carpet, looking for all the world like white wings in the night.

"A flight of swans," I whispered.

It was time to fly away. And it *would* be close to flying, climbing from my balcony to the elm where the white bird from my dream had perched. But I'd done it before. If I left now, I could escape the Queen's guard. My brothers wouldn't have to risk Father's displeasure by protecting me. Perhaps last week's dream had been a threat after all—a promise of what would happen if I resisted the Queen.

I stripped off my finery and went to my garderobe, pulling out an inconspicuous, plain wool dress, perfect for travel. Next came calf-high riding boots.

Then I scurried back to my room and scrabbled under my bed to retrieve Owain's satchel. I'd hidden it there when he fought with me two months ago. I'd held on to that anger for weeks, even after I couldn't remember why we'd fought.

What else should I bring? My chambers were decorated for beauty and comfort—not for provisioning an escape.

I turned slowly, taking in my room, the fireplace—

I snatched my dagger off the mantel and put it in the satchel. It was there mainly for decoration, but surely it would come in handy. I tossed Mother's gold belt in after the dagger. It would be something of hers I could bring with me—something that wouldn't be noticed.

The two lap rugs would travel well. They were sturdy, boiled wool—bulky, but warm. I rolled them tightly, then strapped them to the outside of the satchel.

I'd taken my last few meals in my rooms. I wrapped the remaining bread in a kerchief, shoved that into the satchel, and lifted the bowl of cold stew to my lips. Best to leave on a full stomach.

And then it was time to leave. Just like that.

I went to my writing desk and pulled out a piece of parchment and scrawled "Dear Father" across the top.

I wanted to tell him that I loved him, that I'd miss him, but knew the words would never touch him.

So I sketched three swans flying, necks stretched toward freedom. I was a daughter of the House of Cynwrig, whether he recognized it or not. And *he* was a son of the same house. He didn't belong in bondage, even if it was as sweet as the Queen's enchantment.

Perhaps one day he'd look at the swans and remember who he was.

I straightened and saw the tapestry of Lady Rhiannon in the moonlight. There was one last farewell, after all.

"You don't frighten me anymore," I told her. "But then, I don't think you ever intended to."

Then I slipped out onto the balcony, closing the doors behind me. A moment later, I'd swung myself into the elm and into the dark night beyond.

Chapter 7

My escape from the Queen led me into the forest she'd emerged from.

It swallowed me up. Dead branches clattered and moaned around me, whispering sharp and twiggy secrets to the moon.

I startled at every sound, jumping when fallen leaves rustled nearby.

It's just a small creature, I told myself, pulling my cloak around me, *and happy. It's very happy and very full. It doesn't want to eat the big noisy creature trudging along the path.*

I stopped walking, dust and wind swirling around me, and looked up at the moon sailing through thin clouds. It reminded me of the Queen's face: beautiful and pale and blank.

She's not watching me. She can't be.

But I was too tired to believe my own lies. I tugged my hood over my face so the moon couldn't see me.

I could never be too far from the Queen.

x x x

I heard the hoofbeats too late.

I dashed off the path and huddled among the shadowy trees.

A single rider. Though even one of the Queen's wild guard would be enough.

I sank deeper into my hood and prayed he'd ride past.

The rider slowed, then stopped altogether—right where I'd been standing.

I hiked my skirts and—

"Andaryn! Ryn!"

It was Aiden.

He looked so wild in the moonlight that I thought the Queen had enchanted him again.

"What were you thinking?" He dismounted, and a moment later he took me by the shoulders, punctuating every word with a small shake. "What were you thinking, running like that? You scared the life out of us!"

Not enchanted, then. Just furious.

I didn't care that he was angry. It was so good to see him that I threw my arms around him.

He pulled me close, and hope began to grow inside me. "Father changed his mind?"

Aiden's arms dropped to his sides and he shook his head.

"Oh." I realized then that I'd expected Father would change his mind, that *something* would keep the worst from happening.

"Don't take me back to the castle, Aiden. I won't travel with her awful soldiers."

"I wouldn't give a dog to those men," grunted Aiden. "We have a plan: we're going to hide you until Father comes to his senses."

"Where? And where is everyone else?"

"Mael and Declan went to your room hours ago to beg your forgiveness, even if they had to talk through the door to do it."

"Truly?" I asked. "They're not enchanted anymore?"

Aiden walked his horse to the side of the road. "If one good thing came from the feast, that is it. All of us—even Owain—know the truth about Father's new bride."

"Except Father."

"Yes. Except Father." Aiden's shoulders slumped, but he pushed ahead with his news. "When you didn't answer, we unlocked your door. Gavyn saw your picture for Father and realized you meant to leave for good."

I turned at the sound of more hoofbeats in the gloom. Aiden stiffened, then drew his sword and stepped between me and the approaching horsemen.

I gripped his cloak with both hands and braced for the worst.

As they came within sight, Aiden relaxed. "It's Owain and Mael."

My brothers pulled their horses to a stop. Mael leaped from his charger and swept me into a hug. "I was a fool, Ryn."

I blinked back tears.

Mael released me and motioned Owain forward. "Your turn."

Owain dismounted and looked anywhere but me: the ground, the chargers stomping and chewing their bits, my shoulder. "I was—"

Mael rolled his eyes. "—a complete and utter ass, and I'm . . . ?"

". . . sorry," finished Owain.

I hugged him too, mostly because I knew it would irritate him. To my surprise, Owain hugged me back and whispered, "I *am* sorry."

Mael turned to Aiden. "The others are close by. When we didn't find Ryn on the road to Roden, we realized our best chance was along this trail. This is good. She's nearly a third of the way to Roden."

"I'm *not* going to Roden," I said.

Aiden raised an eyebrow. "Why?"

"I don't want the Queen anywhere near Tanwen."

More horses and riders. It was the triples: Declan, Gavyn, and Cadan.

Declan slipped off his horse and put an arm around my shoulder. "I'll never forgive myself. I knew there was something different in her songs. But I didn't let myself care. And now—"

I snuggled into Declan's side. He was my favorite, he and Cadan, though the two of them couldn't stand each other. I loved Declan because he loved me, and I loved Cadan because he didn't care what anyone thought. I needed that too. I could borrow it and wear it like armor sometimes.

"Gather 'round," said Aiden. "We only have hours.

I was telling Ryn we're taking her to Roden—"

"And I was telling him that I wouldn't put Tanwen in danger," I interrupted.

"You won't stay there," said Aiden. "We can't risk that. You'll stay only a few hours until Tanwen can provision one of our men to take you someplace safe."

"We've provisioned *you* already," said Cadan, tucking a bag into my satchel. "There's food—and a flint and tinder so you're never lost in the dark."

"We should hurry," said Mael. "If the Queen discovers that we're missing, she'll try to turn Father against us. She'll tell him Aiden's trying to take the throne."

Owain tried to act brave. "If anyone questions us when we return, Declan will spin a tale that takes them to the Otherworld and back before they can think."

"There's no story that would explain us going out for a midnight ride," said Aiden. "We tell them we discovered Ryn was missing and went searching—and we buy Tanwen time to hide Ryn away."

"They'll search Roden," I cautioned.

"And you won't be there by the time they reach it," Aiden replied. "Tanwen will have sent you on your way before search parties leave the castle."

He looked off to the west, where Roden stood a few leagues away. "I just wish we'd been able to plan so that we don't look as if we're defying Father. This is risky."

"Let *me* escort her to Roden," said Cadan. "I'll get her safely to Tanwen while the rest of you go back to the castle. The crown prince should be at the castle when Ryn's discovered missing. Let the mean triple be blamed for this, if there's blame to be given."

"If any part of this plan fails, it will settle on Aiden's shoulders—no matter who takes her there," said Mael.

Aiden bent down a little so I could see him clearly. "I'll see you safe to Roden tonight, Ryn, and safe every day after that. I vow it. We all do."

"I vow it," echoed my brothers—all but Cadan.

"I'm so determined to keep you safe that I don't need to waste breath vowing it," he announced. But he smiled at me to show the edge in his words wasn't for me.

In that moment, with my brothers around me, I felt safe again. They were my own fortress, my castle, my home—all six of them. For the first time since Father had returned from the forest, we were united. Perhaps the worst hadn't happened, after all.

Cadan helped me up to sit in front of him, and we started for Roden in silence.

As we traveled on, the night pressed so close that I could imagine the Queen watching me. I should have felt safe with my brothers near, but I didn't.

Declan brought his horse beside us. "Aiden mentioned a dream, Ryn. Tell me about it."

It was always easy to confide in Declan. So I told him about the feather and the words that stopped the Queen and the fire.

"Mother had dreams," said Declan.

"It was just a dream," argued Cadan. "Ryn's didn't stop the Queen—though I almost thought she would, standing there, with the Kingstone in the fire. What a sight that was! But she didn't—so I won't worry about feathers or fires anytime soon."

Declan shook his head and grabbed a hank of his curly hair, tugging absently as he thought.

"What burned, Ryn? What part of the castle?"

"Stone doesn't *burn*," argued Cadan.

I ignored him. "The ramparts—the roof along the ramparts, near the turret."

"Could you tell which side of the castle?"

I closed my eyes. It had hardly been a dream at all, more like images as the strange music tried to pull me into its current.

I looked up, feeling a failure. "I don't know. It wasn't what you see from the courtyard. Do you think that's good?"

"I'll think it over. It might mean something later," said Declan. He rode ahead, still tugging on his hair as he thought.

Cadan shook his head. "Or it might mean nothing at all! Sometimes dreams are just dreams."

He looked over his shoulder at me, serious. "Far more important that Aiden return to the castle as soon as we reach Roden. It's not wise for him to linger. We shouldn't have all come, but we worried for you. The forest isn't safe anymore."

Fortress Roden lay ahead, its towers black against the starry sky. My heart began to pound so I could feel my pulse in my fingertips.

"Ryn?" asked Cadan.

I'd seen those ramparts in my dream. It had been Roden burning, not the castle.

"Cadan, those walls—"

"What, Ryn?" Cadan stood up in his stirrups to better see the gate.

"We're here!" announced Aiden. He turned to call back to me. "Perhaps Tanwen sensed you'd be coming. The courtyard is lit."

We passed through the gate, clattering toward Tanwen, who stood stiffly by Roden's great oak doors—Tanwen, who always ran to greet Aiden.

A shiver of fear ran up my spine.

"Aiden!" Tanwen called. "Run!"

Aiden didn't move, but Cadan pulled our horse up and wheeled it around. The gate was only feet away, but the ambassador's soldiers in Danavirian uniform had already filled the courtyard, circling behind us to cut off escape.

"She's here," I whispered.

The Queen stepped out from behind Tanwen, twisting her arm back till she cried out.

"Welcome, children of the King," the Queen called. "I've been expecting you."

Chapter 8

The soldiers surrounded us entirely.

I'd feared so many horrible possibilities that evening, but even I hadn't imagined that the Queen would meet us at Roden. She must have known the entire time.

My brothers and I sat like statues on our horses, and the soldiers, nearly thirty of them, stood as still as stone.

What were so many Danavirian soldiers doing here in Fortress Roden, with the Queen?

The Queen released Tanwen's arm, and Tanwen stepped away. Her red hair hung in long strands around her face, but she didn't look as if she'd been harmed. She looked furious. But she didn't move as the Queen walked slowly toward us, lifting up her golden skirt with a white hand.

Cadan backed our horse away, while the rest urged their horses between the Queen and me. Even Owain moved to guard me. He almost looked like a man then, and I was sorry for ever being angry at him.

Aiden turned his attention to the soldiers. "Danavir and Lacharra have enjoyed peace for over a century. I have no wish to jeopardize that." He pointed at the Queen, while his horse danced beneath him. "She does *not* speak for our country."

The Danavirian soldiers didn't twitch. Aiden glanced at Mael. What was this?

The Queen drew closer. "They are not yours to command or to bargain with, young prince. They are mine."

Now that we were closer, I saw that the soldiers were not the ones who had visited the castle with the ambassador. These men made me think of winter nights and howling winds.

They were the Queen's own guard, dressed in Danavirian livery.

"Then why do *your* soldiers threaten us?" Aiden demanded.

The Queen laughed, a bright splashing sound, as she approached Aiden. His stallion shied away as if it couldn't bear to be so near the Queen.

"When will you learn?" She reached out a hand to Aiden's stallion. It grew still beneath her touch.

Then she looked over at me. "Step down, Andaryn."

Cadan's hand clamped around my arm. "Don't."

"Come to me, sweet Andaryn," called the Queen. It was closer to singing. "Come! Or my men *will* bring you."

Mael, always more reckless than the rest, drew his sword, and the ring of it seemed the beginning of a ghastly symphony. The soldiers in the courtyard drew their obsidian weapons in response.

Cadan cursed.

"See to the young prince's wife!" called the Queen, and

one of her soldiers drew a sword and moved toward Tanwen.

"Aiden." Tanwen's voice was low but strong. "See to Ryn."

Aiden's hand tightened around his sheathed sword's hilt, but he didn't answer. Just looked at his wife, his face pale.

"Your brothers are fine fellows, Andaryn," called the Queen. "If I have to fetch you, it will not go well with them."

Aiden looked back at me, resignation in his eyes. He knew the cost of defying her. Yet he'd vowed to keep me safe! They all had, even Cadan in his own way. Aiden turned back to the Queen and drew his sword.

Cadan cursed again and drew his own sword.

I wished Father had never found the Queen in the forest's dark corners. I wished I'd never challenged her. I wished I'd never run.

I wished so many things.

But I dismounted from my horse, hands shaking so violently that I gripped my cloak to hide it.

Cadan leaped down after me, and my other brothers followed. "No, Ryn!"

The Queen laughed. "Step aside, princes, or your sister will see you cut down."

Less than an hour ago, I'd thought of my brothers like a wall around me. They seemed so human now, just flesh and blood.

Owain moved in front of me and I put a hand on his back. It seemed important to touch him, to let him know I wasn't mad anymore.

"Let me pass," I said.

"Yes, young Owain! Let your sister pass, and you may live to grow as tall as your brothers."

"Ryn!" hissed Mael, trying to look back at me but keep his eyes on the Queen.

I shook my head. "Not like this."

And I meant it. They needed to be free. I couldn't bear it if they were hurt.

I slipped from behind Owain and stood alone before the Queen. I only glanced back at Aiden long enough to see him lower his sword. The soldier guarding Tanwen lowered his sword in response.

The Queen slipped an arm around me, and I saw that she'd taken the shard of the Kingstone and fashioned a web of gold wire around it and joined it to a necklace. She'd caged the Kingstone and was wearing it around her neck.

It was like wearing Father's crown.

I winced as her hand tightened on my shoulder. "You, of all the king's children, have vexed me the most. His heart is most tender toward you. And you have been most vocal against me."

"Is that what you want? His heart?" I asked, trying to pull away. "Enchanting him into a stupor and threatening his children are funny ways of winning it."

"Do I want his heart?" She smiled. "I want it all, child. Every last morsel. And I want *you* to be quiet."

I opened my mouth to answer, to give her anything but the silence she craved. But the clatter of an approaching horse stopped me.

"Father!" I shouted.

Chapter 9

Father ignored me as he rode to the center of the courtyard and dismounted. He just stared at my brothers—and the soldiers surrounding us.

"What's this?" he asked.

I wouldn't be silent, not when the Queen hated my voice so much. "Father—"

He turned to Aiden. "Tell her not to speak to me!"

I stopped.

Father stepped toward Aiden. "I ask you again: What is this?"

Aiden glanced at Tanwen, as if he could gather strength just from seeing her. Then he bowed to Father.

"Ryn—" Father flinched at the sound of my name, but Aiden continued on, "Ryn ran away after she was sent to her chambers. When we discovered she was missing, we rode out after her. As you know, the forest is a dangerous place."

An awful stillness covered the courtyard.

"You defied me," Father said finally.

There should have been a bolt of lightning the moment we realized Father was truly lost to us.

"No," said Aiden. "*No*! We sought only to fetch Ryn from the forest."

"All six of you?" asked the Queen, her voice as soft as harpsong. "Why did you bring her to Fortress Roden? Devoted sons would have taken her back to the castle."

Father began to tremble. "You betrayed me. All of you."

Mael stepped forward. "*We* have not betrayed you! Look around you, Father! Why does your wife dress her guard in Danavirian livery?"

Father stopped, and the iron hardness behind his eyes faltered.

He turned to his wife. "What is this?"

"My dear one," crooned the Queen, "what do you want? Tell me and it shall be done."

"Father!" called Mael. "Don't let this happen. Look! Look around you. Look at *us*."

Father looked across the courtyard, his eyes traveling over his six sons surrounded by soldiers in ill-fitting Danavirian uniforms. I saw each of my brothers try to hold Father's gaze, willing him to see what was before him. Yet Father acted as if he was looking out over a beautiful landscape with no danger or darkness before him.

He couldn't see what was happening. His gaze returned to the Queen, and she was all he saw.

His body stiffened. "Imprison the princes for their treason. I never want to see them again."

"No! You can't do that!" I scrabbled against the hands that held me.

Father swung to face me. "I can't restore my kingdom

to order? You dare to speak to me after all you have done? You attacked my wife! You defied me before my noble guests!"

He looked at me one last time. "You disgust me."

I couldn't breathe. That's what he thought of me?

"My dear one," said the Queen, "return to the castle. I will see that your wishes are carried out." She waved a hand at her soldiers. "Take the princes to the dungeon, then take up position around the fortress. Attack just before dawn."

Attack? The Danavirian livery made sense now. Her guards would level Fortress Roden, killing the princes inside. And Danavir would be blamed.

I want it all. Every last morsel. Including neighboring kingdoms as well.

Lacharra's nobility had just seen Father give her a portion of the Kingstone. This attack would give her justification to begin an unopposed war against Danavir. And Lacharra would win.

Father adjusted his hold on the reins as if he hadn't heard.

"No!" shrieked Tanwen.

Her voice broke Aiden's control. He swung his sword at the soldiers near him.

"You will watch each other's blood soak this courtyard if you do not do as I command," said the Queen softly.

One soldier raised a sword above Tanwen. Another raised his over Aiden. The Queen meant it—she'd strike them both down and sing while they died.

Aiden dropped his sword, the clatter echoing off the

walls. My brothers, one by one, did the same.

Aiden didn't look away from Tanwen, though she stood across the courtyard. "I love you. Don't forget that."

And then the soldiers swarmed my brothers.

Cadan spit on the ground near one of the guards. The black blade flashed, cutting a slash in Cadan's cheek.

"No!" I tried to dart toward him, but the Queen flicked a hand and one of her soldiers held me back.

A moment later, the soldiers led my brothers from the courtyard.

I swung to face Father, to see what he thought of the Queen's guard cutting his son.

Father mounted his horse as if nothing had happened.

The Queen called to him. "I think Tanwen should ride with you. She will stay with us at the castle. I fear she is ill and confused, but our physicians can heal her."

Tanwen struggled against the soldiers who bore her toward us and the horses, until the Queen said something in her ear.

Tanwen stilled.

I thought the Queen had enchanted her too. But as she walked by, she caught me in a desperate embrace and whispered, "Don't come back, Ryn, do you hear me? If you get the chance, run!"

Then the wild soldiers bore her to a horse.

"Don't let her speak again," the Queen commanded.

Tanwen rode silently as some of the Queen's guard escorted her and Father out the gate. Father never looked back at me.

When the hoofbeats died away, the Queen folded her hands and smiled. "Now we visit the princes. Don't let Andaryn lag behind."

⁎ ⁎ ⁎

Two guards dragged me behind the Queen as we walked to the dungeon.

Part of me wanted to collapse and cry like a child, but I wouldn't let myself. My brothers would already be planning something. I needed to be ready for whatever opportunity presented itself.

Pay attention!

I found that the dungeon was strangely comforting. I'd played there as a child, for Roden hadn't been used as a true fortress for years. It was just as I remembered it: still cluttered with old pieces of furniture, even fragments of wagons—a century's worth of refuse.

Then I saw my brothers. They were in a single cell at the hollow center of one of the fortress's crumbling turrets. I could see the night sky with its fading stars at the very top, but it was too tall to climb to freedom—even if there was time before the staged attack began.

I ran to them and rattled the bars of the door as if I could yank it open.

My brothers crowded near. Aiden's expression was drawn and desperate after seeing Tanwen dragged away. Mael looked murderous and Declan calm. Cadan, his cheek bloody from the wild man's cut, gripped the bars as if he wanted to tear them away. Owain tried to hide his fear. And did, mostly.

"What do I do?" I whispered.

"Leave," said Aiden. "Save yourself, Ryn."

Then I understood: There was no plan. There would be no saving. They didn't want me to see them die.

I gripped the bars tighter. There *had* to be something left to do or say.

"You will face me, Andaryn." The Queen's voice echoed off the stone walls.

Owain reached for my hand, but I had already turned to face her.

She gestured at the dim cell. "Look at what you and your words have wrought, Princess: you, rejected and banished by your father; your brothers, imprisoned moments before my guards lay waste to Fortress Roden. All because you wanted to take back the love your father had given *me*."

Her words beat against me, and I had no armor against them—perhaps because I already believed them: I had created this. My brothers were here because of *me*.

My brothers started shouting, but I couldn't understand them.

All that was left were the Queen's words.

"I had thought to leave you here with them, to suffer their fate. But I think I will take you outside with me. I want you to watch Roden burn—"

"No! You can't make me."

"You dare tell me *no*?" The Queen stepped closer. "You should be begging me for your life."

"Go, Ryn!" shouted Aiden. "Leave!"

The rest of my brothers joined the chorus.

The world blurred around me, as if a giant hand had swept across my vision, smudging all the edges and sounds.

It wasn't supposed to end like this. My words were supposed to *stop* her. She wasn't supposed to meet us at Roden, or enchant our father so that he'd ride away from our deaths without looking back.

My vision cleared, and I could see her pale face clearly. *You should be begging* . . .

But not for myself.

For the second time in my life, I knelt, hands outstretched. "Please. Let them go."

"I can't hear you, Andaryn. But then, all you've done till now is shout."

"I throw myself on your mercy, my lady! Please free them!"

"Be quiet, Ryn!" shouted Mael.

But I didn't care. My behavior at the feast, my decision to run, had put my brothers in the dungeon. I'd see them free if it killed me.

I scrabbled closer to the Queen, grabbing handfuls of her skirt. "I *beg* you, let them go!"

The Queen merely smiled down at me, as if tasting something sweet. "You have learned humility too late."

She flicked her hand and the two guards yanked me back so roughly that I sprawled on the floor. One pressed his boot on my shoulder, ready to stop me if I tried to move.

A sound like a mountain falling. The fortress shuddered once more.

The Queen didn't flinch. "You *wretched*, begging child, with your dirty dress and your foolish attempts to steal your father from me and save your brothers!"

She knelt before me, but there was nothing humble about her. Her fingertip caught me under the chin and tilted my head up so that I couldn't look away.

"Hear me, Princess Andaryn: It is time you knew your place. Look at what your words have wrought. You are merely a breath against a storm that breaks trees. You are a speck of dust to be brushed away. You have become nothing to your father. You are even less than that to me."

The last shard of hope shattered inside me, and her words rushed in to fill the void: *You are . . . dust . . . a breath . . . look at what your words have wrought!*

But I clung to the birthright of every last-born.

I didn't care if we lived—I didn't have the strength for it—but I had all the spite of a child determined to infuriate the person who tormented me. Gods knew I had enough practice with my brothers.

I reached for the words that had enraged her, determined that she'd have no joy in killing us.

"We are the House of Cynwrig." I pushed myself back to kneeling. "We are the flight of swans bearing swords."

"Silence!" She yanked her finger away as if burned, and grasped the shard of Kingstone that hung around her neck as she stood once again.

"*You* are the usurper who came from the darkest corner

of the forest." My voice grew stronger as I remembered what I'd told her at the feast, and I chose words Mother might have used. "You crave the power of the House of Cynwrig. You may wear the Kingstone, but you will *never* possess its authority!"

The Queen's fury blazed up, and just as quickly she covered it—a fire smothered beneath a terrible smile.

"You," she panted. "I have your father and the Kingstone. *You* have nothing I wish to possess."

It was a flash of light in a dark place. I spoke from instinct, not cunning. "You want my silence."

"*What?*"

"You want my silence."

She backed away. "I will have that soon enough, when my soldiers leave you in a ditch along the road. It will fuel the coming war, no doubt, when Roden is leveled and Lacharra's only princess is found murdered by the Danavirian band."

I didn't care what happened to me anymore. Didn't care if her soldiers cut me down on the road. My brothers would not die because of me.

And somehow, I knew what to say. "You would have only my death, then. Not my silence."

"Make her stand!"

The soldiers pulled me up.

"Andaryn!" Aiden's voice seemed to come from a distance. "Go away! There's nothing you can do."

Yes. There was.

"Be quiet, king's son!" answered the Queen. "You cannot protect her from inside your cell."

Aiden fell silent.

My heart couldn't beat any faster, but I felt as light as air. I raised my head. "I will be quiet if you let them go."

I waited several heartbeats, certain she'd never agree to such a bargain.

Her eyes narrowed. "Do you think I would trust them to leave and never return?"

Was she considering it?

I didn't stop to think, simply followed the one chance of saving my brothers. "Your soldiers could escort them away. You are powerful enough to manage it."

"I could *manage* it. And you would be silent. How intriguing! I would see to it that your banishment was revoked. You would live in the middle of the desolation you created . . . but not be able to tell your story." She half-smiled. "Never in my life has someone envisioned my desires so clearly."

I let the idea grow within her—and ignored the unease growing in me.

Finally, she spoke. "It would be a great sacrifice to release your brothers. I would expect something great in return: one year of silence for each of them. Not a word spoken," she raised a finger, "and not a word written, either, for a word that's written can be spoken. The moment you consent is the moment they are free."

"Rynni!" shouted Owain. "Don't you dare—!"

It was like running downhill when you're too fast to stop and all you can do is set one foot in front of the next, even when you're not sure you can.

Even when you can't tell whether you're flying or falling.

"You must promise that they will leave the castle *unharmed*," I said. "And you can't kill me. It wouldn't be fair if I can't say anything."

She laughed. "Your life will be sacred, my dear! As you say, it wouldn't be a gift of silence if you were dead."

I glanced at my brothers. Declan stood by Owain, but Mael had murder in his eyes. Aiden just looked at me, shaking his head: *No, Ryn.*

I turned back to the Queen, determined not to be trapped. "How would you know if I spoke or not?"

The Queen laughed again. "Sweet Andaryn! I won't have a servant press her ear against your door all those years, oh no. A woman who lived beside a knot of rivers taught me the power of words. They *do* have power, you see. Words made the world. They create and destroy."

I shivered as if something cold and dark had brushed past me.

"Your words, if you speak, will go into the air, and the air will know *you*. And if the air recognizes a single word from you these next six years, it will pull the breath from your brothers' lungs as payment. They will die, you may count on it. But you may also be sure that they will go free—and remain safe as long as you please me—the moment you give your word. Your last word."

Another crash, and the fortress shook again, debris falling from the planked roof above us. There was so little time before the fortress fell.

I looked back at my brothers. One last step, both flying and falling all at once. "I love you."

"No!" shouted Cadan as the rest of them threw themselves against the bars.

"I agree," I told the Queen. "Set them free."

The moment stretched out, and though I could see my brothers beating against the bars, I hardly heard them. I waited for the Queen to tell the guards to unlock the cell.

Instead she raised her arms above her, fists clenched. Then she shouted a word I didn't understand and opened her hands wide as if releasing something invisible into the air.

Wind roared down the turret. It made torch-flames dance and plastered my brothers' black capes across their shoulders and backs.

Owain's eyes widened in horror.

Declan shouted in pain, but it wasn't a shout. Nor a shriek, either.

Their cloaks fell to tatters, still pressed against their bodies, and then I saw that it wasn't tatters, it was . . .

Aiden threw back his head, calling my name—and his neck stretched longer and longer and his head grew smaller, the black from the cloak covering his face. He flailed, trying to tear the now-feathered cloak from himself.

And then it wasn't a cloak blowing in the wind.

It was wings, black wings.

Gavyn watched it all, his own neck extending as he turned to me. "What have you d—"

Six great, black birds filled the cell, wings brushing

the bars of the door as they took flight. For a moment, the dungeon echoed with trumpet-calls and the clap of wings catching the air beneath them. Then they rose together and disappeared out of the top of the turret.

They were swans. My brothers had turned to swans—*black* swans—before my eyes. She'd transformed them into something we could never imagine, something that would frighten every soul who saw them.

Even mine.

I turned to the Queen, horrified.

She gestured to the now-empty cell. "Behold what you have wrought! They are free."

I opened my mouth but didn't speak. I didn't say a word.

"Good. Good! I knew you could do it," she said. "Don't be so downcast. Your brothers will be men every full moon, though I do not know where they will travel, for swans fly long distances. You, however, will return to the castle with me. A word from me and the king will show his mutinous daughter mercy. But if you displease me, I will set a bounty for the six black swans.

"For six years, you will stand beside your father but not speak to him. You will bear the pity and scorn of the Lacharran court as they wonder at you, and you will feel your silence open a great chasm inside you."

It *was* like falling into a chasm, realizing what I'd done. And I couldn't even scream.

"Oh yes, I know what it is like to be without words." Her malice was potent, but directed at someone else. "I know what it is to beg for them. Didn't I plead with the old woman for months? But I will be more resolute than she was. I'll hold you to these six years, every last second of them."

Then what? I gripped her arms, my cheeks warm with tears.

"You want to know what happens after six years, don't you?"

I nodded.

"After six years, you may speak without killing your swan-brothers. They'll remain free for the rest of their lives."

And then I smelled the smoke.

The Queen motioned to guards. "Bring her with me."

They bore me out into the fresh air.

Chapter 10

Minutes later, we stood in the courtyard as Roden burned. Some of the Queen's soldiers started fires inside the living quarters, where tapestries and tables quickly kindled. Once the wood-shingle roof caught fire, the fortress truly burned, while the Queen's wild guard and their obsidian swords dealt with any servants who tried to flee.

In one night, the Queen had scattered the royal family and sown seeds of war between Lacharra and Danavir. And I had unwittingly helped her.

Behold what you have wrought!

I closed my eyes as one of the great walls began to tilt. I'd seen the wall fall in my dream—I knew the smoke was billowing in great curls as it toppled, sensed the gaping hole that the flames hadn't yet filled . . .

I heard the crash as the wall fell and opened my eyes. There was the hole, an entrance to a corridor that led to the back of the fortress.

I heard Tanwen's voice*: Don't come back, Ryn, do you hear me? If you get the chance, run!*

Run.

I'd stood so still that the Queen's guards had released me while they watched Roden burn. I would die if I ran into the fire. But returning to my father's castle would be its own sort of death.

The fire would be a relief.

Run!

One last glance at the Queen. And the Kingstone fragment that hung around her neck.

I leaped forward, using my momentum to wrench the Kingstone free. I was beyond her by the time I'd yanked it from her neck. I didn't slow as I tucked my satchel close and dashed into the burning fortress.

The Queen shouted after me.

Let her follow me into the flame. Let her try and find the Kingstone in the burning rubble!

But the hallway was empty of flame—perhaps I wouldn't die in Roden after all.

Run.

I ran on.

The air filling the corridor grew hotter and hotter as I ran, so I dropped to my hands and knees, pressing still farther into the fortress. I could hear the splinter of wood as it gave way in the darkness ahead of me.

If the fire was a monster, then the searing, smoke-clogged air that gusted around me was its breath. It grew thicker till I began to choke, even as I groped along the floor.

Then cool air rushed past me. It didn't cut the smoke that roiled along the ceiling, but it was as welcome as water. I blindly swung a hand toward it, expecting to meet a wall.

Nothing. Perhaps an old chute or window.

A roar echoed down the stone walls, and orange light blossomed behind me: the fire had finally found the corridor. Flames streamed toward me as if driven by a bellows.

I threw myself out of the hole in the wall. Fire and gray sky spun around and around me as I tumbled away.

When I stopped, I lay at the bottom of the embankment, my satchel twisted around me, the Kingstone still in my fist. I looked up at Roden. The portion of the fortress I'd crawled through crumbled as I watched.

Let them think I'd died in it.

I heaved myself to my feet, untangling my limbs from the satchel.

Run . . . run!

Tripping and falling and standing again, I fled into the early morning mist beyond Roden's walls. I stayed in the smoke that filled the forest as I ran. Ran from the Queen. Ran from the flames. Ran from the memory of my brothers being twisted into black swans.

But I couldn't run fast enough to leave *that* behind. It was etched on the back of my eyes. Not even my tears could blur it.

Behold what you have wrought!

⁂

I'd outrun even the hint of smoke when I fell to my hands and knees one last time. I couldn't even crawl. I pitched forward, dead leaves crumbling like old parchment beneath me. Exhausted beyond all measure, I fell asleep.

In my dreams, I saw the dark enchantment seize my brothers. I heard Owain's shriek a thousand times. And through it all, I saw the Queen. Her voice reached inside me and turned whatever it touched to fear.

When I woke, the sun was a few hours from setting, and my cheeks were wet. I tried to wipe my cheeks but gasped at the pain in my hands. They were bruised and covered with cuts. I'd fallen almost as much as I'd run.

I slowly sat, grateful for the weak sunlight that spilled through the trees. The movement seemed to loosen something in my chest and I coughed, throat stinging from the smoke. Coughed and coughed till I vomited what little I had in my stomach.

Even in daylight, I heard my brothers' screams as they turned to swans, the wind as it swept them away. And Tanwen! She was back at the castle, if she was even alive. I saw it all, again and again.

It was the Queen's artwork, drawn just for me. I would never forget any part of it.

I pushed myself to my feet, gripping the nearest tree for support. Then I noticed the Kingstone, still clutched in my hand. It wasn't much to look at: a bit of stone with only a carved feather visible on it.

But it was enough.

Enough to remind myself of that one small victory against the Queen. Enough to tell myself that maybe I'd saved my brothers after all.

Enough to keep going.

I tied knot after knot in the fine chain I'd broken when I tore the necklace from the Queen. Then I hung the Kingstone around my neck and tucked it so that it hung beneath my bodice.

A breeze rattled the branches, and I held my hand out to it. It tickled my bruised palm and then caught up dead leaves as it flowed through the forest.

The wind had taken my brothers from me. I'd follow it until I found them.

I stumbled after the wind.

Chapter 11

Before the first full moon of the enchantment

For days, I followed the westward-moving wind, my mind and heart too numb to do anything but keep walking. When I couldn't walk, I slept where I fell, though *sleep* was too kind a word for it.

Even then, I could still see Roden fall and my brothers fly away.

Finally, days after the food in my satchel was depleted, the wind drifted past a creek. I knelt beside the pool and stared at the water, my mind so frayed I hardly knew what was before me.

I dipped a dirty finger in, felt the water's chill travel up my wrist.

Then my body remembered what my mind could not: I was thirsty. I lapped the water like a dog. When I'd drunk my fill, my stomach was so full of water that I almost didn't mind the hunger.

Almost.

But now that my heart and mind were beginning to wake, something gnawed at the edge of my memory. I squinted up at the nearly full moon. My brothers would change soon. And I didn't know where they were.

I rested my head in my hands, taking handfuls of my hair the way Declan did when he thought. If my swan-brothers were near, they'd be at a lake. Swans were always in a lake.

I had to find a lake.

⁂

When the sun rose, I followed the creek downhill. As I walked, I imagined what it would be like to see my brothers again. Perhaps they'd be able to talk, even as swans. What I'd give just to hear their voices!

After several hours, the creek opened into a small, tree-sheltered lake.

I stood, panting, at the banks, as I searched for black swans.

Nothing.

I slumped onto one of the boulders along the bank, too tired to search for another lake. I'd been a fool to think that in the lake-filled Northlands, I'd find the one where my brothers sheltered.

Using my satchel for a pillow, I slept on the sun-warmed stone.

⁂

I woke to what sounded like voices and jumped to my feet, certain the Queen's guards had discovered me. Instead, six black swans swept low over the lake, their wings beating the air. One by one, they landed in a spray of water.

For days, my only company had been memories of Roden and the Queen's curse. But now my swan-brothers had come. I'd never been so happy to see anything in my life.

Aide—!

I froze. I'd been a breath away from killing my brothers.

I pressed my hands over my mouth, aghast at how easy it would be to break my silence.

All the while, my swan-brothers circled and honked as they explored the lake, unaware of how close they'd come to death.

Unaware of *me*.

I left my boots and the satchel on the boulder and splashed into the achingly cold water, tripping over the weeds that tangled around my ankles and legs. I waded waist-deep into the water where my brothers swam.

There was no reunion. No human speech.

They were just swans. Black swans.

Two of them glanced at me before darting into deeper water. One drifted near, its wings held a little from its body in warning, so close that I could see the white feathers that lined the underside of its wings.

I needed my brothers. Surely they'd remember me if I could just touch them.

I leaned forward, my fingers brushing the glossy black feathers.

Trumpets! Wings! Red beaks pecked at me as I covered

my face. They didn't stop their attack until I splashed, shivering, back to the water's edge.

My swan-brothers were as wild as any other creature.

Or perhaps they knew, even as swans, what I'd done.

At home, someone would have wrapped a blanket around my shoulders. My brothers would have chased away the creatures that hurt me. There would have been warmth and comfort and at least a fire.

Yet this lakeside wasn't the castle, and it was my brothers who had hurt me. The night didn't care if I was the princess of Lacharra. If there was going to be a fire, I'd have to kindle it.

Very well then.

I stood and wrung the water from my skirts. Cadan had provisioned my satchel so many nights ago at Roden. When I dug to the bottom of it, I found the flint.

I knew how to start a fire with flint, thanks to my brothers and a bet that Gavyn could teach me how to start a fire faster than Owain. After some coaching from him, I did.

Twice.

It had been a game then, but it served me well that night. I soon had a merry little fire crackling and sparking.

Near dusk, the swans heaved themselves out of the water, their leathery black feet flapping in the mud and reeds. They hardly noticed me as they huddled at the shore, honking uneasily.

I stayed beside the fire, trying to decide which swan was which brother.

The smallest was Owain, of course. Would the biggest be Aiden or Mael? Mael was taller, but Aiden was broader. One of them kept pecking at another, just the way Cadan picked at Declan, mocking him. And the one who edged so near me could be Gavyn, watching, always watching.

Then I heard wind tearing at the trees on the far side of the lake.

I stood.

The swans' frantic trumpeting was lost in the rush of wind as it roared over us.

Owain screamed.

Cadan's shouts rose above the wind.

As quickly as it had come, the wind swirled itself into stillness while the ghostly shapes emerged from the darkness.

"Father? *Father!*" called Owain.

"Where are we?" That was Gavyn, his voice low.

I froze. They didn't remember what had happened in the dungeon.

I'd have to tell them how I'd tried to outwit the Queen. How I'd lost so horribly and how they—

"Ryn! Andaryn! Are you there?" It was Aiden.

And then it didn't matter that I'd have to tell them. My brothers were *here*. I needed to see them, to have them stand around me once again, even if they hated me.

I gathered my still-damp skirts and ran to them.

"*Stop!*"

The wildness in Aiden's voice rooted me in place. I stood in darkness, just outside the fire's ring of light, waiting for him to explain. He whispered something to my brothers.

Were they already angry?

I took two steps toward them, and Aiden shouted again, "Stay where you are, Ryn!"

I stopped but couldn't hold back a silent sob.

"We're naked, Ryn!" called Cadan, his voice bristling with anger. "Not a stitch of clothing! What in *heaven's* name has happened to us?"

I gasped.

Why hadn't I thought of clothes?

I ran to my satchel and dug through it. I had the two lap blankets and nothing else. I scooped up the blankets and the dagger. They'd have to cut pieces for themselves.

I walked as near as I dared and dropped everything in a heap before darting back.

Pale figures drifted closer, plucking up what I'd dropped.

"How are you, Ryn?" called Aiden. "Are you hurt?"

I couldn't answer, but at least Aiden didn't sound angry anymore.

"Cadan didn't mean to shout," said Declan.

"I damn well meant to shout," muttered Cadan. "I'll not have my sister see me naked as a—"

The sound of a blow landing and a grunt.

"You scared her!" That was Mael.

Through it all, I heard Owain's uneven breathing. It made my own breath catch.

"Andaryn!" Aiden only used my full name when he was worried. "Say something! Let us know you're well!"

How I wanted to answer them! But I clapped a hand over my mouth, worried I'd be as foolish as when I first saw them on the lake.

"Hurry . . . hurry . . ." It was too low to tell who spoke, but not low enough to hide the fear.

A moment later, my brothers stepped toward me. They looked ghostly white in the moonlight, with scraps of blanket tied around their waists.

But I didn't care. No red eyes. No red beaks. It was their faces, their own dear faces, and their dark eyes. I ran to them, tripping in the darkness but never falling. Not once.

"Ryn!" said Aiden. "What happened? What's wrong?"

I threw myself at him.

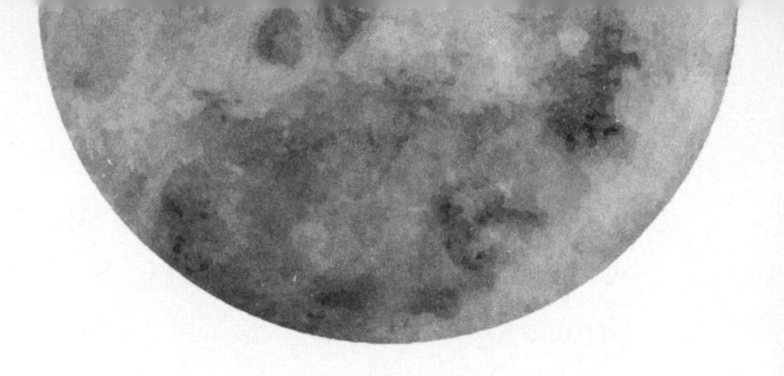

Chapter 12

First full moon

Aiden scooped me up. It was the world set right for a single moment.

I turned my face into Aiden's neck and wept. His arms tightened around me as I cried on, sobs pushing up from my belly. I felt a rain of hands on my back—some gentle, some awkward—as my brothers maneuvered me to the fire. They were so careful that it only made me cry harder, and I kept a hand pressed to my mouth to stay silent.

All the while, my brothers talked among themselves.

"Where do you think we are? How far from Roden?"

"She's gotten thin—how long have we been away?"

One of them made an impatient sound—Declan perhaps? "Let her cry. Ask questions later."

"That's a fine idea," muttered Cadan, "so long as the Queen isn't near."

Hands on my shoulders pulling me back. Cadan's face swam into view, blurred by my tears. "Where is she, Ryn? Are we safe?"

My mouth moved to answer him, but I kept my hand clapped over it and nodded.

Cadan tilted his head, as if trying to figure out what was wrong. "Don't cry, Ryn-girl! We'll set things right soon."

I knew better.

"Get something for her tears!" Mael hissed to the others. "She's dripping all over . . ."

"Where? There's not a scrap of cloth left—"

A ripping sound, and Gavyn pressed something into my hands. "For your face."

I pressed the bit of blanket over my eyes, hiding there for just a moment. *Please, Mother, I don't know how to tell them!*

I pulled in a shuddering breath and looked up.

Mael leaned back enough to see me. "Better?"

No. But I nodded anyway.

Aiden dropped another branch on the fire, then knelt beside me as everyone else crowded around. "What's happened, Ryn?"

The telling felt too big for me. I didn't know how to start.

"Why aren't you talking?" asked Gavyn.

"She hasn't said a word," said Cadan. "Not even when I asked her about the Queen."

"It wasn't a dream, was it?" whispered Owain.

I shook my head. *No.*

Cadan turned to Owain. "The dungeon."

"The Queen." Aiden's eyes narrowed.

"Oh," said Gavyn, who had been the last to transform, "I remember now. You struck a deal with her: your silence for our freedom. That's why we're here. That's why you haven't said anything."

"Ryn!" Mael breathed, disappointment and grief in his eyes.

But Gavyn was piecing that awful night together, trying to remember. "I saw Aiden *change*—"

"Change?" asked Cadan.

"To a swan," whispered Gavyn. "A black swan. We all did. That's why we're here, wherever we are," said Gavyn. "That's why we were naked. We didn't wake up next to a lake—we changed back to men."

"That's not possible." Cadan spoke like Gavyn was a child who didn't understand. "Men don't change into swans. And black swans don't exist!"

No one answered.

Finally Mael turned to me. "Ryn?"

There was a world of questions in that one word! I was almost glad I couldn't speak. I simply pointed to Gavyn and nodded. *He's right.*

Aiden sat still and released a long, slow breath. Owain shook his head. Mael looked from me to Gavyn and back again, as if waiting for someone to say it was a joke. Declan buried his face in his hands.

"What happens if you talk, Ryn?" murmured Aiden.

I shook my head.

"We die," announced Cadan. "She speaks and we die. Even I remember that much!"

Aiden took me by the shoulders. "How long has it been?"

I held up a finger.

"A day?" asked Declan.

Cadan shoved him. "She traveled this far in a day, poet? Not in the real world."

Declan righted himself. "We've gone past what happens in the real world, wouldn't you say?"

"A week," said Aiden, still looking at me. "It's been a week, hasn't it?"

I nodded.

"I don't remember a moment of it," said Gavyn.

"How long?" asked Cadan, his voice expressionless. "How long does this last?"

I held up six fingers, not daring to look any of them in the eye.

"Six . . ." But Gavyn didn't dare finish the sentence.

"Years! Six *years*, Gavyn!" shouted Cadan. He stomped away, then looked back at me, firelight dancing over his face. The small, cringing part of me that couldn't bring myself to face his anger noticed that the cut on his cheek had begun to heal, even while he was a swan. "What were you thinking?"

"She was saving us, idiot!" snapped Declan.

Cadan shot him an incredulous look. So did I. Declan had never spoken to him so, no matter how Cadan baited him.

"Saving us!" muttered Owain. "We were at Roden because of her!"

Mael cuffed him on the back of his head.

Declan turned on him and Cadan. "We were at Roden because Ryn had to choose whether to give the Kingstone to the Queen or defy Father! Would *you* have handed the shard to the Queen?"

Owain swallowed. "No. But I'd have—"

"What *would* you have done, then?" pressed Declan, as fierce as I'd ever seen him. "Because I remember you sitting there while Ryn—"

Enough! Having them fight about me was worse than them being mad at me. I pulled the Kingstone shard from its hiding place beneath my bodice.

My brothers were as mute as I was.

I slipped the Kingstone off my neck and handed it to Aiden.

Cadan crowded close. "You *stole* it from her, Ryn-girl? That's the best news I've heard all night!"

Gavyn gave a low, wondering whistle.

"When did you take it?" asked Cadan. "Did she explode with rage? Please say she did."

"Wait," said Mael. "Let's hear—"

"Ryn can't talk," interrupted Gavyn.

Mael rolled his eyes. "Let's *learn* all that happened. Gavyn, tell us what you remember from that night. It'll save Ryn time. Ryn, you stop him if he's wrong."

So Gavyn described all that happened, beginning with when we arrived in Roden's courtyard. When he reached the part where they were led away, I put a hand on his arm to stop him. They needed to know about Tanwen.

I crouched beside the fire and drew in the dirt with a stick. With enough pictures and pantomime, my brothers understood Tanwen's command that I should run—and that she'd been taken back to the castle.

Then I let Gavyn and his near-perfect memory recount the last minutes in the dungeon when I tried to free them before Fortress Roden fell.

"That was the best I could hear, Ryn," he finished. "You and the Queen were standing far away. Did I miss anything?"

I shook my head. I showed how I snatched the Kingstone from the Queen and ran into the burning fortress to escape her.

The Kingstone—and its fragment—wasn't a signet ring. It didn't impart the ability to make laws, but it meant something, nonetheless. I hoped that even if the nobles of Lacharra became completely smitten with the Queen, it would rankle that Father had chipped off a piece for her. And whether it meant anything to *them* that she lost it, it meant the world to me that I'd kept her from having it.

"You ran into the *fire*?" exclaimed Owain.

I nodded, then sketched the walls falling over.

"She thinks you died in Roden, then," murmured Aiden.

Mael grinned. "I'd bet my chances with any Lacharran maid"—Aiden elbowed him in the side—"that the Queen has those wild men of hers poking through the rubble trying to find the Kingstone."

We were silent a minute.

Aiden handed the Kingstone back to me. "She won't look for you. That's good."

"Unless she hears rumors of you," added Gavyn. "Then she'll hunt you *and* the Kingstone."

Aiden couldn't take his eyes off the Kingstone. "I should have stopped this—"

Mael dropped a hand on Aiden's shoulder. "No more of that! The blame isn't ours alone: Father shouldn't have brought her home. And yet she found him when he was sick. Look what she did to us when we were well and whole."

Aiden blew out a breath. "Very well. No blame, then."

Gavyn cleared his throat. "What happens now, Ryn? How long before we turn back to swans?"

I quickly drew a sun rising over the horizon. *Dawn.*

"We have hours, then." Aiden stood, brushing dirt from his hands. "Let's see to Ryn."

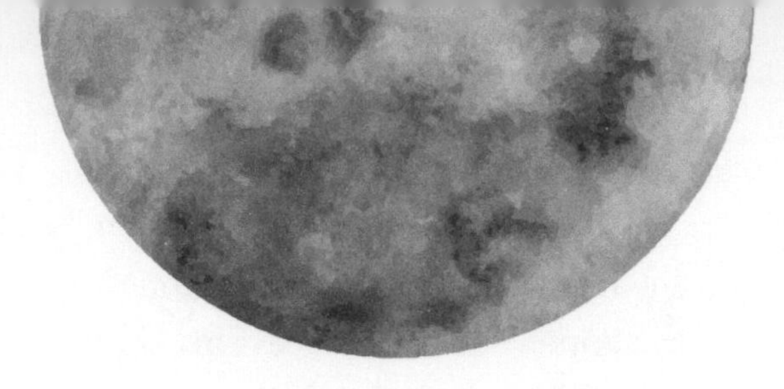

Chapter 13
First full moon

Over the next few hours, my brothers helped me prepare for the month ahead. Cadan and Owain hunted for food.

"No wonder I'm so hungry!" muttered Cadan as they strode away. "I haven't eaten in over a week!"

Gavyn looked up from the time-keeper he was making me. "If we're anything like normal swans, we feed several hours a day. You've probably had four meals today already!" he called to Cadan's retreating back.

Mael rolled his eyes, but I didn't mind Gavyn's talk. Cadan complained to the world when things were wrong, and Declan found refuge in stories and songs. Gavyn didn't feel better until he could explain.

I just felt sorry for whoever had to listen to the explaining.

"Here, Ryn," said Mael, his hands full of vines and longer branches he'd gathered. "We'll make a weir, one small enough that you can carry it on your back."

He arranged the branches into a cone. I held them steady while he wove the vines around it till it looked like a poorly made basket. That was shaped like a trumpet.

I shook my head.

Mael didn't look up from his work. "I saw that, Ryn. It's supposed to look like this. Water goes through, fish don't. Though it won't work in still water. We need to find the rivers that feed into or out of the lake."

He led me along the bank, gingerly, for he was barefoot. And he was already beginning to shiver.

My brothers needed shoes. And clothes.

I resolved they'd have them by next full moon.

Finally Mael found a small river, a dark ribbon edged in moonlight. He made me wedge the weir between two rocks so that water flowed into the wide end. "It won't pull many fish, but it'll keep you from starving."

Gavyn showed me a strip of linen the moment we returned to the fire. "You need to keep track of the days that pass. You don't have anything to write with or on, so this will have to do for the first year, at least. I've frayed the edges. Every night, you must tie a knot in one of the strings: one day, one knot. On the full moons, we'll tie a second knot in that day's string so that we can keep track of those too." He looked down at his handiwork, satisfied. "It's as important as traps and shelter. We can't have you speak too early."

"Or too late," added Declan. "I'd never forgive myself if Ryn stayed silent even an extra day because we didn't keep track."

Mael looked up from his work on Mother's belt. We'd decided that I should use it to buy supplies, but the gold links needed to be broken apart so that it wasn't recognizable.

"I'll keep track of time, don't you worry. The first thing I'll do is strangle the Queen. I don't care if the entire court of Lacharra watches."

"If there still is a court," added Cadan.

Owain, back from the hunt, looked up from the rabbit he was skinning with my dagger. "Keeping time should be the easy part: in six years, we'll be men again."

And then I remembered what the Queen had said: *After six years, you may speak without killing your swan-brothers. They'll remain free.*

She never promised they'd become men again.

I'd condemned my brothers to live as swans. I thought I'd been so cunning, demanding that she let my brothers go unharmed. And all the while, she'd known that my brothers would never see Lacharra in sunlight again.

I nearly jumped straight into the trees when Declan sat beside me.

"Are you cold, Ryn? I'll find more wood for the fire."

Before I could answer, he disappeared into the dark to find it.

"I can't calculate it tonight," said Gavyn, who was still talking. *Had it only been a moment since I'd realized what the Queen had done?* ". . . but I estimate that there will be seventy-five full moons during the six years."

Mael frowned. "I thought there were twelve moons a year: one each month."

"No. Some years, there are thirteen moons. You see, the number of days from full moon to full—"

Cadan flopped down by the fire. "I've suffered enough being turned to a swan. Don't make me endure one of Gavyn's astronomy lessons, Aiden!"

Mael smothered a smile, but we all looked to Aiden.

"Our concern now is Andaryn," said Aiden, "and keeping her safe."

For days, I'd wanted my brothers around me, smiling and happy to see me. But I couldn't bear it. I didn't deserve it, not after what I'd done.

Declan returned with a piece of wood and placed it on the fire. I took another stick to poke at the fire, grateful for an excuse not to meet their eyes.

"There are"—Mael paused, choosing his words—"many dangers in the woods. How do we keep Ryn safe when we are swans?"

For a moment, there was only the pop and hiss of the wood on the fire.

"Maybe we could." Cadan laughed. "Do you remember the time the geese chased Declan when he wandered too close to their nests?"

Declan didn't answer, just took my wrist and held my arm toward the firelight. The bruises from their attack were already visible. "Did we do that?"

I tried to pull my arm away, but he wouldn't release it.

"Why didn't you tell us, Ryn?" asked Aiden.

"Well, there's that bargain she made about not speaking," began Cadan sarcastically, but Mael hushed him.

I pulled my sleeve down over my wrist, but it was already too late: Aiden looked broken. He glanced at the gray eastern horizon and then asked Gavyn, "How do we keep this from happening?"

"If we were dogs, I'd have her leave clothes behind to get us used to her scent, but—"

"We could stay away," offered Aiden. "We don't have to visit her when we change."

"Don't we?" asked Owain. "How else can you explain us landing at *this* lake? Ryn didn't find us—we found her." He still didn't sound happy about it, either.

Silence.

"That's good, then," declared Mael. "It means that part of us knows Ryn, even when we're swans."

"So long as she doesn't try to touch us," said Cadan.

"That could change over time," said Gavyn. "It would, even with normal swans."

"We could work to change it," said Aiden, and I sensed how glad he was to have some task over the next month.

"Can we?" asked Gavyn. My brothers looked at each other around the fire, a silent conversation skipping back and forth between them.

A fool's idea. Cadan didn't hide his disdain.

Gavyn shrugged.

Mael raised an eyebrow. *We'll try. It can't hurt.*

Aiden nodded. "We try to hold onto our minds, then. Even after the change."

My brothers sobered, and I remembered their shouts as the wind found them in the turret. Such a transformation must hurt.

They stood on the edge of that pain again.

Cadan hurled a twig into the fire. "Think of it as wearing feathers, this turning into a swan. I *won't* be afraid of feathers. Not for as many times as it will happen."

"It hurt," murmured Owain.

"So would falling off a horse," said Cadan.

Owain glared at Cadan. "It wasn't like falling off a horse! It was a pain in the center of me."

"The pain was in your bones," said Gavyn. "Birds' bones are hollow. Every time we change, our—"

Cadan cuffed Gavyn on the head.

"—our bones are scooped out?" finished Aiden for him. "How does it help us to know that?"

"It helps *me*." Gavyn glared at Cadan. "I can bear it if I know why it hurts."

Mael shook his head. "Keep your comfort to yourself, Gavyn. I'd rather not know what happens when I change."

I glanced at the horizon, then interrupted them and mimicked walking.

"Where are you walking, Ryn?" asked Declan.

I held up both hands, with an exasperated look. *Exactly! Where should I go?*

"Good question," answered Gavyn.

I shrugged again. *Well?*

"The hunting hut near Cairwyn Lake," said Aiden. "I don't think the Queen knows about it."

Aiden looked down at my drawings beside the fire. He smoothed the dirt with his hand, then sketched a map in the dirt. "If I'm right, we're on the shores of Lake Sandall.

To find the hut, you need to go north along the headwaters, past the town of Etten. The hut will be a good week"—he glanced at me— "two weeks' journey."

I didn't hear the rest. In the middle of Aiden's map, three rivers met.

Three rivers. Why did that seem important?

"—I don't know if we'll follow you as you travel, Ryn," continued Aiden. "But the trek is clear. Now *you* draw the way."

He erased what he'd scratched into the dirt and had me try. After four attempts, I could recreate the way. "Good," he said. "Draw it every morning and every night so that you remember—"

A fierce wind pulled at the treetops across the lake. We all turned at the sound.

Aiden took me by the shoulders. "We're going to hold on to our minds so we don't hurt you. But go to the hunting hut. We'll see you there next moon."

Small waves lapped at the shore, running before the wind.

Aiden stood. "We need to leave now so we don't hurt her again."

Then it was a tangle of good-byes, hands squeezing my own, and fast, fierce hugs.

"Quick!" barked Aiden, his voice ragged. The change was beginning.

They loped to the shoreline, clutching the tied blankets around them.

"Clothes, Ryn!" called Cadan back over his shoulder.

"Have clothes for us next time! It's the worst part of this, opening your eyes and—"

The wind caught them and a shadow streamed over their bodies, blotting them out. Cadan's neck began to stretch. He tried to tear at his throat, but by the time he'd swung his arms forward, they'd turned to wings. Owain's shout turned to a rippling trumpet, and I prayed it didn't hurt him so much this time.

They didn't stop, my brothers. They'd been running as they changed, and in a moment, they were swans hobbling toward the water, wings sweeping the air beneath them.

All except one: Aiden. He paused, then stumbled over his webbed feet as if his body carried him someplace he didn't want to go. The swan looked back at me with its red eyes, but I saw my brother, determined to hold onto his mind.

Then sunlight streaked across the lake, tipping the waves with gold. It touched the swan, and I saw Aiden slip away.

I dropped to my knees.

I'd thought home was the castle, my bed draped with curtains, my window seat that looked out over the fields. But home was my brothers, all six of them, a living castle around me.

My swan-brothers drifted to the far side of the lake. Two of them flipped so that their heads were underwater, their black tails pointed toward the sky. One of the swans righted itself, then pivoted to watch me, neck arched.

I couldn't let my brothers stay swans. I stood, then walked to collect the scraps of blankets they'd dropped along the shore.

I also gathered some of the black feathers scattered there, brushing them across my cheek. I'd tie them together and keep them so I could remember my brothers when I left for the hut. All I had to do was follow the headwaters—

Headwaters. A tangle of rivers. And the Queen's low-burning fury.

A woman beside a knot of rivers who taught her the power of words. Who'd made her beg.

I had to find her. She might be able to tell me who the Queen truly was. And how to stop her.

How to make her beg once more.

I'd meet my brothers at Cairwyn by the next full moon, but I'd find the woman beside the rivers first.

I'd discover how to set my brothers free.

Chapter 14

Aiden's map had made the journey to the hut look so simple: all I had to do was follow the headwaters for two weeks.

I thought there would be a narrow, winding path the entire way.

I quickly learned that following a river meant scrabbling over fallen trees and along steep banks. It meant almost falling into the water a dozen times.

It meant actually falling in twice.

I learned there was a reason travelers carried walking sticks, and I fashioned one out of a branch I hacked from a newly fallen tree. I only fell in the river once after that.

All the while, I thought about the knot of rivers between me and Cairwyn Lake.

A woman who lived beside a knot of rivers taught me the power of words.

Would this woman know how to undo that power?

And would she tell me?

⁎ ⁎ ⁎

Two nights after the full moon, I stopped along a level bit of land beside the river. I'd put off using Mael's weir because . . . I huffed out a breath, ashamed at myself . . . I didn't want to have to clean a fish.

But after two days of travel, I *had* to fill my belly. I set the weir between two submerged boulders where the water moved as fast as a winter wind, and limped back to where I'd left my satchel to start the fire. The blisters had merely stung this morning. My feet throbbed now.

I ignored them long enough to properly start the fire, then gingerly removed my boots. Little wonder my feet hurt: my stockings were bloody. I'd torn the blisters.

If I was home, one of my brothers would have carried me to my room while another fetched the physician. I'd be so busy listening to Declan's scolding or Gavyn's lesson that I wouldn't even notice the physician's ministrations.

Tonight, I would have to be my own physician.

So I peeled off the stockings, then hobbled to the river. There was a dry rock near the weir to sit on, and I lowered my feet into the rushing water. The water sent goosebumps racing up my legs, but it numbed the pain. I kicked my feet in the current until the weir jumped.

When I finally pulled the weir out of the water, I saw two fish trapped in the narrow end of the trumpet shape.

Two!

I cradled the weir like a dripping baby while the fish inside it tried to flop free.

Now what?

The dagger.

I hobbled back to the fire, still holding the weir, and dug through the satchel with one hand. The fire was running out of fuel, so I added a few more branches before taking the dagger and the weir back to the river.

The fish had stilled in those few minutes, and I sighed in relief. Perhaps they were already dead.

They weren't. The minute I reached into the weir, they both flopped around.

A few minutes later, I still hadn't managed to keep hold of a fish. I sat back on my heels.

It was getting dark, with a gibbous moon rising in the east.

The moon reminded me of the Queen, a pale, beautiful face staring down at me from the sky. I could be sensible and brave during the day, but at night the moon—even if it was waning—made me feel hunted.

I imagined my brothers: Aiden stroking his beard. Mael with one eyebrow raised. Gavyn with his finger at the place where he'd stopped reading in his latest book.

And then my mind didn't have room to fear the moon and the Queen.

How long do you plan on waiting, Ryn? That was Cadan's voice. *Till the fish turn to dust?*

A frustrated grunt from Owain. Apparently, he was mad at me even when I imagined him.

You can do this, encouraged Declan. *You'll get used to cleaning the fish—*

I know she can do it, interrupted Cadan. *I'd just like to see it before I'm an old man.*

I laughed silently, right under the rising moon.

Lips pressed together, I reached into the weir. I could almost feel my brothers crowded around me as I wrapped my fingers around the struggling fish and pulled it out.

I'm sorry, I thought. *I'll be as quick as I can.*

Dream-Cadan mocked the silliness of my little speech, but Declan whispered encouragement. And with my brothers looking over my shoulders, I slipped the knife into the gills, sawing till I'd severed its head, my head half-turned away from the gruesome task.

It took more work to slice open the belly and clean out the guts, but I could almost feel my brothers patting my shoulders.

Well done, Ryn-girl! That was Mael.

Next time, you should angle the knife differently, pointed out Gavyn. *It'll make the cut cleaner.*

It *was* easier with the second fish. I remembered what I'd seen fishermen do: I whacked it on the side of the head with a rock and it immediately went still.

It took only a minute to clean that one. After washing my hands and the fish in the water, I returned to the fire. A little later, I ate the fish I'd cleaned and cooked. Plain as they were, I'd never tasted food so satisfying in all my life.

Afterward, I sent my dream-brothers on their way, worried that if I became too used to hearing imaginary voices, I wouldn't be able to hear real ones.

Clothes, Ryn! Don't forget to have clothes by the next moon! called Cadan.

I watched the fire fall to coals, feeling small and alone, thinking of Father.

I quickly sketched the map of my journey in the dirt beside the fire to keep the path fresh in my mind, but I couldn't stop thinking of home.

Don't forget me, Father.

I erased the map and drew the swans from the Cynwrig crest, the long necks stretching toward freedom in the Northlands. The pebbly soil wasn't suited for drawing, and the lines in the dirt were crude and wavering. And yet, drawing pictures in the dirt was almost as good as speech. It let me remember the life I'd left. It let me draw my hope for the future, a prayer for my father and brothers sent into the night.

We are not a game of swans, not anyone's game.

I drew the wide wings riding the air.

We're a flight of swans. And I'm going to help my brothers fly to freedom.

Chapter 15

After a week of walking, I discovered the knot of three rivers. I camped beside the joining, determined to spend as many days as I needed to find the woman.

After five days of searching in widening circles around the camp, I found her cottage.

I didn't even know it was a cottage at first.

All I saw was the rotting thatch roof rising above a sea of weeds, and the top of a half-open door and two windows. There was no smoke coming from the chimney, no movement behind the shadowed windows. The forest had already crawled back into the small patch of land, sending saplings into the overgrowth that filled the clearing.

I turned around slowly at the edge of the weeds, hoping for some hint of life, even though I suspected no one would let a cottage fall into such ruin.

I'd been so sure she'd be here! *What now?*

A flash of movement near my feet.

I jumped away, slapping a hand over my mouth to stop the shriek.

It was just a finch, pecking at the insects that swarmed

among the weeds. He darted away, sending some of the weeds flashing toward me. I pushed them away and nearly yelped at the fire in the leaves: nettles!

I'd fallen into a nettle patch when I was a child and had borne the pain of it for several days. A few stings weren't bad—similar to ant bites—but any more than that could make your skin burn.

Then I heard the scrape of wood against stone as the cottage door moved.

"Who's there?" The voice sounded as rasping as the door.

I dropped into a crouch beside the nettles, heart racing as if the Queen herself had found me.

"I know you're there."

Don't hide here, I thought. *You looked for her!*

I gripped my walking stick—and stood.

The woman in the doorway was shabbily dressed, her clothing and shawl all the same drab color. As soon as she saw me, she shuffled off the step and into the nettles between us, clutching her shawl close to protect herself. She moved through the nettles like a boat through water, her head hunched forward and her eyes on me.

Always on me.

I gripped my walking stick tighter as she neared, horribly aware that it was too skinny to protect me if I needed it.

The woman stopped right in front of me. Her eyes, both faded and too bright all at once, narrowed when she saw the feathers at my belt.

"Black swans," she murmured. "My birds have been chattering of black swans, and I told myself, told myself, told myself that she had nothing to do with it. But I knew better."

I understood the words but had no idea what she *meant*. It reminded me of when Gavyn was trying to explain something. Yet I was certain I'd found the right woman. No one would look at black feathers and think they came from swans.

I slowly extended a hand to her—the only form of greeting I had.

She glared at it, her voice trembling between grief and rage. "And so you've come, Swan-Keeper! What will my snowy one do now?"

I stepped back, confused. Frightened. Who did she think I was?

I shook my head, trying to show I didn't understand.

She relaxed a little, shoulders lowering, gaze clearing. She waved a hand as if dismissing her anger, and I saw she wore gloves. Of course she did, in a cottage overrun by nettles.

"Don't mind an old woman's grief. My snowy one's done harm, but I can't stop loving her, can I? And I can't help hating you. The blackness fills my heart just to see you." She scraped her gloved hand across her cheek. "But I'll tell you what you need to know. Perhaps it will gain me forgiveness for what I've done."

Snowy one, again. Did she mean the Queen?

"Come with me," she said, turning to go back through the nettles. She kept an arm extended to sweep nettles aside for me. "Hear my story."

I'd have turned and run if I didn't think she could help my swan-brothers. So I followed her, stepping where she held the nettles back for me.

But before I took the final step out of the nettles, she released them so that they slapped against my arm and face. I gritted my teeth, holding a hand over my mouth to stay quiet as I leaped out of the nettle patch.

I couldn't help it: I made one of Cadan's favorite rude signs, though I was so ashamed that I lowered my hand before I finished it.

The old woman cocked her head at me, just like the finch. "I know that sign! Many a man has gestured so when he's frustrated by my ramblings. And you, *you* nearly made that same sign, but you've changed it some, I think." She fingered a tear on my dirty dress and laughed. "Of course you would! A princess would be punished for such a rude sign. And I should be punished for letting the nettles touch you, but that's not the last time you'll feel their sting. Oh no."

She pushed the cottage door open and waved me in before her. "Sit, Princess! Sit, Swan-Keeper!"

How did she know I was a princess? I paused on the threshold, the sun warm on my back.

I didn't want to talk to her! I thought she'd be a nice old woman with a cozy cottage. And a fire. And *food*. Real food that I hadn't pulled the guts from only an hour earlier. This woman already hated me and had told me so.

Yet she knew the Queen.

More than that, the Queen knew her—and hated her.

I leaned my walking stick against the outer wall and entered.

The woman closed the door behind us and squinted at me in the dim. "Which will it be, I wonder? Princess or Swan-Keeper?"

She was asking herself, not me, so I didn't sign an answer. Instead, I looked around the surprisingly neat cottage: a dirt floor, covered with fresh reeds; a jumble of potted plants clustered around the two dingy windows; a much-used hearth.

"You are Swan-Keeper, I think! They are your brothers, aren't they? The black swans. Why else would a princess watch them?"

She motioned me to sit at the small table beside the hearth. I slowly sat, and she dropped in the chair across from me, suddenly weak. "It's all my fault. Can you forgive me, child? Can they?"

She started crying before I could answer.

My left hand and cheek burned with the nettle-stings, thanks to her, but she hadn't grieved *then*. I folded my arms, using my anger the way Aiden used a shield.

But she cried on, and I couldn't help but pity her. Finally, I rested a hand on her arm, and her sobs slowed.

"You're a kind one, Swan-Keeper," the woman said. "But then, so was I."

She stood and tottered over to a plant growing on a windowsill. She wrenched a few leaves off and popped them into her mouth, chewing noisily. Then she spat the leafy pulp into her hand. "Put this on the welts. It'll ease the sting."

I shook my head. *No.*

"I live among nettles, Swan-Keeper. Trust that I know how to deal with their sting. And then perhaps I'll tell you what you want to hear."

I held out my hand to her.

She globbed the mess over the welts, then reached to put it on my cheek as well, but I jerked away. I didn't trust her so near me.

She sighed and sat back in her chair, eyes fixed on the cluster of feathers on my belt.

"Black swans. They're safe if they need your silence to survive." Her eyes dropped to the hand that I'd signed the curse with. "Yet you find your way of speaking, too, and all the better for your own soul!"

I didn't care about my soul. I cared about my brothers. I patted the table, impatient for her to go on.

She nodded. "Yes, yes. You want to know about *her.* You've seen her, haven't you?"

I nodded.

"What did she look like?" the woman demanded. "I need to know what my snowy one looked like before I tell you how to undo her!"

Snowy one. So she *had* been talking about the Queen!

I shook my head, unwilling to revisit the ugliness of what had happened.

"Tell me!"

I closed my eyes to steady myself. *Think of it as a barter, one story for another.*

I slowly stood, just as I'd seen the Queen stand, iron

in my spine, ice in my eyes. And I discovered that the iron and ice weren't just from mimicking the Queen. They were in me too.

I *would* get the wisdom I needed from this woman.

Her eyes traveled over me hungrily as she rocked in her chair. "That's her! That's her!"

She seemed so pleased that I took my braid and wrapped it around my head, like a crown.

The woman buried her face in her hands. "So she still wears her hair like that. Surely she does. That's when I knew she was lost to me."

I pounded the table with the flat of my hand to get her attention. When she looked up, cheeks wet with tears, I pointed at her: *Your turn. Tell me what I want to know.*

"I was so lonely, you see, so lonely, and she was a bewitching little thing. She sang . . . she sang my loneliness away." She pointed out to the garden. "She'd sit there, hour after hour, singing and watching me. How could I not love her? How couldn't I give her everything she wanted?"

But she said you made her beg.

The woman wiped her nose with the back of her hand. "The Great Lady was so cruel to her before she escaped—taking, always taking! Sing this! Sing that! Is it so bad that she wanted something for her own? But I didn't give it to her all at once! No, I wasn't that foolish. I knew the cost. How could you wrench so much from nature and not have there be a cost? So I gave her speech, little by little, only a few words at a time. That wasn't so bad, was it?"

I touched my lips with my fingers. *Words? How did you give the Queen words? She was already singing! And where had she come from?*

The old woman tugged on my arm, ignoring my questions with a shake of her head. "Tell me what happened first, Swan-Keeper! Tell me what happened to my snowy girl."

I clenched my jaw. Once again, it was my turn.

I looked around the room, then went to the hearth with the sagging mantel. I swiped a finger through the soot, then began to draw on the empty hearthstone.

The woman joined me and watched breathlessly, head bent over the pictures: The Queen finding Father in the forest . . . her marriage to him . . . an image of her speaking the spell while my brothers stood halfway between human and swan.

Fury and terror grew inside me as I drew, the way my breath pushed for release when I swam with my brothers and stayed too long underwater.

I stopped and gulped in a deep breath, wiping my tears with my sleeve.

The woman stared at the drawings, then looked up at me. She raised a finger to my damp cheek. "How she's wounded you . . ."

I almost relaxed, for her touch was tender. Then the iron and ice returned, and I stepped back. I pointed to her, then touched my lips again. *Your turn. Tell me more about the words!*

"I didn't know what she'd become." The woman

looked at me with such sorrow that I almost softened. Then her grief pulled the madness up after it, and I watched her gaze shift back in time. "After the words, came the day that I gave her her first dress! How she danced, though she was clumsy at first! But she sang so prettily I didn't mind, and how could the Lady have ever refused to give such a pretty thing a way to dance when that was all she ever wanted?"

A dress? Surely she hadn't been naked the whole time! And why would dancing matter so much?

"But that wasn't enough, you see. I gave her words and a dress and feet to dance and then she wanted to dance in other places, places she'd seen earlier. She said they were so small when she saw them." Another sob.

She gave her feet? Had the Queen's feet been hurt? Had the woman healed them somehow?

"She said I didn't love her, if I kept her here. She stopped singing, stopped dancing." The woman covered her face with her hands, her voice breaking. "She said the garden disgusted her! That she loathed me! I, who taught her to dance! Who gave her words! What could I do but let her go?"

A sickness settled inside me. Something awful had happened. Something ugly and dark that shouldn't have seen the light of day.

"I didn't let her leave until I knew she'd be cared for. One day, a man came to my cottage, such a strong and handsome man! He was a king, I think."

Father! This was where he met the Queen.

I pounded the table for her attention, not caring how she cried or whose turn it was. When she blinked watery eyes at me, I pointed to my hair.

Still the woman blinked at me! I motioned as if setting a crown on my head, and then pointed to my hair. *Did the king have black hair?*

After a moment, the woman slapped her thigh. "You're almost as smart as she was, Swan-Keeper! No, the king didn't have dark hair. His hair was gold, gold as his beard. Only a golden king for my girl."

I dropped back into the chair. It wasn't Father, then.

"I told him he'd find his way out of the forest if he'd take my snowy one and marry her. I knew she could show him the way, for she'd seen the path a thousand times.

Her mind was slipping away.

"So I kissed her on both pale cheeks, and I gave her what she wanted. That was before you were born, I think. I've spent all these years here alone."

Who was the man, then?

"I've been so lonely . . . ," sobbed the woman, ". . . no singing, no dancing . . ."

I could've cried along with her from sheer disappointment—for a moment, it seemed like something in the Queen's past might make sense. Yet I still had no idea who the Queen was or where she'd come from.

I couldn't give up. If this woman knew my brothers had been turned to swans, she might know how to save them.

I marched over to the woman and took her by the shoulders. She sobbed a bit, but I made myself heartless and shook her till she looked at me. Then I jabbed a finger at the sooty picture of my swan-brothers on the hearthstone. *What do I do?*

She shook her head and tried to turn away, but I wouldn't let her. Another jab at the picture. *Tell me!*

She finally looked at me.

"I don't want her to come back, that's my secret," she whispered, and gooseflesh prickled my arms at the fear in her voice. "She's not my sweet one anymore. She wants to kill me so she can keep the words and the feet and the dress forever! And I won't have that. I told her so when she came back." She glanced fearfully at the dingy windows.

The Queen came back? *When? Was that when Father found her?*

"That's why I let the nettles grow! She hates them. They remind her of when she'd sit beside the nettles and eat and sing for me . . . when she sang without words . . . before I gave her words . . ."

Another shake, even though I winced at the pressure on my nettle-stung hand.

"When she saw the nettles, she wouldn't come closer. Just shouted to me. And her wolf men couldn't come for me, either."

Wolf men! The wild-faced men who made up her guard. I patted my chest and drew the outline of a leather breastplate, then brandished an imaginary obsidian sword.

"Oh, you've seen them, have you? Beware them, child—I fear for you if she ever sends them after you. She's pulled them from the Great Hunt to hunt for her here.

But she's not so powerful that she can keep them when the Otherworld horns are sounded. She's only strong enough to keep a few near."

Declan told tales of the Great Hunt and the Otherworldly creatures that rode across the earth, hidden by great storms. I didn't remember much—only that I'd shivered with that comfortable sort of fear that disappeared when I pulled my blankets around me.

But mortal or not, I didn't see how nettles would stop anyone. I pointed to the nettle stings on my hand that she'd recently covered and then motioned to a crown on my head. *Why did the Queen and her wolf men fear the nettles' sting so much?*

The old woman wagged her head back and forth. "Oh, you're a stupid one after all, Swan-Keeper! It isn't the sting she fears, it's the remembering—memories of Before, when she sat beside my nettles—that she pushes away. And since the wolf men are here at her call, they fear the nettles too."

She laughed, a sound almost as harsh as her weeping. "I told her I wouldn't let her have her words forever, though 'twas just talk at the time. But lately, I've heard in wind and birdsong that a mite of a girl would undo her. Now that I see you, I know it's true. And I hate you for it, for the hurt you'll bring her."

I stepped back, hoping for a moment that she really had heard truth, that I'd be the one to undo the Queen.

But my mind *wasn't* broken like the old woman's. Not yet. And I knew that dreams could lie.

They can make you lose everything.

"That's how you'll save your brothers," she said, in a voice so sane it startled me.

She gripped my wrist. "Knit tunics for your brothers, Swan-Keeper! Knit them out of nettles. How long did you give her your words?"

I held up six fingers.

"One year for each," murmured the woman. "She always did like words. Little wonder she'd try to collect them."

The woman jumped up and walked to an overflowing cupboard. She trotted back to me and pressed something into my hand without giving me time to look at it.

She took my face in her hands and pulled me so close our noses almost touched. "You can't have those six years back. You cannot speak the word I should have said, oh no, but you *can* save your brothers. Have the tunics ready, and on the day you can speak, have your brothers wear them, the tunics made from nettles. They'll be men and not swans. They'll never be swans again. Do you understand me?"

She released me and plucked at her shawl. "It can be done, Swan-Keeper, those tunics. I made this from nettles, using that spindle."

I looked down at what she'd given me. A slender rod of wood two hands high. It had an apple-sized disk of wood at one end. Wrapped around the middle was a small swell of yarn. Nettle yarn, apparently.

She plucked the spindle from my hands, unwrapped a length of yarn, looped it over a hook at the other end, and set the spindle whirling, disk-end down, as it hung near her knees. The yarn twisted even tighter. "Like this, child. You use a drop spindle like this. No fancy spinning wheels now that you're only a swan-keeper."

Fast as thought, she wrapped the tail of yarn around the spindle and handed it back to me.

I'd sooner be able to spin a spiderweb than understand what she'd just done.

"I made all my clothes from nettles! I don't want her to lay a hand on me. Don't want her wolf men to hunt me the way they'll hunt you." Her head drooped until her chin rested on her chest.

Hunt me? How? I reached for her to shake the answer out of her, but she batted me away, and I saw she was done with me.

"Go away, Swan-Keeper. Go away, Princess. Leave me to my grief. I'll never hear her sing again." Her voice dropped to a whisper as I walked toward the door, spindle in my hand. "I'll never see her again."

Chapter 16

The iron and ice I'd borrowed from the Queen fell away as I stepped outside and snatched my walking stick, dragging the door closed behind me.

Sobs rasped through the door, and I peered back over my shoulder.

She didn't want my help or comfort.

And then the sound of her sobs seemed like every dark thing that had chased me since I left the castle. I clutched the spindle closer and ran down the path through the nettles.

I didn't stop till I reached my little camp by the three rivers: my satchel slung over a tree branch to protect it from animals and thieves, the sooty remains of a fire in the hollow protected from the wind. I had to be at least a league from her cottage, but I still feared I'd somehow hear her cries and that maybe I'd become just like her.

Don't be silly, chided Gavyn. *Think about what you've learned.*

I dropped my walking stick and sank down, my back against a tree. I hadn't learned anything.

I thought the old woman would tell me who the Queen was.

I thought she'd tell me how to stop her.

I thought she'd be *sane*.

Think!

Very well, then. I turned the spindle over in my hands.

I'd learned that the Queen escaped from a mean mistress—or someone she thought was mean. And that the Queen sat by the nettles and sang.

So she hadn't always been royalty.

Then the old woman had given her words . . . and a dress . . . and feet? *Feet?*

I pressed my free hand against my forehead. I wanted to talk! If I could tell someone what I'd heard, I might begin to understand it.

Not speaking was almost like not thinking.

And then I was back in Roden's dungeon with the Queen gloating over all that I'd lost.

She'd said silence would open a chasm inside me.

No.

I leaped up, not minding that the spindle fell to the ground, and made Cadan's rude gesture then—all of it—both hands held up to the pale slice of moon that hung in the blue sky. Let the Queen see *that*!

I'd be quiet, but I wouldn't be empty.

And then I lowered my hands because it really was an awful gesture. Besides, it was time to think, not insult the empty air like a child.

I dropped to my knees, plucked up a flat rock, and

used it to strip moss from the ground. Then I patted the exposed earth as smooth as a piece of parchment.

I drew a pair of bare feet peering from beneath a skirt. Then songs streaming like a summer wind from the Queen's mouth.

She sang without words.

Or perhaps words the old woman didn't understand. Perhaps the mistress the Queen had escaped from was foreign and the Queen needed words to be understood here, in Lacharra.

Feet. What did that mean? She'd been hurt? That made sense, if she'd escaped someplace foreign. How far away was the nearest place that spoke another language? I'd have to ask Gavyn—

How exactly was I supposed to draw *that* question so that Gavyn would understand? I drew more swirls next to the mud-Queen's mouth, thinking.

A dress made the most sense once I considered it. If the Queen had escaped and come to the cottage so hurt she could barely stand, she'd need a new dress too.

And then she wanted to leave?

I'd left the castle seventeen days earlier and all I wanted was a safe place to stay. But she had wanted to leave the woman's cottage after being given so much.

Can you blame her?

Maybe the woman had been mad then. Or perhaps it was the Queen's handiwork.

Regardless, she'd left with a golden-haired man.

"*. . . a golden king for my girl.*"

Was he truly a king? What had happened to the Queen after she left? What did she do?

There was no way to know. But I did know what she wanted.

"*I want it all. Every last morsel.*"

I picked up the spindle again, turning it over in my hands. How could nettle tunics and a spindle stop the Queen?

I remembered the hatred in the Queen's voice when she mentioned the old woman. She'd have killed her if she could. But she hadn't been able to reach the nettle-covered cottage, because nettles reminded her of Before.

Whatever—*wherever*—that was.

The old woman was convinced that nettles would break the enchantment, that the memory was that strong.

Nettles—common weeds!—were such a pitifully small weapon.

Yet remembering had been a powerful thing for Father. *Years* of reading together were wrapped up in the scent of cloves, and the Queen had rightly feared that.

Very well, then. If nettles had stopped her, then I'd make nettle tunics—and pray they reminded the Queen of the Before she feared so much.

I'd harvest *fields* of nettles and use the spindle to spin every last one.

I examined the spindle the way I'd seen Mael look at a new sword, feeling the weight of it in my hand.

The thin rod was nearly as long as my forearm, its wood glossy from being used so often. The whorl—I thought that was what it was called—was a carved wooden disk almost as wide as my fist at the lower end. Uneven yarn was wrapped above the whorl, covering a few small gashes in the rod.

I gingerly touched the nubbly, gray-brown yarn above the whorl with a fingertip.

No sting. It wouldn't hurt my hands to spin it, then.

I let the spindle dangle at the end of the yarn, trying to remember how the woman had used it. It had looked like a living thing in her hands. Almost magical.

Here in the sunlight, however, the spindle looked ordinary and cheap: more like a lopsided top than my best hope of defeating the Queen's enchantment.

I'd imagined a daughter of the House of Cynwrig fighting with a sword, not stinging nettles and a spindle. But if this was my only weapon, I'd wield it.

I looked back over the path to the old woman's cottage. What would happen if she changed her mind and wanted the spindle back? I imagined her bending over me while I slept that night, gloved hands reaching . . .

I gently placed the spindle in the satchel. Then I walked out to the curve of river where I'd submerged the weir. I upended the weir and dumped the fish inside it back into the river before strapping it to my back. There was no time to eat. I'd walk the last few hours of daylight and put as many leagues between me and the old woman as possible.

It was time to save my brothers.

Chapter 17

My brothers needed clothes before the next week's full moon, and I needed supplies for the coming winter. So I decided to travel through—rather than around—the small town of Etten, the last landmark before the hut at Cairwyn Lake.

It wasn't until I stood on a bluff overlooking Etten that I realized how much had changed. How much *I'd* changed. Two months ago, a carriage and armed escort would have brought me into the town. Trusted servants would have been sent to buy anything I desired and fetch it back to me.

Now, I was alone—voiceless, defenseless—with only links of Mother's belt to buy what I needed. Anyone who saw me would easily believe I'd lived out-of-doors for the past four weeks.

It took nearly an hour to scrub myself clean and rebraid my hair. I repacked the satchel, leaving most of Mother's belt links in it and putting only a few in my pocket slits. Then I attached the weir to the satchel and shrugged the satchel onto my shoulders.

I was clean, but I didn't look anything like the banished princess of Lacharra—and all but a small part of me was glad of it.

The road through Etten was crowded with other travelers on their way to the market: a farmer leading a donkey laden with bulging burlap sacks, an old wagon filled with baskets and several stacked coops of various birds.

The press was overwhelming after so many weeks alone. The stamp of horses' hooves took me back to the courtyard in Roden. Travelers shouting to each other reminded me of my brothers calling to me from their cell in the dungeon. I could see the Queen before me, silhouetted in torchlight, even though the sun shone high above.

It was a wicked trick for my mind to play on me. I walked toward the town square with tears at the back of my eyes and fury rising like fire in my chest: I'd lived that night once. Why did I have to keep seeing it again and again?

I was slammed from behind and stumbled, nearly falling under the weight of my satchel. Something caught—or snatched—at my weir.

The wolf men *couldn't* have found me! They weren't even looking for me!

I ducked my head and darted forward, intent on escape, but when I glanced behind me, all I saw was a group of boys my age, laughing as if they'd never seen anything so funny as me scurrying away.

I stopped and stared at them, all iron and ice.

YOU don't scare me, I thought. *You aren't the Queen. You aren't her wolf men. You're just spoiled, bored boys. Even if I had guards around me right now, you wouldn't be worth the trouble of a beating.*

Sometimes, words show on our faces, even when we can't speak them. The boys disappeared into the crowd, and I allowed myself one small smile.

⁎⁎⁎

And then I reached the square and the market that filled it.

"Chawetties!" A woman walked by with a basket of meat pies on her head, a pouch of coins jingling at her waist. "Still-hot chawetties!"

You don't know who made them, cautioned Mael, *or where.*

But Mael wasn't the one with the empty belly.

I chased the woman down. A minute later, I had a chawetty and several tin coins—change for one of the links of Mother's belt.

I savored the chawetty as I walked through the market, noting the different stands and the men and women who worked them. Within an hour, I'd discovered that there were three grocer's stands where I could buy food, and only one where I could buy clothes for my brothers.

But there were lots of spinners. Etten was a wool town—I should have guessed from all the sheep that filled the pastures that surrounded it. Hanks of dyed wool yarn hung like banners, and women wandered the market with distaff and drop spindle, busily spinning as they inspected the wares, the spindles hanging down to their knees like small birds hovering on a short leash. I followed one of the women while I finished my chawetty, watching to see what she did.

Just as I was beginning to make sense of how she spun, she saw me. Her glare sent me scurrying away.

And all the while, language swirled around me. I'd become used to being mute when I was alone. In Etten, I walked through a sea of conversations I could not join.

"It's robbery, I tell you, to ask so much for a—"

"Have you seen the new chandler one street over?"

"All the princes dead in one night—and the Queen herself had to give the news, wailing and tearing at her hair as she did. She loved them as her own, they say."

"Danavirian barbarians! Attacking Roden like that! I hear the widowed princess has shut herself in her rooms and not even the Queen can comfort her—"

I turned to hear more of Tanwen, but the speaker had melted into the crowd. Still, Tanwen was alive! That was some good news, at least.

The novelty of the market dimmed after that. The crowd pressed too close, and news of the castle—all of it lies—pressed closer.

"Princess Andaryn attacked the Queen at the feast, and then word comes that she died at Roden too. No one's said it outright, but some wonder if *she* let the Danavirian savages inside the gate at Roden."

How I longed to stand at the center of the square and shout what the Queen had done! But if I must be mute, I'd be sure that my brothers would live—and speak once they were themselves. That meant clothes and food and leaving Etten and its gossip as soon as possible.

So I bought clothes for my brothers—and boys' clothes for me—and a pack to put them in, along with a tin mug, a blanket, a wedge of cheese, and a small sack of barley. The flash of gold made up for having no voice. I had thought I'd hate giving away pieces of Mother's belt. Instead, it felt like she was standing beside me, pointing to what I should buy, walking away with me if the price quoted was too high.

Mid-afternoon, I passed the hen coops on my way out of the square.

The chawetty had made me greedy. Suddenly, all I wanted were a few eggs to cook at my fire that night.

I caught the farmer's eye, pointed to a basket of eggs, and held up five fingers.

"Five eggs?" he asked, wiping his hands on his burlap apron.

I nodded.

"Show me your money first."

I held up a link from Mother's belt.

The farmer squinted and held his hand out. "That real gold?"

I wouldn't let him hold it—he might not return it. Instead, I stepped forward and bit into the link, showing him the metal was soft enough to bend: real gold.

He nodded. "Only five eggs, young mistress?"

I smiled. Now I was a young mistress.

"For another two links like that, you can have all the eggs you desire. I've a hen who will lay eggs every week."

The idea was tempting, but I had no way to carry the hen to the hut. I shook my head.

"She'll peck out her own food. Eat all the beetles from your bed and give you eggs in exchange."

I'd have eggs. And no bugs.

It seemed like a dream.

Which means that it is, warned dream-Cadan, ever the cynic.

I held up my empty hands, showing I had no way to carry the hen away.

"I'll give you one of these burlap bags. She'll travel just fine in it."

I crouched to peer down at the hen.

She let loose a low, churling sound.

I stepped back. If she was a dog, I'd have sworn she was growling!

"She's a harmless biddy," argued the farmer, reaching inside her coop. "See?"

The hen pecked at his hand, but he ignored it, stroking her head and under her beak. She raised her head, and I saw that she'd lost the feathers on her breast.

I scowled at the farmer. I did not want a mean, half-naked hen!

A chuckle.

I turned to see a matron standing behind me. She hooked a finger, motioning me closer. "She's broody, girl. Thinks she has chicks to hatch, but there's nothing there except the stones she's sitting on. That's why the feathers are gone—she's plucked them to keep the stone eggs warm. But those stone eggs will never hatch and she won't lay new ones while she's sitting on them . . . and there's the problem."

"Morgyn!" bellowed the farmer. "Are you calling me a liar? This hen is one of my best layers!"

The matron laughed and walked away. "Don't take the hen unless you're hoping for a good dinner, girl!"

I crouched again to see the hen. She looked at me with one dark eye as if to warn me away from her eggs.

The poor creature thought stones would hatch into chicks.

And I hoped to defeat an enchantress with a spindle and stinging nettles.

We were both expecting the impossible.

I looked at the farmer and held up two fingers. *Two links for everything.*

He laughed. "You may have her then!"

A moment later, he tucked the real eggs and hen into a burlap bag, closed the bag over her head, and handed it to me. "Keep a loose hold on it so she can breathe while you travel. Hens fall asleep soon as it gets dark—even if it isn't night—so she won't give you any trouble when the bag is closed."

And so I became the owner of a hen and five eggs. After two streets, I opened the mouth of the bag and carefully peered in. She hunkered down on the eggs and blinked up at me, finally settling in the dark.

I wanted to make soft, clucking sounds, to somehow tell her that she had nothing to fear.

You want to talk to a hen, commented Cadan.

I closed the mouth of the bag as guiltily as if he was there to see me. *No, I—*

Then I jolted to a stop. One of the Queen's guard stood farther down the narrow street.

The old woman had called them wolf men, and at that moment, I believed it. He was tall and rawboned, his beard unkempt. Even from across the square, I could see his leather breastplate. I didn't think I'd ever be able to see a leather breastplate again without wanting to turn and run.

Don't run, whispered Mael. *He'll know you're prey for sure.*

And you will be prey if they discover you're still alive. That was Aiden, speaking so steadily, so certainly, that I found a little courage.

I ducked my head and stepped back slowly. I didn't stop until my back was against a shop wall. The hen churled from her bag, as if she could sense my fear.

I put a hand to the bag. *Peace, you silly, broody hen. Peace! He'll hear you.*

And then the guard looked up from across the square. I saw his brow crease, and he lifted his head as if scenting something.

Scenting me.

I ran.

By the time I reached the far side of Etten, I was breathless. I forced myself to slow and match the pace of everyone leaving town. I'd only stand out if I kept running.

But I didn't feel any safer, no matter how much I traveled. I was sure the wolf man must have seen me and was trailing me.

Calm yourself! soothed Gavyn. *He'd have captured you by now if he was looking for you.*

Now there's fine comfort, said Cadan. *Keep reminding Ryn of someone hunting her as it gets dark.*

Alone, neither one of my brothers could have calmed me, but I distracted myself the rest of that afternoon by imagining their argument.

That evening, I didn't dare light a fire. Nor did I need to; my stomach was still full of the meat pie. But as I lay in the fading daylight, I jumped at every sound, certain it was the wolf man. How would I manage to stay calm when it was truly dark?

Think of the hut. Think of four walls and a door that can shut out the night. Think of feeling safe inside it.

It didn't work. A sob caught at the back of my throat.

The hen stood up in her open bag-nest and twisted her head in short, quick movements, taking in our small camp.

A low, comforting roll of clucks.

To my surprise, she stepped out of the burlap sack and onto my chest. Then she settled on me as if I was a clutch of eggs she was determined to hatch. I twisted a little, and she pecked at the air a few inches from my nose.

I didn't speak hen, but the message was very clear: *Be still.*

My breath grew more steady.

I lifted a hand to touch her.

A small cluck.

Slowly, I rested my hand on her back. She didn't move, only wiggled back and forth, leaning so that the featherless portion of her breast rested above my heart.

Oh, she was warm! Or maybe it was that the night was so cold. But I began to feel just a little safe.

You're being comforted by a hen, Ryn.

I was calm enough that I could imagine my brothers then, though it wouldn't have taken much effort to figure out what Cadan would have said.

I don't care, I answered back. *She's warm and clucky.*

That was just to irritate my brothers.

Clucky *is NOT a word!* chided Owain.

Just for that, I said, *I'll call her Owain.*

I fell asleep to Owain's shouts and everyone else's laughter.

Chapter 18

Four days later, in the early afternoon, I found the hunting hut.

No, I found its remains.

My future home was a one-room ruin slumped at the edge of Cairwyn Lake. Half the roof and one of the walls were missing.

And there was no door. No way to shut out the dark.

I dropped my walking stick and sat down—shedding the weir, satchel, and pack full of clothes for my brothers and a little food for the winter. Finally, I opened the burlap sack so Owain-the-hen could hop out and forage for food.

I buried my face in my hands.

I imagined that I was back in my room, with its bed that was always warm and its balcony that looked out over the lakes that my mother had loved when she was alive. I imagined a fire crackling and food that Bronwen had prepared. My brothers crowded around me, teasing. I teased back, with words right there on my tongue and the freedom to speak them.

I didn't want to open my eyes.

And then the words I'd thrown at the Queen came to me—rebuking me for sitting beside the hut's ruins and feeling sorry for myself:

We are the House of Cynwrig. We are the flight of swans bearing swords.

I stood. I was Andaryn of the House of Cynwrig, and it was time to set my new home in order.

The hut itself was well situated, close to the lake and sheltered by pine trees and a rocky bluff just behind it. I smiled. The hut reminded me of myself when I slept: pressing against something solid for protection.

It had been a good hut, once. One that princes might have used when they wished to hunt alone. The roof—what was left of it—was slate, something that wouldn't rot like thatch if it wasn't tended to regularly. The walls had been stacked stone.

I inspected the outside of the hut, stepping silently over the pine needles that velveted the ground. Three walls tilted against scrubby pines that grew beside them, but the wall that faced the lake had collapsed entirely, spilling stones inside the hut. The roof above the collapsed wall had fallen into the hut as well, and the portion that remained sagged dangerously under the weight of the slate shingles.

I found a nearby branch and poked the walls with it, determined not to walk into a hut that might fall on me.

Unsteady as they looked, the walls didn't topple, no matter how I pushed.

I clambered over the collapsed wall into the hut itself, nearly slipping on the pine-needle-coated rubble. Then I

wedged the branch under the sagging end of the roof to support it until I could fix it.

Fix it. I turned in a slow circle, taking in all that needed to be done. There wasn't even room on the dirt floor for me to sleep!

I nodded to myself. That was where I'd start, then.

Even if I could completely repair the roof, I was certain water would seep under the walls and gather on the floor if it rained hard enough. So I moved some of the stones in the middle of the hut to the far corner, creating a raised platform I could soften with branches. Even if the entire floor became a puddle, I'd be able to sleep on something dry—a luxury after these past weeks.

Near the fallen wall, I created a hearth for cook fires, building up the wall behind it so that the fire would be protected. But laying stone for a wall had never been part of my training as a princess of Lacharra—more the pity!—and I didn't know how to keep it from toppling over once I stacked it more than a few feet.

I sat back on my heels and surveyed my work. That would be a problem for another day.

Then I moved the rest of the rubble outside.

By the time night fell, I sat inside the hut next to a fire that I'd built. I ate a bit of cheese and roasted the last egg by way of celebration, while Owain-the-hen cluck-cluck-clucked to herself on the small nest I'd built her. The fire quickly warmed me, and the three walls and roof kept the rising wind from touching me.

I looked out the open wall beyond the fire and watched

the moonlight edge the ripples on the lake with silver. I didn't feel safe yet, not while I was so exposed. Not while I could imagine the Queen's wolf men outside. But I felt safer than I had since leaving the castle.

Tomorrow, I'd find a place for the weir. And . . . perhaps there were different types of doors to make me feel safe. The old woman had talked about how nettles kept the wolf men away. Maybe I could plant nettles around my own hut.

Tired as I was, I didn't fall asleep right away. I'd placed my bed so that I could sleep with my back to the wall, but everything was so new.

Then I saw the dark form hopping across the hut's floor.

Owain-the-hen. She stopped right beside me. In the bit of moonlight slanting through the open wall, I could see her cock her head one way and then another.

What do you want?

Ah.

I rolled onto my back and patted my chest. Owain gave a small cluck, fluttered up on my chest, and settled herself so that the featherless part of her breast warmed me.

You are the maddest hen I know if you think I'm an egg. I rested a hand on her feathery back as I fell asleep. *But I am so glad you do.*

Chapter 19

I'll see my brothers tonight was my first waking thought. *I have so much to tell them!*

I opened my eyes to see Owain-the-hen perched on the half-wall behind the hearth, a beetle struggling in her beak. She bobbed her head to swallow it down, then clucked loudly.

It was a scolding for sleeping late, if ever I'd heard one, and I was grateful for it. After almost two months alone, it was heartening to wake up to a living creature, even if she was a fierce, silly hen. I sat up, blinking in the morning light, and Owain flapped over to me, pecking my toes as a sort of *good morning.*

I smoothed the fine little feathers under her neck as I looked out to Cairwyn Lake through the ruined wall.

This is my home.

I sat motionless as my world rearranged itself around that truth: *This is my home.*

I would live here for six years. Six summers. Six winters. I'd be a woman by the time I left, a full eighteen years of age.

I looked down at my torn dress, my calloused hands.

What would I look like in six years? Would I forget how to be a princess?

And then I remembered that even when I was free of the spell, I wouldn't be free to return home. I was the banished princess of Lacharra. What had the men in Etten said? The princess who had betrayed her six brothers to their deaths in Roden.

I wouldn't be free to return unless I returned with my brothers.

And I would.

I pulled the Kingstone from beneath my bodice, held it so tightly my fingers whitened. The old woman had called the Queen's life at the cottage her Before. The Kingstone shard was mine: a reminder of life when my family and country had been whole.

The Queen fled her past, but I would fight for mine.

In six years, we'd return to Lacharra, all seven of us, the flight of swans flown up from exile. I'd fit this shard back into the Kingstone and make our land whole again.

Six years of nettles and silence were not too high a price.

I tucked the Kingstone shard back into my bodice.

⁂

I walked a portion of Cairwyn that morning, looking for rivers running into or out of the lake where I could position the weir. An hour later, I'd found the spot: a little hollow beneath the lake where the water threw itself down a rocky hill and dashed between some boulders.

I also found nettles, an entire patch of them, running along the banks of the stream and gathered in the ruined stone foundations of some clan that had lived here ages ago.

Funny that nettles—like me—should live among ruins.

The long stalks nearly reached my shoulders, already browned and curling from the cold, lengthening nights. A breath of wind gusted around me, ruffling the nettles till they swayed.

I gently touched one of the browning leaves—and felt the sting. The plants were dying, but not the fire inside them.

I knelt by the edge of the nettle patch to better see them. They were wicked-looking, with rough-edged leaves. What looked like silvery hairs along the stem and leaves were needle-like spikes.

This, too, would be part of my life. I'd harvest nettles for the next six years.

Do it now, I thought, *before you lose your courage.*

I held my hands open in front of me, noticing how they'd become rough and covered with calluses.

It'll be almost like gloves.

It was a bald-faced lie, but it was enough. I drew my dagger and in the same movement, I grasped a handful of nettles and took the dagger to the base of the stalks.

It was like holding hornets in the palm of my hand.

The stalks were tough and didn't give way immediately. I gritted my teeth, held the nettles even tighter, and sawed at the stalks while fire burned my hand.

Finally, they gave way. I threw the clump aside and examined my hand.

White welts already covered my fingers and the tender skin of my forearm.

I sat back on my heels, lips pressed tight against the pain. I couldn't do this today. I still had to catch and prepare the fish for my brothers. I had to cook it.

But first, I had to stop the fire in my hand.

I glared at the nettle patch. *You can't make me run away,* I vowed. *I'll come back again. And again. Until I have all the nettles I need for my brothers.*

Only then did I walk to the river and plunge my hand into the icy water.

⁎⁎⁎

When I pulled my hand from the water, the welts had disappeared, leaving behind tiny red pinpricks. Yet the fire had only burrowed deeper, a flickering, searing pain that burned beneath my skin.

And it burned hours later as I cleaned the fish I'd collected from the weir. The pressure of simply holding the fish made it worse.

I was cleaning my hands in the lake when I heard the sound of wings.

My brothers!

I'd hoped they'd come. I'd expected it. But I hadn't been *sure* of it until this moment.

Six black swans drifted low over the lake's surface,

necks extended as if they'd longed to come to this place. They landed in a spray of water, scattering it like diamonds around them.

For a moment, I forgot my stinging hand while I watched them trumpet and splash as they fed.

We've done it. We've made it this far.

Owain-the-hen came up to me, pecking around my skirts and sending baleful looks toward the water, as if she distrusted the swans. I smoothed her feathers—and saw how dirty I was.

My swan-brothers were far enough away that they shouldn't mind me bathing close to shore.

I stripped off my dress, stopping at the under-tunic. I still didn't know if anyone lived near. Best to bathe in it, just in case.

The water was cold, but the sun was strong. I waded in until the water reached my shoulders, then ducked my head under the water, scrubbing my face with my hands to clean off, then coming up with a gasp.

I unbraided my hair and went under again, running my fingers through my hair to clean it. Soon I found a rhythm—ducking under, coming up for breath—that seemed as natural as breathing itself.

The final time I emerged, one of my swan-brothers waited for me, his red beak inches from my face. He extended his wings a little, startled.

I stilled, releasing my breath slowly. *I'm not going to hurt you.*

Finally, he lowered his wings and trumpeted a

three-note honk that ended on a higher note, like a question. Another swan-brother joined him, and they circled me like they couldn't decide what sort of bird I was.

I remained still—toes gripping the bottom of the lake, arms floating near the surface—and kept my eyes averted so I wouldn't scare them.

A gentle tugging on my arm.

I kept my head averted but watched from the corner of my eye. The swans were nibbling at my under-tunic's sleeve. One saw me watching him and paused, head raised. When I didn't move, he glided over to explore my other sleeve.

A few more honks, and my other swan-brothers joined us—all six black swans circling me slowly. Some nibbled at my sleeves. Others tweaked gently at my hair that floated on the surface of the water.

It was a breathless moment—my brothers so close to me.

Their red eyes and red beaks against the black feathers had seemed monstrous the first time I saw them, especially compared to the white swans I knew. And perhaps the Queen had meant it to be so.

But my swan-brothers were beautiful, with feathers as black as a moonless night—though not all the feathers were black. I'd caught glimpses of white feathers on the undersides of their wings. And the feathers along their wings settled into curled rows when their wings were folded, like ruffles on a dress.

I imagined Cadan in ruffles, jerking a bit as I held back the laughter.

Most of the swans scattered, but one stayed near, watching me.

I watched back.

The swan twitched his head, uncomfortable, but he didn't swim away.

He was Aiden, I was sure of it.

When he drifted by again, I lifted one finger and let it run lightly along his side. Aiden-swan flinched, and his head flicked back as if to bite.

But his beak snapped short of my hand.

We can try to keep our minds, he'd said. Somehow, for a moment, he had.

I'd seen my brother.

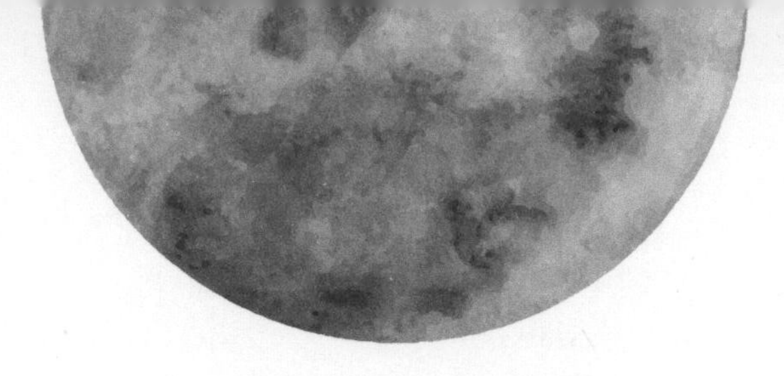

Chapter 20

Second full moon

When I finally climbed out of the water, I slipped into the boy's clothes I'd bought in Etten. Then I darted back to the hut to prepare dinner. I'd created a perch for Owain-the-hen in the corner by my bed, and she settled there, watching me work through half-closed eyes. I hoped the firelight would keep her awake until my brothers arrived.

My swan-brothers grew uneasy as dusk neared. I wasn't sure if their minds pushed against the enchantment that bound them, or if the swans simply sensed the coming change.

As the last bit of light faded, a rush of wind tore through the pines that sheltered the hut. I knew the sound—it was more savage than any storm I'd ever heard. I waited in the hut's open wall as the wind pulled at my still-drying hair and rolled toward the swans.

After a moment, the swans' trumpets changed to men's voices.

I grinned, bouncing on my toes like a little girl, willing them to hurry.

"Ryn, *Ryn*?" called Aiden.

"There's a fire," said Mael. "She's well."

I heard splashing as they stepped out of the water.

Cadan's laughter rolled up out of the darkness as he discovered the clothes I'd set out for them. "Clothes! *Clothes*, bless her! There's sign enough!"

Half a minute later, my brothers ran up to the hut. Aiden scooped me up first, and I was passed from one to the other and hugged close—until I reached Owain. He simply nodded.

Cadan smacked the back of his head. "You'll wear the clothes she brought you, but you won't hug her?"

"We wouldn't need these clothes if she hadn't—"

Cadan reached to smack Owain again, but I grabbed his arm. *Don't.*

"Whatever you want, Ryn. What's for dinner?" Cadan tilted his head back and sniffed. "I've waited all month for this."

I motioned them to follow me to the hut.

Mael paused when we reached the hut. "I thought we were seeing the firelight through a door, not a broken-down wall."

They stepped gingerly over the half-wall, taking in my bed and the fire in the nearby hearth. Gavyn went to the branch that propped up the roof and prodded it, nodding when it held firm.

"BWAAAAK!"

There was an explosion of noise and motion, a glimpse of feathers and beak and clawed feet, as Owain-the-hen launched herself at my brothers.

Cadan bellowed and stumbled backward. Mael reached for the sword that was no longer on his hip. The rest of my brothers dissolved into a tangle of flailing arms and churning legs as they tried to figure out what monster was attacking them.

I darted toward Owain-the-hen, thumping my chest to call her to me. She flapped away from my brothers' reach and turned to me, as if to be sure that I was safe. I patted my chest again, and she flapped up to my shoulder and settled there.

"What was *that*?" bellowed Aiden.

Owain clucked smugly from my shoulder.

Cadan strode toward us, ready to wring her neck. "We're having hen tonight, brothers!"

I kicked out, just as he'd taught me, raking the edge of my boot down his shin.

"Ow!" He rubbed his leg. "That hen attacked us, Ryn!"

I looked at him, eyebrow raised, waiting for him to hear the words he'd spoken.

Owain-the-brother snorted.

"The House of Cynwrig routed by a hen . . . ," mused Mael.

Cadan shook a finger at him. "I didn't say that!"

"But you screamed like it," Gavyn pointed out.

"You all did! I wasn't the only one!" protested Cadan.

Aiden guffawed, but Declan watched Owain-the-hen as she settled on my shoulder. "She thinks Ryn is her chick."

"That's ridiculous," said Gavyn. "I've never heard of such a thing!"

"That coming from a man who was a black swan an hour ago," pointed out Cadan witheringly. "Exactly how many years have you studied hens?"

Poor Cadan. He'd come to the hut expecting a meal and had been routed by a hen instead.

The meal!

I deposited Owain-the-hen on her perch before kneeling by the fire. After making sure that she stayed put, my brothers crowded close, peering over my shoulders.

"You just put all those fish straight on the coals?" asked Mael, poking one with a stick. "The flesh will be burned. It already is."

Aiden glared at him, eyes wide: *Hush!*

"Have you considered skewering them and then creating a frame so that you can roast them *over* the coals instead of on them?" asked Gavyn. "That might produce a better meal."

I rolled my eyes. I'd cooked fish *on* the coals for weeks. If you waited till the coals were just right, the meat cooked perfectly even though the skin charred.

"And our dinner wouldn't be able to look back at us." Cadan scowled at the fish with their wide, dead eyes.

"Since when does that bother you?" asked Aiden.

"Since they got all shriveled from *sitting on the coals.*"

"Oh, for sweet pity's sake," muttered Declan. "You face an enchantress, but *these* fish make you shudder? I could have composed and sung an entire song about your cowardice in the time that you've moaned about them."

He reached down to the coals, gingerly felt the tail of one of the fish, and then tugged it off the coals.

I handed him the dagger. In a few deft movements, he peeled the skin back, revealing tender meat beneath. He looked up at me and saluted with the dagger. "Excellent! May I have their fish too?"

I grinned and nodded.

At the threat of losing their dinner, all my brothers surged forward, pulling fish from the coals and settling into the dinner.

Finally, Aiden wiped his mouth, brushing a few scales from his beard. "It was an excellent meal, Ryn. Never mind what they tell you."

Mael threw the bones of his fish back into the fire to keep pests away. "Now." He rested his elbows on his knees. "Tell us about your journey here."

So much to tell them! But now that it was time, I was frightened. I took a deep breath and tapped my temple.

"That's easy," said Cadan. "You've been thinking."

I drew the Queen, arms outstretched, in the dirt floor.

"About the enchantment."

I nodded, then held up six fingers.

"After six years, we'll be men again," said Cadan, as if reciting a lesson he knew by heart.

One heartbeat. Another.

I shook my head. *No.*

Silence.

"*What?*"

It took a minute to sign that I'd be able to speak in six years, but that they would still be swans. It took much longer for my brothers to accept it, with me signing over and over exactly what the Queen had said in Roden's cellar: *After six years, you may speak without killing your swan-brothers.*

Before they could discuss it, though, I held up a finger and began to sign that the Queen had mentioned the old woman. Then I drew the map Aiden had me follow to the hut, and pointed to where the old woman lived.

"You found her? She knew the Queen?"

I nodded and went straight to the important part, drawing a swan turning to a man on the dirt floor. *She knew how to change you back.*

"How?" asked Aiden.

I went outside and picked up the clump of nettles I'd harvested, using the hem of my tunic to protect my hands. Then I dropped them by the fire.

Gavyn bent over them. "Mint?"

Before I could shake my head, he touched them, then yanked his hand back. "*Nettles?*"

Yes.

"How will nettles—of all things!—break the enchantment?" asked Mael.

I signed turning the nettles into yarn and the yarn into tunics.

"How did you harvest that?" asked Declan.

I held up a dagger.

"And your hands? How are they?"

My left hand and forearm still hurt like fire, but that wasn't the point. Why couldn't they see that nettles were important?

"How do you know it will work?" asked Gavyn.

I tried to explain that the Queen hated nettles, that the nettles around the cottage had stopped her and her wolf men.

"Nettles wouldn't stop warriors." Mael shook his head. "It wouldn't stop *farmers*."

"It stopped Cadan," said Owain. "Do you remember the time you stole Cadan's clothes while he was swimming? And then Cadan took the wrong path back from the lake?"

Cadan raised an eyebrow. "I doubt our Ryn was stung in the same places."

Declan choked on a laugh.

Cadan scowled. "I couldn't sit for a *week*!"

"Nettles make no sense," declared Mael. "And that's not the most puzzling part: How does a forest crone know the Queen?"

Gavyn shrugged. "Actually, I believe that part. We know the Queen was in the forest. Why wouldn't she know someone who lived there? What did the woman tell you, Ryn?"

Finally! One of my brothers was asking an intelligent question.

I began to recount what I'd learned. My description of the woman's ramblings would have been confusing if I could speak, but my signs and drawings only made her sound more crazy, if that was possible.

"She gave the Queen a *tongue*?" asked Owain.

"And feet? How do you give someone feet?"

I tried to sign that I thought the Queen had run away from another land. That the old woman had nettles, and the Queen hated them because they reminded her of the cottage—or of the place she had left. That they were the key to breaking the enchantment.

My brothers just stared at me in silence.

Aiden shook his head. "The enchantment isn't your fault, Ryn. And it isn't your responsibility to save us. That's where the interest in nettles comes from, isn't it?"

I stared at him.

He didn't just think I was foolish. He worried that the nettles were a morbid fascination, a sickness of heart or mind.

I'd fretted about how to explain the nettles, but I never thought my brothers would understand my signs and pictures and still not believe me.

I looked away, heartbroken.

"Then what happened?" asked Declan, attempting to move to safer subjects. "Tell us about Etten."

I explained, but all joy was gone from the telling. They felt it, too, though they tried to act as though nothing had changed. Then I signed that I'd seen one of the Queen's wolf men in Etten and run away.

"Did you see him again?" Mael leaned closer.

No.

"That's good. Very good," said Gavyn. "If the Queen's man had seen you, he would have found you. I'm sure the Queen still believes Ryn is dead."

It was so close to what I'd imagined him saying on the road that I almost smiled.

Almost.

Owain-the-hen clucked in her sleep. I looked at her, grateful for the distraction.

Mael chuckled. "I never thought I'd say it, but I'm glad you have a hen who thinks you're her chick."

"What do you call her?" asked Owain in a snide tone. "Mother?"

I'd wondered whether I should change Owain-the-hen's name, because my brothers would tease Owain unmercifully if they knew.

But Owain made the decision easy.

I pointed at him.

"You named her *Owain*?" Cadan cackled.

I raised an eyebrow and nodded.

They laughed just as hard as I imagined, ignoring Owain's protests.

Finally, Cadan walked to Owain's perch and made a low sweeping bow to the sleeping hen. "My lady Owain, on behalf of my brothers, I thank you for protecting Ryn. I think you are crazy—"

She merely blinked.

My brothers hooted, but Aiden became grim. "We need to end it. Ryn shouldn't have to live like this for six years."

The laughter faded.

Aiden stared at Owain-the-hen, but he wouldn't have noticed if she'd flown straight into the air and turned somersaults. "Ryn should have more than a hen to protect her. And I don't know what's happened to Tanwen. Or Father. I can't not know for six years."

"Then we end it," said Mael. "We end the Queen."

Aiden nodded.

Suddenly, the fire didn't seem warm enough.

"What if killing the Queen makes the enchantment permanent?" asked Gavyn.

"We have to do something! She should be confronted!"

"Ryn will need warmer clothes if she's going to walk back to the castle this side of winter," said Gavyn.

Aiden shook his head. "Ryn isn't going anywhere."

"Isn't she? If you want to face the Queen the next full moon, Ryn must lead us there. It's no mistake that we arrived here after she did. I've been thinking about it: we *follow* her, and we nest where she settles. The only time we won't be able to follow is when we molt in late summer. You see, swans lose their flight feathers and are flightless for several weeks—"

Cadan smacked the back of his head to stop the lesson.

Aiden just pushed the dying coals in on themselves.

"We'd have to time it perfectly," said Declan. "We'd have only hours and we'd lose even that if she locked herself in a room till sunrise. One whisper of black swans, and she'd know we were coming."

Mael had fought too many times to stomach such talk. "What do we do for the next six years, then? Run away?"

I saw the same grief on their faces that I'd weathered that first night at Roden. I picked up a log and threw it on the fire, glad for the spray of sparks that made my brothers stop.

I tapped my chest. *Look at me!*

They did.

I made a motion like a plant shooting up.

They stared blankly.

I made the silly face that Owain and I used when we were little and played war with wooden swords.

Owain recognized it. "We *die*?"

I shook my head, *No!* Then mimicked a plant sprouting up—the opposite of dead.

"We live," said Aiden.

I nodded. *We live.*

I looked at the pile of nettles that my brothers had dismissed. *We live—and I'll make your nettle tunics, whether you believe in them or not.*

Chapter 21

Second full moon

"Well, then," said Aiden after a long silence. "Let's get started with living."

My brothers threw themselves into their work that night. Declan and Gavyn collected wood and stacked it near the hearth, while Cadan and Owain worked to repair the roof itself, scavenging the fallen slate and filling in any remaining holes with a weave of branches that would keep rain away.

Aiden and Mael closed the fallen wall with a basket-weave of branches, while I daubed their work with mud scraped from the lake. It wasn't possible to add a door that would close, but they left a small opening and then wove a frame that could be pushed across it at night.

I watched them, heart sinking. The makeshift door would keep some of the cold at bay, but it wouldn't protect me from what I'd feared ever since talking to the old woman: the Queen's wolf men.

An hour before dawn, we crowded back in the little hut, sitting shoulder to shoulder so we could fit. Our work had closed out the night, but it was still my brothers who made me feel safe—not the new wall. I rested my head against Cadan's shoulder as we sat around the fire.

Mael laid a straight, fresh-cut branch across his knees and began stripping the twigs from it. "I'm making you a cudgel, Ryn-girl. It'll be a proper walking stick as well as a weapon. I'll teach you how to use it every time we change."

Aiden nodded, then said, "Tell us a story, Declan. One of the old ones. It'll fill what's left of the night."

Declan looked down, his chin almost on his chest as he considered what story to tell.

This was my chance to learn about the Hunt.

I ignored the fear that pricked the back of my neck as I tapped Declan's shoulder and pointed to myself. *Could I pick the story?*

He chuckled. "What do you want to hear?"

It took a minute of signs and sketches in the dirt for him to guess the story. "The Great Hunt?"

Yes!

He scowled. "It's a grim story, Ryn."

I insisted.

Declan leaned back, staring at the ceiling like the story hung there beneath the slates and only he could see it.

"Back when the oldest forests were young and the moon was unblemished, before the Bright Ones retreated to the Otherworld, there lived a chieftain whose name has been lost to time. He loved the hunt above all. He'd hunted and killed every creature under the sun and moon, except for a snow-white boar that lived in the center and soul of the forest."

Declan warmed to the story, and I tucked myself deeper into Cadan's side.

"One summer, when enemy soldiers were within a day's march of his own fort, the chieftain learned that the white boar had ventured from its hiding place. He didn't pause. After entrusting his captains with the defense of his home, he rode out with his hounds to hunt and kill the boar. After days of pursuit, he cornered the wounded boar in a cave."

I leaned forward, entranced and horrified by the man's single-minded pursuit.

"He entered the cave, hounds slavering at his side, spear raised to deliver the death blow. As the chieftain approached, the boar spoke with the voice of a man: 'Fool! Your fort is besieged, and yet you hunt *me*, the favorite creature of the Dagda of the Bright Ones? Spare me, and you will return to find your enemy vanquished and your heirs safe. But if you slay me, you will lose all you hold dear, and the Dagda's own rage will follow you the rest of your life.'

"The boar's offer only incensed the chief. Rather than kill it swiftly with his spear, he set his hounds upon it, watching as they tore the creature to pieces."

I shivered as Declan finished the ugly story.

"In the end, the boar lay dead, but not before it tore the chieftain's leg. He returned to the smoldering remains of his fort, where the bodies of his family and captains lay under the blue sky for the birds to enjoy. Even then, he wouldn't acknowledge the part his madness had played. He shouted his fury to the sky and prepared the bodies of his loved ones with his own hands. But before he could take their bodies to the barrow-graves that would receive them, he, too, died."

Declan's voice dropped to a whisper, and even Cadan leaned forward to hear the end. "But he was not granted rest. He was made Lord of the Great Hunt, and he rode with the horse and hounds he'd loved more than life and family. Sometimes the Bright Ones rode with him, sweeping across the land, hunting monsters and creatures that are now lost to time: giants, trolls, and imps."

Something tapped against the slate roof. I knew it must be a pine branch, but I still slid closer to Cadan. If the old woman was right, then the Queen's wild men—or wolf men—weren't men at all but Otherworlders who'd joined the chieftain's madness ages ago.

But Declan wasn't finished.

"And still they ride. Terrible storms hide the Great Hunt from human eyes. They *look* like banks of clouds running across the land, but legends claim that storms are the garments that hide the Hunt—and that if you listen close enough, you can hear the voices of the Hunt-Lord and his riders in the wind as he travels the ancient barrow roads. And if they ride over a mortal, that person will be swept up into the Hunt, forced to ride with them until he"—Declan glanced at me—"or she is released."

No.

No. The old woman couldn't have meant the Queen pulled her wild men from the Hunt. I couldn't let myself believe it, not when I didn't even have a proper door between me and the night.

Cadan pulled me from my thoughts, chafing a hand over my arm to warm me. "Don't you worry, Ryn-girl! It's a creeping sort of story, but it's just a story."

It's just a story.

Wouldn't I have said the same thing about an enchantress turning men to swans?

But the truth was as relentless as driving rain: Mortal men wouldn't have been stopped by nettles. Mortal men would have metal weapons, not obsidian blades. Mortal men wouldn't have made our skin crawl just to see them.

The Queen's Hunters—I couldn't think of them as anything else now—weren't from this side of the Veil.

And I couldn't tell my brothers. They hadn't believed what the old woman said about nettles. They wouldn't believe this.

It was just me and the Hunters—and the nettles that I prayed would keep my brothers and me safe.

Chapter 22

The next day, I returned to the nettle patch, more determined than ever.

The fire in my left hand had burned for hours after harvesting yesterday, finally fading late in the night. What would happen after any real amount of time?

I closed my eyes and was back at Roden, saw the curl of smoke, the darkness open up in front of me. I remembered Tanwen's command to run and the breathless moment when I decided I would.

I had escaped the Queen once by running into fire. The burn of the nettles was no different.

It was time to run into the fire once more.

I tugged my sleeves down to my wrists to protect my arms. Then I gathered a handful of nettles and began. I tried to imagine my brothers free of the enchantment, standing as men in the daylight, but that didn't help. If my brothers knew what I was doing, they'd try to stop me.

So I imagined Mother instead. And when my left hand felt too stung to hold the nettles, I switched hands, holding the dagger with my burning hand, and gathered the nettles with my good one.

Twenty minutes later, I had a pile of nettles beside me.

I rocked back on my heels, staring at the pile as I cradled my throbbing hands on my lap for a few moments. Then I sheathed the dagger, scooped the nettles into my arms, and carried them back to the hut.

By the time I reached the hut, my hands hurt so badly I couldn't think of anything except stopping the pain. I dropped nettles and dagger outside the hut and ran to the lake, plunging my hands into the cool water, hoping it would help as it had the day before.

I held them in there, grateful for the numbness that crept up my arms.

Gavyn had been right about nesting wherever I settled. My swan-brothers glided across the lake, unaware of me as I crouched at the bank.

Think how good it will be to have them be men again. Remember that the nettles will be like armor against the Queen's Hunters!

One of the swans swam close, and that little thing heartened me. I knew I'd soon be able to stand—or swim—close to them. I'd learn their markings and mannerisms.

I pulled my hands from the water, and the burning returned immediately. So I plunged them in again, still watching the nearest swan as it drifted by, preening.

A month ago, between his lessons on birds' hollow bones and the number of full moons a year, Gavyn had described how swans' feathers must lie just-so for the water to flow over them. Owain had fallen to the side, letting loose a snore that sounded like a wall collapsing. By the time my brothers stopped laughing, Gavyn swore he wouldn't say another thing about feathers.

So why couldn't I stop thinking about them? What was it about feathers that—

Feathers all lying in one direction.

I jumped up and ran to the pile of nettles.

I used the dagger to push aside the leaves to look at the stalk. The nettles' stingers looked like fine hairs all tilted outward and upward.

Declan used to say you could pet a porcupine if you knew which way to stroke it. He'd been talking about humoring Cadan, but the saying might also apply to nettles. I reached a fingertip toward one of the nettle stalks. I touched it at the base, brushing my finger from where I'd cut it up to the top of the stalk.

Nothing. Not one sting.

I grinned and stroked the stalk with my fingertip one more time. So that was how it should be done!

Now I knew how to cut the nettles without being stung.

Next I had to strip the stalks of their leaves. I'd harvest the fiber from the stalks for yarn and save the leaves for tea. Even I remembered old wives' tales of witches sipping nettle tea.

I looked down at the dagger in my still-dripping hand. It would take forever if I stripped the stalks with it—even if I managed not to cut them entirely.

What if . . . ?

I held the base of one of the stalks firmly in one hand. Before I could think better of it, I pinched the stalk with my other hand, between finger and thumb. Then I ran my pinched fingers up the stalk, following the direction of the fine hairs, stripping all the leaves off in one sweeping motion.

Not a sting.

I leaped up and tilted my face toward the sun.

I didn't trust myself to confront the Queen. Every attempt had led to someone getting hurt: my father, my brothers. The kingdom of Lacharra itself.

I wouldn't be the one to challenge her again. But I *would* be the one who set my brothers free. And when she saw them as men, when they returned to take back all she'd stolen, she would know that I was behind it.

This was how I'd wage war. And I *would* win.

⁂

I harvested and stripped piles of nettles that fall—all without my brothers' knowledge. I dried the leaves for tea and soup for the coming winter, but I lost nearly all the fiber hidden in the stalks.

Nettles were greedy with their fiber. You couldn't just pull it from the stalk. I vaguely remembered flax being retted—the long, slender stalks left out in the fields under the sun until the plant rotted away, leaving the fiber behind.

But the nettles I left out rotted entirely.

I took another portion of nettles and set them in still water, weighted down with branches to hold them under the surface. But the stalks rotted there too. And the smell! The little pond smelled like a chamber pot left in the sun.

In the end, I learned how to ret entirely by accident. I was so furious with the water retting that I rinsed some of the stalks after only a day in the water. Bits of the plant were already falling away, and I could just see pale strands of fiber beneath.

So I rinsed all the stalks and then left them in water for one more day. Then I carried the pulpy mass to one of the streams and let the running water wash away the excess. I was left with a dirty pile of fiber strands, full of bits of plant, but I'd done it! I'd finally collected the fiber. That was it, then: ret them one day, rinse them, then ret them just one day longer.

I couldn't have been happier if I'd found gold itself. I'd learned how to harvest nettles. I'd learned to ret them. This winter, I'd teach myself how to spin them.

Chapter 23

Five months later, I still didn't know what to do with the fiber I'd retted. I felt like I'd discovered a sword but still couldn't swing it.

All through that first winter, I tried to turn the sticky clumps of nettle fiber into a yarn that could be knitted. I couldn't finger-comb it, and the clumps of fiber were as thick as a baby's fist—too big to twist by hand.

I didn't ask my brothers for help. They'd have no patience for what they considered an unhealthy fascination. So every full moon, I hid the spindle and nettle fiber in Owain-the-hen's burlap bag and tucked it under my bedding.

By midwinter, I decided to travel to Etten. I'd seen so many women with drop spindles when I'd traveled through it. Someone there must know what to do with nettle fiber. I had only to decide when it would be safest to travel.

I'd teased some meaning from the old woman's ramblings and Declan's story: the woman claimed the Queen pulled Hunters from the Otherworldly Great Hunt, and

Declan said fall and winter storms hid the Great Hunt as it swept across the land.

Which meant I was safe during late fall and winter—when storms made it impossible to travel.

I settled for the next best thing: I left for Etten as soon as the snow melted, despite the freezing nights. It had been two weeks since the last storm, so even if the Hunters had already joined the Queen at the castle, they probably wouldn't have traveled as far as Etten.

And yet I still worried I was too late.

⁂

I huddled over the fire I'd kindled near a small outcropping, only one night from Etten. I used a stick to poke one of Owain-the-hen's eggs. She'd begun laying just before the weather turned cold. Those eggs and the nettle stew had kept me from starving. I dug the egg from the coals and dropped it in my lap, holding my rag-wrapped hands over it. It would cool enough to eat soon, but before it did, I'd soak up what warmth I could.

My tin mug rested on a flat stone on the coals, the water inside it steaming. I pulled a bag of dried nettle leaves from my satchel and dropped a handful into the mug. I sipped the tea as I ate the roasted egg.

Finally, as darkness spread around me, I sprinkled nettle leaves around where I'd spread my blanket. I feared the Queen's Hunters even more now that I knew who they were. The old woman had sworn they hadn't been able to walk through the nettles around her cottage. I was defenseless here without the walls of my hut—or the crazy hen who thought I was her chick. I hoped the dried leaves would provide some protection.

I lay down, my hand over the shard of Kingstone beneath my tunic.

After a long while, I slept.

The next morning, I walked the final leagues to Etten.

⁂

It didn't take long to find the part of Etten devoted to wool-craft. Three streets from the square, I discovered a broad, sunny shop with great swaths of yarn and thread wrapped around things that looked like upright pitchforks.

I gathered my courage and walked in. It was full of light, shadows gathering only in the corners. One side of the room was devoted to a large loom, with a heavy wooden frame that held threads fine as spider silk.

"My brother is at the fair today," said a low voice from a corner.

A woman stood next to an opening to a side room, a distaff in her hand. Her dress was covered in fine wool fluff the way a cook would be covered in flour. There were even a few stray bits of wool in her black hair, which had a single streak of gray. Her hair was pulled back in a tight knot at the base of her neck, but she didn't wear a wife's cap.

"I'm in no mood for pranks today, boy," she said as she sat at a spinning wheel, setting the distaff in its holder.

"You're new to Etten, or you'd know that already."

There was something in her low voice that would have quenched even Cadan.

I stepped closer.

She began pedaling the treadle, and the spinning wheel sprang to life. She knew its motion so well that her hands guided the fiber while she glared at me, eyes narrowed. "I told you to leave."

She had such authority that I almost turned and walked out the door.

Instead, I gritted my teeth and stepped closer, pulling the nettle fiber from my satchel.

That caught her attention, and she tilted her head as she studied it. "So you've come to ask something of the spinster of Etten? Ask it, then!"

I'd have given a year's worth of eggs to have words in that moment! I felt sure she'd chase me out of the shop if she thought I was making fun of her.

So I touched my throat as I shook my head, hoping she'd understand that I couldn't speak.

She nodded tersely. "Bring the fiber closer so I can see it."

I stepped so close I could touch the spinning wheel.

She glared at the fiber while she worked the treadle and fed a thin stream of wool into the whirring wheel.

"It's not wool, of course. But it's not flax, either." She glanced up at me. "What is it?"

I motioned harvesting a plant, then winced as I touched my hands and wrists.

She watched me, silent.

After a few moments: "Nettles?"

I nodded.

She raised an eyebrow.

I held a dry, sticky wad of fiber up and tried unsuccessfully to tease it apart. Then I pointed to the spinning wheel and moved the nettle fiber closer to it.

"You march into my shop and demand that I spin nettle fiber for you?" The words were cutting, but there was laughter deep in her hazel eyes.

I shook my head and dug into my satchel again, pulling out the old woman's drop spindle and a link of Mother's gold belt. I held the drop spindle up and pointed to her and then to myself: *I want you to teach me.*

Then I held the gold link out to her. *And I will pay you.*

She half-smiled. "And here I was thinking the commission from our new Queen wasn't enough and wouldn't a little bit of gold be just what I needed?"

I thought I'd lost some of my fear of the Queen, but hearing someone else mention her made it hard to breathe.

The spinster studied me as fiercely as she'd examined the nettle fiber. "Now why would mentioning our Queen make a boy like you turn white?"

I ignored the question. I *had* to learn how to spin the nettles. So I pushed the fear down so far I could almost ignore it and straightened my shoulders. Then I held the gold out one more time. *Will you or won't you?*

"My grandmother told us of how her family spun yarn from nettles. How the nettles had strength and warmth for those brave enough to grasp them." She cocked an eyebrow at me. "She'd lost her mind by then, of course."

I took a chance and tossed the fiber to her. She caught it with one hand and stilled the spinning wheel with the other. "I suppose that's my answer, clever lad. I'll give you three hours—till mid-afternoon. That's all."

I nodded.

"Why isn't your sister here?"

I shook my head, confused.

"This is woman's work, spinning. Why isn't she here?"

I showed her the gold link again in reminder that I was paying her.

She laughed, a full-throated sound that made me feel safe, somehow.

"Any spinner who lives in Etten learns wool first. We'd be fools not to. But I have tools for flax somewhere, and they should work for nettles as well." She pointed to a low, three-legged stool before disappearing into a back room. "Sit there while I fetch them."

So I sat.

A moment later, she returned with the most villainous tool I'd ever seen. It reminded me of the spiked maces knights of old used—except this was a block of wood, with one side covered in wicked-looking iron spikes. I bolted to my feet. She pushed me back to sitting.

"You're the oddest boy I've had the misfortune to meet. Your *sister* . . ." She lingered over the word as if she doubted it. ". . . harvests stinging nettles, but you've never seen a hackle before."

She dropped it onto a nearby worktable, spike-side up. "Nettles and flax produce strong fibers that don't lie straight easily." She held up half of the nettle fibers and, working from the end of the hank, began to yank them across the bed of spikes.

I thought the nettles would tear over such a ferocious comb, but they began to lie straight as she worked them farther up the hank. It reminded me of the way the ladies-in-waiting would brush my hair starting at the ends first.

"There." She handed the fiber to me. "You do it."

So I did.

She made me comb the fibers again and again, till the flecks of stalk and leaves that had clung to the fibers fell away. After a while, the fibers lay straight and long.

"Now, again." She handed me the second half of the nettle fiber.

I worked that entire hank. Seeing the fiber lie smooth and straight was nearly as exhilarating as the first fire I kindled for myself.

Then she showed me how to wrap the fibers around a stick to create a distaff I could rest against my shoulder. "Now let me see your spindle."

It took the spinster a full half-hour to get me to just hold the distaff and spindle properly and another to show me how to join the new fibers on the distaff to the old yarn left by the old woman. She taught me to lick my fingers to moisten the yarn and hasten the joining, something I'd never have thought of on my own.

Still, I never felt so stupid as when I looped the yarn

over the hook at the end of the spindle and let it hang before me. I couldn't keep it spinning to save my soul. When I could finally keep it spinning, I couldn't feed it fiber fast enough: the yarn thinned till it broke and I had to start over again. Or I'd feed too much fiber into the twist and end up with thick, clumpy yarn right after a length that was nearly as fine as thread.

Still, the spinster seemed pleased—though she didn't smile—as she watched me labor. "It's a matter of work, now. The yarn will become more even the longer you practice."

I looked up, heartened.

She glanced outside, then pushed the spiked hackle across the table to me. "And now you should go."

I shook my head, confused. Had I offended her?

"I think that a boy who pales at the mention of the Queen would not like to meet her soldiers when they come to ask about my progress on the Queen's commission."

I leaped to my feet, tumbling hackle, spindle, and fiber into my satchel. I felt in my pocket for the link of Mother's belt I'd promised as payment and pushed two links into the woman's palm.

"Two?" she asked.

I pointed to the hackle, its spiked outline visible even in my satchel. Then I pointed to myself and held a finger to my lips.

She handed me back the second link. "If I intended to mention you, a little gold wouldn't stop me."

I stiffened.

"But I won't, and so you may keep your money."

I drew myself up—the way I used to when I was a princess—and pressed the link back into her hand. I pointed to the hackle and bowed my head just a little. It was the closest I could come to a *thank you*.

She raised an eyebrow but accepted my gratitude with a nod. "Now go."

I darted out the door, expecting to see Hunters any minute.

Don't be silly, I scolded myself as I hurried up the street.

And yet it hadn't stormed in weeks. I could feel the change in the air—the new strength in the sunlight, despite the cold nights. The Queen could have called her Hunters across the Veil by now.

And sent them to Etten?

I turned a corner and ran into the answer.

I was face to face with a Hunter's leather breastplate.

I ducked my head in apology and backed away, scanning the street for any others.

I didn't see any, but there were several knots of people—and an entire gathering around a vendor selling rolls. I turned on my heel and darted into the crowd. When I was a street over, I began to run.

Even then, I could hear the Hunter when he finally scented me. "Princesssss!"

The voice was more howl than speech. My legs trembled just to hear it, but I pressed on, threading narrow alleyways. I tried to imagine what my brothers would say, but I couldn't hear anything.

Think. Think!

I couldn't outrun him. And I suspected he had ways of tracking me that no human could thwart.

Hide.

I almost moaned at the stupidity of the thought. How was I supposed to hide from an Otherworlder?

And then I knew.

At least, I *hoped*. It was my best chance. I dug into my satchel, feeling for the nettle leaves, nettle fiber . . . *anything*.

Too late. I heard footsteps behind me.

I swung to face the Hunter.

He tilted his head to one side, grinning so that his teeth showed. "Princess!"

I ran, still desperately digging through the satchel.

He caught me within two strides, grabbing a handful of my cowl and wrenching me around.

My fingers closed around a tangle of fiber. I yanked it free and threw it in his face.

He collapsed, clawing at it and howling when his hands closed around it.

I backed away. His whole body seemed to be shaking, rippling—

Don't let him get up! Cadan's voice was clear.

I threw a second handful on the Hunter . . . heard his howl in my bones . . . and dashed out of the alley. His howls were the last thing I heard as I ran from Etten.

Chapter 24

Sixteenth full moon

When I returned to the hut, I feared the Hunters would follow me. Find me.

But they didn't. The nettles hid me more than I'd dared imagine. So when my brothers changed two weeks later, I didn't tell them what had happened. I didn't want them to insist on finding another place to live.

I didn't want to be distractd from *finally* spinning the nettles.

I never signed a hint of either Hunters or nettles to my brothers during the warm nights when we gathered around a bonfire, grateful to be free of the cramped hut.

I spent the days harvesting and retting nettles, and the nights combing the retted fiber and practicing with the spindle. By the time autumn arrived, I had a bag full of nettle fiber and several lengths of yarn.

My future at Cairwyn Lake stretched before me: summers and autumns gathering and retting the nettles. I'd spend the winter months safe from the Hunters, spinning the fiber and knitting it into tunics.

⁂

On the morning of the sixteenth moon, I learned we couldn't hide forever.

High clouds raced across the sky, promising rain later. My breath fogged in the air as I walked to the weir. My brothers were always hungry after they changed, and I wanted to gather fish for them before the sky opened.

Then I saw the black swan—far from where my swan-brothers normally fed.

Something was wrong—the angle of its head, perhaps. I couldn't even tell which of my brothers it was.

Was it sick?

I took a step toward it, but the swan didn't move—not a flick of wing or tail.

And I realized it wasn't a swan at all.

It was a decoy, like what duck hunters near the castle used. They'd fold and bind river reeds together into the shape of a duck. Then they covered the reed-form with feathers.

I watched the swan decoy bob in the water. Someone was hunting swans.

Black swans.

I dropped to a crouch, right there in the reeds, and tried to reason the panic away.

But I knew better.

The Hunters had found us at last. The Queen's promise guarded me against harm, but my swan-brothers were defenseless.

I pushed back images of Hunters and black feathers and blood. *Think, Ryn!*

If I left Cairwyn Lake, my swan-brothers would follow. They'd finished molting months ago and would be able to fly to wherever I settled—if I could somehow escape.

But I had to leave *now*. I knew it so deeply that I didn't have room for panic.

Go! That was Mael, urging me back to the hut.

I stood.

No shout. No sound of footsteps. Nothing but the hum of insects and the whisper of water lapping against the reeds.

I crept along the edge of the lake, back toward the hut, cutting through the pines behind it to the portion of the lake where my swan-brothers nested. I'd scare them away before I left. By the time they wanted to return to the lake, instinct would urge them to follow me.

Yet I saw nothing when I stepped out of the pines and onto the bank.

No swans.

I waded softly in the shallows to see farther.

Still no swan-brothers. I didn't dare call them and draw the Hunters to this part of the lake. All I could do was to leave and pray my brothers followed.

I darted back to the hut and slipped inside, thumping my chest with the flat of my hand when I entered, hoping Owain-the-hen had returned from her morning hunt for food.

No answer—and there was no time to find her.

I started shoving everything into my pack and satchel: my brothers' clothes, my blanket, my dagger, the nettle yarn, the spindle, and the hackle the spinster gave me. The pack went on my back, the satchel over my shoulder. I snatched up the burlap bag I'd used to carry Owain-the-hen from Etten. I had no time to look for her, but if I found her . . .

Then I took Mael's cudgel and stepped out, walking to the back of the hut, toward the rocky bluff.

I felt a pricking between my shoulder blades and knew someone watched me.

Don't act like prey. Don't run.

I hitched the satchel higher on my back, moving toward the hill's rocky shoulder and the wilds beyond.

I heard a scuffling in the brush ahead of me and tensed.

The bush trembled again and Owain rushed out, chasing a bug.

I took two long strides toward her, ready to scoop her up.

Then I heard a branch break behind me.

I dropped into a crouch by the remains of the fire circle my brothers and I gathered around on warm nights—only a stride from Owain.

It's an animal, I told myself. *Just an animal.*

But no animal was heavy enough to break such a branch.

My breath came fast—I didn't have courage to look behind me. Instead, I watched Owain, just out of reach, as she stretched her head up, eyeing whatever was behind me. She didn't growl or spread her wings and attack. She just stood there.

I wanted to run, but it was like Gavyn was there, his hand on my shoulder: *Stay quiet, stay still.*

I heard a whisper of leaves brushing against something off to my right. I turned toward the noise. Three bearded men stood at the edge of the pines. They wore leather breastplates.

Two other Hunters appeared ahead of me, near the outcropping.

Five, now.

I closed my eyes. I'd lose my courage altogether if I saw any more of them.

"Princess?" asked one in a voice that sounded disused. "We mean you no harm, she-child. The Queen would have our heads."

She'd found us.

Me. She'd only found me. I had to keep her from finding my brothers.

The same voice spoke again, smoother this time, as if he'd grown used to speaking. "Are you hungry? Thirsty? We are here to serve you."

My body relaxed. They weren't allowed to kill me. The Queen had agreed that night in the dungeon. Maybe I could let the Hunters take me back to the castle. I'd be safe, and it would be better than trying to fight them.

No. I'd be a decoy. The Hunters only had to hold me until my brothers arrived by day's end.

I couldn't fight, but I could run.

Even a rabbit can run, murmured dream-Declan.

It was time.

I patted my chest. *Don't make me leave you, Owain!*

She huddled in front of me—just out of reach. Could I use the cudgel to sweep her close? I looped the burlap bag's makeshift strap over my shoulder, afraid even that small movement would bring the Hunters down on me.

I glanced over my left shoulder. Two other Hunters appeared from the trees.

Seven Hunters, now.

I looked back at the man who'd spoken. His voice was gentle, but his eyes held violence.

Use the cudgel, Ryn. That was Cadan.

I adjusted my grip on the cudgel. Then I slowly scooped up a handful of old ash with my free hand.

That's right! Teach them not to touch a princess.

More stirring in the trees around my camp. Two more Hunters in front of me. Nine in all.

They'd nearly surrounded me. The only reason they hadn't was because of the tumble of boulders ahead and to my right. I'd run to that. Run to it and up it. And push down that tangle of tree limbs onto any following Hunters once I passed it.

"Rest easy, Princess. Come, eat with us. The White One desires only your company—and the Kingstone you stole from her."

One . . . , counted Mael, and I focused on the boulders a few strides beyond Owain. *Two . . .*

"Princess?" The voice wasn't comforting now that I'd

seen his eyes. "Let us help you." His eyes kept darting to the other Hunters behind me.

. . . three!

I launched myself toward the boulders, terrifying Owain-the-hen, who flapped straight up.

Please . . . please! I swept open the lip of the burlap bag, and Owain tumbled into it.

I ran straight over the remains of the fire, dead coals crumbling beneath my feet. And in that moment—with the ash billowing around me—I wasn't afraid. I wasn't courageous. I simply listened for my brothers' voices as I ran.

Even a rabbit can run.

Faster. Only a few strides more.

Two of the Hunters stepped in front of the boulders, and I pulled the cudgel back, ready to strike.

Not the face, Ryn, said Cadan. *Be smart!*

The Hunter to my right put his hands before his face to block the blow. But Cadan's voice reminded me of a better strategy. I swung the cudgel down and brought it up between the Hunter's legs.

He dropped to his knees.

I threw the handful of ash into the other Hunter's eyes. He swung out blindly, tearing my cheek, but it bought me the sliver of time I needed to shoot past him and onto the boulders.

The next moment, I'd scurried halfway up the rocks. A hand caught my foot, but I shook free. A quick shove sent the dried tree down onto whoever tried to follow me. I was running before I heard the frustrated shouts behind me.

"Get her!" There was nothing gentle in the voice anymore. "Remember, the Queen wants her unharmed!"

I was at the far end of the boulders now, and I listened for more shouts as I ran.

Nothing. That scared me even more. They didn't want to give away their position.

A whistle behind and to my left rang out, their way of communicating.

I stopped at the end of the rocks, scanning where to go. The Hunters could easily outrun me.

Think! Where can you hide?

I could climb a tree, but if I stayed there, my brothers would still return to Cairwyn Lake that night.

And they'd be killed.

Then I saw the nettle patch a quarter mile away.

I ran for it, pack beating against my back, satchel and burlap bag sagging almost to my knees.

Another whistle off to the left. They were trying to flank me.

Run! Run and hide! It became a prayer I sent into the forest, something to focus on instead of my aching lungs and burning throat.

As I ran, I yanked one of my brother's shirts from my satchel. I threw it over my head, wrapping a sleeve around my exposed neck for protection. The patch was already wilting from frosts, but they could still sting.

I hit the nettles without breaking stride, my cudgel

held before me, scattering the plants to either side.

More whistles off to my left.

One or two behind me—not in the nettles, though.

I knelt and pulled the shirt up around my mouth to muffle my breath. I kept expecting to hear Hunters crashing into the nettles, but there was silence.

More whistles off to my left, growing softer over time.

The nettles were protecting me once more. I listened as the whistles retreated. Were they hiding me too, or were the Hunters toying with me? I stayed hunched in the nettles until my breathing grew even and the forest grew silent.

I couldn't be here when my brothers changed. The Hunters would find them.

Slowly, I pushed through the nettles till I found the far side of them, determined to run as far as possible before my swan-brothers joined me.

I froze again at the sound of footsteps. Had the Hunters found the edges of the nettles?

I looked up, saw clouds racing across the sky.

Then I heard a sound so deep that I felt it in my bones.

A minute later, the sky gathered itself into one great storm that threw itself at the world. Wind drove the rain in sheets that swept across the nettles. If I had any chance of slipping away from the Hunters, it was now.

I darted forward, moving as fast as I could until I found an already-swollen stream. I waded into the center of it so I wouldn't leave any evidence behind: no footprints, no crushed plants.

One look back.

I couldn't see far, and I could hear nothing over the roar of wind and rain. But there was no evidence of the Hunters. The storm had given me the chance I needed.

I hitched the pack higher up onto my shoulders and began to hike upstream.

Chapter 25

Sixteenth full moon

That evening, I sheltered at the edge of a gray lake, praying my brothers would find me.

The storm had abated a little, but I couldn't see the middle of the lake. The wind roared through the trees endlessly, making it impossible to distinguish the wind that heralded my brothers' change—if they were even here.

Finally, when the world was a sweep of gray, I saw six black shapes approach the shore. My swan-brothers pulled themselves onto the bank, trumpeting protests. I quickly set out their already-soaking clothes and stepped back into a copse of nearby trees.

One moment, my brothers were swans, huddled against the storm. The next, they were ghostly figures nearly hidden by the rain as they scrambled to gather their wet clothes.

I beat my cudgel against a stone so they would know I was there—and follow the sound to find me.

"What happened?" demanded an already-soaked Mael. "Why aren't we at the hut?"

I motioned as if pulling back a bowstring.

"A bow?" asked Owain.

"Hunters, you fool," hissed Cadan. "Even I know that."

"Why would hunters make you run?" asked Gavyn. "I'm sure they'd move on soon enough."

I saw the moment when my brothers realized that it was the Queen's men doing the hunting.

"How near?" asked Mael, already peering out into the darkness.

I shook my head.

Declan caught my chin and turned the cheek I'd been trying to hide. "They were close once, at least."

Cadan's sigh was more a hiss than anything.

"We need to find shelter," said Aiden. "And then you'll tell us everything."

It would have been hard to see through such heavy rain during the day, but to search for shelter in the dark with no fire or moonlight?

We ended up huddled at the base of a small bluff, where sheets of slate reached out into the night to cover us. There was no getting away from the rain, but the bluff protected us from some of the wind.

Nothing protected us from the cold. We crowded together, my brothers in a circle around me and Owain-the-hen cowering on my lap in her burlap sack.

"I never thought I'd be this close to a hen," muttered Cadan.

I put a hand over Owain's head and scowled at Cadan. I'd never admit it, but it felt good to argue with him. It was the only normal thing on that wretched day.

"It was the Queen, wasn't it?" said Aiden.

I nodded.

He cursed.

"How do you know, Ryn?" asked Mael.

It was difficult enough to communicate with my brothers when I had dirt to write in, but that night, with the rain streaming down, I had only my hands. I was hungry and tired and if it hadn't been for Owain sitting on my lap, the rain's cold would have settled bone-deep.

It took a full five minutes for one of my brothers to understand that there had been a black swan decoy.

"Black feathers on the decoy?" confirmed Gavyn.

I nodded.

"Only the Queen would know about black swans," said Aiden.

Mael nodded. "Then what, Ryn?"

The rest was pantomime. Cadan especially liked how I'd used the cudgel. "Well done! He won't walk straight for a few days, I'll wager!"

But Aiden remained grim, the rain running in small rivers down his temples and into his beard. "Now she knows you didn't die at Roden."

"How did you lose the wild men?" asked Gavyn. "They would have been faster than you, better trackers."

I pantomimed a nettle patch—and me running into it.

Owain whistled. "You ran into a nettle patch?"

Yes.

"That wouldn't stop them." Mael said.

It would if the Queen hated nettles.

"You still think nettles will save us," said Declan.

I know it.

Why didn't they believe me? Escaping the Hunters was proof that the nettles would work.

Gavyn squinted, trying to understand. "Even if nettles would hold her wild men at bay, how did you get out of the nettle patch? Why weren't they waiting for you?"

I'd pondered that as I slogged through the creek, and I thought I knew. If I was right, we were safe.

The sound I'd heard before the storm hadn't been thunder. It had been the horn calling the Hunters back to the Great Hunt in the Otherworld.

But before I could answer, Aiden asked, "You've been harvesting nettles all this time?"

This was my chance. I'd show them all I'd done.

I scooped up Owain and plopped her in Cadan's lap. Before he could protest, I pulled out the nettle fiber, the hackle, the spindle, and the yarn I'd spun. I'd come so far in this year!

I knew my brothers wouldn't exclaim over the handiwork. But I thought they'd at least look at it.

"Where did you get this?" asked Mael.

I motioned that the spindle had come from the old woman.

"And that?" he asked, pointing to the hackle. I signed that it had come from Etten.

"You traveled into Etten? Did anyone see you?" asked Aiden.

He saw the answer on my face before I could hide it. "Her men saw you there, didn't they?"

I clenched my fists. Why couldn't they see the entire story? That I'd found a way to save them? Hadn't I proved it today when the Hunters couldn't follow me into the nettle patch?

But Aiden's face was set. "They saw you there?"

I nodded.

"So the Queen knows that you're alive . . . and her wild men know where we are . . . because a crazy woman told you to make us clothes out of stinging nettles?"

I stood silent.

He waved an arm out to the storm. "Her men are out there, and we can't protect you once the sun rises!"

I tried to sign that I was safe, that I was sure this storm meant that the Hunters had been called back to the Otherworld, but Aiden wouldn't look at me.

"No more," he said in a low voice. "I want you to stay safe."

Stay safe? I had stayed safe in the wilds for over a year. A year *after* I'd stolen the Queen's Kingstone and escaped the destruction of Roden.

Since then, I'd grown a few inches taller—not that they had noticed. I'd learned to handle a woman's monthly flow without a breath of help from *anyone.* And I'd done it all while surviving winter and summer in a hut. While feeding myself and watching over my swan-brothers.

But I didn't sign any of that to them. I wasn't the child

I'd been a year ago. If they couldn't see that, I wouldn't try to change their minds.

So I simply tilted my head at Aiden. *Anything else?*

"Nettles will not fix this, Andaryn. You will not endanger yourself." He picked up the hackle and swept the rest of the nettle goods into his arms. Then he strode away into the rain.

I lunged after him, but Declan held me back.

"It's for the best, Ryn." Declan pulled me closer as I beat against him. "We didn't know the hold it had on you. We can't let you hurt yourself."

And then I was crying, tears mixing with the rain on my cheeks. Aiden was throwing away the only things that would save them! A year's worth of work!

"It's not just you, Ryn," said Gavyn softly. "There's no breaking the spell if something happens to you. We need you."

Cadan put a hand on my shoulder. "He doesn't want you to hurt yourself for *us*."

I shrugged his hand away.

I pulled Owain-the-hen into my lap and ignored my brothers. After a while, they stopped trying to talk to me or explain what they'd done.

When Aiden returned an hour before dawn, his arms were empty.

Chapter 26

It took me two days to find everything that Aiden had thrown away that night. I waded the shore and scrabbled along the banks to recover the few lengths of yarn and the hackle and spindle. The fiber was half-rotted and useless by the time I found it.

After nearly a month of travel north and a trip through a nearby town for winter provisions, I found a new home near Lake Rhywar. There was no living to be had on the bank of the lake, but there was a nearby cave in an old mining pit. My swan-brothers followed me to the lake, nesting along its rocky banks.

The cave—I later learned it was called the Horned Man's Mouth—seemed a dismal place after the hut by Cairwyn Lake. But I needed shelter from the coming winter. The pit, as broad as a merchant's house, *did* look like a rocky-sided mouth opening in the forest floor, with the cave openings in the pit walls looking like an open throat. There was one wall that slumped down to the bottom of the pit: the Horned Man's tongue. It served as my entrance into the pit.

⁂

Ten months later, the morning after the twenty-fourth full moon, I picked my way down into the Horned Man's tongue, my satchel full of my brothers' clothes. The temperature dropped as I descended, for the pit was as deep as five men, and it acted like a bowl for cold and damp long into the day. By the time I reached the bottom, I was in dim once more, for the rising sun touched only the top of the pit.

At the bottom of the pit, there was only mud and three rough arches in the pit's wall. There, ancient miners had burrowed into the earth, never knowing they were creating shelter for a banished princess of Lacharra centuries later.

I walked into the opening on the left. It had the lowest arch—better to keep cold winds out—and a level antechamber, where I lived.

The jagged walls of the antechamber were their own sort of shelves. I quickly tucked the satchel on one of the outcroppings to keep it safe from mice or insects that might have escaped Owain-the-hen's pecking.

There were sometimes human visitors to the Horned Man's Mouth—that was how I'd learned the name. Most people avoided any place with a name like that, but some ventured down to see what Otherworldly creatures inhabited it.

I'd found my own way to deal with them. As rumors of a spirit haunting the cave had grown, there had been fewer and fewer visitors.

I dragged an old stump I'd scavenged from the

surrounding forest over to another of the outcroppings. I clambered on the stump, stood on tiptoe, and reached to the very back of the outcropping, my fingers just brushing the nettles.

I always hid the nettle-fiber, the hackle, the spindle, and the yarn on this outcropping. If I pushed it back far enough, even my brothers couldn't see it when they stood in the antechamber.

I'd vowed they'd never see it again until it was time to wear the tunics.

I pulled the spindle and a distaff dressed with combed nettle fiber from their hiding place. The hackle followed them, though I wouldn't need it that day for fibers. Then I moved the stump to the center of the antechamber and sat on it. I'd spin a few yards of yarn before I slept.

I'd spent that night of the twenty-fourth moon with my brothers. We were a third of the way through the enchantment, and I still didn't know whether to celebrate or mourn.

I tried to shift the heaviness in my chest. Best to just spin.

I licked my fingers to dampen the yarn before holding it to the fibers I'd already teased from the distaff. I looped the yarn around the hook on the spindle and let it hang before sending it spinning. The yarn twisted, taking the new fibers with it, and I slowly fed the fiber into the twist as the twirling spindle moved closer and closer to the ground. When I'd spun nearly a foot's length, I wrapped the new yarn just above the whorl. Then I looped the yarn over the hook and sent the spindle spinning once more.

The spindle occasionally faltered in my hands, and sometimes the yarn was so thin it broke or so thick it became lumpy. But my skill was increasing. Every time I took the spindle out, I reminded myself that this was how I fought the Queen—*this* was how I resisted. I might not be able to face her in six years, but I'd set my brothers free so that we could reclaim Lacharra.

I'd almost spun another foot-length of nettle yarn when someone approached the cave, stepping through the dry twigs I'd spread near the opening so no one could catch me unaware.

I snatched up the hackle, distaff, and spindle and dashed deeper into the shaft.

A soft voice, as if the speaker was frightened. Very different from the bold calls of those who wanted to brave the spirits of the Horned Man's Mouth.

I set down everything except the hackle.

When I heard the voice again, I pressed the iron spikes against the wall and dragged them, making an unearthly music. I trailed the hackle closer to the antechamber, as if something was rising out of the depths.

Only silence after that.

I paused just outside the antechamber, listening.

Nothing.

I counted ten slow, deep breaths, then peered around the corner.

A red-haired woman stood there, her fine clothes smeared with . . . *blood*? . . . and her face streaked with dirt.

She stepped forward. "Ryn? Is that you?"

Chapter 27

Tanwen.

I drew the hackle back, ready to use it like a weapon.

Had the Queen grown so strong that she could send phantoms to us?

I looked behind her, expecting to see Hunters pouring into the pit, obsidian blades drawn.

The sun had risen high enough that its light almost touched the arch. Any moment now, light would reveal that this wasn't Tanwen, just a trick of the Queen.

The apparition took a step closer, half-laughing as if she couldn't believe it was me, and I saw the dimple in her left cheek. She held a hand out to me. "Ryn, it's me. It's Tanwen."

Tanwen!

I dropped the hackle and ran to her.

She caught me close, and when I opened my eyes, sunlight filled the antechamber, pooling at our feet.

She took my face in both hands. "How I've searched for you! You've no idea what it meant when the Hunters reported that you were alive!"

She called them Hunters too?

Tanwen sobered, fear bright in her eyes. "And Aiden? I have to know for certain, Ryn."

What I'd have given to say, *Yes! He's alive!*

But Tanwen saw the truth in my face.

She pulled in a great, shuddering breath and pressed shaking hands to her mouth. After a moment, she collected herself. "Where are they? I must see Aiden."

Then she noticed that I hadn't spoken. "Are you well?"

I nodded yes, then touched my throat. It was the easiest way to let her know I couldn't speak. She seemed to understand that I'd explain it later.

Right now, it was time to show her Aiden.

I quickly returned the nettles, spindle, distaff, and hackle, then gathered a small handful of grain from my food stores. I led Tanwen out of the pit, up into the forest, and along the short path to the banks of Lake Rhywar.

Tanwen craned her head once we reached the lake, barely able to contain herself as she looked for Aiden.

I pulled off my boots and motioned that she should stay at the banks. Then I rolled my leggings up and waded into the shallows. I'd grown used to the cool water and my feet were tough enough that I hardly noticed the stony lake bed.

Six black swans glided across the smooth water. I waded out a few more steps, then slapped the water the way a beaver does when danger approaches. The swans stilled, heads held high to better see me. One trumpeted to the others, and then they all swam to me.

I looked over my shoulder at Tanwen, saw her forehead

crease as she tried to make sense of me calling six black swans when all she wanted was to see Aiden.

And then I saw the moment when she understood.

My swan-brothers surrounded me, gently tweaking my sleeves or hair, stretching close so that I could stroke their long necks. I opened my hand and showed them the bit of grain, grinning at their trumpets and calls. They followed me as I waded out of the water and sprinkled grain at Tanwen's feet.

She watched, pale-faced, as the swans pecked around her feet. "Which one is—?"

I stroked Aiden-swan's neck. Then I took her hand and poured the last of the grain into it.

She extended her hand to Aiden. He backed away, neck curling in the funny way of theirs. Finally, he nipped at her fingers, testing her, but she didn't flinch. After a moment, he stretched his neck forward and began to eat from her hand. She raised her other hand and, with her fingertips, traced the curve of his neck . . . the breadth of his back . . . felt the ruffled feathers of his folded wings.

Aiden raised his head from the grain and looked at her for a long moment.

Then the rest of my swan-brothers pressed close, pecking each other and trumpeting. Tanwen scattered the grain on the bank and stepped back, leaving the swans to their meal.

"I hoped I'd be able to see him, and I have." She smiled and wiped her eyes with the back of her hand. "You must tell me everything that has happened, and I will do the same. And then, you have to leave."

Chapter 28

I motioned Tanwen to follow me to a place along the bank with exposed dirt. Then I drew all that happened at Roden: how I exchanged my speech for my brothers' freedom, the enchantment, how I stole the Kingstone and ran into the fire.

Tanwen was patient, carefully watching my dirt-sketches and asking questions that reached to the heart of the matter.

Once my story was told, she nodded. "That's why she hunts you so fiercely. You saved them—I'm sure she believed you'd speak by now. Or she thought that if you remained silent, you'd be a living doll in her court. Yet you *all* escaped, and you took the Kingstone with you!"

I hadn't thought of it as besting the Queen. I'd thought of it as survival.

"And then she discovered you were alive! I thought her fury would consume her." Tanwen leaned forward to rest a hand on my arm. "She hunts you, Ryn. She hunts you *all*. Her guards? They aren't even men."

I'd known it for nearly a year, but I still shivered to hear it spoken in the morning light.

Tanwen nodded grimly. "There are some things better left in the dark, but you need to know about the Hunt—"

I held a hand up to stop her, then pressed it to my chest as I nodded. *I already know.*

I quickly drew the Hunt with a squiggly line between it and me—a veil that separated the two. Then I circled one of the riders and pointed to our side of the veil: I knew the Hunters were Otherworlders.

"She hasn't called Otherworlders, Ryn. She called their *hounds*." Tanwen's face crumpled in disgust. "White hounds with burning eyes and crimson ears and muzzles. She fashions them into men who do her bidding here."

I sat back, horrified, remembering Declan's story of the chieftain who'd set his hounds on the snow-white boar.

Tanwen swept a hand over the Hunt. "The day after I was carried back to the castle, soldiers reported that Roden had fallen to Danavirian soldiers and that Lacharra's six princes and one princess were slaughtered in the attack."

She shook her head. "The ambassador was thrown into prison and the entire country mourned. The Queen came up with an elaborate story of how she'd lost the Kingstone in her escape, though she never explained why she was at Roden in the first place. I lived somewhere between sleeping and death for months. It was grief, but I also knew that if I was myself, I'd draw the Queen's attention—and her ire.

"Then, last spring, her Hunters arrived from Etten with news that sent her into a rage. Had they seen you?"

I nodded. That was when I'd visited the spinster.

"So I secretly sent two of our most trusted soldiers, men who mourned Aiden, to Etten to search for you, though I knew nothing except that you were alive. The Queen sent more of her dog-men to Etten to hunt you, and I prayed my own would find you first. Her Hunters never returned—they'd been called back to the Hunt before they could report to her."

I nodded, remembering the sound of the call as I hid in the nettles so many months ago.

"The Queen can only pull hounds from the Hunt if they're not needed elsewhere. They're summoned by the first great storm, and once they're wanted for the Hunt, they must answer its call. I think the only reason she can pull them here is because of a kindness to the Hunt's leader: she once sang a song that soothed his horse.

"Now, tell me how you hid when they found you at the lake. The Hunters said you hid where they couldn't sense you. They said something about blackness, blindness."

So the nettles had hidden me as well as protected me!

I signed and pantomimed my escape, ending with how I'd hidden in the nettles.

Tanwen leaned forward, elbows propped on her knees. "Why nettles?"

I signed the story of the old woman to Tanwen, trying to show her madness and her fierce love for the Queen. How I'd been told that the Queen hated nettles, because they reminded her of Before, whatever that was.

"I wondered if the Queen was an Otherworlder, for how could a human call the hounds like she does? But no

Otherworlder would mind nettles like she does! Iron, perhaps, but not nettles."

I'd puzzled over that a thousand times.

"Perhaps she was one of the women caught up into the Hunt ages ago," said Tanwen, "when the Veil between the worlds was thinner."

I nodded. It would explain how the Queen seemed so old sometimes. And her story of escape from a stern mistress.

That reminded me: How had Tanwen escaped? I tried to sign the question, and when she understood me, the smile fell from her face.

"Her hound-men spent the winter in the Great Hunt and didn't return to her until a few months ago. They brought news of your escape—and of the soldiers I'd sent to search for you. The men didn't talk before they died, but it was easy enough for her to guess that I'd sent them."

I shook my head, imagining the Queen's rage.

Tanwen smiled grimly. "She said if I longed to find you, I should travel with her Hunters. She surrendered me to their Hunt—and I became a human decoy for the ones who hunted my husband and his kin."

We'd been discovered again. I leaped to my feet.

Tanwen tugged me back down. "You're safe, Ryn. For a little while, at least."

How long? I wanted to ask. But I didn't dare interrupt her.

"I traveled with them for months. They hoped that rumors of the widow of the crown prince would draw out your family—and I learned their secrets." She shuddered. "I've seen them as hounds on new-moon nights.

"And I listened in each town we traveled through. When I heard about a spirit that haunted the Horned Man's Mouth, I wondered if you'd found shelter here." She smiled at me triumphantly. "I was right!

"Now listen: you must leave. The Hunt—and the hounds she pulled from it—are limited to the lands between the old barrow roads they traveled in ages past. The last barrow road stretches across the moor. You must travel beyond their reach, even though that may not protect you in coming years. If the Queen suspects you've hidden beyond the barrow roads, she'll negotiate with the Hunt-Lord himself to send her Hunters there.

"But that is a matter for another year. You must leave here now. *Today.* You only have a little time."

I sketched a Hunter in the dirt. *What happened to the Hunters you traveled with?*

"I sent them back to the Otherworld."

I shook my head, confused.

"They were close to discovering you. So I gathered a drug from the forest to make them sleep. And as they slept, I put one of their swords through each of them."

I studied the smears on her skirt. One was the shape of a hand. She'd wiped her hands on her skirt.

"I'm not a warrior," faltered Tanwen. "To pierce them through till they changed from men . . . to hounds . . . and finally returned to the other side of the Veil . . . I'll see it till I die, and perhaps beyond.

"The Queen will call them back to this side of the Veil soon, and then they'll sweep here, all of them. I've bought you time to flee beyond the moor's barrow road, but you must leave *now*."

It was nearly time for my swan-brothers' yearly molt. Once they began to lose their white flight feathers, they wouldn't be able to fly and follow me beyond the moor. Tanwen was right: we needed to leave immediately.

It took less than an hour to pack. My brothers' clothes and all the nettle fiber, the yarn, the spindle, and the hackle went into the pack. I filled my satchel with what we'd use each night: blankets, the tinder box, and the few handfuls of dry tinder. Owain-the-hen's latest eggs and the last of the grain would sustain us as we traveled, and I'd bring two of the five weirs I'd woven.

It would be a lot to carry, but manageable with Tanwen's help.

As I rolled the last of the blankets, she introduced herself to Owain-the-hen, who'd wandered in for a mid-afternoon roost. Owain maintained an uneasy alliance with my brothers, but she immediately warmed to Tanwen, who discovered that the hen loved to be tickled under her wattle.

I tied the weirs to the pack, then shrugged into it, handing the satchel to Tanwen. Finally I patted my chest, and Owain-the-hen fluttered to my shoulder.

Tanwen shook her head as she looked at me, her lips twitching a bit at Owain. "I thought I'd find the girl I knew two years ago. Instead I find a young woman. You've escaped the Queen twice now, and you're closer than anyone else to knowing her secret. I'm sure of it."

She kissed my forehead and handed the satchel back to me. "I'm not worried for you, Ryn. You'll do just fine."

I stepped back as her words sunk in. I jabbed a finger at her and then pressed my hand to my chest. *You're coming with me.*

"No. I'm not. It's so much for you to carry, but it's better this way. The Queen's Hunters believe I've desecrated their Hunt. When she calls them back, they'll come for me. I won't have you beside me when that happens."

I dropped the satchel on the ground. Then I sat down on the tree stump, arms folded.

"Don't be foolish, Ryn!"

Foolish? *Foolish*? I hadn't been this angry since the Queen first came to the castle. How dare Tanwen give up like this?

Tanwen looked just as furious. She always did have a fine temper. Good. Maybe she'd learn sense as well.

"I'm not going with you."

I shrugged and made myself comfortable on the stump. *As you wish.*

"Ryn, you don't have time for this!"

I raised an eyebrow. *So you say.*

Silence. I stared down at my feet.

Finally, she whispered, "Don't ask me to endanger Aiden. I won't."

I pressed my fingers to my stinging eyes, knowing I'd do the same thing, trying to think of an answer.

Nettles!

I drew Tanwen in the dirt on the floor. Then I drew Hunters approaching. Finally, I drew nettles between Tanwen and the Hunters, then covered her with my hand.

Hidden. Safe.

"You don't know for certain that they could hide me."

I do. I pointed to myself. They'd hidden me. The chief Hunter himself said that I'd disappeared.

She hesitated.

I wished I had words! I wished I could write. I wanted Tanwen to know how much Aiden needed her. How much I did.

But all I could do was stand and hold my hand out to her.

One breath, in and out. Another.

Finally, Tanwen put her hand in mine.

Chapter 29

Before the twenty-fifth full moon

By the end of the third day of walking, we stood at Cadair Tor, a turret of weathered granite atop the low mountains that bordered Fawryn Moor. Both Tanwen and I had to shield our eyes from the glare of the setting sun. Even Owain-the-hen, perched on my shoulder, hid her head under her wing.

"There." Tanwen pointed to a dark line stretching diagonally across the moor. "That's one of the old barrow roads the ancients traveled to bury their dead." I remembered the chieftain who'd become the Hunt-Lord, how he'd been called to the Otherworld before he could take his family and captains to the barrow. "Even now, the Hunt respects that road. So the Queen's hound-men respect it as well, for tracking you is their own twisted Hunt. If I understand aright, there's another barrow road beyond this one. If we can cross that road, you'll be safe—at least for a while."

I glared at her.

"*We* will be safe," she amended.

That night we didn't build a fire. There was little fuel for it on the moor, but even if there had been, we wouldn't have used it. The Hunters would be able to see us creeping along like insects if they stood on the mountains. There was no need to draw further attention with a fire.

We crossed the second barrow road after four days and kept walking beyond that. We needed to find a lake for my brothers—and nettles. Passing beyond the barrow roads offered us protection for at least a year. Nettles would shield us after that.

⁂

We traveled a week till we found a town where I could buy clothes and other supplies for Tanwen. She remained hidden while I went into the town. I didn't dare risk having her with me: her red hair was too memorable if someone came searching for her.

After another week's travel, we'd found a hiding place among the ruins of the ancients who built their fortresses on great mounds. The ruins sat at the top of a tree-covered hill near the sea. The west side of the hill sloped down to a rocky beach and the sea beyond. On clear days, we could see the shores of Eyre like a gray cloud on the horizon. The east side of the hill sheltered a lake that would, in turn, shelter my swan-brothers.

I'd heard tales that stinging nettles loved old stone, and they were right: nettles grew throughout the ruins and crept in long swaths down the hill. Tanwen and I cleared the nettles out of a ruined foundation and built a small shelter against the tilting remains of a wall. I knew my brothers would help us build a sturdier home before winter.

But first, my brothers needed to know that Tanwen was *here.* I wondered if their swan selves would guess the miracle, for Tanwen watched them for hours once they reached the lake.

Finally, the night of the full moon, Tanwen and I awaited the transformation. The roar of the sea filled our lives now, and I'd thought I'd heard the wind that heralded my brothers' change at least twice only to discover I'd been mistaken.

Tanwen squeezed my hand till it hurt. "How much longer, Ryn? I don't know if I can—"

And then the wind caught us, blowing down from the hilltop, making the nettles bow and dance, catching my swan-brothers and—

"Ryn? *Ryn!*" That was Aiden. "Where are we?"

". . . clothes are here . . . ," said someone. "She's fine."

I tugged on Tanwen's hand: *Say something!*

Yet the only sound was the scuffling and murmuring of my brothers as they dressed.

"Aiden." Tanwen's voice broke, and I felt her pulse pounding in her fingertips.

Silence, then. Not a word, not even a twitch from my shadowy brothers.

Then I heard footsteps. Slow. Wary.

Aiden emerged from the dim by the lake's edge, carrying a branch like a weapon. He stiffened when he saw the figure beside me, drawing the branch back to deliver a blow.

"It's me, Aiden." Tanwen released my hand and stepped toward him.

He turned to me, unbelieving.

I nodded.

He covered the distance between them in two strides. Tanwen reached up, pushed his hair out of his eyes, and smiled up at him. Then Aiden crushed her close, as if that could make up for all the time they'd been apart.

My other brothers crowded around them. Gavyn touched Tanwen's shoulder, just to be sure it was her. Owain grinned, and Cadan brushed at his eyes.

But Aiden and Tanwen didn't notice any of it. After a moment, Mael said, "Lead on, Ryn-girl. Let's give them a little while to themselves."

Declan nodded and shooed Gavyn and Owain toward us. I led them up the hill, on a path we'd cleared through the nettles, to the fire and food Tanwen and I had prepared.

How we celebrated when Aiden and Tanwen joined us! The Kingstone was passed from hand to hand as we pieced together all that had happened since the enchantment was begun. After spending time among the Hunters, Tanwen could finally tell my brothers who the wolf men were and how the Queen called them here when they were not required at the Hunt. I tried not to look smug as she confirmed that nettles did somehow thwart them and that she believed they limited the Queen's power too.

I knew that it must be easier for my brothers to understand—and believe—the details of the enchantment when it was explained with words rather than signs, when

Tanwen could answer their questions directly. But I still savored the moment when they realized that I'd been right all along about the nettles and the Hunters.

I grinned when Tanwen scolded Aiden for throwing away the spindle, hackle, and fiber—the things that would save him!—nearly a year ago. But Aiden wasn't anywhere near crestfallen. I think he would have borne a beating with a smile just to have Tanwen near again.

To their credit, my brothers apologized in grand style, exclaiming over the work I'd completed. Then Declan told every embarrassing story he could remember of all of them just to make Tanwen and me laugh.

And laugh we did—my hand pressed over my mouth so no sound would escape—till Owain-the-hen flapped down from her perch and wandered out into the night so she could find a little peace.

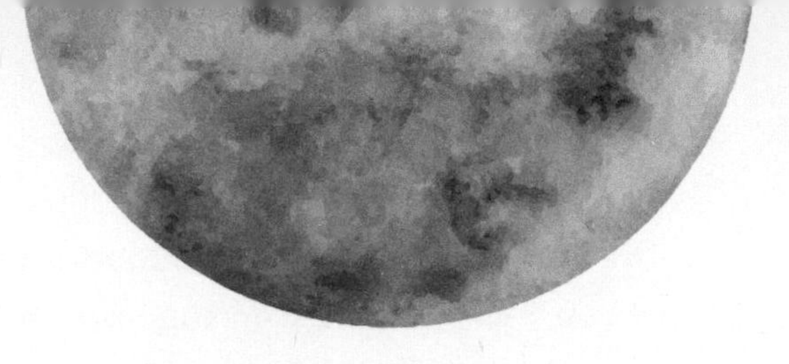

Chapter 30

Thirty-eighth full moon

Tanwen had waited for my swan-brothers to change on eleven different moons, according to Gavyn's time-keeper, but I would have thought this was the first. She'd grown thinner the past year. Owain-the-hen supplied eggs and the weirs provided fish, but we still walked the knife-edge of hunger. I saw it in the hollows in Tanwen's cheeks.

Yet her eyes burned bright. I'd grown used to hearing human voices only once a month. To have Tanwen fill the days with speech and song, to have a companion, was a gift as valuable as food.

She nervously smoothed her hair back from her face, and her hand slid to her belly. She had news for Aiden, and I prayed he wouldn't be a fool about it.

I clutched her arm the moment I heard the wind, and she grew silent.

The wind tore at us, and my swan-brothers batted their wings at it until they weren't wings at all.

"Tanwen?" called Aiden. "Tanwen!"

"I'm here! We both are!"

Ever since that first night, Aiden called to her first. She was the wife he thought he'd lost. I knew that, in the half-second when he first changed back to a man, he always feared that he'd lost her again.

I heard a few chuckles in the dark. "Hurry, brother! Don't keep her waiting."

"If he knows what's good for him, he'll take a dip in the lake first," said Tanwen.

"What?" called Aiden through a chorus of everyone else's laughter. "You haven't objected before!"

"You'd come to your wife after a month, unwashed?" Tanwen called. I saw her nervousness in the way she bounced on her toes, but there was laughter in her voice too.

"Unwashed? I spend my life in that lake!"

The rest of my brothers guffawed.

"Never fear, my lady!" That was Mael. "We'll give him a dunking for you."

A tree toppling would have made less noise as they threw Aiden back into the lake. And he must have taken as many of them with him as he could. Finally, they splashed up out of the lake, dressed, and joined us, shaking the water from their hair. Owain caught me up in a hug, and I traveled from him to Gavyn, to Mael, to Declan, to Cadan, to . . .

Aiden. But Tanwen had already taken his hand and led him from the moonlight and into the forest.

Something inside me twisted to see them go. What would it be like to have someone call for me the way Aiden called for Tanwen? For someone to be happy just to have me near?

Cadan must have seen me watch them. "He missed her so, Ryn. But don't you worry: I'll always call for you."

I smiled up at him and patted his cheek. It wasn't a brother I hoped would call for me, but it helped ease my loneliness, nonetheless.

Cadan winked, then announced, "Let them go! But I won't hold the food for them."

We'd hardly settled around the fire and the fish before we heard Aiden's exclamation. Mael jumped to his feet, but I pulled him back.

"They could be in danger, Ryn!" he protested.

I shook my head.

Mael peered at me. "What do you know?"

I shrugged with exaggerated innocence. He'd have to wait his turn with the rest of my brothers.

When Aiden and Tanwen joined us a few minutes later, I studied Aiden's dumbstruck expression, anxious to see how he'd taken the news.

But Tanwen nodded to me, smiling so wide that I grinned back.

"I heard a shout," said Mael.

Aiden spoke slowly. "There's going to be a baby."

A moment of silence, then my brothers leaped up, hugging Tanwen close and slapping Aiden on the shoulder.

"When will the newest member of the House of Cynwrig arrive?" asked Mael when the chaos had calmed.

"About five months, I think," said Tanwen. "It's hard to know without a midwife."

Aiden looked at our improvised house, grieved. "This is a poor place to birth a child."

"Hush!" she chided and pulled him down to sit beside her. "I'll do what must be done—and Ryn will be here."

Aiden pulled her close and handed her some food, but the worried look didn't leave his eyes. Our own mother had died giving birth to Owain and me.

"It'll be a challenge," said Gavyn. "There's a great deal that can go wrong that we must prepare for."

Everyone fell into stunned silence.

What Gavyn said was true: childbirth was dangerous enough in a castle with midwives and maids to assist. And I knew the way Gavyn helped was to look at the worst and describe it so he could begin to fix it.

But *still*!

"No!" blurted Gavyn. "I meant—"

I'd set the most recent nettle tunic near the fire so that my brothers could try it on for size. Before Gavyn could speak another word, I held up the tunic and pointed at Gavyn.

He seemed relieved by the change of subject. "My tunic?"

I nodded. Then I made a cutting motion with my hand, as if snipping off a sleeve. Then I pointed to him.

"You'll cut my sleeves off . . ." Then he looked up at me. "But why?"

I widened my eyes and pointed to Tanwen. *Think!*

"Any more comments about childbirth," said Owain, "and your tunic will be missing a sleeve."

I flapped an arm.

". . . and you'll be left with a wing for an arm," completed Owain.

More silence as Gavyn stared up at me. "I suppose I deserved that."

Tanwen snorted a laugh.

Aiden guffawed.

And then everyone was laughing, even Gavyn, who didn't breathe a word about childbirth after that.

Aiden pulled me aside the next morning, just before the sun came up. "You'll look after Tanwen, won't you? This is almost as bad as the Hunters, for there's nothing I can do."

Yes.

I would protect Tanwen and this new member of the House of Cynwrig.

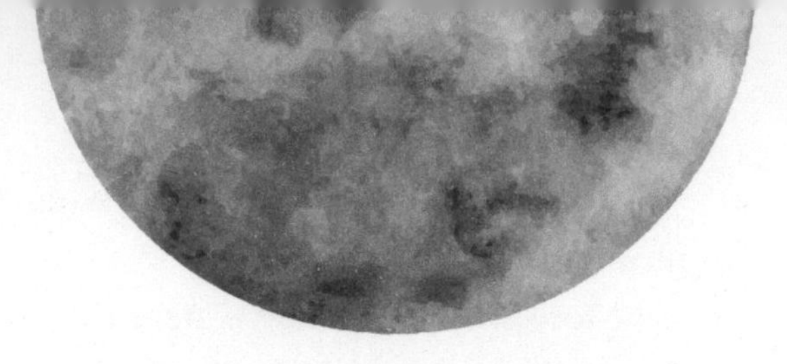

Chapter 31

Forty-fourth full moon

Carrick ap Cynwrig was delivered the day before the forty-fourth full moon of our enchantment, while a winter storm tore at the coast and beat against the house my brothers had built from the ruin's stones. The savage storm comforted Tanwen and me, a reminder that the Great Hunt traveled the barrow roads far from us on the other side of the Veil.

And a good thing it was too! For little Carrick bellowed fit to match the storm when he was born. The fire blazing in the hearth seemed to leap up in surprise that the little man could make such a great noise.

When Tanwen and Carrick lay drowsing afterward in the firelight, I hid my face in my hands and silently wept every bit of fear I'd held inside me the last five months.

By the time Aiden and my brothers ran up the snowy path the next night, I felt only joy. Aiden sat beside Tanwen all night and couldn't seem to decide whether to watch her or little Carrick's every movement. Mael praised the little man's hearty cries, while Owain and Gavyn observed the festivities with shy smiles.

Declan sang Carrick the songs we'd heard as children.

I think I missed my voice most when my brothers and Tanwen joined in. I'd found a way to speak to those closest to me with signs and pictures. But Carrick should be sung to and murmured over and blanketed with the soft voices of those who loved him.

And I could do none of that.

Chapter 32

A sound pulled me from my sleep.

I lay still, listening in the darkness.

A rustle as Tanwen turned in her sleep. Then a moan. She was dreaming again.

A prickle of fear raced along my skin, as if Tanwen's fear was contagious. I could sense it, even in the dark. And I knew, somehow, that she was dreaming about the Hunters.

I lay still under the blankets and forced my breath to grow even again: in and out, in and out. *We are safe here. The barrow roads and nettles have shielded us for over two years. We're safe.*

Another moan from Tanwen.

I threw back my blanket and crawled over to her. Even in her sleep, she was careful of the bundle near her: Carrick, or Little One, as I signed him. He squirmed in his swaddling, disturbed by Tanwen's distress.

I felt around until I found the pile of nettle tunics I'd knit in the past year and a half. The knitting needles had been one of Tanwen's contributions to the nettle tunics:

she'd carved two pairs from small branches. Aiden's tunic lay on top. I plucked it up, shook it open, then gently draped it over Tanwen.

Tanwen pulled in a shuddering breath, then stilled. I sat back on my heels, ready to wake her if the dream touched her again. It didn't. Tanwen's chest rose and fell in a regular rhythm.

But Carrick remained restless. He'd managed to pull an arm free from the swaddling, and he waved it as if fighting off nightmares of his own.

I reached for the nettle cloak Tanwen had knit me.

"It'll protect you, Ryn," she'd said. "A nettle-cloak will keep the Hunters at bay."

I felt the truth of it every time I pulled the cloak across my shoulders. Then I gathered Carrick up, tucking him close, his head under my chin.

He quieted immediately, and I smiled.

I stepped lightly out of our hut. That night, I needed to *see* the nettles that surrounded us. I needed to stand in the middle of the plants that guarded us from the Hunters.

I followed the narrow path through the nettles, not minding how they caught at my clothing. Finally, I reached the wall that had completely collapsed. I sat on a massive, moss-covered cornerstone that rested against a young tree. It was my favorite place to sit: the ancient cornerstone tilted to a comfortable angle by the upstart tree.

I sat with my back against the tree and rearranged Carrick's swaddling before settling him against my chest. He stirred, then his breathing grew even once again. I pulled the edge of the cloak over him.

Tanwen had been dreaming more and more often throughout the summer—and they were not good dreams.

I looked over the nettles that stood, silver-edged, in the moonlight. We were safe here, safe in the nettles that protected us from the Queen and her Hunters. Tanwen's dreams were only dreams. Fear wasn't the same as a warning.

We were *safe.*

Yet I sat on the fallen cornerstone for the rest of the night, flinching at every sound. I didn't sleep till nearly dawn.

⁂

"Ryn?"

Carrick's weight on my chest lightened, and I pulled him even closer to me.

"Let me have him, Ryn! He's safe," said Tanwen. "Were you here all night?"

I nodded, squinting up at her in the morning light.

"Why?" Tanwen cuddled Carrick close.

I waited till she looked at me: *Dreams.*

For a moment, I thought she'd pretend and ask about *my* dreams. Then she sobered. "I woke you?"

Yes.

"I've been dreaming of the Hunt," Tanwen said. "I can see them clearly now."

She watched the sunrise. "I didn't know how to describe what I saw before when I traveled with them, but I think I can now. Because of these dreams. They're here only because the Queen has pulled them here, and it's like being caught between two tides. They don't belong to this world. It's only her will—and it's such a powerful hunger!—that keeps them here. The Hunters are balanced on a knife's edge, belonging neither to this world nor to the Otherworld. It means that the slightest thing"—she shook her head—"no, the *right* thing can send them off the path they walk. I think that's why the nettles are so powerful. No Otherworlder would mind nettles. But they mean something to the Queen, and so they stop the Hunters as well."

She raised an eyebrow. "As the dreams roll on, I keep hearing a word at the back of my mind, and I think . . . if I could hear and remember it . . . and then speak it to them, it would send them back."

It was too near my dream of the Queen to comfort me. I'd lost everything when I challenged the Queen, thinking that a word—my words—could somehow defeat her.

Tanwen put a hand on my arm. "You'll remember that, won't you, Ryn? The Hunters and the Queen have all the power that belongs to any Otherworlder. But their standing here is precarious. The Queen isn't as powerful as she'd like us to believe. When the time is right, she will fall."

Carrick began to cry, and I wanted to. This conversation sounded too close to a farewell. Let Carrick cry on and distract her!

Tanwen bounced him on her hip. "We can finish the tunics with what we harvest this year, don't you think?"

The nettles that surrounded us were waist high—and just beginning to seed. Truly time to harvest.

Yet Tanwen had been so frightened in her dreams. When a farmer harvests his fields, he gathers his treasure to him. But when Tanwen and I harvested nettles, it was like lowering a castle's walls.

This was the first year that it felt truly dangerous.

"If we harvest them now, we'd have new growth before the frosts," said Tanwen.

I hesitated as dread grew inside me. We shouldn't do this. Not this year.

"Don't try to talk me out of this, Ryn," said Tanwen.

I stood, ignoring the stiffness from sitting so long, and jabbed a finger at little Carrick. *Think of him.*

She tilted her chin. "I am. I'm thinking of all of us."

I held up one finger. *Enough for one tunic.*

Tanwen cocked her head as if considering an offer.

I shook my head. It wasn't a suggestion, and I wouldn't negotiate.

I'd grown stronger in mind and body since fleeing the castle four years ago, but I had not grown less afraid, and that was a good thing.

Tanwen and I both knew what hunted us.

Chapter 33

Two afternoons later, we began our harvest. I'd already walked the edges of the nettle fields, determined to harvest those areas that had the most nettles. I wouldn't let careless harvesting create a chink in our nettle armor.

In the past, Tanwen sang as we worked, both to cheer us and to let me know where she was. In the morning, she'd sing ballads of valor. As the day wore on, she'd sing the bawdy songs that Cadan loved. I grinned every time I heard her sweet voice carry such uproarious songs.

This year, we harvested in silence, Tanwen working as quietly as me.

We laid two mats of woven nettles on the ground beside us, then cut the stalks at ground level. I quickly stripped the leaves and let them fall on the first mat. The stalk was thrown on the second mat. We dragged both mats with us as we harvested.

It was grueling: the ache spread from my arms to my shoulders, then to the small of my back. But every time I wanted to complain, I'd think of my brothers.

Sometimes, I'd even think of my old dream that had started this in the first place, remembering how the Queen's face had crumpled in defeat. That defeat wouldn't come by me challenging her, but through the nettle tunics. Still, I imagined the look on her face would be the same as when my brothers confronted her.

⁎⁎⁎

By noon the second day of the harvest, I was frightened for Tanwen. Her dreams had intensified, and the shadow of them stretched into the day.

She was convinced that the dreams were a gift and that she'd be able to make out the word soon. I was not so certain.

I used the day's chill as an excuse for Tanwen to wear the nettle cloak. And since she wore Carrick before her in a sling she'd made from her old dress, the nettle cloak covered them both.

"It's good to harvest the nettles, Ryn," she said during our midday meal of roasted eggs. We sat in the middle of the portion we'd cleared. "I spent so long with the Queen, and then with—" She shrugged her time with the Hunters away. "But now I feel like I'm striking at her with every stalk I harvest. I don't care that my arms ache."

I smiled and took Carrick from her so she could stretch.

"How he's grown!" Tanwen arched her back, easing the soreness from it. "I should have known better than to choose a name for him that means 'stone.'"

She traced a finger over Carrick's round cheek.

A bug whirred close to my face, and I batted at it.

It wasn't a bug—an arrow struck the ground nearby.

Then I heard the whistle that had haunted my dreams since the encounter at Lake Cairwyn years ago.

Hunters!

And Tanwen and I sat in the middle of a patch we'd cleared.

I tried to hand her Carrick, but she pushed him back to me. "Keep him! They're bound by the Queen's oath not to harm you."

Another arrow flew past, near Tanwen's shoulder, not mine. She grabbed my arm and pushed me ahead of her, placing herself between me and the Hunters. "Run!"

We dashed down the path until we reached the uncut patch of nettles. I pulled the sling up over Carrick's face to protect him and dashed into the thick of them, hardly noticing the stings.

Still the arrows followed us.

Tanwen pulled me to a stop and swung the nettle cloak over my shoulders. "I think I know the word that can stop them. I can give us a few days. You run with Carrick—I'll meet you at the ruins."

The fear in her eyes disappeared when she looked at Carrick. She brushed his fuzzy hair back and pressed a fervent kiss to his forehead.

"Protect him!" she whispered.

I took her by the sleeve to make her look at me, then signed, *Come back!*

I held her gaze and prayed she understood*: Do what you must, but don't you dare leave us!*

She nodded, then turned back to the Hunters. And as I ran toward the ruins, I heard her sing one of the songs she loved when we harvested nettles: a warrior's song.

Tanwen was hunting the Hunters, gathering them to her, as her voice rose in a ferocious melody.

Then the melody was cut short.

I stopped, gasping, waiting to hear her song once more. *No. Please, no. She's not hurt, she's—*

Tanwen's voice rose once more, a savage shout: one word I couldn't understand that was lost in the howls of the Hunters. I saw a glimpse of a snow-white hound with crimson ears, staggering through the clearing. After one last yammering howl, it vanished.

Then utter, complete silence.

I pressed Carrick to me and wept.

I wouldn't hear Tanwen's voice again.

Chapter 34

Fifty-first full moon

I knew Tanwen was dead the moment I found her. For more than two years, she'd been fire and voice filling my days.

Now she was so quiet. Not a sigh. Not a sound.

I stepped farther into the clearing, my stomach twisting at the odd angle of her limbs, the arrows in her chest.

I checked that Carrick's sling was still pulled over his face. Young as he was, I didn't want him to see Tanwen this way.

I crept closer, aching to say her name! *Tanwen. Come back. We need you. Aiden needs you. Carrick . . .*

I knelt beside her, hoping like a fool—like a child—that she'd stir. She didn't move when I touched her shoulder. She didn't blink her wide-open eyes when I pushed her hair back from her face.

I gently closed her eyes and straightened her limbs.

Then I looked up at the sky. It was already afternoon.

Aiden would be here in hours.

Tanwen had sent the Hunters to the Otherworld one last time, but I didn't know how long it would be before the Queen summoned them back—or sent others to find us here.

We—*I*—didn't have much time. Tanwen must be buried, and Carrick and I must run again.

By the time the sun set, I'd brought Tanwen's body to the camp. I removed the arrows and threw them into the fire, then wrapped Aiden's cloak around her.

Good, I could almost hear her say. *I'm proud of you. Don't give in to fear now.*

I hadn't. Fear and hurt disappeared when I was preparing her. There wasn't room for it.

She looked pale, but I'd washed her tear-streaked face. I didn't want Aiden to see that. More than that, I knew Tanwen wouldn't have wanted him to.

And then it was dark. I heard the beating of wings and finally the low voices of my brothers.

"Ryn?" whispered Mael. "Why is there no fire? What happened?"

But Aiden knew, I think. He knew the moment he changed. "Tanwen? Tanwen!"

I just stood there, with Carrick still in his sling against me and everything edged in cold, blue moonlight.

Aiden rushed up to me with only his trousers on. I'd long wished I could erase the image of my brothers' first transformation, but Aiden's face when he saw Tanwen was even more horrifying.

He scooped her into his lap and buried his face in her hair, rocking her back and forth. His shoulders shook, but I couldn't hear anything.

Not a thing.

The rest of my brothers rushed up. Mael stood beside Aiden, a hand on his shoulder, his cheeks shining with tears in the moonlight. Gavyn sat with his head in his hands.

Cadan bellowed words I couldn't hear, his fist raised toward the trees, until Declan ran to him and wrestled him into stillness.

It wasn't till Owain put his arm around me that I seemed part of the world again. I could hear Cadan's gruff sobs and the murmur of Aiden whispering something into Tanwen's hair.

"Was it the Hunters, Rynni?" Owain asked.

I nodded.

"You did all this? Brought her here?"

I nodded again.

He led me to a stone near where I normally lit the bonfire. I rested my head against his shoulder and wondered if I would ever feel my heart again.

After a while, Mael's face swam in front of me. "What happened, Ryn?"

Numbly, I drew and acted out all that had happened.

Mael sat back on his heels. "How is Carrick?"

I opened Carrick's sling and he peered up at his uncle with curious eyes. Mael's gaze softened as he cupped his hand around Carrick's head. "Ah, Little Man! How brave you are tonight."

Then he went to Aiden and whispered something to him. Aiden nodded but kept holding Tanwen.

Then Mael walked over to my other brothers.

"It's time," he told them. "Cadan and I will dig the grave. The rest will gather the stones."

Stones to keep the wild animals from reaching Tanwen.

Cadan brushed his sleeve across his eyes. Then my brothers began their awful tasks.

I kissed Tanwen's cold cheek before we laid her in the ground. And I cut a lock of her hair.

"What are you doing?" grunted Cadan.

I held the lock close to the sling to show that it was for Carrick. When I had my voice, I would tell him how she saved him. I would show him the color of her hair and I would tell him how her laugh was as warm as fire on a cold night.

We laid the last stone in place only hours before dawn.

Aiden looked as if his spirit had been poured from him—but I needed my brother back for what I was about to ask of him.

So I loosened the sling and gave Carrick to his father. Aiden looked at his son blankly for a moment, then gathered him up so quickly I was afraid he'd crush the child. When he looked up, something fierce burned at the back of his eyes.

Good.

I knelt to smooth the dirt at my feet and motioned that he should watch.

I drew our shoreline, and Eyre across the channel, then pointed to Eyre and made the sign for *safe.*

Aiden nodded. "But how—?"

I drew a raft with a girl and a baby in it. Then I drew

six lengths of rope from the raft, up into the air. Finally, at the end of each rope, I drew a swan.

Aiden stared at what I'd drawn: six swans, towing a raft across the water.

Then he called, "Mael! Cadan, Gavyn, Declan, and Owain! Come here!"

They all came running.

"The Hunters will come back for Ryn and Carrick. We have to take them to Eyre."

"You want to send them to live among those barbarians?" asked Declan.

"We can hardly see Eyre from here!" argued Gavyn. "And only when the weather's good!"

"I need you to make a raft, Mael." Aiden's voice was granite.

Gavyn shook his head. "It's at least twelve leagues to Eyre! We don't know the currents. They could be swept beyond Eyre and out to sea!"

Aiden looked at me, asking if I was certain that I wanted them to attempt to tow us so far.

Yes. I'd never been more sure.

Aiden turned back to Mael. "*Can you make a raft?* That's what I need to know."

"We'd need rope."

I darted away and returned with length after length of nettle yarn. We could braid it into a rope. There would be enough to tow the raft.

Mael took it from me, then nodded. "I can fashion a simple raft. It wouldn't last long, though."

Aiden pointed to my drawing. "We don't need it to last long. We'll tow them across the sea. Six swans harnessed to the raft, flying for the far shore. It's the only way we can guarantee their safety." He pulled in a shallow breath, mouth pinched against the pain. "We won't leave Ryn and Carrick to the Hunters. We can't."

"This is *your* idea, Ryn?" asked Mael, incredulous.

Yes.

"Even if we could make harnesses, no swan would suffer itself to be harnessed!"

"The swans would follow if one led the way," said Aiden.

"You?" asked Cadan.

Aiden nodded. "I won't let myself go."

"You'll hold on to your mind for that long?" asked Declan. "It can't be done, Aiden. Think of something else."

I took his arm and shook my head. *There is nothing else.*

Finally, Mael nodded. "I say we do it."

Cadan grunted approval. "Better they die with us in the sea than fall into the hands of the Hunters."

"There will be no dying," said Aiden. "I can do this. I know it."

I nodded, then gathered Carrick from Aiden so his hands would be free. There was so much to do before sunrise.

Cadan stood. "Gavyn should rig the harnesses and think of a way to get them on us. The rest of us should see to the raft. It'll need to be provisioned too."

Chapter 35

Fifty-first full moon

We could not work fast enough as we tried to outrun the dawn.

Mael oversaw the raft while Gavyn played with the nettle rope to create some sort of harness. I sat with him to show how big they were in swan form. Gavyn hated planning for a body he had never seen, even if he spent most of his days in it. Yet every time his frustration rose, he'd glance at Aiden, who silently gathered branches for the raft. Then he'd return to work.

"It isn't even the harness," Gavyn murmured. "It's getting it *on* us. It must be big enough that a man can position it, but not so large that a swan could slip out."

In the end, Gavyn created moss-padded harnesses that tightened when pulled against. "We just have to pull in the right direction."

As soon as he knew how to make it, Cadan helped him fashion the other five, all the while checking the eastern horizon for the first hint of the coming day.

Declan collected enough food and water from our stores to last a few days on Eyre until I could gather provisions there. Mael, Aiden, and Owain built the raft, using vines and the nettle rope to hold the branches together, and piled our belongings on it, including the weirs. Gavyn and Cadan attached the harnesses to lengths of rope, then tied them to the raft.

Minutes before dawn, they pushed the raft into the shallows, with Carrick, me, and Owain-the-hen aboard. Each brother hugged me. Finally, Aiden bent over his son and whispered something to him.

I hugged Aiden as tightly as I dared with Carrick already in his sling. Then I pointed to the shadow of Eyre on the horizon. *I'll see you there.*

He nodded and kissed my cheek. "I'll take us across, Ryn. I promise you."

"Turn away, Andaryn," called Gavyn. "We'll have to get out of our clothes before the change."

A moment later, shirts, pants, and boots were tossed onto the raft, and I quickly stuffed them into my bag.

Splashing, my brothers waded out into the water.

"Put the harness here. Like this . . . ," said Gavyn. He called instructions while Cadan cursed the cold water. Aiden never spoke. I didn't have to see him to know what he was doing: he was looking across the water, bracing his mind for the day ahead.

And then I heard the wind.

"Move forward *now*!" called Gavyn. "We need the harnesses to tighten properly!"

The raft lurched farther into the water, sending a spray up my back. A moment later, the splash of my brothers wading disappeared into the sound of wings beating, feathers brushing the wave tops.

They'd changed.

Please! I sent the prayer winging out into the salt spray. *Let this work!*

I turned around to see them, clutching both Carrick and the side of the raft. The swans were free of the water now. The harnesses had worked, tightening across their breasts and keeping the rope free of their wings. The lengths of rope rose from the water as my brothers flew out across the sea . . .

And then the ropes snapped taut.

I gritted my teeth, imagining how much it must hurt.

No natural bird would suffer such a jolt and keep flying. But none of them faltered. None of them turned back.

Not one of my brothers had let go of his mind yet. I could tell by the way they pulled. I heard it in their silence. That was always the sign. A man had no desire to trumpet like a swan. I think it reminded them of how they'd lost their voices.

One of the swans trumpeted then, and I knew that one brother had slipped away. However, every swan followed Aiden's dark body as he pressed silently toward Eyre.

In the next few minutes, the rest of my brothers surrendered their minds. They trumpeted complaints—one even faltered as if to go back—but still they followed Aiden.

The swans followed Aiden until the sun rose noontime-high above us. The sea was choppy and the wind strong.

Once, it tumbled poor Owain from her perch, and I tucked her beside me to keep her safe.

The land across the water was plainly visible, though it was still a few leagues away. By then, my brothers' trumpeted complaints grew louder. Aiden answered them with a trumpet of his own.

A trumpet.

My heart turned. Aiden's trumpet wasn't a scolding: he was slipping away.

We were leagues out still, too far for me to swim. And what would happen if the swans dropped into the water? They'd become tangled in the twine, unable to fly away. We'd drown, every one of us.

I longed to call to Aiden, to give his mind something to hold to. Then I looked down at Carrick sleeping against me. Heaven forgive me, I pinched his plump little arm until he wailed angrily.

Aiden's head reared up, then thrust forward again. He flew toward the shore as silently as before.

I comforted poor, confused Carrick. *I'm sorry, Little Man. So sorry.*

I watched Aiden throughout that last hour, and every time I saw him falter, I'd jostle Carrick or pull back his blanket until he howled.

I knew of no other way to save us.

Aiden held to his mind long enough to direct his brothers away from the rocks and to a gently sloping bit of shore. Then he let go of his mind. By then, land was so near that the swans didn't need Aiden's guidance to push for it.

I pressed my hand over the Kingstone hidden beneath my tunic, willing my swan-brothers strength for the last portion of the journey.

As the shore drew near, I checked that Carrick was secure in his sling and then pulled the dagger free. Gavyn had warned me to cut them free once they landed. They might injure themselves if they became tangled.

The moment the swans dipped toward the ground, I leaped from the raft. The cold water reached well above my waist, drenching Carrick's legs. I looped one arm over the edge and tugged the raft the last distance toward land, the dagger still in my other hand.

I reached the coast when my swan-brothers did. Gavyn hadn't reckoned how weary they'd be, for they didn't struggle against the harnesses. Instead, they lay down just beyond the reach of the waves, wings half furled.

One by one, I cut them free, hacking against the braided rope. I reached Aiden last, for he'd flown the farthest inland. He lay on the shore, head and neck extended along the ground. After I eased the harness from him, I stroked his head, smoothing the feathers.

Carrick's safe, Aiden. We're both safe. You did it.

But I could not see my brother in the weary red eye. The swan honked softly—the three-note trumpet that sounded like a gentle question.

I sat on the beach that morning, cudgel across my knees, while my brothers slept, heads tucked under their wings. They'd carried Carrick and me to safety.

It was my turn to guard them.

Chapter 36

Sixty-first full moon

I moved quietly through the woods near the lake. I'd collected enough fish for dinner, but I wanted to visit one more weir before nightfall. Carrick, riding in the pack I'd arranged on my back, squealed and tugged my hair. I winced and pulled his hand away. He immediately gathered up another handful.

I'd swear he thought I was his horse.

I stood still a moment, listening to be sure we were alone. This final weir was within half a league of a trail. I wouldn't set Carrick down if there was a chance the barbarians were near.

Nothing.

I reached behind me and pulled Carrick free.

Oh, he'd grown in the year since we fled here to Eyre! His red-brown hair—an inheritance from Tanwen—was just beginning to curl, but he had Aiden's brown eyes. And he was truly walking now.

Carrick laughed the moment I set him down, and he reached up for his stick.

For the past week, he'd wanted one to match my

cudgel and I'd found him a slender branch of his own. I'd learned the hard way not to let him hold it while he rode in the pack.

I pulled his stick from my belt and handed it to him. Then I took his free hand and followed the trail once more, moving more slowly now that I had to match Carrick's pace.

A moment later, I heard the shouts.

I dropped to a crouch and pulled Carrick down beside me—tapping his mouth gently three times. I'd rehearsed this with him since he'd taken his first, staggering steps, practicing in our little cave home. Whatever he was doing—even if he was babbling—he would stop and sit when I tapped his mouth three times.

At least, he would most of the time.

His eyes widened when he heard the distant shouts. He stood, smiling, and tapped his fists, one on top of the other—my sign for Aiden.

He thought he heard his father.

I shook my head and tapped his mouth again three times. *Sit. Be still.*

He sat.

And sprang up again when he heard more shouts. When I reached for him, he scowled.

I scowled back and tugged him down. His face crumpled, and he pulled in a wobbling breath.

He was going to cry.

I reached into my satchel, found some berries, and popped one into his hand. He looked up at me, thoroughly distracted. I nodded, and he lifted his dirty hand to his mouth, grinning.

I fed him, berry by berry, until the shouts faded away and the forest grew silent again.

Then I snatched him up and ran back along the deer trail. I didn't care about the weir. It wasn't worth it, even for a week's worth of fish. I'd been foolish to venture so close to the barbarians' trail.

What would I tell Aiden if something happened?

Carrick squirmed in my arms, pressing sticky hands to my face. "Wyn . . . Wyn . . . !"

No. No!

His first words, speaking my name, and I wished I could snatch them out of the air, out of his throat, so that the barbarians would never hear us, never find us.

I couldn't keep Carrick safe if I couldn't keep him quiet.

I looked down at his berry-smeared face. His smile that was so like Aiden's. He even thought the jolting ride back down the trail was a game. He laughed up at me—a low, throaty chuckle he'd inherited from his mother.

His mother.

Tanwen would have known what to do. *She* could have spoken back to him. She would have celebrated his first words, not tried to smother them. I shifted Carrick to my other hip and kept running.

He's the son of the rightful king, I thought. *He should walk proudly through the forest. And I'm teaching him to hide.*

⁂

I'd found our home soon after fleeing to Eyre. It was a small cave in the rocks above a lake. It wasn't a cave, really. More a room-sized hollow in the heart of an ancient landslide. But it meant the entrance was difficult to find—even when you looked straight at it—and it provided shelter against the weather. A crack in the ceiling of the cave acted as a chimney, drawing the fire's smoke on all but the windiest days.

The cave hid us, and the nettles that crowded the cliff above us protected us from the Hunters—though I'd neither seen nor heard a hint of them since we'd come to Eyre.

I reached the cave as daylight faded, with barely enough time to prepare food for my brothers before they changed. I quickly set the fish on the coals, then picked up Carrick and clambered down to the shore.

I set Carrick by the water just as the black swans neared us. Carrick shouted to see them and waved his ever-present stick, but I held him back.

Finally, the wind came whistling over the rocks. Moments later, I heard my brothers splashing as they strode toward the shore.

"Ryn!" It was Cadan, still calling for me as he had promised so many years ago.

I rapped my cudgel against the stone to signal that all was well. I'd used it ever since Tanwen's death. There wasn't anyone to tell my brothers all was well.

"Carrick!" called Aiden.

Carrick squealed, tapping his fists as he signed his father's name.

After a few moments to dress, Aiden leaped up the rocks toward us. He scooped Carrick up and held him above his head, tossing him up and catching him until Carrick shouted with laughter.

Mael joined them. "Ah! He's grown so!"

Cadan put an arm around my shoulders, squeezing me close. "Where's the food, Ryn? What else besides fish?"

That had been the berries I'd fed to Carrick in the forest. I spread my hands and shrugged.

"What?" complained Cadan. "I've waited a month for this meal!"

Declan kissed my cheek. "Don't mind him, Ryn. Is everything well?"

I forced a smile and pointed to Carrick, then signed something coming from my mouth.

"He talked?" said Owain, who towered over me.

I nodded, then reached up to playfully pat his cheek. I pulled my hand back, surprised his cheek wasn't smooth anymore.

He grinned down at me.

"He *talked*?" said Aiden, joining us. He lifted Carrick up over his head and settled him on his shoulders. "What did he say?"

I pointed at myself.

"Ryn?" asked Aiden.

I shrugged and grimaced. *Almost.*

Declan looked up at Carrick, who had buried his hands in Aiden's dark hair. "Who is that?" he asked, pointing at me.

Every one of my brothers waited for an answer, silent. Carrick stared back at them with round, expectant eyes.

"Is that Ryn?" asked Mael, also pointing at me.

"Can you say Ryn?"

"Ryn?" prompted Declan.

My brothers were a chorus around me, chanting my name while Carrick watched from his perch on Aiden's shoulders.

Nothing.

"I smell fish cooking," said Cadan, finally.

I nodded. They'd burn if I didn't turn them soon.

"Wyn!" shouted Carrick into the silence.

My brothers erupted into cheers. "Wyn!"

Cadan reached up and plucked Carrick from Aiden's shoulders. "That deserves a meal. Let's go."

We followed Cadan up to the cave.

⁂

After the meal, my brothers played with Carrick till he fell asleep, exhausted by the attention and from staying awake so late. He slept sprawled across Aiden's lap, thumb in his mouth.

It was cool in the cave, despite the fire. I draped Carrick's blanket over him. Then I pulled my nettle cloak around my shoulders.

Aiden's gaze lingered on the cloak Tanwen had knit for me years ago, and he silently rubbed a fold of it between his fingers. Then he sat back, resting his hand on Carrick's back.

"How are you, Ryn?" asked Declan.

For the first time in nearly five years, I was glad I couldn't answer. Carrick was healthy, yes. But he was so skinny, nothing like the fat little babies I remembered at the castle years ago. And my brothers wanted to celebrate his new voice, but I feared I might not be able to hide him anymore.

"You're worried about the barbarians," said Owain.

I looked up at him, shocked.

"Don't be ridiculous, Ryn," said Cadan. "Even I could see that."

I could feel my eyes filling, and I blinked the tears away. Finally, I pointed to Carrick, who looked so darling asleep, and signed his speech, hands fluttering out to show how loud it had sounded.

Mael nodded. "This is a remote enough place, Ryn."

"Is it?" murmured Aiden, rubbing Carrick's back.

"It *is*," answered Mael.

"And good thing too," said Gavyn. "I saw white feathers on the bank as we dressed. We're molting, aren't we?"

I nodded. It would be weeks before they regrew their flight feathers. There'd be no leaving the lake if anyone discovered them.

"Speak for yourself," muttered Cadan around a mouthful of fish. "*I* do not molt."

"We're safe, Ryn," Declan reassured. "The Queen won't find us here."

Gavyn did not look convinced. Instead he asked, "How are the tunics?"

I went over to the satchel I hung from a jagged outcropping near the cave's ceiling. Wild goats roamed these hills. When I'd first made a home in the cave, I'd returned from a walk to find goats there, nibbling a blanket. So I'd rigged a way to hang the satchel from the ceiling. It spared the precious tunics from the damp of the cave—and from the goats.

I released the satchel from its rope and tossed it to Owain.

Owain peered in, counting. "Five! So close, Ryn."

Gavyn pulled out the strip of linen I used to count time—a knot for every day that passed, and two knots for each full moon. "We have a little over a year left. Thirteen moons, as best I can tell."

"And then we return to Lacharra," said Aiden. "We free Father and reclaim what is ours."

My brothers nodded, faces grim.

Thirteen moons would pass like mere weeks for them: only thirteen nights until we could travel home and confront the Queen. The thought of so small a wait comforted my brothers, but thirteen moons stretched too far for me. Thirteen moons' worth of harvesting and retting nettles to finish the last tunic. Thirteen moons of chasing Carrick, of fearing he'd speak and feeling guilty if he didn't.

He was almost two. He should be able to say so much more than *Wyn*. But how could he when a mute cared for him?

Mael stood, stretching the stiffness from his limbs. "Come, Ryn. Time to spar. I don't believe the barbarians will trouble you, but let's be sure that they'll regret it if they do."

He was a taskmaster that night, claiming it would burn the fear out of me. We practiced with the cudgel again and again, then I grappled with Owain until just before dawn.

I was so weary and sore the next day, I could hardly move. It wasn't till that night that I realized Mael's sparring had nothing to do with it—for a fever had begun to burn.

I gathered food and water while I still had strength. And when I had to lie down, I piled branches across the cave's opening so Carrick couldn't leave. I made sure his stick and the few toys my brothers had carved for him were nearby.

I didn't let myself sleep till he lay down.

Chapter 37

When I woke, I knew the fever had broken. I tried to make sense of scattered, heat-singed memories: stumbling to the water, then back to my blanket . . . Carrick patting my blankets to make me play with him . . .

How long had I been ill?

It took all my strength to raise myself on my elbow.

Owain-the-hen watched me from her perch, but Carrick wasn't in the cave. The branches across the cave's opening had been pulled aside. I sat up, vision swirling from the sudden movement. I touched Carrick's cool blanket. He'd left his bed a while ago.

I stood, gripping the side of the cave as dizziness swept me. I pulled on leggings and boots, then grabbed my cudgel and stumbled out of the cave and down the boulders. I stopped at the edge of the lake, expecting to see Carrick chasing the black swans he loved so much.

I saw my swan-brothers, but not Carrick.

Surely he hadn't gone into the lake.

No. The swans wouldn't have been so calm. During Tanwen's pregnancy, Aiden had been protective as a man—and intolerable as a swan, acting as if there were eggs somewhere that he needed to protect. His swan self remained just as protective around his human son.

Carrick wasn't in the lake. So where was he?

Damn the Queen for taking my voice. And damn me for giving it to her! How would I find Carrick if I couldn't call him? *Think . . . think.*

The deer trail.

I walked as quickly as I could, desperate for any sign of him. When I reached the point in the trail where we'd heard the barbarians, I stopped for a moment and listened:

The sound of the lake lapping over stones.

The sound of wind pushing through the trees.

The distant sound of hooves.

Barbarians!

For Carrick—precious, curious Carrick—sounds in the forest meant that Aiden would come striding through the trees, arms open for his son. Carrick didn't know the forest could bring men besides his father and uncles.

I ran toward the sound of horses.

As I ran, I beat the cudgel against the trees, praying it would call Carrick: *thwack, thwack!* Each impact shuddered through my fever-sore body, and my small store of strength began to drain from me.

I pressed on, imagining Carrick trampled under the horses or surrounded by barbarians on horseback. Each image flung loop after loop of fear across my chest, tightening my breath.

If you can hear me, Tanwen: help!

I heard men's voices ahead.

"Hey there, child!"

"Make way!"

"Catch him!"

I ran even faster, beating the cudgel against the trees, trying to call Carrick back. I thought I heard him shout my name, but I wasn't sure.

I burst onto the trail, cudgel held before me. Eight horses surrounded me, dancing at my appearance. Their riders glared at me, torn between surprise and settling their horses.

"Wyn!"

I whirled toward Carrick's voice, nearly slamming into a horse that stood behind me.

Carrick stood on the far side of the trail—struggling against the barbarian who held him. I darted through the dancing horses and reached for Carrick, felt his fingers brush my hand . . .

The barbarian holding Carrick twisted away.

I raised the cudgel and charged, landing one good stroke across his shoulders.

He grunted at the impact but didn't release Carrick.

I struck him again, even though it took all my strength. That time, he hardly flinched, and he shifted Carrick so that he was even farther from me.

I pulled the cudgel back for another strike, but before I could ram it into the barbarian's ribs, someone yanked it away. And then I realized whatever vessel had been holding my strength had emptied itself.

I fainted.

Chapter 38

I opened my eyes and saw a ring of faces above me.

They were not kind.

Eight or more barbarian warriors encircled me. Each had a short sword strapped to his side or an ax slung on his shoulders. They wore no armor. Some wore short leggings just to their knees. They didn't even wear boots—only leather sandals protected the soles of their feet.

Were they warriors or bandits?

I didn't care. All that mattered was Carrick.

I sat up, looking for him, and heard the metallic hiss of a sword being drawn over my left shoulder.

"I'd urge you to rethink attacking the *Ri*, lass."

I'd left Lacharra years ago, but all the arrogance of my royalty surged up in me. I didn't even look at the man who spoke. I wouldn't give him the dignity of a hearing. Not when they'd taken Carrick.

"I don't think she can hear, Finn," said another voice.

Good. Let them think I was deaf. I'd learn more if they talked among themselves.

And then I heard Carrick's squawk. It took every bit of

strength not to go to him, but the sword tip was too close.

It didn't matter. A moment later, Carrick barreled through the men who surrounded me. "Wyn!"

I pulled him close, as if I could shield him from swords and evil.

From barbarians.

Then I felt the heat of fever. I leaned back, saw Carrick's pale lips, his flushed cheeks.

No. I'd barely survived the fever.

I pressed him to my chest, my cheek against his forehead. He settled against me with a whimper, pressing the hidden Kingstone into my ribs. I looked up at the men around me, all arrogance gone. I needed to take Carrick back to the cave. *Now.*

"Something's wrong with the child," said the one who'd drawn the sword. He had a fierce, craggy face, faded gold hair, and a forked and braided beard. Yet he knelt beside me and gently pressed the back of a gnarled finger to Carrick's forehead. "Fever. Little wonder. How long did the crazy witch let him wander in the woods?"

The circle of faces above me retreated. Who were these men? The clothing had looked shabby at first glance, but no peasant could afford the blues and greens that these clothes were dyed.

Then I saw that the old one who'd touched Carrick wore a leather breastplate.

Hunter!

I scrambled away, crablike, with Carrick clutched close, until I ran into a tree behind me.

"Careful!" the old one shouted. "She's mad—and her child bears the fever!"

His eyes were fierce, but not wild.

I scanned the other men's eyes. These were barbarians. Not Hunters.

I sagged in relief—until the tree behind me moved.

I jumped so violently that Carrick whimpered. I'd backed into a barbarian, not a tree. But I kept my head down, watching him from the corner of my eye as he joined his comrades. His pale linen tunic was embroidered in a twisting design of purple and crimson thread. I didn't need to look any higher. His clothing announced that he was the leader of these men.

I kept my head bowed over the burning Carrick. *Leave. Just leave us!*

There was only the sound of horses stomping and huffing and the slow steps of the head barbarian. I swear I heard the grind of every pebble turning over, the snap of every twig that broke beneath his shoes.

"We should go," said the old one. I already recognized his voice.

Yes! Leave! All would be well once I took Carrick back to the cave.

"The child's sick, Finn," said his leader.

"He's with his mother now. She'll tend to him."

I heard men mounting the horses and a wooden groan as the head barbarian stepped onto . . . I looked through my eyelashes . . . a chariot.

"Tend to him, how? The fever takes most of the children it touches."

Still I didn't move.

Carrick burrowed into me, his face buried against my neck. He was hot, so hot! And his breath seemed to grow weaker by the moment.

The fever takes most of the children.

I realized then that I couldn't care for Carrick. Not here. Not by myself. I wasn't strong enough to carry him back to the cave. I'd fainted after swinging the cudgel a few times.

I needed to go with the barbarians. *I'll keep him safe, Aiden. I promise.*

I thought of the five nettle tunics hanging from the cave ceiling and swallowed back the fear. I had to protect Carrick first—I'd return to the tunics in a few days.

The barbarians mounted their horses, some in a single leap.

They were leaving. If I wanted to go with them—

I shifted Carrick to my hip and stood, weaving in my weakness.

"Careful!" It was the old one: Finn.

More swords being drawn. What did they think I could do?

I kept my head bowed to show I meant no harm, then reached toward the chariot: *Help us. Take us with you.*

Silence.

I stepped closer to the chariot—free hand extended, then patted Carrick's head: *Help him.*

Finn dismounted and stood between me and the chariot. "We'll not have you bring fever into Fianna, lass."

Fianna. I knew Eyre was divided into seven kingdoms. The kingdoms were different, but even I knew that all of them valued honor and hospitality.

Very well. I'd use that.

"I said: go on with you." Finn's voice was gentler than I expected, as if he didn't like keeping me away but meant to enforce it all the same.

But I wouldn't let Carrick die because I couldn't care for him. I *would* go with the barbarians, and this Finn wouldn't stop me, even if he did carry a sword.

I took another step toward the chariot, gesturing to Carrick: *Help him!*

Finn didn't budge. He simply called over his shoulder. "Ride on, *Ri*. I'll stay with her till you're past."

What sort of man was a *Ri*?

I didn't care. If the *Ri* wore fine clothes and rode in the chariot, he was the one whose word would stand. I'd appeal to him. I darted around Finn and knelt beside the back of the chariot, almost inside it, hand extended to the *Ri* himself.

Finn shouted a curse, and his hand fell heavy on my shoulder—

"Wait," said the *Ri*.

Finn released me. "She's mad—don't mind her!"

I wasn't mad. I was desperate—and I knew exactly what I was doing. I tugged a corner of the *Ri's* cloak over my bowed head: *Cover me. I ask your protection, your hospitality.*

"She doesn't know what she's asking!" I knew Finn didn't believe his own words. "*Leave her*, Corbin. For your own sake. You cannot afford to bring fever to your people. Connach will be all too happy to use it to challenge you."

"How is honoring a plea for hospitality foolhardy?" The *Ri*'s voice grew rough.

"You don't even know that she asks it! But your people? All they'll know is that you plucked something evil from the forest and brought it to Fianna!"

I *did* know what I was asking. I wanted the *Ri* to see it in my face.

I tugged on his cloak and raised my face to him: *Shelter us . . . help us—*

He was young. Cropped gold hair, close-trimmed beard. Brown eyes that pitied Carrick. I could tell that much.

I lifted Carrick a little higher and looked up at the *Ri* as if I was still the princess of Lacharra, as if I could demand hospitality and expect that it be granted.

His eyes widened, startled, and something like recognition flew between us. I held his gaze a moment longer so he could see that I knew what I asked.

Carrick stirred in my arms, and I looked down again.

"She comes with us," said the *Ri*. "I won't refuse her."

I expected Finn to explode, but he spoke quietly, as if he knew he'd already lost. "She could be a slave, running from her master, or a criminal! No good can come from bringing this woman from the forest!"

I waited for the *Ri*'s response, my heart roaring in my chest.

"She asked my protection," said the *Ri*. "And she'll have it. Help her into the chariot. And then give her the cudgel."

"My *Ri*!"

"Now."

Finn sighed and extended his hand to steady me as I climbed in, holding Carrick. It was a small chariot, and I was close enough to touch the *Ri*. Finn leaned in as he handed me the cudgel. "If you strike him as you did earlier, lass, you'll deal with me."

"Finn, she can't hear you—and those are *not* your words to speak! Do you hold my hospitality so lightly?"

Finn stepped away, head tilted in the slightest bow. "No, my *Ri*. I've never seen a man hold to justice like you."

"And isn't this part of justice?"

Finn massaged his neck. "I'm captain of your men. I won't have you hurt, and this? *This* will hurt you. You're meddling in something best left in the forest." He studied the *Ri*'s face. "You feel it, too, don't you?"

Finn spoke the truth, more than he knew.

The *Ri* sighed. "She comes with us, Finn, no matter the consequences."

Chapter 39

I didn't bow my head as I rode in the *Ri*'s chariot. I watched every bend of the road through the forest, studied every turn he made, determined to retrace the path as soon as Carrick recovered. I wouldn't leave the nettle tunics unguarded.

Carrick's fever only grew hotter, his breathing more shallow. I pressed him into my shoulder and wished I could speak to him, call him back as he slipped further and further away.

He'd never been so still.

Despite his threat, Finn didn't look at me even though he rode near the chariot. The barbarians rode differently, with only one rein threaded through the top of the bridle and a rod they held in their free hand. Finn touched his horse's flanks gently enough as he directed his mount, but the horse-rod had an ugly hook on it.

Maybe he planned to use it on the mad girl if he needed to.

The *Ri* acted as though we weren't there—eyes fixed on the narrow road ahead of us. Occasionally, I'd look away from the path and study him, trying to learn what I could about this man who had promised us shelter.

He caught me watching him once. He transferred the rein to one hand and, with the other, loosened something from his belt and held it to me. A waterskin.

I hesitated. He offered it again.

I took it.

The water revived Carrick, and he cried softly after a few sips. I poured water onto the hem of my shirt and used it to wash his face, praying it would slow the fever.

The road opened onto a plain, fertile as the lowlands in Lacharra. Despite the overcast sky, the low rolling hills were a brilliant green.

I studied the land we traveled, looking for landmarks, watching to see if the road branched off. Making sure that I could find the way back home.

Finally, the chariot approached a hill that rose above the others. At first, all I could see was a wall crowning the rocky hillside and glimpses of a tower and castle beyond. I sighed in relief. I'd heard that the barbarians of Eyre couldn't make even a simple building—that they didn't even know how to mix mortar to build a wall.

But that wasn't the case here in Fianna, at least. Proper walls might mean proper physicians as well, and all the better for Carrick.

The chariot and riders pulled alongside the hill so that I had to crane my neck to look up to the walls. A spring flowed out of the rocks and gathered itself in a river, rushing out toward the plains. Once we crossed a bridge over the river, the road curved back around the base of the hill and up toward the castle.

Half a minute later, the chariot heaved itself over the brow of the hill as we swept through the gates.

The walls we'd just come through circled the top of the hill. A castle, smaller than our castle in Lacharra, rose before me, with a single, soaring tower on the southeast corner. Small stone buildings clustered against the wall that protected the hill, and people peered out of them when they heard the clamor of the chariot and horses.

This Castle Hill must be the seat of Fianna, then.

The chariot stopped between some of the buildings and the castle itself. A group of servants greeted us, bowing.

I realized then what a *Ri* was.

Hadn't I seen this a thousand times in Lacharra?

Ri meant "king."

I'd begged hospitality from the barbarian king of Fianna. After I attacked him with a cudgel.

The *Ri* stepped over me and leaped from the chariot. He pointed to me as he spoke to one of the older men who waited for him. The man wore a richly embroidered tunic, and different keys hung from his embossed belt. The steward, perhaps.

The man nodded, then motioned for something or someone. I held Carrick tightly and pressed myself back into the chariot. I hadn't been surrounded by so many people in years. My ears rang with the noise of the busy courtyard, as if I'd stood too close to a cannon when it fired.

Then I looked down at Carrick, flushed with fever.

This was not the time to be afraid.

I slid off the edge of the chariot and stood, legs trembling from weariness, studying the people who crowded around us. *Who will help us*?

They backed away, and I saw the fear and distrust in their faces:

Madwoman.

Witch.

I'd become the witch-woman from the forest. Like the Queen. Like the old woman with her nettles. For a breathless moment, I realized how far I'd come from my life as a princess, how much I'd lost.

I held Carrick closer and reminded myself of how much I'd gained.

I didn't care if I frightened these people. All that mattered was helping Carrick.

Then the *Ri* approached with a woman not much older than I. Her red-gold hair was plaited into many small braids, some pinned up into elaborate designs. Each braid was tied with a small silver bell that gave a shiver of music every time she moved. She walked as tall and straight as a birch—and didn't try to hide her suspicion.

"She and her child will be given all the hospitality of this house, Ionwyn," said the *Ri*. "You'll see to them?"

I held Carrick out to her: *Help him!*

Her expression didn't soften, but she looked at Carrick. Then she gestured to someone behind her.

A stern-faced woman stepped forward and plucked Carrick from my arms.

I lunged after her, but Ionwyn blocked me. "She's come to help him!"

I didn't care. I wouldn't leave Carrick among strangers. I tried to push past her and reach Carrick.

The *Ri* held me back. "She's deaf, Ionwyn! She doesn't understand you—!"

Let them think I was deaf. Let them think I was a witch. But I would *not* let them separate us!

Ionwyn swung in front of me and took my face in her hands, forcing me to look at her. Her expression was so fierce that I stopped. Not furious, but fierce, as if she would meet any challenge I brought.

Somehow, it made me trust her.

I stilled.

"Your son will be safe here," she said, then glared over my shoulder at the *Ri*. "Help me! How do you explain *safe* without words?"

She didn't wait for an answer but pretended to cradle an imaginary baby. *Safe*.

I nodded.

Her gaze flashed up to me, intent, scrutinizing. Did she know I could hear?

I dropped my gaze.

"I'll see that she's bathed," I heard Ionwyn tell the *Ri*.

Then she turned and led me into the barbarian king's castle. I slowed to trail behind, but she immediately took my elbow and tugged me to walk beside her.

She didn't want me to walk like a servant.

I glanced at her, curious, but she studied me so intently that I ducked my head once more.

"What was he thinking," Ionwyn muttered to herself, "taking in a creature that's wild as a fox? She's ugly, too, with her mat of hair and dirty face."

My cheeks warmed as shame rolled over me, tugging anger close behind it. Who was she to criticize me so?

When I looked up, Ionwyn was staring at me. She'd seen the blush.

Was that why she'd spoken so unkindly? To see if my face revealed that I could hear her? I immediately looked down, and though she continued to talk, I ignored her. I concentrated on our footfalls on the stone floor, the hum of conversation of the people we passed. The swish of Ionwyn's fine dress, and the braided design embroidered into the hem of her dress: two strands—maybe three—looping over each other endlessly in a braid as beautiful as any Lacharran artwork.

She showed me to a little room with a wooden tub.

"For you. Someone will fill it soon." She pointed to the table beside it that held linens to dry myself and a dress similar to hers, but without the embroidery.

I didn't move.

She sighed and narrowed her eyes. Then she pulled me to the tub and mimicked washing herself in imaginary water. "To bathe."

She raised her eyebrows: *Do you understand?*

Finally, I nodded.

"Who are you?" she said, more to herself than me.

I just stared at the wall and rocked on my heels like a child who needed comforting. I didn't want her to know that I could hear or think, that I'd take Carrick away as soon as I could.

"You're safe here. You and your boy." Her voice was gentle now.

My heart turned over. No one had spoken to me like that in years.

But I knew we weren't safe, and no one could protect us. So I kept rocking and looked through her, as if she wasn't there.

Her gaze dropped to the black feathers tied to my waist. She reached for them, but I batted her hand away. She yanked it back and watched me a few seconds more.

"You're safe, Bird-girl." She turned to leave. "But I wonder if we are."

Chapter 40

If I hadn't been so worried about Carrick, I'd have bathed all night. After washing in lakes for five years, that wooden tub seemed extravagant. And the barbarians had soap! Real soap. I savored the chance to wash away the filth and work the tangles from my hair with one of their carved bone combs.

As soon as I was clean, I left the bath so Ionwyn could take me to Carrick. She led me into the cool evening, across the courtyard, and into one of the stone buildings against the wall.

A woman tried to hold a thrashing Carrick in her lap.

Of course he fought her, sick and separated from every face he'd ever known! How could I have enjoyed the bath while he was alone?

I rushed to Carrick and snatched him from her.

He still thrashed as I sat, but I just tucked him close and bent my face close to his.

He was so hot!

I stroked his cheek and red-brown curls, damp with sweat.

“Wyn? Wynnn—” He stopped beating against me. One small hand gathered a handful of my dress, the other tangled itself in my wet hair.

I didn’t care if he pulled my hair out by the roots. I kept rocking till he grew still, his weight pressing the Kingstone against me—a reminder of who we were, even in this strange place.

Keep fighting, Little Man, I thought as I rocked Carrick. *A prince of the House of Cynwrig does not surrender easily.*

When I finally looked up, Ionwyn crouched near. “Here, Wyn.”

So she’d heard Carrick’s name for me.

She held a cup, motioning that it was for Carrick.

I took it, wary. Finally I sniffed it, then took a small sip, ignoring the older nurse’s snort.

“The wench thinks it’s for her!”

But Ionwyn silenced her with a hand on her arm.

They’d added willow root to the water in the cup. I knew the taste—and that it would cut the fever. I lifted the cup to Carrick’s lips.

After a moment, he drank, too weak to protest the bitter drink.

Within an hour, he’d emptied the cup. And then another. But his fever didn’t break. He burned against me as he grew more and more restless, more and more distant.

I was losing him. The fever burned too bright.

I reached out into the dark and brought Ionwyn’s hand to Carrick’s forehead.

She gasped. "He's burning up."

"We can bathe him," suggested the nurse. "I'll get a basin." She scurried out.

Bathe him. Hadn't the *Ri*'s chariot splashed through a river as we approached the castle?

I stood with Carrick, wincing at the tingling in my now-numb legs. Ionwyn watched me, ready to act if I—what? What did she expect me to do?

I didn't care, so long as she let me do what I wanted.

I motioned her to follow as I stepped into the night, listening for the sound of water.

To my amazement, she walked with me: past the gate that guarded the wall, down the road that sloped along the hill's side, to the river the chariot had driven over.

I walked along its banks until I found a suitable place. I handed the motionless Carrick to Ionwyn, then scrambled into the river, positioning myself so that the cool water rose nearly to my shoulders.

I held my arms up for him.

After a pause, Ionwyn knelt and gave him to me.

He moaned as the cool water rushed around him, then quieted. I pulled him to my chest, his cheek against my collarbone, and felt the fever burn on.

The waning moon hung low in the sky, as if the Queen was reaching across the water for Aiden's son. I held Carrick closer, hand over his cheek, so even the moon couldn't find him.

I would not let the Queen have him.

I concentrated on the sound of water surging against

stone, against me. It became a prayer I chanted over and over: *Keep him safe . . . keep him safe . . .*

And still Carrick burned.

Ionwyn tried to take him from me once, but I pushed her away with weak, cold hands. I alone would stay with the little man. Throughout the night, I held him close as the water waged war against the fever that burned inside him.

The moon had neared the western horizon, paling as the night turned gray, when I realized Carrick's cheek had cooled.

Or perhaps I'd grown so cold I couldn't feel anymore. I tugged on Ionwyn's skirt, motioning her to check.

She pressed a hand to his forehead, eyes widening, then called over her shoulder, "He's better!"

Had others been keeping watch with us?

Ionwyn held her arms out to Carrick. "Let me take him."

I didn't understand at first, her words dancing like snowflakes inside my head: shifting, never landing.

Ionwyn held her arms out again. I didn't want to give her Carrick, but my arms were so weak.

I nodded, my jaw clenched against the ice in my bones.

She had a difficult time reaching him, for the river had tangled my skirt around him. But she freed Carrick and gently lifted him.

He wailed at the sudden change.

The sound tore at me, even though it meant he'd grown well enough to cry.

I struggled to climb out of the river. My legs buckled beneath me, and I couldn't close my hands around anything to steady myself. Or were my hands already fisted shut?

I didn't know I was falling until the water closed over my head.

I flailed for air. And then my head was above water, a hand tugging at my dress. "Help me. *Help me!* I can't hold them both!"

I gulped a few breaths before I fell again, the water splashing my face as I tried to keep my feet under me. Then boots kicked up dirt on the bank beside me. I heard cursing, felt hands pull me from the water and onto the bank.

I retched up the river water I'd swallowed. I couldn't find air, though I felt it all around me. The nearby voices turned to buzzing.

My throat finally opened, and I pulled in one deep breath. Then another.

I looked up for Carrick, saw Ionwyn hurrying away with him.

I pulled myself up to my hands and knees, but my entire body shook as though trying to fling the cold away from me.

I fell again.

And was lifted into the air, held like a child.

I peered at the face of the man who held me, but my eyes wouldn't focus.

"How's a man to hold someone when they shake so?" he muttered.

I knew the voice: Finn, the *Ri*'s captain. The one who'd threatened me.

I didn't care. And *why* wasn't he warmer? Why didn't I feel a whit warmer for being held so close?

"Someone get a blanket!" he shouted as he began to carry me back to the castle. "She's going to shiver herself free from me!"

⁂

I woke a full day later, with a healthy Carrick tucked beside me.

That evening, Carrick and I joined the evening meal in the *Ri*'s hall. We were given a place far from the main table, but I was satisfied. That evening—and every day after that—he was swept up by young sons of other chiefs who visited the castle. I ached to be away but couldn't regret the chance Carrick was given: after just a few days with his playmates at the castle, he was already babbling more.

One of the young boys was also named Carrick. Ionwyn saw Carrick's head lift when she called the other boy and was canny enough to realize he recognized his name. From that day on, Carrick heard his name spoken every day, even if it was in the oddly lilting accent of the kingdoms of Eyre.

Carrick spent his days with other children of Fianna, but he spent the nights with me, sleeping close to my side. The bed was soft, but there was nothing to press my back against, no gentle clucking from Owain-the-hen during the long nights. I thought at first that having a room to ourselves was a luxury, but soon discovered that none of the maids who worked in the *Ri*'s household wanted to share a chamber with the mad girl and her son.

I learned more of the Fianna those days while Carrick and I recovered. I learned they had their own systems of honor, and that, fierce as they were, there was a kindness about them too. I wished more than once that I didn't have to pretend to be deaf and mute, that I could walk among them with open face and heart and listen to all they told me.

I also learned that Ionwyn was the *Ri*'s cousin, though I'd already guessed as much. There was an easy familiarity between them that reminded me of my brothers and me. I suspected that few people could scold the *Ri* the way Ionwyn sometimes did.

However, I had not guessed that she was a bard in the *Ri*'s household, respected among the chiefs of Fianna. The third night that we ate from the *Ri*'s table, he called her to the front. "Ionwyn! Won't you gift us with a story this evening?"

She'd walked to the center of the hall, the bells at the ends of her many red-gold plaits making quiet music around her. Finally, she stood with her head tilted to the side, as though already hearing the story.

And then she told us the story of a warrior determined to avenge his dead father. I'd never heard anything like her telling of it: the power in her voice, the promise that if we dared follow her into this story, we would encounter a place as fierce and beautiful as the Otherworld itself.

For that one moment, I wished Carrick and I could stay.

Yet the nettle tunics waited—and my brothers!

The black swans were molting. Without their flight feathers, they wouldn't be able to follow me to a nearby lake this full moon. When they changed, my brothers would find a deserted cave.

I couldn't let that happen.

⁂

Nearly two weeks after the *Ri* brought us to Fianna, I decided it was time to go. If I'd had words, I would have thanked the *Ri* for his kindness, but I feared we wouldn't be allowed to leave. So we walked out of Fianna after everyone broke the night's fast, hidden in the busyness of the early morning.

Ionwyn and two young men found us not three leagues down the road and escorted us back to the castle.

Her signs were choppy, frustrated as she pointed to Carrick. "You can't leave! The *Ri* himself has contracted to foster your son for a year." She threw her hands in the air when I merely blinked at her.

She tried again, motioning some sort of shelter over Carrick's head.

"Foster? Do you understand?" Her tone was almost caressing, but her words were pointed as swords. If I hadn't been so determined that she believe I was deaf, I'd have laughed. Her performance reminded me of something Cadan would do. "Of course you don't. For the next year, you and your son will be fed. He'll be educated. Corbin won't be paid the foster price of even a cow for his troubles because I doubt you've seen that much wealth in your entire life! And even if you owned a herd of cows that gave cream instead of milk, Corbin wouldn't take it because you begged his help."

She took me by the shoulder and began marching me toward the castle. "You were smart enough to do that, but stupid enough to walk away from it. I wish to heaven he was wise enough to let you go."

I knew then there was no escape. The *Ri*'s hospitality had trapped us in Fianna.

Chapter 41

Sixty-second full moon

Carrick and I did not greet my brothers the night of the full moon.

I imagined Aiden peering up at the cave, looking for firelight. I could almost see Cadan searching the bank for their clothes—the clothes that hung in their satchel from the jagged outcropping in the cave, right beside the tunics.

My brothers would believe the Hunters had followed us across the water and found us. Their hearts would break again and again throughout the night, and there was nothing I could do.

I thought I'd go mad with grief.

So when Carrick fell asleep, I slipped out into the night.

Moonlight spilled across the castle with its round tower, and the courtyard was quiet. Not a candle burned in any of the houses. But the walls still surrounded me, holding me from my brothers.

I paced in wider and wider circles, going beyond the castle to the ruins of a small building, my vision blurred by angry tears. Aiden shouldn't have to suffer a night like this. He'd endured so much already—

And then I saw them: nettles, clustered around the ruins.

They like old stone.

The nettles were tall, just beginning to seed, as they should this time of year. If I was at the cave, I'd harvest them for Owain's tunic.

The last tunic.

What would I do if I couldn't return to the cave in time? How would I—?

I wouldn't be thwarted this close to the enchantment's end.

I ran to the stable and gathered a small knife and a torn horse blanket, then dashed back to the nettles.

I'd start the last tunic here. Now.

I looked up at the full moon.

It had always reminded me of the Queen, always made me feel she was watching. But I was glad it shone down on me. Let her see me. Let her learn that for the last five years I'd worked to free my brothers. Every nettle I'd harvested had been my way of taking up a sword against her.

I raised the knife to the moon in salute, then turned to the nettles.

I'd worked with nettles so long that I hardly thought about running my hand up the stalks before gripping them. Harvesting them was second nature, and I barely noticed the few stings as I tossed the stalks on the blanket I'd spread on the ground.

And all the while, I sent prayers into the night that my brothers would somehow know Carrick and I were safe.

After an hour, the blanket was lost beneath the nettles. There'd only be a little more light before the moon set, and I still needed to ret the nettles.

There wouldn't be any ponds this high up the hill, and I didn't dare set the nettles in any of the drinking water for animals, for the retting made the water foul as any chamber pot. But I could at least hide the harvested nettles till I could find a pool near the base of the hill, even if I needed to dam off a shallow portion of the river.

One of the far stone houses was deserted. I could hide the nettles behind it for the rest of the night.

I returned to the nettle patch and gathered the corners of the blanket to drag it away.

"What's this?" The rough voice came from behind me.

Fear jolted through me, but I didn't stop. The people of Fianna thought I was deaf, so I kept walking.

"Don't ignore me, chit. What are you doing?" A thick paw of a hand turned me around.

Two men stood there. The smell of beer and a stronger brew hung around them like a fog.

Don't provoke them. They may just move on. I'd left the knife at the patch, but I held nettles in my hand. I squeezed them so tightly that they stung me. I found courage in that: the pain was a reminder of what I could endure.

I was no longer a child scared of the night.

These men, though? They feared the forest witch who harvested nettles under a full moon.

"Does the *Ri* know you're out here working forest evil?" slurred one.

I shook my head, hoping they'd think I didn't understand them.

"He'll shelter anyone," said the other. He looked a little like Aiden—an arrogant, heartless version of Aiden. "Doesn't care what this witch does to us."

Fear blossomed inside me. This man was bent on proving something, and he was going to use me.

The first grabbed my arm so tightly I winced. "You should be inside, witch."

Mael's grappling holds flashed through my mind, but it wasn't yet time to use them. I might get free from one of them, but not both.

The man in front of me nodded to something behind me, and—

An arm snaked around my waist from behind, lifting my feet off the ground.

Three men, now.

I tried to twist away—

"Be still!" A slap caught me on the cheek. My head slammed against the shoulder of the man who held me.

Another slap, and another.

I kicked out, grimly satisfied when my foot slammed into the almost-Aiden's face.

"Moyle's nose! She got his nose!"

They must have struck me with a fist next, for everything went dark. I swear the moon dropped from the sky and danced in front of me.

But I didn't drop the nettles. *Be still*, I heard Mael say. *Lean back into the one who holds you.*

Attackers never expect that someone who wants to escape will move closer.

I slumped against the chest behind me, heard him chuckle. "The *Ri* ignores the evil you're working, but we won't. We'll beat it out of you."

My gaze flew to the castle.

Moyle, holding his bleeding nose, staggered up. "She's too canny for a mute. Go ahead, witch! Tell us why you're out here."

I shook my head as if I didn't understand.

The first one backhanded me and laughed at my silence. "See? Silent as death, Moyle. Stupid too. You can beat the evil out of her, and she won't say a word. The *Ri* won't know who to thank."

"He's too weak to consider it a kindness," said Moyle, wiping the blood from his face with the back of his hand.

The first one leaned close. Oh, he was ugly, and his delight made him uglier. "What did you do to the *Ri* that made him bring you here, wench? Did you—"

Now!

I caught him across the face with the nettles. He howled and fell back.

I twisted the way Mael had taught me, and the grip on me loosened. I elbowed the man behind me, and he released me so fast I fell.

I scrabbled away and leaped up. Moyle caught my sleeve and yanked me close enough that I could drive the edge of my hand into his throat. His eyes widened in surprise as he dropped to the ground.

My sleeve ripped as he fell, and I ran.

I heard footsteps and shouts behind me, but the castle was so close. Only a few more steps—

A figure loomed up out of the dark, cutting me off. Were there more of them?

I darted around him, expecting to feel his hands any moment. Then I heard the ring of a sword being drawn.

I tripped over a tuft of grass and sprawled on the ground. I rolled to my back, with only a handful of nettles to protect myself against the swordsman.

But he moved between me and the men who pursued me.

"Stand back!" he barked, his sword tip flicking like the tail of a cat.

It was Finn.

The men stopped. "She attacked us!"

Finn didn't take his eyes off them. "The *Ri*'s *guest* attacked you?"

The men muttered among themselves.

Finn whistled two short shrills, and several men joined him.

"What happened?" asked Finn.

Moyle tried to talk despite his bloody nose and bruised throat. "We had a few questions for her."

"I don't like your way of asking questions. Seems she didn't, either."

Moyle flinched.

Finn turned to the men beside him. "Take them to

separate cells. I don't want them to talk to each other before the *Ri* sees them."

He sheathed his sword, then walked to me. "No," he muttered, "she won't be any trouble at all, Corbin. Not a bit. Never mind that your rival's son wanted to beat her."

But he didn't show a breath of anger when he knelt beside me, holding up his hands to show he meant no harm.

Finn didn't like me, but he was fair. When he held a hand out to me, I tossed aside the nettles and took it. He pulled me to my feet.

Ionwyn joined us a moment later. "What happened?"

"Moyle and his friends found her by the ruins. You see what happened next."

Ionwyn held her lantern aloft, and I blinked in its glare. "Wyn," she whispered. Her gaze dropped to my torn sleeve. "Did they . . . ?"

I shook my head. *No, they hadn't.*

Ionwyn's eyes widened, and I realized my mistake: I'd answered a *spoken* question.

I looked away, wagging my head from side to side, hoping she'd think the gesture had been one of pain and terror—not a response to her question.

Ionwyn tried to speak to me again, but I ignored her and stood.

"Wyn—" she sighed. She took my arm, but I shrugged away.

I couldn't go back to the castle yet. I couldn't just sit and be still.

I held up a single finger. *One thing.* I prayed Ionwyn understood. *Let me do one thing.*

Ionwyn nodded. "I think she wants me to follow her, Finn."

I left them, determined to find the blanket of nettles I'd harvested. Lantern light danced behind me as Ionwyn ran to catch up.

Finn joined us. "Is she mad?"

"I don't think so. Did you see them, Finn? Three against one, and she still escaped—and bloodied Moyle! I *like* her."

"What is she doing now?" muttered Finn.

I found the blanket of nettles where I had left it and started dragging it to the gate. I'd take the nettles to water tonight if it killed me.

"Let her pass!" called Ionwyn to the warriors guarding the gate in the wall.

They opened the small wooden door beside the huge gates and let us pass. Once, Finn tried to help me by picking up a corner of the blanket.

Just as quickly, he cursed and dropped it. "Nettles! What's the crazy lass doing with them?" But he picked up the corner once more and helped carry the blanket the rest of the way.

The three of us walked down the curve of the great hill. There was only the castle with its one round tower, standing like a guardian above us—and the sounds of the small bells Ionwyn tied to her braids, and Finn's muttered curses.

Finally, I found a small section of the river where the water circled slowly, separate from the rush of the rest of the water. I upended the blanket, sending the nettles into the water. A few long branches I scavenged pinned the nettles underwater so they wouldn't float away.

"I think she's retting them," said Ionwyn, holding the lantern high to see. "Though we use a different technique with flax."

"Why nettles?" asked Finn.

"I don't know," said Ionwyn.

And I couldn't tell them.

Chapter 42

I dreamed of blood that night, perhaps because I fell asleep tasting the blood from my swollen lip.

In my dream there was blood on my clothes and hands, but I hardly noticed because I watched my brothers fall mid-flight. Black wings faltered against the blue sky, my swan-brothers tumbling as they plummeted to the ground. My attackers were there too, somehow responsible for my brothers' fall.

I wrapped my bruised hands around my cudgel and attacked—

"Wyn . . . *Wyn*!"

I flailed out.

Ionwyn bent over me. "I know you can hear and understand me! For the sake of all you hold dear, don't ignore me now."

I sat up, wincing at the soreness in my shoulders—they'd wrenched my arms behind me. I looked up at her and held her gaze.

"Corbin brought a claim against your attackers today for harming someone under his hospitality. Moyle's father,

Connach, claims his son caught you in some evil last night and that you attacked *him*. We must answer him."

Every time I'd flinched at some sound in the darkness last night, I'd told myself that I was safe, that the men who'd beaten me were captive. I'd reminded myself that I was under the protection of the *Ri*'s house.

It seemed that even that might not be enough. But Ionwyn did not see my dismay.

"I've been appointed your advocate," she continued. "I'll speak for you."

I touched my throat and nodded.

"I'll speak for you because you are mute, yes. But Corbin has asked me to speak in your defense. You won't stand alone, do you hear me?"

⁂

Ionwyn brought me a pale blue linen gown that hung straight from my shoulders to the ground. It was embroidered around the cuffs and hem with bright purple and crimson thread—the colors of royalty, and of those sheltered by it. Then she fastened a belt embroidered in the same pattern around my waist, arranging the folds of the full tunic so that it looked like water cascading around me.

We walked to the hearing, every sense so sharpened that I would have sworn I heard the wind sweep each blade of grass.

The hearing was held in the base of the round tower, "the oldest part of the fortress," Ionwyn whispered to me as a warrior opened a thick wooden door for us with a respectful nod.

I couldn't see anything of the dim room at first. There were slashes of white in the gloom, where daylight leaked through arrowslit windows.

As my eyes adjusted, I saw a ring of the *Ri*'s chiefs standing along the walls. The three men who had attacked me stood between two chiefs. There were others there, too: youths with their fathers, and even an old man sitting on a stool.

Ionwyn led me to the center of the tower, near a gristled chieftain with a face set like stone. I felt his fury when he looked at me, like heat rolling off coals.

"Connach," murmured Ionwyn to me. "The father of Moyle, whose nose you bloodied."

The tower reminded me too much of the hollowed-out turret where the Queen had imprisoned my brothers. Every awful memory of the night rushed over me until I could hardly catch my breath.

The *Ri* stood at the far side of the tower and motioned that Ionwyn and I should come farther into the circle. As we neared, I witnessed something I hadn't seen in him, even when I attacked him with the cudgel: ferocity. When he saw my swollen mouth, his own thinned. His hands clenched, and I could almost see him rooting his feet into the floor of the hall. He would not be moved.

And somehow, his fury gave me strength.

My fear dissolved as anger threaded my spine. I remembered the dream Ionwyn had pulled me from, how

I charged the men who watched the swans fall: the men who stood across the room.

"Will you speak for her?" the *Ri* asked Ionwyn. It was spoken as a formality, the beginning of the hearing.

"I will."

The chiefs nodded solemnly.

I glanced around the room, amazed. Women never spoke in Lacharran court, except to testify. Even then her husband or father had to vouch for her, as if she couldn't find the truth on her own. Yet no one here doubted Ionwyn could speak the truth—certainly not Connach, who fingered his tunic nervously.

I'd thought they were barbarians.

"The woman Wyn and her son are my guests, guarded by my house," began the *Ri*. "Finn, the captain of my men, discovered her, a woman who couldn't cry out for help, running from these men last night. She'd been attacked. I demand the restitution due a member of my household. I have brought Wyn to stand before you so that the details of her attack may be made plain. She remains under the protection of my house"—he glanced at Connach—"and she will not suffer another grievance."

When he finished, the king nodded to the old man beside him.

"An elder," whispered Ionwyn. "The Advocate who will judge our claims."

Advocate for whom? And then I realized: this judge was viewed as the advocate for the laws of Eyre's seven kingdoms.

Another surprise.

In Lacharra, Father's word was law. Here, even the *Ri* stood beside a judge.

My fate lay in the judgment of a man with short, curling gray hair and a clean-shaven face.

The Advocate bowed his head in acknowledgment, then turned to Connach. "Tell us once more what happened. Take care that the story matches what your son told earlier. It seems particularly changeable."

"When my son Moyle and his friends saw her working in the dark, they asked her what she was doing. When they asked again, she struck out with stinging plants. She broke Moyle's nose and used her arts to wound the rest. The *Ri* claims that she is under his protection, and we respect that. As he learned years ago, though, the law doesn't allow him to protect a menace."

"And how did she break the law?" pressed Ionwyn. "You have yet to explain that, Connach."

The Advocate turned to Ionwyn. "Tell us what you know."

"She was harvesting nettles and preparing them for retting, Honor."

The Advocate raised an eyebrow. "At night?"

Ionwyn nodded. "It was important to her. She wouldn't allow me to tend her wounds until she'd taken the remaining nettles to be retted."

The Advocate nodded. "No one has worked with nettles for generations. It is an ancient craft."

Connach nodded. "But *why* was she there at night? If it

was so innocent an activity, why wait till dark?"

"Only those who are scared of the dark distrust it: children and fools," shot back Ionwyn. "Would your son have been frightened to see a woman harvesting nettles in the daylight?"

A ripple of laughter moved across the room.

The Advocate raised his hand for silence. "Continue."

"How do you know she was the one who was mistreated?" Connach asked. "You have a good but weak heart, *Ri*. She bloodied my son! Those who stalk their prey are silent. She acts more like the hunter than the hunted."

"She can't *speak*!" thundered the *Ri*.

Connach raised an eyebrow. "We don't know that. She has a tongue. Her child can speak. Who else but her would have taught him?"

Silence fell over the room.

"Until today, we thought she was deaf, yet your cousin Ionwyn whispers in her ear this morning! Why do you doubt that she might also be able to speak?"

He spread his arms in appeal to the assembled chiefs.

"It is my son's honor that is assailed, *Ri*! You claim he attacked the woman Wyn, but none heard the cries which would be evidence of that attack. I cannot believe she is silent. Even a man with his tongue cut out can scream. I fear, my *Ri*, that you have chosen to protect the wrong person once again."

Once again? Who had he protected the first time?

I saw the Advocate's guarded expression, and all hope of justice fell from me.

Connach pushed harder. "Indeed, I could ask for payment from you, *Ri*. Your guest attacked *my* son and his companions! And I hear they are not the first she has attacked." He bowed to the Advocate. "I request, Honor, that you question him about this."

The Advocate nodded. "*Ri*, have you witnessed any violence?"

The *Ri* looked at me, his shoulders square but his eyes full of defeat. "I have."

"What happened?"

"I was holding the boy, Carrick. We'd found him alone in the forest. She attacked me with a cudgel—trying to protect *him*."

The crowd began to murmur. I couldn't hear the words at first, but then snatches became clear: "Sorceress. Enchantress."

I looked at the chiefs around me. They believed I might have attacked all three men. I wasn't a mute victim—I was the assailant.

"She has a tongue. She could have screamed for help," said one.

"Why was she working with nettles?"

"Her hands aren't stung. More enchantment!"

The *Ri* raised his hand for silence, his face like fire and thunder.

The chiefs grew silent.

He turned to the Advocate. "What do you rule, Honor?"

The old man raked Connach with his gaze. "It has become the word of one against another. And the witness we have"—he nodded to Finn—"did not see the actual attack."

"I saw her fear, Honor," insisted Finn.

The Advocate nodded. "Powerful, indeed. But not enough. This I know: the truth will manifest. We will reconvene in a week's time and trust that lies will be exposed."

We couldn't afford to wait so long! I might be attacked again. I might be imprisoned. Or kept from the nettles. Or from Carrick. If anything happened to me, my brothers would bear the consequences.

Fear pressed in, a certainty that I'd lose everything. These people would not let the mad girl from the forest go unpunished.

And then I remembered who I was. I was Andaryn of the House of Cynwrig, who'd stolen the Kingstone fragment from a usurping enchantress. I was the Swan-Keeper, protector of my brothers until they were freed from their enchantment.

I saw my dream once more: black swans falling from the sky. I felt the cudgel in my hands as I charged my attackers.

The answer came in a flash: not a cudgel, but a cane.

I broke away from Ionwyn and snatched the cane of the old man sitting on the stool.

He shouted a protest, but I was already approaching Connach.

Several chiefs stepped forward, but when the *Ri* held up a hand, they let me pass.

For once, the people around me were as quiet as me.

I stopped in front of Connach, heart thundering so I could barely breathe. *Please, let this work. Please let me be strong enough.*

I held the cane out to him. He didn't respond, so I offered the cane again.

After a moment, he took it.

Before he could say anything, I held up five fingers. Then I knelt with my back to him and pulled my braid over my shoulder.

I didn't want anything between me and the beating to come.

I think the *Ri* understood my challenge before Connach did. He looked down at me, eyes wide. Something in his face reminded me of Aiden on that first full moon, when he realized the black swans had bruised me.

He walked to me and knelt on one knee so that his face was level with mine. For the first time since I'd begged hospitality, I met his gaze.

He didn't say anything, just studied me as if he needed to be sure of something. Of me.

"I know you understand me." He spoke too low for those gathered around to hear. "Hear me now: He'll not pity you because you're a lass, nor gentle his blows because you're under my hospitality. If you challenge him to this, I cannot shelter you."

I knew it. Connach would refuse me altogether or throw all his strength behind the beating.

And either way, I would win.

I tried to let the *Ri* see that I could do this. That I must.

The moment drew itself out, and in the space between heartbeats, I remembered the last time royalty had knelt before me: the Queen in Fortress Roden. I remembered my fear and horror as she turned her full attention on me. Her gaze had stripped my soul.

But the *Ri*'s gaze gave me armor. He believed I could do this—more than that, he would let me.

Finally, he nodded. "As you wish. I will support you, even in this."

Then he rejoined the Advocate.

Connach, who had watched us, smiled.

When the *Ri* pinned him with a glance, his smile faltered, then died altogether.

"Beat her," the *Ri* commanded. "Five blows."

"*Ri* . . . ," breathed Connach.

The Advocate spoke, triumph in his eyes. "It is a proper challenge, Connach. You have argued that her silence is a deceit, that she used it to accuse your sons. She has given you a chance to prove your argument."

I rested my hands on my knees, fingers digging into skin, preparing myself for the blows.

The king's voice filled the room. "I would not wish this for Wyn, but if she demands it . . ." He turned to me, and I nodded, one last time. "You have a choice before you: pay the fines due an attack on someone under my hospitality or give her five blows, as she has demanded. If she cries out, you will prove she attacked your son and that the beating is deserved."

He paused and used the silence like a weapon. "But

hear me: if she remains silent, if you beat an innocent, then Moyle will pay the fine and his standing among the men of Fianna will be reduced to a servant's."

Connach sighed. "My *Ri*, perhaps I spoke in anger."

I sensed the release in his body, heard the scuff of leather against stone as he stepped away. I looked over at Ionwyn, who was smiling.

And saw Moyle, the one who had hit me, break away from the guard near him. Two long strides, and he reached me, wrenching the cane from his father.

I had a heartbeat to prepare before the blow landed across my shoulders.

Pain has a color: this was blinding, noon-white light. The curved walls of the tower room disappeared in the fire, and I fell over my knees, mouth open in a cry I would not voice.

After a moment, the light pulled back, and I could see again: see the *Ri* holding up a hand, telling Ionwyn to stand back. I heard the roar of the people around me as the Advocate held up one finger.

Four more blows.

Moyle was vicious. He let me wait for the next one. Finally, I heard the whistle of the cane cutting through the air. The blow caught me low on the ribs, when I'd been expecting it across my shoulders like the last one.

More light. More fire wrapped around my side till I thought I'd lose myself or go blind in it. I dug my fingers into my legs, concentrating on that small pain to pull me out of the mist.

The Brehon held up a second finger. The room grew so silent I could hear my ragged breathing.

The fear didn't help. I hadn't known it would hurt so badly. I longed to put something in my mouth to keep from screaming, but I couldn't. Those watching would guess that I could speak.

I glanced up at the *Ri*, and he held my gaze as if that alone could give me the strength I needed.

Three more.

I pulled in a deep breath, distracting myself by wondering where Moyle would hit again. Low on the left side, close enough to the ribs he'd just bruised, but in a new enough spot to spread the pain.

A shout and the whistle of the cane cutting through the air.

I'd guessed aright: the blow fell low on my left. I smiled as the white rolled across my vision. He was so predictable—

A breath later, another blow fell across my shoulder blades. I felt my skin split. The pain pounded my back with every heartbeat, as if the pulse beat at me from the inside. The only coolness was on my left cheek.

I'd fallen on my side, face on the cool cobblestones, mouth open as I dragged air inside me. But it hurt to breathe, too, hurt so much that I wondered if I could bear it.

I looked at the *Ri*, fury and pity warring in his face . . . at the Advocate with his four fingers held up.

There was only one more.

One more.

The pain made the dream so much closer. Once more I held the cudgel in my hands, wood smooth against my palms as I neared the man who watched the black swans fall from the sky. I wouldn't let him hurt my brothers. I wouldn't let him dishonor or imprison me when I was so close to finishing the tunics.

One more blow and I would unravel Moyle in front of these people.

I pressed my palms to the cool stones and pushed myself upright, panting around the pain, wincing as my dress clung to the blood on my back.

I turned my head, even though the white light burned the edges of my vision, and stared at Moyle. He was sweating from the effort of the blows, face flushed. If I were younger, I'd have made the gesture Cadan was so fond of. But I didn't have to anymore.

I met his glare.

I wanted him to know he would lose. I wanted him to see I knew how small he was inside and that his whole community knew it too.

I saw the moment he understood. His eyes widened, his shoulder rose as he drew back his arm—

I looked away. He was cowardly enough to try to break my jaw.

The cane landed between my shoulders, near the base of my neck. The white light engulfed me one last time, darkness dancing between it like night sky behind a fire, and the room disappeared.

In my dream, I saw the black swans' wings catch the air beneath them. My brothers flew away.

I had won.

"Five!" thundered the *Ri*.

Then Ionwyn was kneeling in front of me, holding my hands, keeping me from falling.

"You did it, Wyn!" She wiped the tears from my cheeks. "Can you stand?"

My body seemed distant from me, trembling and broken. But I nodded. I wouldn't be carried from the room. I pulled in as deep a breath as I dared, looking around. Moyle was being dragged away, his face slack with losing. Connach looked shattered.

And the cane lay beside me where Moyle had dropped it.

I curled my fingers around it. How could such a small movement hurt so much?

Then, leaning on Ionwyn, I stood. The white light flickered for a moment, and I swayed. But I didn't fall. I didn't drop the cane.

I limped toward the *Ri* and the Advocate, Ionwyn supporting me. The room quieted with each step until I stood before the *Ri*.

I pressed my free hand to my heart, my only way of thanking him.

I saw that he understood, as if I'd been signing to him for years.

Then I turned to Finn, who stood beside the *Ri*, and handed him the cane.

"My lady." Finn took the cane in his huge hands and nodded at Moyle. "I'll put this to good use."

My eyes filled. It had been so many years since I'd been called a lady.

"Tend to her, Ionwyn," said the *Ri*.

Ionwyn supported me as I walked from the room. As I passed the chiefs, I saw that I would never have to stand trial before them again. Some had eyes bright from tears they would not shed. Others nodded as I passed. None looked at me coldly.

I'd earned a place for Carrick and me among the Eyre.

If I chose to claim it.

Chapter 43

I woke to a dark room. Carrick had been given to a different caretaker for the night, and I hadn't protested. I could barely move, let alone care for him, and I didn't want my injuries to frighten him.

The pain had settled to a dull red color, only flaring to white when I tried to move. The nurses had insisted I sleep on my stomach, and the pain pinned me there.

I couldn't feel the Kingstone. Where was it?

Finally I saw the pale smudge of gray on the low table beside my bed.

I pulled in several deep breaths to smooth out the pain. One of the maids who had bandaged my ribs remained in the room—and so did Ionwyn. Her mouth was settled in a firm line while she slept, as if she was guarding me even in her dreams.

I still didn't feel safe.

Then I realized that I'd hoped the *Ri* would be there when I opened my eyes.

Don't be a little fool. I turned my face back into the blankets, wincing at each breath.

I've earned it. For one night, I'll let myself be a fool. With the darkness pressing in, I closed my eyes and imagined I rested beside the *Ri*, my back not against a tree or stone, but him. I imagined he held me close enough that the pain didn't matter anymore.

⁎⁎⁎

"How do you feel this morning?" Ionwyn asked when I next opened my eyes.

I rolled my shoulders, trying to see where the pain lay. I felt brittle as a brown leaf, cracked in a million places. But I would heal.

I smiled.

"Good," she said. She watched as the maid smoothed more salve over the cuts on my back and rewrapped the bandages around my ribs.

When they'd fed me and left, Ionwyn sat on the floor beside the bed, her face level with mine. "Wyn, I must ask you something."

I nodded, worried. Had something happened to Carrick?

She spoke slowly, as if feeling her way along a path. "Your lips moved in your sleep last night. You could speak once, couldn't you?"

The question drove the breath from me.

She didn't stop. "And the women last night, they said that Carrick couldn't be your son."

Anger and fear burned bright in me. I wouldn't fail

Tanwen by losing her son. I balled a hand into a fist and held it against my heart. *He is mine!*

Ionwyn didn't look triumphant. Just determined. Perhaps a little sad. "You don't have the body of a woman who has borne and suckled a child."

I wouldn't let them take him!

I pushed myself up, shrugging away her attempts to help. And then the pain from my back and ribs was so great that I sat hunched there, unable to sit or lie back down again.

"Lie down," said Ionwyn. "Nothing will happen to you or Carrick."

I put my hand on my chest again, pressing it to me, as if it could touch my heart. *He's mine.* Carrick was the child of my heart if not my body. I wouldn't fail Tanwen by losing her son.

"I know you love him," whispered Ionwyn. "Come. Let me help you lie down."

I let her help me, even though I hated how much I needed her assistance. Then I turned my face away from her.

I heard her sit beside the bed again.

I expected her to push for answers that I couldn't give. But she waited until I grew calm.

Finally she spoke, her voice low. "You frightened me the first time I saw you. You were a wisp of a thing, this Otherworldly lass Corbin had brought from the forest." She paused, a laugh in her voice. "I know it sounds foolish."

I remembered our fear when Father brought the Queen from the forest—I couldn't blame Ionwyn for hers.

Whether I liked it or not, I'd brought some of the Queen's evil with me.

I heard her dress rustle again as she settled her skirt around her. "In every tale, there is a sentence or word where the story turns—earth and sky trading places. A good bard knows that place in her soul. She may not discover it until she tells the tale a hundred times. But once she knows the turning point, she tells the story with even more power and wisdom."

She paused, as if hoping I'd face her.

I didn't, though sadness crept over me. Another time, Ionwyn and I might've been friends. But I couldn't let her into this story. Tanwen had become part of this story, and she had died.

Please, I thought. *Leave us in peace. Leave us alone.*

"You are that turning point, Wyn. I knew it the moment I saw you."

Father. My swan-brothers. Tanwen. I had changed the story for so many lives, and none of them was the better for it.

She sighed, as if she knew I wouldn't face her.

"Corbin has given so much for his people. After his father lost everything, Corbin paid everything to reclaim it."

She put a hand on my shoulder, so very lightly.

This is when she tells us to go, I thought, just as I'd predicted where Moyle's blows would fall. She was worried I'd hurt the *Ri* somehow. I couldn't fault her for it. Connach had used me to challenge the *Ri*.

But while I waited for her to tell me to go, I realized how much I wanted to stay.

"I worried for Corbin until yesterday. You turned the story. In one action, you disgraced a family that has challenged Corbin ever since he first wore the crown. I'm convinced you're supposed to be here. You were meant to step into our story, Wyn. And I think—I hope—that you will turn it in a way we never could have imagined. It's already begun. I'm glad Corbin brought you here."

The words were balm, soothing heart-wounds I'd borne for years.

I turned to face her.

"Who are you?" she asked.

I'd been so many people: princess, swan-keeper, prey, wild girl from the forest. I tapped my chest with a finger. *Myself. I am myself.*

"Will you tell me why you're here?" she asked.

I shook my head.

"But you could speak before?"

It was such a small question! If someone had found out last night . . . but I would trust her with it.

I nodded.

She raised her eyebrows. "So you could have cried out?"

I nodded.

She laughed. "Oh, it would break Moyle to know that! He cried like a child after Finn's third blow." She shook her head. "Finn was as angry as I've ever seen him, and so was Corbin. But then, so was Moyle."

She smiled. "Do you know what it means to be *Ri* here?"

I shook my head.

"It means that you protect your own. More than anything. Above anything. You act like a queen. Carrick is your own. And yesterday, you acted as if *we* were your own. You protected Corbin too."

Ionwyn's praise left me breathless.

"You have many secrets, and I won't demand that you share them. Not after yesterday. But I insist on this: if one of them threatens us, you must tell me."

I will.

"We have an understanding." She raised an eyebrow. "Rest well, Wyn. This afternoon, you will walk out with me."

Chapter 44

Ionwyn and I walked near the castle that afternoon. No one looked at me askance. No whispers followed me.

"Wyn!" A patter of feet against stones, and Carrick wrapped himself around my knees.

He'd have knocked me over if Ionwyn hadn't steadied me.

How I'd missed him beside me last night! I signed Carrick's name, and he held his arms up to be held. I gingerly knelt down to be closer to him.

His arms wrapped around me before I'd lowered myself to the ground, and once more, Ionwyn's hand kept me from falling. I smiled my thanks up at her.

It wasn't Ionwyn.

It was the *Ri*, and he kept his hand on my shoulder. I ducked my head quickly, blushing that I'd let myself dream of sleeping beside him the night before. But Carrick didn't care about blushes or smiles. He burbled on in his mix of new words and signs, and I savored the sight of him. His cheeks were fuller, his arms almost chubby. He'd been such a skinny child ever since Tanwen died.

I pulled him close and kissed his cheeks until he squirmed free and trotted off to collect a stick. Ionwyn helped me stand.

I dipped my head in acknowledgment to the *Ri*.

"Good afternoon to you, Lady Wyn," he said.

I looked up, startled.

"The 'Lady' surprises you?" he asked.

I nodded.

"It suits you," he said.

I stared at him. He'd seen me burst from the forest like a wild animal. I'd let everyone in Fianna think I was deaf and mad, more a creature of the forest than a girl who merely lived there. And yet the *Ri* called me *Lady*—as if I was still in Lacharra, with my servants and finery around me.

For a moment, I felt as if he'd given my kingdom back to me. I straightened, despite the pain in my ribs, and stood as if I wore a crown once more. I could see the *Ri* knew, somehow, what his words meant to me.

Carrick tugged at my skirt, and I looked down, grateful for a reason to turn away.

Up, signed Carrick, a stick clutched in his grimy hand.

I shook my head. I wouldn't be able to hold him till I healed.

"Here," said the *Ri*, and he swung Carrick up onto his shoulders so that he could be nearer me. "Come up here."

Carrick squealed to be up so high and rested his dirty hands in the *Ri*'s gold hair.

How many moonlit nights had I seen Aiden carry Carrick so? It was like seeing a ghost.

And it was a reminder that no matter the *Ri*'s hospitality or kindness to me, I didn't belong here, no matter how they welcomed me. I had my brothers to save. We had a kingdom to reclaim.

"I meant no harm, I assure you." The *Ri* had seen my grief. "He's a sturdy lad."

I forced a smile, but the *Ri* wasn't convinced. He reached up and plucked Carrick from his shoulders so quickly that Carrick dropped his stick. Carrick fussed, and the *Ri* tucked the boy under his arm like a sack of feed.

Carrick laughed and signed for more. Then he actually said it: "More!"

I smiled, despite the tightness in my chest.

The *Ri* looked at me, asking permission. I nodded.

"Well then." He swung Carrick from one side to the other, then threw him over his shoulder for good measure. Carrick laughed and beat his fists against the *Ri*'s back. He wasn't a small boy, but he looked tiny, draped over the *Ri*'s broad shoulder.

The *Ri* glanced at me again, almost like a boy himself, and when he saw my smile, he grinned. Grabbing hold of Carrick's ankles, he let the boy slide down his back till Carrick dangled down almost to his waist. Carrick's face was red from hanging upside down for so long, but he shouted and laughed till I couldn't help but laugh silently.

"What's that I hear? Where's Carrick?" The *Ri* spun as if looking behind him so that Carrick swung out behind him, laughing his delight. The *Ri* did it again and again. Finally, he reached behind him and pulled Carrick up over his shoulder and into his arms. For a moment, Carrick stopped clamoring for more and laid his head against the *Ri*'s chest. The *Ri* looked down at the boy lying still in his arms, surprised, then smiled up at me.

It was as intimate as a kiss.

Not once had I ever felt that way watching one of my brothers play with Carrick.

And that's a very good thing, Cadan would have told me. *What a way for a sister to feel about her brother! Though I am a fine-looking man one night out of the month.*

I smiled just to think of it—and realized not even Cadan would speak so glibly this close to the end of the enchantment.

Not now, he'd say. *For pity's sake, Ryn, not now.*

I looked down, ashamed I'd let myself go so far. Dreams were one thing, but to watch the *Ri* like that . . .

The *Ri* put Carrick down, and Carrick scurried after something else.

Ionwyn's gaze danced between the *Ri* and me. "I'll watch him," she said, then followed Carrick.

"Will you walk with me, Lady Wyn?" The king extended his arm to me, a question in his eyes.

How I wanted to walk with him!

I wanted to reach up and smooth the tawny hair that Carrick had rumpled when he rode on his shoulders. I wanted to find some way to thank him for sheltering us here, for trusting my courage enough that he let me challenge Connach, for calling me *Lady*.

I wanted it—all of it—so desperately. I realized I was already a heartbeat away from staying in Fianna.

No. I was a heartbeat away from wanting to stay with the *Ri*.

I couldn't afford that, not when I was so near the end of my brothers' enchantment and our return to Lacharra.

So I smiled and shook my head and pointed back at my room.

Anger erased the *Ri*'s smile, and I stepped back.

Then I saw he was angry with himself.

He sighed and lowered his arm. "You should have been safe as my guest, Lady Wyn. Instead, you bore an attack and a beating." His gaze dropped to my still-swollen lip. "I don't wonder it's hard to walk with me—I've a hard time bearing it myself. But believe me when I swear I'll settle this debt between us."

Debt? He thought he was in my debt?

He turned away, shoulders rounded just a little. They'd been so straight and strong when he'd played with Carrick.

Then he stopped and turned back. He straightened his shoulders and met my gaze squarely. "I've fought with sword and battle ax and spear. I've even seen battle with cudgel, which you are familiar with." He smiled ruefully and brought a hand up to the shoulder that I'd struck. "But I've never seen battle joined with only a cane—and it *was* battle, what happened yesterday with Moyle, even if you began by giving him the only weapon. It was one of the finest pieces of fighting I've ever seen. You have my respect, Lady Wyn."

I saw him pull his kingship around him. "I hope one day I'll have yours."

If I'd had every word known to man spread out before me and the freedom to speak whatever I chose, I still would have been mute before the *Ri*'s fierce kindness.

And in that moment, my heart went out to him, all at once.

But I didn't move a step toward him. I didn't dare, not with so few moons left before the curse was over.

The *Ri* nodded once, as if satisfying himself that he'd said everything he needed to say. "Ionwyn!" he called. "The Lady Wyn is weary. Will you escort her back to her room? I will take Carrick to his playmates."

I kissed Carrick good-bye and watched as the *Ri* swung the boy up into his arms once again, my hands clasped together to keep them from shaking.

What had happened?

Years ago, I'd seen a just-hatched gosling peer into the face of a goose that wasn't his parent—and it followed that goose from that day on. Was that what I'd done? Looked in the *Ri*'s face too long to take my heart back afterward?

Had my heart somehow slipped away from me?

Then I took myself firmly in hand: I was *not* a gosling. I was the Swan-Keeper, the only one able to reclaim my brothers from the Queen's enchantment.

And I would.

Nothing—not Connach's son, nor the *Ri*'s kindness—would stop me.

Chapter 45

As I healed, I reminded myself daily of my brothers, the nettle tunics I had to retrieve, and the final tunic I had to make. I'd lost the nettles I'd collected the night of the full moon. They rotted before I was strong enough to travel down to the river to check on them.

But that didn't mean I couldn't harvest more.

Here. In Fianna.

A wild hope had begun to rise in me: What if my time bearing this burden alone was ending? I'd been granted shelter, and since the trial, I'd gained respect among the people of Fianna.

Perhaps Carrick and I could spend this last year among friends and allies. I imagined the people of Fianna meeting my brothers on the moonlit nights, of Aiden telling our story to the *Ri*.

For the first time, I considered telling Ionwyn our story. If I told her, I'd have her help retrieving the tunics—no more trying to sneak away to the cave.

I had three weeks before the next full moon. So for several days, I turned our story over in my mind, deciding how to tell Ionwyn. I even practiced the pictures I'd draw in the dirt outside the castle.

Finally, when I could hold it inside me no longer, I found Ionwyn.

"Wyn!" she exclaimed when she saw me. "What is it? You're shaking."

I was. If I could properly tell my story, everything would change. *This* was the turning point Ionwyn had told me about, earth and heaven changing places if only I could make her understand.

So I led her to a grassy corner near the far edge of the wall. I'd already scraped some of the grass aside and smoothed the dirt beneath it, my own parchment ready to be written upon.

I carefully knelt there and motioned her to sit beside me.

One last time, I ran a trembling hand over the smoothed dirt as I sent a prayer into the air: *Help me . . . help me . . .*

Finally, I looked at Ionwyn, then pointed to myself.

"You're going to tell me what happened, aren't you?" she said.

Yes.

Then I began to draw what I'd rehearsed for days:

First the figure of a man for Father. I'd decided not to draw a crown. I didn't want Ionwyn to know that much. Then I drew my mother, my fingertip sure and steady through the dirt. Then five boys. Finally, I drew another boy and a small girl beside them. I pointed to the girl and then to me.

Ionwyn looked up, tentative. "That's *you*. You have six older brothers—"

I nodded, then I smoothed out the woman.

"—and your mother died?"

Yes.

She nodded, pleased with herself. "And then what?"

I drew a woman beside the tallest son, then drew a bundle in her arms and pointed back at the castle.

"Carrick!" said Ionwyn. "His mother?"

I nodded.

"He's your nephew, then."

Yes.

I drew a line across the dirt-Tanwen. Even that small reminder hurt.

Ionwyn saw my wince. "She's dead?"

I nodded. Then I drew another woman beside Father: *a new wife.*

I'd thought how to tell this next part—how to explain just what the Queen had done. I drew fine lines over my brothers: prison bars.

Ionwyn shook her head, confused. So I brought my hands up as if gripping imaginary bars.

"Your brothers were imprisoned?"

Yes.

"By whom?"

I pointed to the Queen.

Ionwyn nodded. "Go on."

I pointed to the Queen again, so Ionwyn would know who I mimicked. Then I stood just as she had, with her iron posture and scowl. I raised my arms, mouth open in a silent imprecation—the exact image of the Queen when she spoke the word that turned my brothers into swans.

Ionwyn watched, wide-eyed. Before she could speak, I crouched and returned to the sketch of my brothers. I drew the change slowly, the way I saw it in my nightmares: I showed necks stretching, arms turning to wings, legs dwindling . . . *Turn the story, Ryn. Turn it!*

She looked at the picture, then up at me. "Swans? What does that mean?"

I pointed to the swans flying, then up at the sky.

Please, please understand!

Ionwyn reached a hand to touch the picture, as if that could pull her into the story. "She killed your brothers? All of them? Is that what your kin believe? That the souls of the dead fly away like birds?"

I sat back on my heels, cursing my stupidity.

Of course she'd think my brothers had died! Who would assume that men had been turned to swans? My story would be hard enough to explain—and believe—even if I could speak.

I tried to draw the change one more time, tried to show Ionwyn the truth.

Ionwyn watched me closely, but she didn't understand. How could she?

"She killed them. Is that it, Wyn?"

There'd be no turning the story, no allies this last year. Just me, the Swan-Keeper.

So I nodded. I let Ionwyn think my brothers had died.

She leaned forward. "Is this woman nearby? Do you fear her still?"

A stretch of ocean separated me from the Queen, but it couldn't lessen my fear. Another thing I couldn't explain to Ionwyn.

No.

"Good!" Ionwyn's smile faltered, as though she sensed there was more.

But she helped me stand and walked with me back to the castle. How I longed for the hackle and spindle! To have something to do with my hands, as if I could make my life as smooth and even as the nettle fiber I wanted to drag across the hackle's spikes.

I'd been a gosling all over again. There would be time—and words!—for explanation later. I should have been satisfied with a full belly for Carrick and me. I could safely complete the last tunic here.

And I would.

But first, I needed to retrieve the other tunics. The people of Fianna were used to me coming and going. They wouldn't immediately pursue me as they had before.

It would take only a day to find my cave and gather the tunics. I'd return on the second. Carrick would be safe till I returned.

Chapter 46

Hope makes your pulse jump, your breath come quick. But there's steadiness in disappointment—a certainty of your place in life, even if you never wanted to be there.

So it was easy to leave the next morning, striding across the fields between Castle Hill and the forest. My duty was clear: I'd retrieve the nettle tunics and bring them back to Fianna, where I'd make the sixth tunic. I wouldn't share the truth of my brothers' enchantment with anyone. And when my brothers were free, we would return to Lacharra.

I'd be content with the gift of a people who were happy to have Carrick and me live among them. I'd never expected any help before—why was I so disappointed now?

I swung my cudgel in a savage arc through the air, cutting the heads off weeds that grew beside my path.

At least I'd see my swan-brothers after so many weeks! I'd stroke their sleek feathers and hear their trumpeting across the lake. I'd tickle Owain-the-hen beneath her wattle.

I would hold the tunics in my hands again and know that the work of five years hadn't been lost.

And yet . . . I missed the castle. I missed Carrick.

I shook away thoughts of Ionwyn and the *Ri*, focusing on the journey ahead. Now that I'd reached the forest, I worried whether I could find where the cave's deer trail met the road. I'd been so anxious to find Carrick a month ago that I hadn't looked about me, simply burst out into the road.

My plan depended on finding that trail quickly.

I walked through the day, keeping a sure and steady pace, eating my trail bread as I walked, and never stopping.

But I overestimated my ability to find the trail. By nightfall, I knew I'd passed it.

I also knew I'd never find it in the dark. I'd have to sleep in the forest, where a search party might find me—though I hoped there wouldn't be one. The *Ri*'s honor was bound primarily to Carrick. So long as Carrick was safe, there'd be little reason to pursue me.

I moved off the road and into the trees, using my cudgel to be sure there were no animal burrows in the brush.

It had been years since I'd slept alone in the forest.

The size and darkness pressed against me all over again. Every creak of a tree, every rustle, every call from one animal to another seemed foreign. I lay down, pulled Tanwen's cloak around me, and prayed that sleep would come soon.

⁎ ⁎ ⁎

As soon as the sun rose, I retraced my steps. Two hours later, I found the trail curving off to my right. I darted down it, almost running. I'd lost so much time.

Please let the tunics still be there!

I heard the voices not long after.

"Lady Wyn!"

"Lass!"

I turned, my heart sinking when I saw the *Ri* and Finn.

I cursed missing the trail, cursed the muteness that kept me from explaining my errand, cursed whatever devilry had helped the *Ri* find me so quickly.

Then I saw the horse-rod in the *Ri*'s hand as they walked toward me. Of course. If they'd left Fianna before dawn, they could have found the trail not long after I had. Finn's tracking skill would have made sure of that.

"Ionwyn told us you'd not returned late last night, and we've chased after you ever since!" Finn settled into the scolding the way a runner finds his stride. "What were you thinking, leaving your babe like that? And the *Ri*'s honor? What will chieftains and folk alike say if the one he shelters is lost in the forest?"

I only grew more determined. My anger was like a stone inside me, and I held to it. It was time to fetch the tunics—nothing else mattered.

I pointed down the trail toward the lake. It wasn't a question, only an explanation: *I will walk there.*

Finn grunted. "This isn't the time for exploring, lass."

I glared at him, almost wishing he'd refuse to let me go farther. I'd use my cudgel and feel nothing but satisfaction if only I could land a single, good blow.

Instead, I stalked down the trail, leaving them behind.

The *Ri* leaped ahead and planted himself in the trail before me. "Why are you here, Lady Wyn?"

Why am I here?

What I would have given to be able to shout! *I'm here because you wouldn't let me go! Because there aren't enough pictures and signs in the world to explain what has happened!*

I softened a little at the concern in the *Ri*'s eyes. *Because it's best that you don't know.*

Then I pointed down the trail again. *I WILL go there!*

The *Ri* didn't blink, though his mouth compressed, just a little, as if he was holding back a flood of words.

I hardened my heart to it.

When he spoke, his voice was even. Calm. "Ionwyn told me your story, as much as she understood: you saw your six brothers slaughtered by your father's wife, and you escaped that blood-feud with your brother's son. You signed to her that you were safe, but Ionwyn said your eyes told a different story." He made no effort to hide his irritation. "*How* do you expect me not to worry when you leave without protection?"

This wasn't about his honor, then.

I wanted him to leave. I didn't want him to see where I'd lived, to have any opportunity to understand the enchantment—or become convinced of my insanity.

But I needed the nettle tunics. So I pressed my hand over my heart and pointed down the path. *There's something dear to me.*

"There's naught but a lake down this trail," said Finn.

"There's something else, isn't there?" asked the *Ri*. "That's why you kept trying to leave."

Yes!

Finn raised his hands to the sky in mock entreaty. "If she wanted to come here, why didn't she ask—?" He dropped his hands. "Ah. There's the difficulty."

He finally understood. Before I could think better of it, I kissed him on the cheek.

Finn slapped a rough hand over the spot, whether to press the kiss closer or keep it from settling, I couldn't tell.

The *Ri* chuckled at Finn's discomfort, then grew serious once more. "Finn and I will walk wherever you wish to go. Lead on, Lady Wyn."

Lead on to everything I'd tried to hide for five years.

I had no choice: I motioned them to follow me.

⁎⁎⁎

An hour later, we reached the lake, and I forgot my anxiety for a heartbeat. I'd missed the way the sunlight scattered on the water! I held a hand to my eyes to shield them from the glare and saw my swan-brothers at the far end of the lake, all six of them.

But no Owain-the-hen.

I had to be sure of the tunics before I greeted my brothers. I didn't think I could face them, even as swans, until I knew all was well.

I held up a finger to the *Ri* and Finn—*Wait*—then

scampered up the boulders to the cave. I paused at the opening till my eyes adjusted, then slipped inside. The floor was covered with wild goat droppings. Torn and chewed bedding lay strewn around the cave.

But the tunics still hung in their satchel from the outcropping, right next to the bag that held my brothers' clothes. I dashed to it, dodging goat droppings as I went. A moment later, the satchel was mine. I rummaged through it to be sure of the spindle, the hackle, and all five tunics, then hugged it close, careful of the hackle's spikes.

Then I saw that the bag of clothes was knotted differently from how I usually closed it. I tugged it down, imagining my brothers here the last full moon: alone, scrabbling in the dark, empty cave to find their clothes. Find *me.*

I couldn't think of it. I'd have clothes for them this time, when they settled at the lake near the castle.

A flash of dark in the entrance, a rush of feathers—

Owain-the-hen launched herself at me.

My arms were full, but Owain took no notice. She perched on top of the bags and pressed her head against my cheek, clucking and scolding as if she'd never forgive me.

I dropped something to free a hand, scooped her closer to me . . . and cried silently, head bent over her feathery back.

My brothers would want answers when they saw me next. But Owain-the-hen? She just wanted me. So I let her scold and I let myself cry for just a moment longer, soaking up the comfort she offered.

The light streaming in from the cave entrance dimmed.

Finn and the *Ri* stood in the entrance—two black shadows against the light.

I shifted Owain-the-hen to my shoulder and swiped a sleeve across my eyes. Silly as it sounded, I felt better able to answer his questions.

The outline of the *Ri* moved as he looked around the cave. "Your refuge, Lady Wyn?"

Refuge. Of course. He imagined me the lone survivor of a blood feud.

And perhaps he saw it more clearly than most.

I nodded slowly.

Finn stepped into the cave, cursing when he trod in goat dung. The *Ri* followed him, moving more carefully, taking in all the details: scattered blankets, a basket overturned and slightly eaten . . .

. . . the hen on my shoulder, pecking at me as if she was a mother smoothing her child's hair.

"I never," muttered Finn.

I raised an eyebrow, daring him to mention Owain. He turned his attention elsewhere.

"I don't understand," said Finn, nodding toward the bag I clutched. "You came all this way—you left your babe—for bags?"

I glared at Finn. If he thought I was going to reveal the things I valued most just because he asked, he'd be sorely disappointed.

The *Ri* picked up the satchel I'd dropped, wincing when his hand closed around the hackle. I quickly gathered it from him, pulling out a few of the tunics and rearranging the contents so the hackle wouldn't spear anyone.

When I looked up, the *Ri* was fingering the sleeve of one of the tunics. "Is it made from nettles?"

Suddenly, the cave seemed too small, my secret too big. I needed to go. I needed to leave *now.* I plucked the tunic from his hands and stuffed it back into the satchel.

"How many shirts do you have?" he asked.

Refusing to answer might make him even more curious. After a moment, I held up five fingers.

"And you've already gathered nettles for one more shirt, haven't you? Six shirts for the six dead brothers Ionwyn told me about. Am I right?"

He thought the tunics were simply part of my mourning.

Yes.

"Ionwyn says you were the youngest of these siblings?"

I smiled to hear such a common question—as if there wasn't an enchantment or Hunters or a Queen we hid from.

Yes.

"You were! Aye, that makes many things clear—including why a lass would wield a cudgel so well."

He swept an arm toward the light at the cave entrance. "We'll follow after you, Lady Wyn. Unless you have anything else you wish to take?"

I looked around the cave one last time. Goat-chewed blankets. A weir I'd been repairing weeks ago. I scooped up one of Carrick's toys, settling it into the satchel with my brothers' clothes.

Then I walked into the light and down to the lake, hurrying down the boulders so that I reached the shore ahead of Finn and the *Ri.* I set the bag and satchel on a boulder and attempted to lift Owain from my shoulder, but the hen would have none of it.

Finn joined me, and I held a warning finger up to him so he would leave the satchel and bag alone. He held his hands up, and I realized it was all I could hope for. So I stripped off my boots and twisted my skirts up above my knees. Then I waded into the shallows and slapped the water, watching my brothers at the far end of the lake.

Several turned toward me. I slapped the water again.

My brothers sprang to life, wings beating the air as they skimmed over the water toward me. Owain did not like to have my swan-brothers so near. She ruffled her feathers in alarm, her toes digging into my shoulder. A moment later, the swans surrounded me, their wings splashing so much water that I gave up any thought of staying dry and let my skirt fall into the shallows.

One of the swans—Declan, I thought—swam close enough that I could stroke his neck. He chortled and clucked with pleasure, angling his neck first one way and then another so that I could scratch every inch. The others were close too, and I could see as they swirled around me that their white flight feathers had grown in. They could fly now, though I wasn't certain I liked the thought. They'd follow me to the castle just before the full moon as they always had, and then nest there. Would they be safe at the lake so near the castle? What would the people think of black swans?

What would the *Ri* think?

I turned to face him, a hen on my shoulder, my wet skirts clinging to my knees while my swan-brothers swam graceful circles around me. He watched the swans intently, and I knew he was trying to make sense of the story Ionwyn had told him: brothers and swans and something evil.

"Black swans!" Finn stomped up to the lake's edge and eyed them with mistrust. "What natural beast has red eyes?"

"They'll follow you, won't they?" asked the *Ri*.

Yes.

"Don't worry for them, Lady Wyn," he said. "We'll make sure no harm comes to them when they venture closer to the castle."

I nodded again.

"That'll be a chore and a half," said Finn. "But no doubt Ionwyn will have a clever idea to help. How many are there?"

"Six," said the *Ri*, never taking his eyes from my brothers. "There are six black swans."

Would he guess the truth? Or decide I truly was a girl from the forest, driven mad from witnessing a blood feud? I'd have sooner stood before the *Ri* naked than wait to see which of the two he decided.

I splashed to the lake's edge, wringing the water from my skirt. I was almost grateful I was mute—it saved me from having to explain all that the *Ri* and Finn had seen.

But the *Ri* continued to watch my swan-brothers.

Six brothers.

Six swans.

Five nettle tunics, and nettles for one more.

"When I first saw you"—he turned to me—"I thought you were mad. And then, I thought you were frightened. And now I think you are guarding something. Carrick, of course. But there's more, something else you try to keep safe." He shrugged. "Perhaps it is yourself, but I don't think so."

I waited for him to ask a question I couldn't answer. I waited for an accusation of witchcraft.

Instead the *Ri* watched me as if he could see past skin and bone. It was like when I'd begged him to take Carrick and me with him, praying he would see *me* and not the crazy girl who'd burst from the woods and attacked him.

Once more, the *Ri* offered me shelter.

"Hear me, Lady Wyn, without kin in this world: I will protect you as you have protected me. And even if you hadn't begged my hospitality so many months ago, I would protect you still. My honor on it. My life on it."

Chapter 47

Sixty-third full moon

I stood knee deep at the lake only a league from the castle, skirts tucked up into my waist, and swished the handful of nettles through the water. The motion washed away the rotting stem, leaving tangles of pale fiber in my hands.

Then I heard the three-note trumpet of my swan-brothers and saw the sweep of black wings above the tree-tops. I'd been waiting for them, knowing that the coming full moon would draw them soon.

I splashed ashore and tossed the sodden fibers into the basket with the rest that I'd collected. Then I waded back to greet my brothers, sweeping my hands through the water to remove the stench of retting nettles. My swan-brothers wouldn't mind the stench, but I hated to touch them with dirty hands.

They quickly surrounded me. One of them—probably Cadan—nipped at the others as if jealous of my attention. They were less swan-like today, especially Aiden. I knew that he, more than my other brothers, worked to reclaim his mind the earliest. On the days just before the full moon, the enchantment wore thin at the edges, and Aiden's strong heart and determined mind pressed against those boundaries.

Perhaps that was why Cadan-swan became contentious—more like his human self—the closer we came to the full moon.

I reached out to Aiden, stroking the short, silky feathers along his cheek, hoping that some part of him would know Carrick and I were safe.

He nibbled the inside of my wrist.

I thought of how Carrick was growing chubby and speaking like any of the other children. How, now that I didn't have to scavenge for food, I had so much more time to harvest and ret nettles for the final tunic. My earlier foolishness aside, it was good—right, even—that we be here in Fianna.

I just didn't know how to explain that to my brothers.

⁂

That afternoon, I signed to Ionwyn that I would leave that evening—alone. I'd spent days wondering how to explain I'd be gone all night.

And then I realized I should simply draw the truth.

In the hearth soot of the great room, I drew that I'd visit with my six brothers that evening—under the full moon.

I could see her try to make sense of what I'd drawn, then: "You keep vigil for your brothers during the full moon?"

I'd known she would supply a better answer than I could ever create.

Yes.

⁂

The lake was too far for Carrick to walk, and I couldn't carry him with my ribs still healing, so I'd planned to get to the lake early and draw that Carrick was well.

I quickly found the part of the lake where the swans waited and laid out my brothers' clothes. Perhaps if they found their old clothing, they'd know all was well. I didn't dare light a fire, but I set my muted lantern down on the bank and began to sketch all that had happened since they'd seen me last.

But I wouldn't tell them about the trial or caning. I couldn't explain it, or how it had earned me respect among the people I thought were barbarians.

At dusk, I heard the wind roar toward us. My swan-brothers were already at the lake's edge, wings spread as if to snatch their change from the air.

When the wind stopped, I didn't hear my brothers' voices.

I tapped my cudgel against a nearby tree three times and lifted a shutter on the lantern so my brothers could see my face.

"Ryn?" called Cadan, softly. "Please let it be you!"

I tapped again.

"Thank heaven!" That was Aiden in a choked voice. "And Carrick? Where's Carrick?"

After a mad scramble to dress themselves, my brothers gathered around, hands reaching out as if they needed to be certain of me, only—

Aiden stared at my empty arms. "Where's Carrick?"

I signed *safe*, but he was looking past me into the dark.

"Where's Carrick, Ryn?" A panicked note seeped into his voice. "Where's my son?"

I took Aiden's face in my hands and made him look at me. Then I held my arms as if rocking a baby and signed *safe*.

"Then why isn't he here?"

But I knew Aiden was seeing Tanwen's death all over again. I took his face again, prayed he'd be able to see the truth in my eyes. *Believe me. He's safe.*

After a moment, he stilled. "What's happened? Tell me where he is, and where *we* are. I have to know, Ryn."

I took his arm and tugged him to sit beside the history I'd drawn, the lantern's light streaming over the pictures.

Me sick in the cave . . . begging hospitality for the sick Carrick and myself . . . Carrick among the Fianna.

"I knew you were too close to the barbarians!" said Aiden. "How is Carrick now? Why isn't he here?"

I nodded, signed that he was sleeping, then puffed my cheeks out a bit and patted them.

Aiden shook his head, confused. I put my hands on my belly, then pulled them out slowly, as if I was getting fatter.

"I know you're not telling us you're with child, Ryn,"

said Cadan in a flat, calm voice. Too calm. "Please tell me you're not expecting a child."

I hit his shoulder. Hard.

"Oww!"

"Shhh!" hissed Mael.

I put my hands back over my cheeks, rounding them so my cheeks looked fatter.

"He's gained weight?" suggested Owain.

I gestured at him with both hands: *Yes!* I picked up a nearby twig and waved it around.

"He still has a stick?" asked Aiden. "He's healthy, then?"

I nodded.

"And Ryn is not pregnant," reiterated Cadan.

I scowled at him.

"The tunics?" asked Gavyn. "They were there in the cave last full moon. How did you get them? And how far are you from the cave?"

I'd known they would be too unsettled to believe me, so I'd brought one of the tunics with me. I pulled it from the satchel and handed it to Gavyn.

"They're all safe?" asked Mael.

I rolled my eyes—a perfect imitation of Cadan. I signed *Carrick*, then pointed to myself and the tunic and signed *safe* once more. *We are all safe!*

"But how?" pressed Mael. "How can you be sure you are safe?"

I made a motion of a crown, even though the *Ri* did not wear one.

"The king keeps you safe?" asked Declan. "Can you

trust that? You're a maid with a child among barbarians!"

The word *barbarians* seemed razor-sharp in his mouth. I felt the edge of it. They had no idea how wrong it was.

I pointed again to the picture of me begging hospitality.

Mael just shook his head.

"The kings of Eyre value their honor above all else," said Gavyn. For the first time, I was grateful for one of his lessons. "When they offer hospitality, the honor of their house is at stake. Ryn and Carrick's welfare is tied to the barbarian king's honor. She's safe."

He glanced up at me. "But I still don't like it: you, just . . . here."

Here? What did they think I did all the other nights of the month? I wanted to scold, then I remembered how I felt when I was away from Carrick. I knew I couldn't completely protect him, but I *felt* that I could if I was with him.

My brothers must feel the same about me.

I signed *safe* once more.

"So Carrick is safe"—I interrupted Mael with a gesture at a full belly—"and fat, and the tunics are safe."

"And our Ryn is not pregnant!" finished Cadan.

Before I could brace myself, he caught me up in a great hug, squeezing the sore places in my ribs.

I couldn't help it—I yanked myself away.

Every one of them leaped to their feet.

"What is it, Ryn?"

"What happened?"

"Let me see."

Before I could wriggle free, Declan had pulled the

back of my dress back an inch, revealing the top of the still-healing wounds from the caning.

Cadan took one look, then gestured to the castle on the hill. "We take Ryn and Carrick away tonight, and when we are men again, we burn it to the ground!"

"This is your idea of *safe*?" Aiden thundered.

I yanked myself away from them again, straightening my dress. *Yes, safe!*

Declan, sweet Declan who always tried to make peace, would have none of it. "How could you let yourself stay in this place if *this*"—he waved a hand at my back—"is their king's idea of hospitality?"

And there I was again, in the space between heartbeats, with my life running in two different courses around this conversation. These people were *not* barbarians, and the *Ri* . . . ?

I saw him again as he knelt before me at the trial, telling me he could not protect me if I challenged Connach, but letting me do it anyway, even though it might diminish his honor. I remembered—no, I *felt*—the strength of his gaze all over again, his confidence that I could do it, and how it had bolstered my own determination.

A woman would be a fool not to love him—or to lie to herself and say that she didn't. And I knew, in that still, quiet space, that love for him had been growing all along. I couldn't deny it any more than I could hold back the sun once it started to rise.

What gosling would want to hold back such light and color?

"Ryn!" said Mael. "Don't you understand us?"

And then I was among my brothers again, and I no longer felt like a child.

What had the *Ri* said? *It was one of the finest pieces of fighting I've ever seen.* The marks on my back weren't punishment. They were battle scars, and I wouldn't apologize for them. When I had words, I'd explain everything.

Until then, I would not cower like a child.

I stood in the center of them, felt their fear and fury, but it couldn't reach inside me. I stood straight and tall and waited till my brothers grew silent. Then I pointed to myself with both hands and jabbed my fingers at the ground I stood on, as if the motion could plant me there.

I WILL stay here!

Before they could speak, I signed it again: *We are safe. Safe!*

Aiden looked shocked. I saw his chest rise as he pulled in a great breath. And then a quick shake of his head. "I can't—"

"No."

I spun to face Owain. But he wasn't talking to *me.* "I believe her, Aiden."

"This isn't a matter of believing her!"

"Isn't it?" Owain squared his shoulders. "She was right that Father was enchanted. And she was right about the nettles. But we didn't believe her until Tanwen told us all that had happened."

"Because she's—"

"The youngest? Our sister?" pressed Owain. "She was all those things. And she was still right. So when she says that she and Carrick are safe, I believe her."

I'd have been less surprised if Cadan had started reciting Declan's poetry. I could tell my brothers were just as shocked. But Owain smiled at me and shrugged, a gesture that was both apology for the past years and embrace all in one.

"But there's Carrick."

"That's why I believe her," said Owain. "She'd never endanger him."

After a moment, Aiden nodded. Mael laughed under his breath as if he'd seen a miracle and couldn't quite believe it yet.

I looked at Owain.

Mael *had* seen a miracle.

Aiden cleared his throat. "It's awful, Ryn, to step into a world you can't control—not knowing what will be waiting for you—and stay there only a few hours. You have to leave just as you're making your place in it all over again."

It was his own apology. When he finally met my eyes, I smiled at him.

"This is all I ask: no matter how safe you think you are, don't tell them about us," he said. "Don't let them find out. I'd rather you leave our clothes here at night—so we can know you're safe—and stay at the castle than come here and draw attention to us."

After a moment's hesitation, I nodded. My attempts to explain the enchantment hadn't worked anyway.

"Keep the both of you safe. And this barbarian king, you are more than just his honor. I pray he knows that."

Heaven help me, I prayed the same.

Chapter 48

"You know that birds are creatures between the worlds of earth and air, and that in the days before remembering, they served as emissaries between the Otherworld and this one. You have heard of the *adar rhiannon*, the birds of the Otherworld's Great Lady. At her command, they sang the dead to life and enchanted the hearts of her guests with songs that satisfied every desire . . ."

For one moment, I was back in Lacharra, looking at Mother's tapestry of the Lady, hung in my room.

But it was Ionwyn's voice that pushed the darkness away. She looked around the great hall, waited until she had gathered up the gaze of every soul in it. Then she raised her hands as if giving a gift.

"Hear now the story of the Children of Lir."

ҳ ҳ ҳ

Finn had said Ionwyn would protect the swans, but I'd not known she'd sing a place for them in the heart of every person who heard her tale.

And what a tale it was—so close to the truth I wondered if Ionwyn knew our story after all. Lir's three children were turned to swans—white swans in this tale—by a jealous stepmother, and for hundreds of years after that, their voices and songs touched the hearts of those who heard them.

Even the chiefs had wept at the tragedy, and as I looked around the hall, I knew my swan-brothers were safe. There had been talk about the black swans before that, but Ionwyn's story—and Finn's outright threats afterward—guaranteed their protection.

x x x

That night, as the hall emptied, I set aside the knitting I'd brought with me. Then I saw the hearth: soot-lined edges and the smooth hearthstones.

Ionwyn's story of Lir's children burned inside me. This was its own sort of pregnancy, I thought, to have something inside you that should live out in the world.

I dipped a finger in the soot and began to draw.

It was different from the drawings of my childhood. No ink. No parchment. But my fingers shaped the swan just the same: black lines on the flagstone, and it was a relief like laughter or tears to see it there.

"You're drawing Ionwyn's story, aren't you?"

The *Ri* crouched down for a closer look.

I swept my hand over the drawing, frightened he'd guess the truth of my own story.

He sat beside me on the stone floor and gently batted my hand away. "Let me see, Lady Wyn. It's a fine swan. Why would you be ashamed of it?"

I blinked at him, sooty hands held in front of me.

I'd decided days ago that loving the *Ri* was no excuse to hope he'd love me—or reason to falter in my goal. My brothers weren't yet free. The last tunic wasn't finished. I'd hold my love inside me the same way I'd held my words. I'd ask nothing of him, expect nothing from him, for what could I give in return? Silence? A nettle tunic?

Best to hold him at a distance.

And yet I still blushed to be caught like a child, playing in the dirt.

The *Ri*'s gaze dropped to my dirty hands, and he half-smiled.

"Here in Eyre, our artists do not—" He stopped to think and swiped a broad finger through the soot. "They don't create animals or people like the swan you've drawn. At least not as you see them." He swept an arc on the stone before him. "But the plaits they draw!"

He dipped the forefinger of his other hand in the soot and swept another arc near the first, creating one of the complex knots I'd seen in their books and metalwork that merchants had brought to Lacharra.

Though *knot* could hardly describe what the *Ri* drew. It was fluid as a river as it curled over itself. He continued to expand the knot, and I was grateful it required his attention. I couldn't concentrate when the *Ri* watched me.

"Ionwyn," he continued, "would tell you our knots

represent people whose lives are twined together." Another curling loop. "The priest would tell you of two worlds, tumbled over each other. And I?" He paused, looking down at what he'd created. "I wonder what it would be like to walk the braid like a path. To turn and turn again and cut back over the road you'd just walked. You might never see the pattern of it—you'd be too close." He cleared his throat, then looked up at me with a soft smile. "Or perhaps, Lady Wyn, our plaits are something lovely to look at, a reminder that life isn't all sweat and soot."

Did he think I was lovely to look at? Surely not.

He laughed and returned to his artwork. "Ah! I've done a poor job of it, Lady Wyn."

I didn't know whether he meant the compliment or the knot.

"A true artist would have joined the two ends so that they looked like a single cord."

The braid seemed perfect to me. I reached out to trace it myself.

"I ask a boon of you, Lady Wyn," said the *Ri*. "Draw me a story."

I looked up from the soot-braid he'd drawn.

"Draw me part of *your* story."

Images of swans and curses filled my mind. But I couldn't show him that. It was too close to the truth.

"Your father?" prompted the *Ri*, his question soft, as if he feared he'd frighten me. "What was he like?"

I stared down at the stone before me. If the *Ri* had spoken again—if he'd even sighed—I would have refused.

But he sat so still I could almost believe he wasn't there, that I wasn't revealing a secret.

And then I knew what to draw.

I dipped a finger in the soot and sketched a few lines on the stone before me.

"A *book*," said the *Ri*. "He read to you?"

I understood his surprise: only the wealthy possessed books. Now he knew that about me. But that one small image opened a floodgate. I drew a stack of books. Then, heart in my throat, I drew a girl in her father's lap, a book before them.

It was a horrible sketch—the rough texture of the stone made the lines swim. But it was a gift, somehow. It was the first time I'd remembered Father—his true self—before the Queen arrived.

The *Ri* smiled at the picture. "No wonder Ionwyn enjoys your company. Anyone who loves books will be a friend of hers. And is the stone you wear from him?"

I looked at him, puzzled.

"Around your neck," he prompted.

The Kingstone fragment. I leaned back, hand covering where it lay beneath my bodice as if I could protect it from questions.

I shook my head. *I can't tell you any more.*

He held a hand up. "I didn't mean to cause you pain, Lady Wyn! Will you tell me of your mother instead?"

I paused, but eventually drew a woman, belly swollen with child. I pointed to her belly and then to me. Finally, I swept a hand over the woman so that she became a blur.

"Ionwyn told me she died birthing you?"

A nod.

After a moment, he said, "I think, Lady Wyn, there must have been goodness in her, to bring you into the world."

I smiled. *Yes.*

The *Ri* looked down at the smear, seeing something else.

I swept my hand over the nearby stone to pull him from his thoughts.

He looked up, and I tapped my temple.

"Your head?"

No.

I closed my eyes as if concentrating, then opened them again.

"You mean thinking?"

Yes.

I *could* have pointed at him. I should have. But perhaps I felt bold because of the dim room or the story I'd just heard.

Instead, I touched his temple, right where his gold hair curled back from his face.

The *Ri* grew completely still, as if any movement would send me back to the forest.

And perhaps it would have.

"I don't know what you're asking, Lady Wyn," he whispered, his gaze dancing from my face, and then to my hand, still close to his own face.

After a moment, I tapped his temple again, then pointed to him.

"My thoughts?" he asked. "You want to know what I was thinking?"

Yes.

He sobered, and I saw that the stillness inside him had fled. "I asked you to draw me a story, and you have, so I'll not deny you. But I fear you'll think me a brute."

I half-smiled and shook my head, fist over my heart, reminding him of his honor. He chuckled.

"Very well then, Lady Wyn." He met my gaze squarely, as if facing a judge. "I was thinking your memories of a good mother are better than the presence of a heartless one."

I blinked at him. What had his mother been like?

He pressed on, resolute. "And I envied you your memories. Now, will you still suffer the hospitality of such an ungrateful son?"

I nodded.

"That's a relief, then," he announced.

And I could see that it was. Before I could move, he pointed to my temple, where I'd tapped it. "You left soot on your face, trying to explain yourself to an idiot."

His fingers were as soot-covered as my own, but not his palms. He gently wiped the heel of his hand against my temple.

If I'd grown up as a princess, I'd have been used to flirtation. I would know how to hold a man's gaze, or what to whisper to make him laugh—or come closer. I might have even managed to escape the notice of all my brothers and meet a suitor for a breathless kiss in a corridor.

Yet there I was, nearly eighteen summers, past marrying age, and I blushed to feel the prince's hand on my face.

The *Ri* smiled. "There you are, Lady Wyn."

Before I could move, he stood. "I'll leave you in peace. But I thank you for your stories. I hope you draw more."

And then he was gone.

The next morning, parchment and ink were delivered to my room.

Chapter 49

"Lady Wyn."

I looked up from my spinning, lowering my work so that the drop spindle touched the ground.

It was Finn, hands clasped behind his back, a wretched expression on his face as if he could barely hold bad news inside him.

I leaped to my feet, my nettle yarn and spindle in a heap at my feet.

Carrick?

"No, lass! The little man's playing in mud like an otter." Yet he looked down, shifting his weight from boot to boot.

Was the man sick?

I touched his shoulder. *What's wrong?*

Finn squared his shoulders. "It's the *Ri*." He saw my alarm and rushed on. "He's well too, Lady Wyn, never you fear."

I held my hands out, palms up. *What, then?*

Finn scowled fiercely, working up to *what?* I imagined he'd looked more pleasant going into battle beside the *Ri*.

"I can't do this, Lady Wyn. I shouldn't. I bid you good day." Finn turned on his heel and marched away.

I grabbed his arm and jabbed a finger at the bench. *Sit!*

Finn did, reluctantly. I sat beside him, but he just clasped and unclasped his gnarled hands. Finally, he looked me in the eye. When I saw his grief and resolve, I almost told him to forget what he was going to say.

Instead, I gathered the nettle yarn and spindle, grateful to attend to something else.

"Aye, that'll make it easier, I think. You watch your yarn. I'll watch the horizon and tell you what must be said."

I nodded and set the spindle whirling as if the seven kingdoms of Eyre depended on it.

"I've come to tell you about Corbin," began Finn. "If I had Ionwyn's way with words, you'd hear harp music as I spoke. And you should, lass, for it's the story of a good man."

I watched him, intent to hear Corbin's story. I motioned that Finn should go on.

"Corbin is a king disgraced, and his people love him for it. I've loved him as if he was my own son since his father died."

Finn seemed uneasy with me watching him so closely, so I made a show of concentrating on the cloud of nettle fiber as it slid toward the drop spindle. Finally, Finn relaxed.

"Corbin's father was a good man. His goodness was in his marrow, and Corbin inherited that from him.

His mother was a stranger to us, her kin unknown, but Corbin's father couldn't look away from her." He met my eyes. "I confess, lass, there *was* something about her—a glory you couldn't get enough of. You didn't mind her reaching into your heart, until you discovered her fingers were tangled in your heartstrings and she didn't care what she tore. I learned not to listen to her, and so I kept my heart safe. Other men were not so lucky."

I nodded.

He spoke as if the words had an unpleasant flavor. "Seven years ago, a man Corbin's mother had taken as a lover was found dead, stabbed in the back. She didn't deny that she'd lain with him or that she killed him. She vowed he'd threatened her—as if any man could make *her* fearful!—and that she killed him to protect herself. There were no witnesses to the killing, and the man was known for his vile disposition." Finn shook his head. "But the *back*! There was a vileness about that, as well. So the Advocate decreed that the queen should be banished for five years and an honor price be paid to the man's family. I think the king's heart shattered. He died the day he learned all his queen had done."

I looked up from my spinning. *A judge would rule against the royalty?*

Finn saw my astonishment.

"Ah, at times I forget you're not of Eyre. No matter which of the kingdoms, the *Ri* is subject to an Advocate's ruling, just as any man. But an *althech fortha* can bear the judgment for royalty: the honor price is paid, yet the king's honor isn't belittled. The cousin who could have acted as the dead king's *althech fortha* refused. He wouldn't risk the farm his sons would inherit to cover the queen's dishonor.

"Corbin wouldn't leave the price unpaid, so he became the *althech fortha* for his dead father. At fifteen summers, he surrendered almost half his father's land as payment. Connach saw the opportunity as a chance to rule himself, and the chiefs might have chosen him to be the new *Ri*, if not for the raiders. But the raiders struck before the chiefs could choose. Corbin fought bravely—and with a poor man's sword. No raider could pass him, and I was proud to fight beside him."

Finn stretched his legs before him. "The chiefs chose him as their *Ri*, even though he had borne the weight of the judgment against his father."

I signed a question.

"No, his mother never returned, so much the better for Corbin! And he's been a good *Ri* ever since, though Connach never made it easy for him, as you can guess."

I could. It explained Connach's bitterness, why he'd pushed so hard to challenge the *Ri* after Moyle attacked me.

And I couldn't help but love the *Ri* a little more.

Finn gazed at his boots. "Ah, lass, out of respect, I'll say this quickly—a clean cut by a sharp blade. Do you understand me?"

I fed the nettle fiber into the twist created by the whirling spindle, saw the cloud of strands tighten into yarn, but all I could hear was the grief in Finn's voice.

I nodded.

"You're not good for the *Ri*." He inhaled through his nose. "I see his face when he looks at you, and don't I know his face and his moods well? I've been father and mother to him all these years."

Any other time, I'd have laughed at the idea of Finn mothering anyone, but I couldn't think beyond *You're not good for the* Ri.

A clean cut, indeed. And deep too.

"There's been muttering among the chiefs about the *Ri* favoring a girl without kin or speech, despite me knocking heads together. Not all of them, mind you! But enough, enough."

The nettle fiber still slid through my fingers—I'd spun too many years to let the yarn thin and break—but my vision blurred till I spun by feel alone.

"You won a place among us when you confronted Connach. But a place beside the *Ri* is different from a place among his people, and you know it. Corbin's strong enough and stubborn enough that he'd choose you anyway."

I blinked once . . . twice, till the yarn came back into focus. The world blurred, as if the spindle stood still and everything else turned. But I was proud—so proud!—that I'd kept the yarn smooth and even.

"So please, Lady Wyn," said Finn, "don't let him choose you."

I caught the spindle and wound the new yarn around the base. Then I set it spinning again, feeding the fiber into the twist as if nothing had happened.

Finn sat still, though I knew he was watching. Waiting. He rubbed the back of his neck.

"I won't press you for an answer, Lady Wyn. I know you think me rough, but I'm not cruel. Just know he needs the support of all his chiefs. There's rumor of war in the air."

I looked up.

"There's a country across the water. Lacharra—"

The spindle fell, still spinning, to the ground and danced there for a moment like a top. *Lacharra.* So the Queen had her wars after all.

I quickly gathered the fiber, spindle, and yarn into my lap.

"—the king of Lacharra is stretching his borders the way a child spreads his arms when he wakes. I fear we'll have to deal with them soon, and Corbin can't afford to have his chiefs divided." He put a hand on my arm. "He himself can't afford to be divided."

Divided! I felt *I* was being torn to pieces: the *Ri*, the chiefs, my brothers' tunics, the enchantment.

I looked down at the spindle in my lap.

I'd been a princess. I was sister and aunt. Mad maid from the forest. Connach's challenger and victor. And perhaps the *Ri*'s love.

No. I was the Swan-Keeper—and when my brothers were men, I'd be the princess of Lacharra once more.

This time, I would not forget it.

When Finn walked away, I lifted the spindle with shaking hands and set it spinning again. There was a familiarity to the action that steadied me.

I couldn't help Lacharra until I freed my brothers. In the meantime, I could free the *Ri*. Ionwyn had said that royalty in Eyre protected their own.

The *Ri* was as much a part of me as breath and blood—I would not have him hurt.

I would not let more countries suffer as the Queen waged her wars.

So I spun the nettle yarn the rest of that afternoon and into the evening. When the *Ri* asked me to draw for him, I did not set the yarn aside.

Chapter 50

I took my time that winter, spinning the yarn for Owain's tunic. It helped to have the spindle whirling before me when the *Ri* asked me to draw. All I had to do was shake my head *no* and nod at the yarn as my excuse.

I longed to look up and explain myself, but what had Finn said? *A clean cut by a sharp blade.* So I remained bent over the yarn. Besides, I didn't want him to see the tears in my eyes. One night, when the wind beat against the walls of the great hall, he saw the spindle and didn't even speak to me.

Once the yarn was spun—more than enough for one tunic!—I knit so slowly I was ashamed of myself. But my slow pace kept the *Ri* respected among his chiefs. It kept him safe from me.

I finished Owain's tunic the spring night before the *Ri* left to visit the chiefs who ruled beneath him. While Ionwyn spun a story about the beautiful maiden Deidre and the wars waged by the men who loved her, I joined the sleeves to the body of the tunic. I spread the tunic across my lap with trembling hands as the last words of her tale hung in the air.

I was finished.

Here was the last of my brothers' redemption, spread out on my lap. Conversations became a low thrumming, like bees deep in their hive. That seemed right, somehow. The tunics had been created in silence. How fitting that they would be finished in it.

Finally, I looked up—and met the *Ri*'s gaze.

He'd seen me finish the tunic. I plucked up the tunic and checked it for any holes or thin spots that might keep Owain from becoming a man again. I didn't look up till the last footsteps had faded from the hall.

I wasn't alone.

The *Ri* hadn't been fooled. He stood near the fire, waiting for me. "You've finished the last one. I'd have known from the look on your face, even if I hadn't watched you make it all winter."

I didn't answer, by look or sign.

"You could've made it in a month's time. But you didn't want to, did you?"

He'd known all along!

He crouched before me so his head was level with mine. "One last night, Lady Wyn, when you've spent so many on this tunic. Will you draw me a story?"

There was such kindness in his eyes that he seemed the safest place in this wild, cold world.

Shake your head—a clean cut by a sharp blade.

I couldn't tell him no, but I didn't dare agree.

So I shrugged.

"Tell me *no*, but don't shrug! Don't look away. It is an

insult to my hospitality, a fear that I'd harm you if you deny me." He softened a bit, his voice dropping to a whisper. "And it is an insult to *your* courage, Lady Wyn. Do what you have in your heart to do, and don't fear the consequences. I've seen too much of you to believe you would cringe from the path you've chosen."

I sat perfectly still, caught by the truth he'd spoken. And the honor of it.

And I saw that he waited for me to tell him to leave.

I slowly folded the tunic. The last tunic. The last night before the *Ri* left for months. The last moon of the enchantment might come before he returned.

Very well. I would do what was in my heart.

I walked to the hearth and knelt beside it. When the *Ri* joined me, I swept a fingertip through the soot and drew one last picture.

I drew the swans from the Cynwrig crest.

I drew the necks stretched for freedom. I drew the wings spread against the blue background. I drew it with all the hope of a daughter who believed she could reclaim her father. I drew with the innocence of a girl who has not yet learned grief. I let the *Ri* into the heart of my family's wretched story, even though he'd never know what he saw.

When I finished, he sat back on his heels. "Ah, here's speech enough, if only I knew how to hear it. Thank you, Lady Wyn."

I waited for him to ask about the three swans, but he didn't. He simply looked down as if memorizing the lines, while silence surged between the two of us like a river.

"Will you ever speak again?" The question flew through the dim like an arrow.

I stared at him. No one had asked before.

"It was wrong of me to ask." He stood abruptly. "Sometimes you look as if you're saving words, like a bard gathering a story. So I wondered, and I h—"

Hoped?

I stood too, but I couldn't leave, couldn't move toward him. It was like the moment the Hunters had found me so long ago while I knelt by the hut, every fiber of me stretched to hear them coming.

Here I was, years later, listening again. Perhaps this time, I wanted to be caught.

The *Ri* looked wretched. "I'm sorry, Lady Wyn. I won't ask again."

I nodded.

He half-smiled. "You won't hold it against me, then? The question doesn't cheapen my hospitality?"

How like him to laugh at himself to blunt the moment's edge.

I put a hand on his arm and waited till he looked me in the eye. Then I nodded again, willing him to understand the question I was answering.

"You mean it? You'll speak again?"

He'd grown still beneath my touch, every bit of him poured into the way he looked at me. I released his arm and stepped back.

But the *Ri* closed the distance between us.

"Soon?" he asked, his voice so low that I felt it more than heard it.

I nodded, wondering how I managed even that.

"Truly? You'll be able to speak soon?" His gaze danced over me. "What will you say, my lady Wyn, when you have fulfilled your vow? Will you shout a ballad? Will you gossip with the old wives until even they chide you for talking too much?"

I grinned. I'd thought of it a thousand times: speaking to Carrick for the first time, telling him how Tanwen had loved him. I'd call each of my brothers by name.

The *Ri* leaned closer. "I wonder what you will do that day."

The laughter left his brown eyes, but not the warmth, not the fire.

I didn't think of the Queen. I hardly thought of my brothers. I just looked up at the *Ri*.

He'd seen me when few else had. He'd sheltered Carrick and me.

What would I do? I'd tell him my name, and I'd hear him say it back to me: *Andaryn*. I'd tell him about Father and home, and I'd introduce him to my brothers, but not before telling Cadan to mind his manners. I'd—

I reached up and framed his face with my hands. His eyes widened, but he didn't move. He didn't have time to. I stood on my toes and kissed him, right on the mouth, soft as a sigh because my courage failed me at the end.

Then it failed me entirely. I turned on my heel, ready to run as if the Hunters themselves chased me.

The *Ri* caught my wrist and tugged me gently back to face him, the hint of a smile pulling at his mouth.

He released me carefully, watching me as if he feared I'd run again. "That's not fair, my lady Wyn," he said, so low, so soft. "Not fair at all to kiss a man and then leave him to wonder at his good fortune."

He stepped closer, a question in his eyes, asking if I minded.

I didn't mind at all, but I looked down anyway, thoughts of my brothers rushing back over me. Now wasn't the time. Why had I let myself become so distracted?

Think of Aiden, of Mael and—

He brushed a finger against my jaw.

All thought fled as he bent close.

"In Eyre," he whispered, "a man is taught respect for a woman. If she doesn't wish his company, she has only to say so. If he presses his attention, he forfeits his honor. So hear me, Lady Wyn: much as I want to kiss you, I won't." His voice dropped to a breath against my cheek. "You can't tell me to leave while bound to silence. And I won't kiss you if there's a chance that you don't want me to. Perhaps that will be something you do after you fulfill your vow."

I opened my eyes then, and leaned back to look at him. He watched me, his expression asking if he should step away.

He was such a good man.

I lifted my hand to his face. He raised his eyebrows, still questioning. "Wyn, you don't have to . . ."

I wanted to—how I wanted to! But I couldn't move.

Slowly, he brushed his lips against mine, his own way of asking. It was fire and moonlight poured inside me, and if his arm hadn't tightened around me I might have flown away.

He pulled back to see if I had minded, looking like a boy uncertain of himself.

But his mouth was too far away, so I stood on my toes again, just to be nearer. He smiled down at me, all boyishness gone from his eyes.

His next kiss wasn't a question.

But mine *was* an answer—my chance to speak without words, to tell him everything I'd held inside me. Even when we stopped and I stood breathless in his arms, I did not feel mute.

"Ah, Wyn," he said, his voice a rumble in his chest, "I wasn't sure."

I lifted my head and raised an eyebrow. *Sure of what?*

His arm tightened around my waist. "What was I supposed to do after you ran from me? I couldn't let you go, but I couldn't catch you up in my arms like I wanted."

I silently laughed into his tunic to hear him talk so. Foolish, foolish man.

His hand rubbed my shoulder in wide sweeps, and he whispered, "It wasn't fair of you, my lady Wyn, my heart." He pressed a kiss against my hair, and I heard the smile in his voice. "It wasn't fair. I might have lost my honor."

Chapter 51

The *Ri* left the next day to begin the circuit of the chiefs who ruled beneath him. He wouldn't return for perhaps four moons. Four moons without him urging me for pictures from my life. Four moons without the awareness of him in the room.

Four moons before I could kiss him again.

In five moons, my brothers and I would be free, and they would be ready to return to Lacharra.

For the first time, my heart ached at the thought of traveling back with them.

⁂

I couldn't just set the tunics aside those months. So I took the remaining nettle yarn and dyed it black with the ground shells of green nuts so I could embroider the tunics. Perhaps it was my way of drawing for the *Ri* while he was away. I embroidered each of my brothers' tunics with my dearest memories of them—or my dreams for them:

I embroidered Aiden on a throne, with Lacharra established once again and Carrick nearby, waving his stick.

I embroidered Mael on horseback, his sword held high.

I embroidered Gavyn surrounded by the earth below him and the heavens above—all within reach of his curious hands.

I embroidered Declan with a harp in his lap and songs that poured from him like a river.

I embroidered Cadan on the lake's edge, calling for me. And I embroidered the three swans from the Cynwrig crest flying away. Perhaps I put them there because Cadan was the most contentious of my brothers, and I hoped this prayer for my father would travel farther if it rested on Cadan's tunic.

I embroidered Owain as tall as his brothers and with a beard. My twin *was* different; the change in his body was no smaller than the change toward me.

Every full moon, my brothers asked to see the newly embroidered tunics, exclaiming over each new addition. Once I was sure that my vigil with my brothers was respected by the people in Fianna, I brought Carrick too. Together, we kept watch as the last moons waxed and waned through spring and summer.

All the while, I embroidered the tunics. For years, I'd drawn with dirt and soot. Now, the yarn made each story permanent—hope that could not be erased with a sweep of the hand. Each tunic became a prayer sent into the heavens: *This is what was. Let it be once more. Let me see my brothers again in the sunlight, with my own eyes.*

Chapter 52

Seventy-fourth full moon

On the second to last full moon of the enchantment, I held the lantern close to Gavyn, inspecting his tunic inch by inch.

In a month, my brothers would wear their tunics and never become swans again. I'd brought all the tunics, insisting that they try them on. I wanted to be sure that no tunic was too small or possessed a hidden hole.

It was time-consuming work, and I'd been half-tempted to leave Carrick behind with Ionwyn. But I couldn't bring myself to abandon him when the time came. We expected the tunics would work. We knew they would.

But if they didn't, I wanted to make sure Aiden had every last minute with his son. So Aiden sat with Carrick sleeping in his lap while I completed my work.

Gavyn turned, trying to look behind him.

I smacked his shoulder and pushed him till he stood straight again.

"Keep twisting like that, Gavyn, and you'll be here all night," said Cadan. "Let her finish."

Gavyn remained still, but I could feel the impatience

vibrating through him. "As still as you were? Mael practically had to sit on you."

"My job is to keep you all from growing bored. And I succeeded."

"I inspected my tunic while she was busy with the five of you!" protested Gavyn.

He had, but I needed to see it with my own eyes. Finally, I stepped back and motioned that Gavyn could remove the tunic.

I folded it carefully and set it on the other tunics in the satchel. Cadan rooted through the bag I'd brought their food in.

"Are you sure that's it, Ryn? There's normally more."

I'd left one of the bags at the castle by mistake, but Mael changed the subject before I could sign an answer.

"You're sure the old woman didn't tell you anything else for breaking the curse?" asked Mael.

Any other time, I'd have rolled my eyes, for Mael had repeated this question the last six moons. But I understood his worry. So I shook my head and signed, *Tunics*.

"This is the last night we'll turn back to swans," said Declan.

"We *hope* this is the last night we change," corrected Cadan.

Aiden rested a hand on Carrick's back as he shifted in his sleep. "We'll do as we've planned: Ryn will be waiting for us with the tunics. We'll wear them and wait till the sun rises. We'll know then if the old woman was right. And then, Ryn will take us to this king who's sheltered her."

"If that's what they call it," muttered Mael. He hadn't been able to forget—or forgive—the cuts on my back.

"And then back to Lacharra," said Aiden.

Traveling back to Lacharra should have felt like a sunrise, the first ray of light in six years, but I shrank from it. The *Ri* would return soon, and I ached to see him again, to finally *speak* every word I'd wanted to say to him.

And then there was the Queen.

I'd challenged her three times: in the library, in the Great Hall, and in Roden.

And three times, I'd lost.

My brothers might be ready to face her, but I worried I was not. Hadn't the past already proved as much?

Declan misunderstood my sober expression. "Don't torture yourself, Ryn. The nettles will work. They stopped the Hun—"

Cadan nudged him. None of us could mention the Hunters without thinking of Tanwen.

Gavyn was anxious to change the subject. "I hope you won't find trouble for stealing so much food from these people."

Cadan snorted. "Oh, this is a cheerful gathering, indeed! Perhaps you should ask Ryn if she's been beaten again recently, or—"

"You didn't take the food then?" interrupted Gavyn. "Someone *gave* it to you?"

I nodded slowly.

"They don't mind giving you enough food for six men?" asked Mael.

No. I wished I could tell them that I was safe, truly safe, that I was given food because the *Ri*'s household believed it was how I kept vigil for my dead brothers.

I wished I could tell them how good the *Ri* was. If they could only meet him!

"Who gave it to you?" pressed Gavyn.

I put a hand to my cheek, felt the warmth of my blush.

"Why would you be embarrassed, Ryn?" asked Gavyn. "There's no shame in—"

"Oh-ho!" chortled Cadan. "You can be so stupid for a scholar, Gavyn! It's not that she's *taking* the food. It's who's letting her have it."

Suddenly, I was the center of my brothers' attention.

"Is that so, Ryn?" asked Mael.

Cadan grinned. "He's the cook, I bet."

I slapped his shoulder.

"Not the cook, then. A knight? Do these barbarians even *have* knights?"

I folded my arms.

"Ryn!" said Aiden. He'd have leaped up if Carrick wasn't in his lap. "Is Cadan right?"

"A month isn't soon enough for us to change back, if you ask me," muttered Mael.

I smacked him too.

"So there *is* someone?" asked Owain.

I almost shrugged, then remembered the king's rebuke. He was right. I'd faced the Hunters. I could face my brothers.

So I smiled. Just a little.

"Has he been *respectful*?" demanded Aiden.

I would have laughed if I hadn't been the center of their questioning. I knelt beside Aiden, waited till I had his full attention, and nodded. He raised an eyebrow, still doubtful.

"I still say we kill him. On principle," said Mael.

"Oh, that's rich, coming from *you*," said Cadan. "Though you may have a point. We'll have to see this man for ourselves before we decide." Then he turned to me, eyes full of fun. "So, Ryn. Who is he? This man-who-is-not-a-cook-and-not-a-knight?"

"I don't think the people of Eyre have knights," said Gavyn. "Chiefs, maybe."

"Oh, keep up, Gavyn!" chided Owain.

I scooched to the middle of my brothers and settled there.

Very well, then. We would play. I was grateful for the distraction, anyway.

I held up six fingers.

Cadan rubbed his hands. "You'll let us guess?"

I nodded.

"One for each of us," said Owain.

Yes.

We spent nearly an hour in the game, almost as if we were children again. It was our own way of setting the uncertainty of the future aside for a while. By the time dawn approached, each of my brothers had enjoyed his fill of laughter, and I'd smiled until my cheeks hurt.

Given all that lay ahead, we needed it.

Chapter 53

The wind caught me from behind, tugging my skirt as it swept over my brothers. They shrank into shadows that swept out over the water.

If all went well, they'd never change to swans again.

I collected their abandoned clothes, imagining the moment, while Carrick slept nearby.

Next time, they'd wear the nettle tunics as the sun rose, Aiden with his face set. Declan would smile to keep me from worrying. Owain wouldn't try, because he'd know I was worried anyway.

I scooped up another pair of leggings, folding as I went.

Gavyn would finger the sleeve of his tunic, trying to figure out how nettle yarn would stop his bones from hollowing. Mael would whistle. Cadan would joke about cutting the sleeve off someone's tunic, just to make us smile.

I plucked up the last shirt.

The sun would rise, and there'd be no wind to catch them up, just silence. But we wouldn't trust it at first. Not even they would dare to speak. Then the sun would shine full on their faces for the first time in six years. Owain would laugh. Cadan would shout.

And I would—

"What did I just see?"

I spun on my heel, almost dropping the clothes.

I saw that Ionwyn knew my secret, and all my befuddled mind could think was that I mustn't drop my brothers' clothes.

Ionwyn walked closer, a bag from the kitchen in her hand. "You left this behind and I thought you might need it. So I—" She shook her head. "What happened, Andaryn? *Andaryn*. It's what they called you. *Wyn* was just all that Carrick could say."

I set the clothes down slowly.

Her breath shuddered in and out, and I saw she pressed her lips together to keep the fear from showing.

"Tell me! Don't you dare stare at me like nothing has happened! Six men just turned into swans!" She walked to the shore and looked out at the swans. One of them—Cadan, perhaps?—turned his head to the side and studied her, with a soft three-note honk. Then he flipped his bottom up into the air to hunt breakfast.

Ionwyn looked at me over her shoulder, eyes wide. "I think I need to sit down."

And she did—suddenly, as if she might fall down.

"It's all true, isn't it?" she asked. "You don't believe that your dead take the form of swans. Your brothers were *changed* into swans."

Aiden had asked me not to tell, but perhaps Ionwyn

was supposed to know. She'd sheltered me. She had spun the story of the Children of Lir to keep my brothers safe when she thought they were only swans.

Perhaps I needed someone to walk these last weeks with me.

So I nodded. *Yes. It's true. It's all true.*

I pulled my knees against my chest and sat quietly beside her, giving her the time to consider all she'd seen.

She looked straight out over the water as the swans glided into the shallows on the far side of the lake. My brothers looked majestic when they swam, but not when they hunted for food on the bottom of the lake, tail-feathers swaying like a hand waving.

Finally, Ionwyn looked at me. "How long have they been enchanted?"

I held up five fingers and half-raised another.

"Over five years?"

I held up the sixth finger.

"Almost six years?"

Yes.

She looked back over the water, and I could see her trying to make sense of everything, trying to recall the story I'd drawn so many months ago. "Why the nettle tunics?"

Gavyn would like her direct, logical questions. And Owain would be jealous that she read my face so clearly.

I found a spot of dirt nearby and crouched beside it. Ionwyn joined me.

It took the better part of an hour to try to explain the enchantment: that the Queen had demanded six years of silence . . . that next full moon, those six years would be over . . . that, somehow, the tunics would keep my brothers from changing back to swans.

Ionwyn finally sat back. "And then?"

I drew the Queen—and me and my brothers standing before her. Challenging her. I almost drew a crown on her head so Ionwyn would know that nations were at stake. But I honored Aiden's request. Ionwyn didn't need to know all our secrets.

"She's still alive?"

I nodded.

"And you must stop her."

I thought of what Finn had told me: how the Queen waged war farther and farther afield, tearing other families, other nations apart. We couldn't let her. Even if it meant leaving the haven I'd found here in Fianna.

Yes.

Chapter 54

Three nights before the full moon, neither Carrick nor I could sleep in our small room among the stone houses. Not even Owain-the-hen sleeping on her roost in the corner could calm me. Our lives would change in days, and there was nothing I could do but wait.

So I played with Carrick, who was nearly as restless as I was. After nearly an hour of playing with the carved toys I'd brought from the cave, he hadn't settled a bit.

Enough. We'd walk outside, and if that didn't calm us, we'd slip into the hall and draw pictures in the hearth's soot. I scooped Carrick up and took him out into the cool night.

The night wasn't as quiet as I expected.

I could hear the rumble of a carriage approaching the gates from the road that wound up Castle Hill. The warriors at the gate hailed them, and after a moment, the gates swung open. I bounced Carrick on my hip and pointed to the company riding into the castle.

The nearly full moon had already risen, so Carrick could watch the horses, even from a distance. The riders didn't notice the little man near the wall, and I was happy for it. I knew I was protected by the *Ri*, but I still hadn't forgotten my moonlit beating over a year ago.

Once the travelers had disappeared into the castle, I led Carrick closer to the carriage so that he could see the horses. He'd not seen horses until we came to Fianna, and he was determined to make up for the time lost.

Carrick was already calling ahead to the horses when I saw the livery on the carriage: three slashes of white in the night's darkness.

No.

I crept closer, not believing my eyes.

A flight of three swans.

The Cynwrig crest, here in Fianna.

I tapped Carrick's mouth three times to sign that he should be quiet, even though he hadn't yet made a noise.

My thoughts scattered like a frightened flock of birds.

Had war come so close to Fianna that we were accepting ambassadors from Lacharra?

I stood rooted to the spot. Perhaps the ambassador would recognize me and listen to reason once my brothers were free of their enchantment. Or perhaps he was completely under the Queen's influence and even traveled with her Hunters.

I had to tell Ionwyn.

I waited another minute, giving the visitors from Lacharra a chance to be escorted to their quarters, then slipped into the castle through a smaller entrance. The guards knew me well enough to simply nod as I passed.

Ionwyn's quarters were only two turns away when I saw the candlelight dancing in an adjoining corridor.

Steal just one look at him, I told myself. *You'll be able to plan if you know who the Queen has sent.*

I tapped Carrick's mouth first to remind him to be quiet before I peered around the corner. A delegation of people standing with their backs to me. The ambassador stood straight, but not as straight as the woman beside him, with her moonlight hair braided around her head.

The Queen.

With her Hunters as escorts. I recognized their restlessness, the way they tipped their heads as if searching for a scent.

I backed away. It wasn't fear I felt: it was scalding terror. I almost crumpled under the weight of it. Every nightmare of the last six years stood only strides away—and my brothers were not here beside me.

At that moment, Carrick saw one of the Hunters' swords and called out, waving his toy knight.

I could move again. And move I did, darting around the corner and running down the corridor, praying I'd be fast en—

"Andaryn?"

It was the Queen.

I stopped and turned slowly, my arms tight around Carrick.

Chapter 55

The Queen smiled and stepped closer. "Andaryn! For all my plans, I never thought I'd see you here."

Plans? What plans? Had she ever thought to bring me here?

She smiled at my dismay.

I shuddered.

Her face was the last thing I saw the night Roden burned. In every nightmare where I died, she was looking on.

She lapped up my fear the way a dog drinks water.

I was a woman of nearly eighteen. I'd escaped the Hunters. I'd buried Tanwen. I'd let myself be beaten to force Connach's hand.

Yet I felt like a helpless child when I met her gaze. I pulled Carrick closer.

The Queen laughed and reached out to touch him. I put an arm over his face, and her fingertips brushed my cloak instead.

She yanked her hand back. "Nettles!"

Her pain gave me a moment's courage.

She looked at Carrick, then back at me. "Don't think that cloak will protect you. If you are unkind to me while I am here, you *will* pay."

She didn't try to touch me again, but she circled around me as if looking for weakness. "Your son doesn't wear nettles. You can't hide him forever."

Let her think that Carrick was my son. What would she do if she knew he was Aiden's son? Even if she killed Aiden, or if he remained a swan forever, he had a son and rightful heir of Lacharra.

Still she circled. "Oh, you've grown, Andaryn! You were a girl when you left, and here you are, a woman! With your own son!"

She stepped close to study Carrick, but I covered his face with the cloak. He squirmed, but I tapped his mouth again and he stilled.

The Queen looked at me, head tilted. "You found yourself a man! Or perhaps he found you. Some men prefer women who won't speak, who will just let them do whatever they will."

I shivered. She made everything sound so ugly.

"Was it hard for you? Did you want to tell him to stop? Or did you hope he never would?"

I swung the edge of the cloak at her face. It brushed her cheek, and she shrieked and stumbled back.

"You don't want to talk about it," she said when she'd composed herself.

She watched Carrick but kept talking to me. "I loved the time I carried my son." She inhaled as if pulling a scent she loved. "He anchored me to this earth the way no other person had. Not once did I change. I thought I had finally been given what I wanted!"

Change? Had she been enchanted like my brothers? What would she have changed into?

"I didn't mind the pain of childbirth! How my son delighted me in those early days! And then . . . that first dark night . . . I returned to my old self."

What did she mean? The old self that the woman in the forest had known?

She pressed her lips together. "I learned no man can give you what you desire. Not even the most innocent man-child."

I kept backing away, down the corridor.

She darted forward and put a hand on Carrick's shoulder. Her touch broke whatever reserve the little man possessed. He dug farther into the cloak and wailed, "Wyn! Wyn!"

"No son calls his mother by her given name." The Queen's mouth hung open. "The prince's son! He's your nephew, isn't he?"

I turned and walked away.

"Stop, Andaryn! You *will* stop!"

But I didn't. In that small way, her words had no power over me. She'd send the Hunters after me. I had minutes, if that. And I needed to take Carrick with me.

I fled to Ionwyn's chamber.

"Andaryn!" Ionwyn closed the book she held. "Is Carrick sick?"

I handed her Carrick, trying to think how to tell her.

How could I sign it? I'd never drawn the Queen with her crown.

Finally, in desperation, I pointed a finger as if casting a spell, then mimicked a swan flying away.

Please . . . please!

Ionwyn's face paled. "The woman who enchanted your brothers?"

I nodded and pointed to the ground. *She's here!*

"Did she see you?"

When I nodded, she plucked up her cloak and peered out her door. "We need to go."

I tapped my chest and mimicked pulling on a shirt. I needed the tunics in my room.

Ionwyn nodded, and I followed her down the hall and out into the courtyard, past the carriage with the Cynwrig crest.

Ionwyn lit a candle as soon as we were inside our room in the stone house. I plucked up my satchel and stuffed in a few of Carrick's clothes. Then the tunics and spindle.

I pulled the satchel over my shoulder and motioned that she should give me Carrick.

She traded me Carrick for the satchel. "I'm coming with you two."

She threw the satchel over her shoulder, and the three of us crept out into the dark once more.

"Corbin would want us to use the horses." She pointed to the stables.

I followed her there. She pulled two of the chargers

out of their stalls and threw riding cloths over their backs while I retrieved the bridles and the horse-rods.

Moments later, she led one of the horses near a block so that I could mount while holding Carrick. Then she mounted as I'd seen the *Ri* do—with a quick leap from the ground.

She tapped her horse's flank with the horse-rod, and we were off.

We stopped by the lake first. I handed a whimpering Carrick to Ionwyn before going to the bank. My swan-brothers heard me coming, several raising their heads from under their wings with a sleepy honk.

I went straight to Aiden-swan, wishing it was closer to the full moon. Then I rested both hands where his strong wings joined his body and prayed he could sense the warning in my eyes: *Fly. Fly to the lake by the cave!*

For a moment, I felt something jolt through his body, as if he recognized my urgency. So I signed what my brother would know: *Fly!*

But Aiden-swan, who always pushed so hard against his enchantment, was just a swan again.

Please! I don't want to chase you.

We had so little time before the Hunters came here.

Forgive me.

I stood and quickly found a long branch. Then I struck Aiden-swan. Not so hard that it wounded him, but a sweeping blow along his flank that sent him toppling. He righted himself and turned to face me, wings spread, neck arched—the way he'd meet a predator.

Good, I told myself, ignoring my breaking heart. *Good.*

I swung the branch again, smacking his breast, and he trumpeted. My other swan-brothers woke with curious squawks and honks. Two even recognized me and waddled up to greet me.

I struck them.

And then everything became a blur of moonlight and black wings.

I blinked back the tears and charged my brothers, thwacking Aiden-swan again and again. If he flew away, the others would follow. A few more sweeping blows and the swans retreated to the water. I followed them into the shallows, swinging the branch again and again, until all six took to the sky.

I tossed the branch aside, cheeks wet with tears, then ran back to the horses.

"Where to?" asked Ionwyn.

I was so grateful she knew our story! It took only a minute to sign that I wanted to go back to our old home—the cave by the lake. There were enough nettles there that we might be able to hide there.

She nodded. A moment later, we galloped down the moonlit road.

Hours later, we'd traveled into the forest and reached the beginning of the trail I'd marked. I gathered Carrick close while Ionwyn loosed the horses to find their way back to the castle.

Then we plunged down the trail to the cave.

Chapter 56

Even as we hurried down the trail in the early dark, I knew we wouldn't outrun the Hunters. Fear crept up my legs, into my belly, making it harder and harder to run. We'd hear the whistles first, then the footfalls would grow closer and closer until we heard their breathing as they scented us.

My mind traveled to when they caught Tanwen. I saw her turn to me once again, her fear disappearing as she handed me Carrick.

Protect him!

A Hunter's whistle shattered the memory.

Ionwyn looked over at me, her breath ragged from running, a question in her eyes.

I nodded.

Her eyes widened, but she kept running. I looked around in the moonlight, trying to find my bearings. The nettles before the cave were a good half-league away.

The Hunters might reach us before then.

On I ran, though my breath rasped in my throat. Carrick had never felt so heavy.

Another whistle. Closer this time.

I hated that I wasn't as strong as Tanwen had been when the Hunters had cornered us. She'd been fearless. Then I saw what I hadn't before: Tanwen was frightened—but she dreaded losing Carrick more.

My breath came steadier then, even though my blood danced inside me.

I slowed. Ionwyn wouldn't do this unless I slowed.

Sure enough, when she realized she'd run ahead, she dropped back. "Give me Carrick," she said. "I can carry him for a while."

I nodded, praying my face didn't betray me. Carrick wrapped his chubby arms around her neck when I handed him over. Before Ionwyn could run, I took my nettle-cloak off and threw it over her shoulders.

Understanding dawned in her eyes. "No, Ryn. I won't leave you."

I put a hand on her arm and felt the fear retreat. Was this how Tanwen had felt?

I tied the nettle-cloak around Ionwyn. Then I opened the satchel, revealing the tunics inside. I signed that Ionwyn should follow the trail to the cave and stay there. My fingers brushed something hard, and I pulled out the spindle, still wrapped with nettle yarn.

"I know what the tunics mean to you and your brothers. I'll see that they wear them." She swung the satchel over her shoulder. "You think they'll come to their nests at the old lake after you chased them away, don't you?"

I hope so.

I prayed so.

If Aiden had been able to peer through the swan's eyes just long enough, he'd know where to fly. If not, they might have returned to the lake by Castle Hill. The Hunters might have already slaughtered them.

I swallowed the fear and pressed the spindle to me.

"It's a miserable weapon," said Ionwyn.

I nodded. But it was all I had left, and it seemed right to keep it as the enchantment ended.

I pressed a kiss to Carrick's cheek and pointed down the path. *Run.*

"Ryn . . ."

Another whistle. Ionwyn put a hand over Carrick's head and pressed him into her shoulder.

Run!

She ran.

I let her go until she was out of sight, then I followed at nearly a walk so that the Hunters would catch up to me. When the path branched, I took the side that led away from the caves. *Then* I ran faster, not caring how much noise I made.

More whistles, and I realized that they'd followed me down this branch of the path.

I'd done it.

Carrick and Ionwyn should be free for a little while longer. Perhaps the cloak would hide them from the Hunters all night. The thought gave me courage and I ran on, the spindle clutched in my hand to remind myself that the Queen and her Hunters were vulnerable.

Not that the spindle would stop them. They'd snatch it away as soon as they saw it.

But I wouldn't let them simply have me—or the spindle. As the whistles grew closer behind me, I broke the whorl off the spindle and tossed it aside, never breaking stride. I tucked the remaining part of the spindle down the front of my dress, the nettle yarn over my heart.

It happened just as I thought it would: as the night deepened, the whistles grew closer and closer. Finally, I heard the Hunter's snuffling breath.

I choked back a sob and ran on.

Footsteps behind me—lighter than any human could run.

Only moments now.

I longed to stop, to let myself be caught and end the suspense.

Then I thought of Ionwyn and Carrick. They needed every moment I could give them.

I felt a tingling in my hand as I brushed a plant. Nettles!

I turned and ran into the patch.

I heard the crash of foliage as a Hunter followed me, then an Otherworldly howl funneled through a human throat.

I didn't feel the stings after that as I ran on, pushing nettles out of the way.

The whistles stopped, or were drowned in howls as my pursuers encountered the nettles.

I slowed, giving myself a chance to gather my breath, but I didn't stop. The Hunters still howled their pain.

I could double back to the cave before they recovered, guaranteeing that my swan-brothers would follow me to the lake beside the cave.

It was worth the risk.

Go!

I burst from the nettles and surged forward again. As I ran, the sound of the howls receded into—

A shadow leaped out from the trees.

Chapter 57

The Hunter threw me to the ground, my face in the crumbling leaves beside the trail. I pushed myself to my knees, but a heel between my shoulder blades shoved me down.

"Curse it again and again," the voice growled over me.

More footsteps as other Hunters joined us.

"She is untouchable," said another, more human voice. But it didn't comfort me. I could hear the growls threading their voices. And through it all was the panting, as if they were wolves just finished running.

My breath came in shallow gasps, fear so tight I could barely breathe, the boot on my back pressing my face into the leaves.

I began coughing, inhaling dust and crumbled leaves.

Hands pulled me up, but I remained doubled over, tears streaming down my cheeks as I gasped and coughed.

As soon as I could breathe, the Hunters tied my hands behind me. "March, Princess."

They led me through the forest at a grueling pace, offering no help except to pull me to standing whenever I fell.

At first I looked for nettles, thinking I could dive into them. But the Hunters would not be fooled again and led me clear of the nettle patch I'd run through earlier. A stinging tingle had begun in my hands, though I couldn't be sure whether that was from the nettles or the too-tight binding around my wrists.

A wisp of wind curled around me, and I looked up as if I could follow it out of the forest. The moon was rising. In two more nights, it would be full. The following morning, the six years would be completed.

I shuddered. That meant two days with the Queen.

She'd only needed one to destroy our lives.

I stared at the moon, willing it to grow fuller as I walked. I needed my brothers!

I couldn't face the Queen alone.

What evil would she work this time? I stumbled to a stop, paralyzed.

"Move!" growled a Hunter.

I couldn't. *Breathe . . . breathe.*

A shove from behind. So vicious that I stumbled forward.

Run.

It was as if every prayer I'd sent out into the night had been gathered up—image by image—and this was the reply. It wasn't till the Hunter shoved me again that I understood the command: Run *toward* the Queen.

No. I shook my head. *I can't. I'll fail. I'll fail and they'll all die.*

It's time. Run toward her.

I waited for the fear to break, for my terror to ease. It did not.

Run!

I took one step. The fear didn't break, but it did not grow stronger.

Another step.

Another.

You are that turning point, Ryn. I knew it the moment I saw you. You will turn this story.

And then I was striding toward the castle, walking so fast that the fear couldn't catch me. I looked up at the moon and felt the anger wax inside me.

I'd run from her for six years. I'd taught Carrick to run. And that would have been fine if my own heart hadn't been fleeing. I'd run once more, but this time I would meet the Queen, not flee her.

She would not hurt my brothers or take Carrick.

Chapter 58

The Hunters skirted the edges of Fianna, avoiding anyone who might question them. Even once we were on Castle Hill, I knew there'd be no Finn looming up out of the darkness to stand between me and my captors. Yet somehow, that comforted me. It meant that the Queen needed to hide. And well she should! When the *Ri* returned . . .

Hunters surrounded me entirely once we reached the castle, giving me no chance to attract anyone's attention. They took me to a dark, empty chamber in the guest quarters. I hardly had the strength to care—or to take advantage of the fact that they'd loosened my hands. I'd run far and fast as I led the Hunters away from Ionwyn, and then I'd been marched back.

It was a wonder I could stand.

But I stood straight as a soldier when the Queen walked into the room, followed by—

Father.

I threw myself at him.

My fingers had barely brushed his tunic before I was dragged back.

"Who is this maid?" Father gazed at me pityingly. "Why does she cling to me?"

"She's gone mad, I think," answered the Queen. "Poor child."

"I leave her to you, dearest." Father smiled as he turned to leave. "Perhaps you can save her as you saved me."

I couldn't call out, so I clapped my hands.

Father swung to face me, puzzled.

I gestured toward myself. *Look at me!*

His polite expression faltered, and I thought he might recognize me. Finally, he nodded: not a father, but a king bestowing a benediction.

Then he left.

The Queen waited before speaking, giving fear room to blossom.

"After six long years, Andaryn, have you not learned how futile it is to defy me?" She leaned close. "How dangerous?"

Stand, said the voice inside me. *Just stand.*

So I stood, legs trembling beneath me, and learned that sometimes standing is its own form of courage.

The Queen once again circled me slowly, like a snake throwing coil after coil of its body around me.

"Where is the child?" she asked the nearest Hunter.

"No child," he snarled.

Her gaze flashed to me. But I looked straight ahead, counting the building stones on the wall behind her.

She drew her hand to slap me but stopped. "I swore your life would be sacred, and I will extend that vow even further. I will not touch you until our agreement has been met."

"Strike her," she told one of the Hunters.

He backhanded me.

I stumbled back, fire and fear streaming through me. But it was a release too. I didn't have to wait for the worst to happen anymore. I knew where I stood.

I glared at her as I licked the blood from the corner of my mouth and realized: the Queen was scared. I knew fear—I'd lived with it for years—and I saw it in her face.

I regained my footing and stared at the wall opposite me, mentally tracing the odd shapes of the stones and the mold that mottled it.

Snake-like, the Queen's hand flashed toward me. She didn't strike, oh no. She yanked the chain that held the Kingstone fragment around my neck.

I flailed out, trying to regain it, but she'd already taken it. A half second later, she'd knotted it around her own neck.

The Queen traced a feather-light finger over my shoulder, but I didn't look from the wall. "No more nettle cloak. No Kingstone. And no boy-child."

She spoke a single, harsh word, and the Hunter dropped to his knees, whimpering with pain.

The Queen turned back to me. "How did *you* learn about the nettles? What else did you make from them?"

I didn't answer.

"Miserable old woman! My only regret is that she was dead before we found her. What did she tell you?"

Finally, I looked at the Queen.

I slowly brought a finger to my lips, the lips she'd closed six years ago. *Shhh.*

The Queen reared back, livid, and grabbed the cloak of the nearest Hunter. "Find the child! Kill anyone who shelters him, and bring him to me." She slanted a glance at me. "You are not required to bring *all* of him to me—but he must be alive."

I dove at her, slapping her face with all the strength I could muster. She fell against the wall, and I rushed forward to strike her again.

The Hunters held me back, and the Queen raised her hand to—

The door was flung open. Finn strode through it, followed by the *Ri.*

He slowly took in the scene before him: the Queen with my handprint on her cheek; me held back by two Hunters, blood on my lip. I'd spent the night running for my life through the forest, through nettles. I must have looked as wild as I had when I first rushed out of the forest.

I waited for him to set everything right.

Instead, the *Ri* stared at the Queen, pain so plain on his face that I thought he'd been wounded, even though there was no blood on his tunic.

And the Queen? Something washed across her face: longing and . . . love?

"Son," she whispered.

No. It couldn't be.

But the *Ri* didn't tell her to take back the lie. His face

paled, and I realized there *had* been a wound. It was just that the blood didn't show.

The Queen was his mother, banished from Fianna after killing her lover. And the golden-haired king who took the Queen from the old woman's cottage?

That was Corbin's father.

Finally, the *Ri* looked at me. I let him see my fear, tried to show that the Queen—his *mother*—was the one I'd been fleeing all along. I needed him to ask why my lip was swollen and my clothes were torn, but his gaze was closed to me. Vacant.

Father had looked that way when he returned from the forest.

The *Ri* opened his arms to the Queen. "Mother! What happened here?"

It would've hurt less if he'd struck me. I sagged against the Hunters who held me.

"Keep her away from me!" The Queen clung to him. "Do you see what she's done?"

Finn didn't believe a word. Hadn't he told me he'd learned long ago not to listen to her? He watched me instead, as if he could see all that had happened in my face.

I prayed he could.

"I know this girl," continued the Queen. "I met her in the forest years ago. Her name is Ryn or something equally ridiculous."

Finn muttered a curse under his breath. Even the *Ri* seemed surprised, though he didn't speak, as if he too had given his tongue to the Queen.

"She had a baby with her. I think she'd stolen it from some poor peasant, for it wasn't hers."

When the *Ri* didn't speak, Finn did. "That child is the *Ri*'s ward."

The Queen looked horrified. "I saw her steal him away tonight and sent my guard to bring them back! They returned with her alone. When I questioned her about the boy, she struck me!"

And still the *Ri* didn't answer.

"There were men who walked with her, sometimes. I fear she's taken your ward to them." Her voice faltered in the *Ri*'s silence.

Perhaps he *hadn't* lost himself to her. Perhaps his silence only masked his fury.

The Queen's eyes filled with tears, and she looked up at her son. *Her son!* My skin crawled at the thought. "Have I displeased you? I thought only of the boy."

"How many?"

"What?" asked the Queen.

"How many men walked with her?" The *Ri*'s voice cracked under some great strain.

The Queen smiled to hear the jealousy in his voice. "Six men. If my guards find them as they search for the child, they'll see to them."

"You sent your own men out to hunt them?"

Hunt. Perhaps he was not under her power yet.

"To *rescue* the child who is your ward."

The *Ri* nodded slowly, as if absorbing the news. "Where is Ionwyn?"

Finn didn't take his eyes off the Hunters, his hand resting on his sword hilt. "No sign of her, my *Ri*."

The *Ri* didn't blink.

Think! I wanted to shout. *You know there's a reason Ionwyn isn't here. You said your mother was heartless—why do you trust her now?*

But I'd seen my father. I knew why the *Ri* trusted his mother.

"You're sure the girl walked with six men?" He spoke thickly, as if half-asleep.

"Yes. Six. But I do not believe she lay with *all* of them."

I lurched forward to give her other cheek a matching slap, but the Hunters kept me pinned between them.

The *Ri* turned away from his mother and stood before me.

I turned my head away. How could he lose himself to her so quickly?

"Listen to me." Something bright as fire threaded his voice.

I looked back, startled. His gaze was as real as touch, asking me to understand. "Lady Ryn, I cannot shelter you."

This wasn't how I'd hoped it would be: the first time the *Ri* spoke my name, to tell me he'd leave me under the Queen's power.

I cannot shelter you.

Then the memory of the trial rolled over me. Once more, I felt flagstones under my knees, the weight of my braid pulled over my shoulder. Saw the *Ri*'s face as he knelt and warned me, *If you challenge him to this, I cannot shelter you.*

And I heard, just as clearly, what he dared not speak with the Queen so near: *I will support you, even in this.*

Even if it looked like he was leaving me.

"Do you understand me?"

I nodded.

One last look, asking if I could meet what was before me.

I can. I will.

He pressed his lips together and turned to his mother. "I'll see to the search for Carrick myself. Ryn will remain in the dungeon until I return tomorrow."

The Queen melted with relief. "I will send some of my own men to ride with you. How wise of you to understand so quickly, son! You are like your father."

The *Ri* flinched but covered it with a half-smile.

"High praise indeed." He nodded to Finn. "Bring Ryn. I'll imprison her myself. And then, we'll set my house in order."

Chapter 59

The *Ri* himself put stone walls and an iron door between me and the Queen before he left that morning.

I stood in the middle of the dim cell, my unsteady breath echoing off the walls. I was filthy from my flight through the forest, but the floor of the cell was worse: stinking and slick with something I dared not touch.

I walked to the cell door and pressed my hands flat against it. The *Ri* would be back in a day. He'd promised. He'd find Ionwyn and Carrick and the tunics at the cave—surely he'd know to search there!—and Ionwyn would be able to explain everything.

It will only be a day.

And all I could do was wait. I had some hope, though. Perhaps my swan-brothers had reached the old lake. I knew if the Hunters had found them at the lake near the castle, the Queen would have delighted to show me their bodies.

I shuddered.

What I'd have given to tell my story! Instead, I'd stood mute before the Queen while she talked about hunting those I loved most.

I turned back to the cell, with the weak light slanting through the tiny window.

I'd tell my story anyway. I'd tell it here: a prayer for those I loved and a defiance to the Queen. Whoever came tomorrow would see my story in this cell.

I twisted my skirt and tucked it into my belt so that it wouldn't drag in the muck. Then I crouched and reached a finger to the floor. I recoiled from the slime at first, but the story inside me was stronger. It was my way of fighting.

I drew a girl in a library with a book in her lap.

I drew a woman made of iron and ice with a voice that reached, like smoke, into the king's heart and mind.

Then the girl again, with her voice pulled from her like a snail from its shell, while six swans took to the air around her.

I drew the wind that turned the swans to men and back to swans again.

I drew Tanwen, fire and voice in the dark of the enchantment, and her final victory over the Hunters.

I drew the swans towing the girl and a babe across the sea, their three-note trumpets streaming in the wind behind them.

I drew the *Ri*, who opened his home to the girl and her boy, whose words in the great hall helped her stand before Connach. I traced one of the *Ri*'s knots around him and the girl, turning over and over itself so that even I couldn't tell where one began and the other ended.

And finally I drew a lake with six men standing beside it.

I stretched out my finger to draw the sun above the

horizon, its light streaming over the men for the first time in years.

But I couldn't draw it. Not yet. I couldn't tell whether it was cowardice or wisdom.

I looked over the pictures and saw that for the first time, I'd drawn sound and voice: the Queen's, the voice I'd lost, Tanwen's, even the swans'—their voices like banners in the pictures.

The Queen. My brothers. Even the swan-children of Lir in Ionwyn's story had voices.

Enchanted voices. Otherworldly songs. And the Queen at the center of it.

I felt like I stood on the threshold of a great secret, but I didn't know how to step across.

I looked up at the window. The light was failing toward evening already. I'd spent hours over my picture-prayers. I remembered the certainty of the night before—that it was time to run toward the Queen.

Before the last of the light faded, I drew the sun shining down over my six brothers, standing as men.

Sometime that night, I fell asleep.

I awoke to a scratching at the door, then the shriek of metal scraping against metal. I pressed myself back against the wall, hoping that it was the *Ri* himself, back like he'd promised.

Let them be safe. Let them be alive.

But it was not a Hunter come to fetch me. Or the *Ri* come to free me.

It was Father.

Chapter 60

I stood slowly, not trusting my eyes. Had the Queen sent him to break my heart again?

"I don't wish to alarm you, child," Father said, standing in the open doorway. "But your face reminds me of something. Though I don't know what it is."

I looked down, saw the patch of light cast by the window, and stepped slowly into it, trying to smooth my hair into something that would remind him of the daughter he'd banished so long ago.

He stepped closer, unable to look away. "She said I was being foolish, my wife, but I don't think I am. It's just that sometimes, I can't think clearly and she feels she must make sure I'm not taken advantage of." He smiled. "There are so many who would abuse their favor with the king, you know."

I nodded. *Yes, I know.*

Another step closer, and I lowered my gaze, afraid even that would frighten him.

"Perhaps it is that you remind me of someone," he said.

I smiled then, to keep from crying.

"There!" he exclaimed. "There it is! Your smile. It reminds me of my first wife, my first love . . ."

He remembered Mother?

He shook his head. "It was very long ago, but she smiled like you. Perhaps that is what I saw earlier."

He looked around the dark cell, noticing it for the first time. "What have you done, child, that she sent you here? She is merciful. I know this from my own life, how she saved me from, from—"

Your sons and daughter? Your throne? Your sanity?

He shook his head, as if trying to remember. "No matter."

I looked down at the untouched muck illuminated in a square of light, the previous day's drawing hidden in shadow. I thought of sunlight streaming through the library windows so many summers ago. I thought of the sound of Father's voice as he read to me from *The Annals of Lacharra.*

And for a moment, I smelled cloves.

There are spaces between heartbeats and breaths. Between the smallest moments of time. Sometimes, you can step into those spaces and live there for a little while.

Just long enough.

I touched Father's shoulder so that he would pay attention and slowly knelt beside the patch of light.

I remembered the scent of cloves and the scent of books and the way the east wind made the library fireplace smell of smoke in the winter. I thought of the Cynwrig crest above the alcove where Father read.

And in the muck on the floor of the cell, I drew three swans, wings unfurled.

I drew the broken chains around their necks.

I drew the flight of swans as if they'd spring up from the muck and find freedom once again.

Father crouched to see the swans better and reached a finger toward them. Then he whispered:

And so, a game of swans, bearing swords, flew up from the south.

The House of Cynwrig settled among the lakes of the north and all the lands in between, establishing their fortress at Roden.

Every prayer I'd ever drawn or sent out into the night was answered as Father recited from *The Annals of Lacharra.*

"It's from a very old book, you see. A favorite of mine, though I'd forgotten that too," he murmured. "Perhaps you wouldn't have liked it, but—"

He looked up at me—and what I saw filled the empty spaces between years of heartbreak.

"Andaryn?"

If I could only talk to Father about home and the library and Lacharra, the enchantment would fall from him—but I couldn't answer him!

So I nodded and smiled up at him.

"You have your *mother's* smile."

I nodded again, then glanced behind him to the open cell door. I wanted to dash from this place with Father, but

I knew I'd lose him if he met the Queen again. He was returning, but not fully. He still didn't seem to notice that I was mute.

So I pointed to the swans, asking him to tell me more.

And he did.

He told me how the Cynwrig brothers fled, but the King of Brisson followed, determined to kill the entire house for denying him their sister. His voice grew strong, and I was in the castle library again, the scent of books and cloves more real than the dark and slime that surrounded me.

The flight of swans, bearing swords, met the King of Brisson and his allies in combat.

And all the while, I watched Father's face as he slowly returned. His hair was as dark as it had ever been. I'd expected the lines around his eyes and mouth to be deeper, but he looked younger than I remembered. It reminded me of the Queen, as if somehow his soul had aged rather than his body. But I pushed the fear aside and held my father's gaze as he spoke on.

Father's voice grew stronger as the patch of daylight grew brighter. I watched him and the door behind him as hope rose inside me—until Father's voice faltered.

I glanced at the partially opened door behind him, expecting to see the Queen or one of her Hunters behind him, but there was no one. But Father wasn't looking out the door. He stared at me.

"What's happened to you, Andaryn? Why are you *here*? Why can't you speak?"

Father looked around at the cell, truly seeing it for the first time.

Seeing *me* for the first time.

He raised a hand to his face. "What's happened to *me*?"

I wanted to hug him but didn't dare—I was covered in filth. But he caught me up anyway and pressed me close.

It was better than sunlight. Better than speech.

"I haven't been myself these past few weeks," he whispered against my hair, just as he used to when I was a girl. Then he released me and studied my face, slowly shaking his head. "No. Not weeks. It's been years, hasn't it? How many years has it been?"

I held up six fingers, and his face crumpled in shame and disgust. But he mastered it quickly. "Now is not the time to grieve it. It is time for me to make it right. And I will, Rynni. I—"

The door screeched behind him.

The sound of a hiss.

Father gasped and a moment later, the tip of an obsidian blade protruded from his chest.

Father's eyes widened, and his hands lifted to the sword as if touching it would make it go away. I saw the Hunter behind Father, eyes wide with bloodlust, and caught Father by the shoulders.

The Hunter yanked his blade from Father, and all that was left was blood.

Father fell back into the cell and tried to pull himself up on one of his elbows. The Hunter stood in the doorway, the evil blade still in his hand. I launched myself at him, clawing and kicking. He stumbled back, flung the blade to the floor, and fled.

The blade shattered, sending sparks into the dim.

I knelt beside Father. Blood already covered his tunic.

So much blood.

I put my hands over the gash in his chest, wishing I could push the life back into him. But still it spilled out, a warm pool spreading beneath him.

All the while, Father looked up at me, his breath catching and burbling in the back of his throat.

I wanted to wail. I wanted to scream.

But his hand came up and caught mine as he tried to speak.

I leaned closer.

"—love you."

I felt the life streaming from him, saw the lines the years *had* cut into his face, and I couldn't stop crying, great silent sobs, and tears so thick I could hardly see him.

Then I felt his hand on my cheek, and I cupped his hand with my own.

"You . . ." Father's breath rattled in his chest. ". . . will finish what . . . could not. Don't—" He closed his eyes, and I thought I'd lost him. ". . . give her any—thing. Don't . . . say . . . *yes*."

I kept nodding against his hand just to keep him close, keep him with me.

"Andaryn."

The last word my father spoke to me was my name.

Chapter 61

My whole body shook as if my sobs had settled in my bones.

I wanted to lie down beside Father and wait for the Hunters to kill me too. I wanted to close my eyes and believe that when I opened them again, I'd see sunlight and smell cloves.

I wanted the past six years to be only the nightmare I woke from.

But there were my brothers. And Carrick. And Ionwyn.

I couldn't die. Not before the six years were over.

I wiped my eyes and picked up the shattered obsidian sword, my hands slipping on the blood-slicked hilt. There was enough blade left to cut someone, enough weapon to help me fight my way out.

I lived between moments one last time, every detail knife-sharp and shining: the one spot of blood I couldn't wipe from the blade handle, the strands of gray in Father's beard as I bent to kiss his forehead, the way the stone wall bit into my palm as I pulled myself to standing.

I pulled in a breath once, twice, while time stood still around me.

It was time to find my brothers.

I'd walked ten strides when I heard shouts from rough throats—Hunters.

But they weren't hunting me. They were raising an alarm. "Murder! Assassin!"

And then time flowed too fast, seconds streaming past like water pouring over a cliff, beating me senseless beneath it. I tried to run, but I was too slow.

The *Ri*'s warriors found me. They saw my open cell door and my father lying dead over the threshold. They saw his blood on my skirt and smeared on my hands.

I tried to fight, but the Hunters and the *Ri*'s warriors were too strong, and I was still shaking.

And still time poured on, and above it all rang the Queen's wails: the piercing keening of a woman whose heart could never break.

I was thrown back into my cell. I trembled so much, I could hardly move. I slid down the wall, felt the rough stone of the wall dig into my shoulder blades.

Father was dead . . . Father was dead . . . Father was dead . . .

My brothers were scattered.

And the *Ri* had not come.

I was alone.

Chapter 62

Two Hunters pulled me from the cell as the light was fading. I was taken back to the small room, where the Queen waited for me.

I looked for any sign of Ionwyn or Carrick.

"She is a small thing," said the Queen, "but she stands too tall for my taste."

I hadn't eaten for nearly two days and could hardly stand. Grief had numbed me. But at the Queen's words, something sprang to life inside me: I was also the princess of Lacharra. I would not dishonor my dead father.

I straightened as if I wore a crown.

"Make her kneel," commanded the Queen.

One of the Hunters swept a foot against the back of my knees, and I dropped to the floor. Hands fell on my shoulders and pressed me there.

I couldn't rise, but I did not bow my head.

"The chiefs of Fianna know that you killed the king of Lacharra: an act of war against a peaceful kingdom. I could demand your death as payment."

Did she want me to beg? To speak?

She couldn't kill me until the six years were over. As long as Ionwyn and Carrick were safe, the Queen couldn't make me do anything.

I would not speak and kill my brothers.

"You must think I want you to break your vow, Andaryn," said the Queen. "But I am not so cruel as to ask that of you! I have a simple request: I ask one more year of silence."

The unexpectedness of it was more confusing than a threat.

"Ah. You've misunderstood me, poor child. I've not brought you here to hurt you. I ask so little. So very little. You see that now, don't you?"

Her voice was so sweet, so gentle that I wanted to beg her forgiveness for doubting her.

Look at her!

I looked once more, saw her pale face that was too young and too smooth for such old eyes. My senses returned, and I remembered what Father had said: *Don't say yes.* So I filled my mind with my own words, the things I would say the moment I could speak.

"Will you give me one more year of silence, Andaryn?"

No.

I knew somehow that words were important to the Queen. I'd given her my speech once. I would not do that again. She couldn't compel me.

The Queen held out her gloved hand—why was it gloved?—and one of the Hunters beside her put something in it.

My satchel.

It couldn't be. Ionwyn wouldn't have dropped it, unless . . . had they captured her too?

"You don't think it is yours?" The Queen stepped into the light. And I saw that it *was* mine. "Ah. Now you recognize it."

She opened it and tugged out Cadan's nettle tunic. Hadn't I sewn the picture of the swans onto it?

NO!

I lunged at her to take it back, but the Hunters made me kneel, their hands digging into my shoulders.

How had she gotten the tunics? What had happened to Ionwyn and Carrick? My brothers?

Where was the *Ri*?

The Queen laughed. "Perhaps now you will reconsider my offer. I ask for your silence—a year, only a year!—for these tunics."

Tonight was the full moon. My brothers would become swans again without the tunics. There'd be no one to challenge the Queen.

Don't say yes.

There would be no one to challenge her—except me.

I shook my head.

"Choose wisely, sweet Andaryn." Anger edged her voice. "I *will* burn them."

She reached a gloved hand to me until her finger touched my head. I resisted, but she pushed my head down until I bowed my head, my entire body bent so that the hidden spindle dug into my side.

"You stand accused of the murder of the king of Lacharra. I could demand your blood. And I will." She leaned close, whispering. "It will be just like this tomorrow: you kneeling, head bowed. Except there will be a Hunter with a sword. And when the sun rises tomorrow and your vow of silence is completed, he will take your head."

I tried to look up, but I couldn't. There was an Otherworldly strength about her. Fear filled me, as if she was pouring it into my skull.

"You will not speak the day your vow is fulfilled, Andaryn. You *will* remain silent, either by choice"—she chuckled—"or by death."

Why had I believed that I could meet her, strength for strength, and not endanger those I loved?

I stopped struggling, and she lifted her finger from my head. When I looked up, I saw the satchel of tunics in her hand.

Those I loved would suffer anyway.

I would not give her what she wanted. It was Father's request, and I half-believed that if I refused, her power might be broken. I might see it shatter, here in this room, if I denied her what she most wanted.

And for a moment, I thought she *would* shatter. Her fine voice cracked, as if she were given only so many words and was running out. "Will you promise me a year of silence, Andaryn? I would not be so cruel as to demand that you speak your answer. A nod will suffice."

I shook my head.

The Queen did not shatter. And she did not falter.

She motioned to one of the Hunters, who plucked a torch from the wall and held it at waist level. With one motion, the Queen held my satchel over the torch. The sleeve of Cadan's tunic—still dangling out of the satchel—caught fire first.

I fought the Hunters, but they held me back, no matter how I struggled. And as my satchel burned, they dragged me back to my cell.

Chapter 63

Seventy-fifth and final full moon

Even in my cell, the stench of the nettle-smoke stung my nostrils and clung to my clothes.

She'd burned them. Six years of work turned to ash just hours before my brothers needed it.

The Queen had to be stopped.

My brothers would wish it, as long as Carrick was safe—and I *had* to believe that he was. She would've murdered him in front of my eyes if she thought I'd give her what she wanted.

For some reason, she wanted my silence.

It was time to speak, then. In what little time I had left between sunrise and my death.

But I would not just let her have me—or them.

I pulled the spindle from my bodice, studying it in the moonlight that filtered into the cell. It would never spin nettle fiber again after I'd wrenched the whorl off it. I gripped it, wondering if I had the courage or the strength to stab her with it. But I could hear Cadan's laugh in my head. *You'll have to do better than that!*

I looked back down at the spindle, with the small swell

of nettle yarn wrapped around it. Hadn't she worn gloves just to touch the tunics?

The nettle yarn was such a small thing compared to the tunics, but I'd use it.

I sat in the corner, cross-legged so I could rest the yarn in my lap. I set a loop in the yarn, put it on the thumb of my left hand, and continued to twist and knot.

I made three arms' length of cord before I unwound the last swath of yarn. It was the first time the spindle had been empty of yarn. Such a plain piece of wood!

For a moment, I imagined breaking free of my captors and binding the Queen with the cord, but that was as unlikely as stabbing her with the spindle. The spindle itself could have no power. I ran my fingers over it.

The old woman had carved something into the spindle. Poor, mad woman! A spindle should be smooth, with no rough edges that might catch the yarn.

She'd not even bothered to sand down what she'd engraved.

You can't have those years back. You can't speak the word that I should have said. But have the tunics ready.

She couldn't have meant there was actually a word that could be spoken that would stop the Queen.

What *had* she engraved?

I wrapped the cord I'd braided around my hand and scrambled to my feet. I took the spindle to the window and read the word in the dim light.

diladh

It looked like the old tongue, the one Declan claimed

was spoken when people still moved freely between here and the Otherworld.

I stared at the word, wishing I knew its meaning.

But I could read it. I could *speak* it, if I was given time.

Tanwen had dreamed that a word would send the Hunters back to the Otherworld. And whatever she had spoken had been enough to do just that. But they'd been pulled here by the Queen's call.

What could a word do against the Queen? She hadn't been called to this world—she was already part of it. The old woman had given her many things, true, but she hadn't called the Queen here.

Then I heard the Queen's voice as she mourned changing that first dark night after Corbin had been born.

Changing again.

I held the thought inside me, let it grow till I could see it fully. So much of her power involved change: Otherworldly hounds into Hunters, my brothers into swans.

What if the Queen, too, had changed?

The old woman had given the Queen feet. *Human* feet.

She hadn't always been human.

I curled my fingers around the spindle, pressed it to my lips. Was this what the old woman had done? Worked the Queen's destruction so that someone else could accomplish it?

Would a word be enough? It was such a small thing.

Small as the cloves that reminded Father of how he'd loved me. Small as the Kingstone fragment that reminded the Queen that we would always oppose her.

A word couldn't send the Queen away, but perhaps it could undo all the old woman had given her.

And that would be enough.

Somehow, I'd speak the word—the one small word—that would defeat the Queen.

I stood beneath the window until the light faded, tracing the word with my fingertip, until I'd memorized it. Even if I never saw it again, I'd be able to speak it.

When the full moon rose, I sat in the corner, praying my brothers would forgive me for losing the tunics. And I planned how to remove the Queen from our lives.

I was sitting in the same corner when the Hunters came for me, nearly an hour till dawn. They took me from the castle, down the hill, to the lake where my swan-brothers had nested.

When I saw the Queen, in the pre-dawn light, I didn't flinch. Instead, I rehearsed the path before me. I could not afford a mistake.

"Your brothers did not return to the lake last night, as swans or men. Nor have the Hunters I sent after them." She pulled a breath deep inside as if inhaling perfume. "I expect that my son and the Hunters will return with the carcasses of six black swans."

I didn't move. There was nothing I could do except hope the old woman's madness had not led me astray.

"Will you not reconsider?" asked the Queen. "I will be merciful if you choose to be silent for one more year."

No.

I wouldn't betray my brothers if they were alive. And if

they were dead, I would join them. I'd speak the word the moment before the sword dropped.

"Bring her to the water's edge," said the Queen. "It's a powerful place, where land and water mingle. Two worlds flowing over each other."

The Hunters pulled me so close to the lake that my feet sank into mud.

"Good," said the Queen. "If the swans *are* here, they will come."

We stood there, while the sky brightened around us.

Finally, the Queen asked once more. "Will you vow silence, Andaryn?"

I straightened, willing my shaking to still. I wanted to look her in the face one last time. I wanted her to know that I would accomplish what I couldn't six years ago in Roden's dungeon: I would not give her what she desired.

I feared her, but I wouldn't let it overtake me. I wanted her to see it, to remember *that*.

And she did see it.

"Make her kneel."

The Hunters did.

"Make her bow."

They did, sweeping my braid off my back so that my neck was exposed. I could feel the morning's cold.

I wouldn't have time to speak my brothers' names before the sword fell, so I recited them in my head, holding them to me like treasure.

"It's nearly time," breathed the Queen.

I heard the dull rasp of a sword being drawn.

The light intensified, though trees hid the horizon from view.

I heard the whisper of the sword being raised.

There was time, still. I could feel that the sun hadn't yet risen.

Hands pushed me down so that I couldn't lift my head.

But I didn't intend to.

Move with the attacker, not against him, whispered Mael, and I was glad to have him with me at the end.

Now!

I dove forward, as if to somersault, my forehead to my knees. The Hunters' hands fell away, and the edge of the sword scraped my shoulder blade.

"Stop! Wait for my word!"

Red-edged pain clouded my vision, but I rolled away and stood. One of the Hunters pulled me to him.

I let him yank me close, and lifted my arms like I wanted to embrace him. And when I was close enough, I dropped a nettle-cord collar around his neck.

The Hunter howled and fell back, releasing me.

He writhed as he changed to a hound: his true Otherworld form. My stomach roiled to see the white beast with crimson ears. And while the hound tore at the collar around his neck, another Hunter caught my wrist.

I spun closer to him, plucked a nettle collar from the front of my dress, and wrapped it around his neck.

He, too, fell away.

"Take aim!" commanded the Queen, and one of the Hunters nocked an arrow to his bow and leveled it at me.

Before he could release it, the Queen stopped him with a hand on the arrow.

She wasn't sure if she could kill me yet.

Run. Run toward her.

I ran. I should have dropped the last nettle collar over the Hunter's neck, but I wrapped it over my right fist, once, twice, three times, till it was tight as a mitten.

The Hunter kept the arrow level. The Queen kept her hand on the arrow and her eyes on the sunrise, waiting for the light that would release both of us from our vows.

"Not a word, Andaryn, my dear," she called as I neared, "or your brothers die!"

I didn't even break stride. My nettle-covered fist caught her on the temple.

She was weaker than I expected. Perhaps it was the nettles. Perhaps it was my fury. She stumbled back, and I struck her again, then spun to face the Hunter with the arrow.

With two arrows. One was buried in his chest.

I looked at the far end of the clearing. Finn reached behind him and nocked another arrow. The *Ri* broke from the forest behind him, sword drawn, running toward us.

My brothers were not with him.

I gathered up my grief, used its strength for what lay ahead.

I tugged the nettle cord from my fist and threw it on the Queen, who shrieked as if it burned her.

Another glance at the horizon. Not yet! But there was someone else who could speak—

I ran to Finn, pulling the spindle from the front of my dress as I went.

"Lady Ryn!"

I caught him by his tunic and pressed the spindle into his hand, pointing to the writing. He looked down, trying to make sense of it, of me.

I pointed again. *Read it, read it!*

I heard the Queen approaching, and still Finn didn't speak.

READ IT! I jabbed my finger at the writing.

The *Ri*'s hand plucked the spindle from me.

"Son!" called the Queen.

He stilled, and dread settled in my belly. He said he'd come. He said he'd save my brothers. Had she won him over after all?

"Do you see what she's done? Let me have it." Her voice was a caress, full of warmth I was certain the *Ri* had never felt from her as a child. "Give it to me."

She extended a slender white hand.

He locked eyes with her.

And he extended the spindle to *me*, just as I felt the sun finally rise.

I didn't touch it, didn't even look down. I simply spoke the word the old woman had carved into the spindle. "*Diladh*!"

Silence as deep as the ocean engulfed us.

Then a flash of light—a thousand sunrises all at once. I turned to it, wincing at the blaze.

The Queen had fallen to her knees, hands raised to protect herself. A line of dark threaded the brilliance at the far end of the clearing and widened, like a curtain being pulled apart. The Queen scurried away from it, crablike, as a silhouette appeared in the light.

A woman so magnificent that the Queen seemed a silly sham. She spoke a single word, and the Hunter-hounds dashed into the brightness and disappeared.

I knew her.

The Lady Rhiannon. Her face and dress were nothing like the tapestry that had been pulled from Mother's chambers. But the queenliness was the same.

And so were the two birds with mother-of-pearl feathers perched on her shoulders. Their song seemed as close as thought and as distant as the stars all at once.

The *adar Rhiannon*. The three Otherworld birds that sang whatever songs the Lady Rhiannon requested.

Until one bird had tired of singing her mistress's bidding.

The Queen had fled to this side of the Veil, where she'd sat by the nettles and sung for the old woman. Sung with all the power she'd been endowed with until the woman had given her human form and speech.

The Queen screamed, but there were no words in it.

Lady Rhiannon extended her hand to the Queen.

It was not a request.

One final scream, dwindling to a screech. A mist gathered around the Queen, shadows given form, hiding her from us. Then a flash of ivory. Mother-of-pearl wings spread wider than a man could reach and caught the air. It was the bird that sang outside my window so many years ago.

The Kingstone dropped to the bank the moment she changed—the moment there was no longer a human form to wear it.

The bird shrieked and circled, trying to escape but unable to fly away from the Lady.

Finally, she flew to the figure who stood in the rift.

When the white bird touched her Lady's hand, both disappeared. The rift closed. The light dimmed.

The Queen had returned to the Otherworld. To her Before.

Chapter 64

I was free for the first time in six years, but I greeted the dawn alone. The tunics had burned—my brothers would not stand as men in the morning sunlight.

I gathered up the deserted Kingstone fragment with trembling hands and slipped it over my head. It was a hollow victory to wear it again without my brothers beside me.

I turned to the *Ri*, who stared at where the rift had closed, like a man stunned. Of course he was stunned. He'd seen his witch-mother in her true form, and I'd been the one who sent her back to the Otherworld.

But my brothers!

I ran to the *Ri*, motioning to the empty lake. *Where are they? Where's Carrick?*

"We didn't go to the cave immediately, Lady Ryn. We couldn't afford to lead my mother's men there. Finn and I led them from it and then disposed of them well away from Ionwyn and Carrick. We didn't reach the cave till after dark. Your brothers fought valiantly against the other soldiers who were already there, but—"

I saw the grief on the *Ri*'s face.

I didn't want to hear the end. I rushed to the lake and waded into the shallows, the mist curling around me. I slapped the water, calling them as I had so many times.

No answering trumpet. No sound of wings.

Nothing.

I almost shouted for them but stopped. I didn't want to speak if my brothers weren't there. Perhaps that was a good thing. There were some stories that should never be told.

"Lady Ryn." The *Ri* took me by the elbow, tugging me back from the water.

I pulled my arm free and waded farther into the lake. I'd let him tell me all that had happened soon. But I couldn't hear it now. I needed to stand in the water, skirts billowing around me, till I was sure my brothers wouldn't return.

"Lady Ryn!" He caught me again.

I pressed farther into the water. If I looked at the *Ri*, I might cry and never stop.

"Ryn!" a voice shouted.

I didn't believe my ears at first, but I stopped, the water past my knees.

"Rynni!"

I swung to face the sound.

Aiden stepped into the clearing. He wore a nettle tunic.

No. I gulped in a shuddering breath. *No, it couldn't be him.*

I looked back over the lake and saw that the sun had truly risen, the horizon a wave of light behind the trees.

"Ryn," said the Aiden-ghost, "we're here."

I heard the *Ri* shouting something about it being over as I dashed from the shallows.

I didn't care.

Only a fool would walk toward the Queen's enchantment, but I did. The man looked so like Aiden, and the others who stepped from the trees looked like my brothers. But they couldn't be.

They couldn't. She'd burned the tunics.

Aiden-ghost stopped in front of me, chest rising and falling as rapidly as my own. But he just stood there and let me look up at him.

Brown eyes. Carrick's eyes. He seemed taller in the dawn, my forehead only reaching his shoulder.

I touched the tangle of stitches on the right cuff of his tunic. I hadn't had time to rip the rows out and make them straight, for it was the first tunic I'd made. I'd simply finished the sleeve, working a few extra stitches into the gap so that Aiden wouldn't be left with feathers on his arm.

I stepped back, hand pressed to my forehead. *I saw the tunics burn!*

I closed my eyes, trying to remember. *No. I saw Cadan's tunic burn.* Had the Queen only found Cadan's and used that to threaten me? I opened my eyes, looking behind Aiden at the figures emerging from the trees.

No. Please, not Cadan—

He, too, stepped from the trees.

"Ryn? Ryn!" he shouted and ran up to me. "Didn't I promise I'd always call for you?"

I watched him approach, shaking my head. When he stopped in front of me, I gripped his tunic in both hands. *I saw it burn!*

"Ah," he said and smiled down at me. "The Queen showed you mine, did she?" He nodded to the trees, to Ionwyn and Carrick. "Ionwyn—now there's a fine woman!—dropped the satchel in the last desperate run to the cave. She discovered later that she had gathered up all the tunics but mine. No time to snatch it up before the Hunters reached it. It's a good thing she had your nettle cape, isn't it?"

I looked closer at his tunic. It had no embroidery and was cut, the sides joined in a rough seam. One of the sleeves fell down over his hand, and he shook it back, pushing it farther up his arm. He winked. "I think she was worried she'd cut the sleeves too short and I'd be left with half a wing—"

But I didn't believe my eyes. I closed them against the dream, shaking my head to clear it.

The *Ri* was talking to Aiden, telling him it was over, the Queen was gone.

"Rynni," said Owain, using my pet name, "you're not dreaming."

When I looked again, I saw Ionwyn. She held Carrick in her arms.

Finally I turned back to the Aiden-dream. I lifted a hand to his cheek and touched his tunic one more time and felt his warm arm beneath the sleeve. He wasn't a ghost risen from the grave to break my heart.

He was real.

"It's me, Ryn," he whispered. "I promise. I'm so sorry we were late. We fought so long and traveled to the castle as soon as we could, but the Queen had already brought you here."

I covered my face with my hands and cried.

But he wouldn't let me cry, oh no. Aiden crushed me to him and laughed into my hair, that soft chuckle of his that let me know all was right with the world.

The moment he released me, Cadan held me at arm's length. "You were right, Ryn! Right about the nettles and the tunics and maybe even your bargain with the Queen, do you hear me?" There were tears in his eyes too. They he caught me up with a whoop and swung me in circles. "I've never been so glad for nettle-nonsense in my life!"

And then to Gavyn and Declan and Owain, dear Owain who had grown so much taller than me. But I threw myself at him and felt him lift me high. He'd been a boy when this started, a boy with smooth cheeks who thought he'd outgrown his twin.

Finally I turned to Mael. He pulled me close.

I felt the brush of feathers and looked down.

Mael had wrapped a black wing around me.

No.

Mael shook his head and smiled. "The tunic was perfect, Ryn-girl. But it was torn in the fight at the cave, and I didn't notice until we were running here. And I wasn't about to make them stop and find some solution.

We guessed you might have only seconds, and we were right, Finn says."

I shook my head.

Mael swiped away my tears with his thumb. "None of that. You gave us six years. A wing is nothing, you hear me?"

Then he glanced over my shoulder at my brothers gathered near and smiled. "It's your turn, Ryn. What do you have to say?"

I looked up at him, my breath stuttering in my throat. For six years, I'd waited to speak. I'd imagined what I'd say a thousand times, the words I'd throw at the Queen, the curse I'd send out into the world.

I'd given her six years of speech. I wouldn't let her have those first words too.

The first light spilled over the treetops and across the land until my brothers were blinking in it. Aiden held a hand against the sunrise but didn't look away. It was the first time he'd seen daylight in six years.

I walked to him and spoke his name, nothing more. "Aiden."

It was enough.

The wind didn't roar over us to pull them away. They didn't turn back into swans.

I could speak!

I turned to Mael, grasping the front of his nettle tunic in my excitement. "Mael." Then the rest of my brothers: "Declan. Gavyn. Cadan. Owain."

Each name was like a spring thaw, melting my frozen throat after all these years.

I turned back to Carrick, still in Aiden's arms, and took his dear face in my hands. "Carrick!"

His eyes opened wide and he held his arms out to me. I took him, and he buried his face in my shoulder. "I have so much to tell you," I whispered against his hair. "I want to tell you about Tanwen."

I closed my eyes against the tears. I'd longed to speak her name to Carrick for so long.

"Andaryn."

I kept my lips against Carrick's soft curls, even though the *Ri*'s voice made me want to laugh and cry, run and stay all at once.

"Andaryn. That's your true name, isn't it?"

I turned to face him, and Aiden plucked Carrick from my arms.

Oh, he belonged in the sunlight! He was gold all over, the sun warm on his skin, his hair looking like the spun gold of Ionwyn's stories.

The *Ri*—Corbin—glanced at Aiden and dipped his head as a sign of respect. Aiden nodded.

So they'd spoken already. I'd expected my brothers would demand an introduction, that I'd have to tell Cadan to behave and Mael not to kill him—

Suddenly I wished I could, just so I could get used to words on my tongue before having to talk to the *Ri*.

The way he smiled at me made it hard enough to talk anyway.

"Ryn," began Cadan, and I turned to him, relieved at the reprieve. But Cadan was mock-scowling at me. "You can talk now. It may just be me, but I think he'd love to hear what you have to say"—Cadan saluted the *Ri*—"and frankly, I think he'd be happy with *anything* you have to say."

He gave me a gentle shove toward Corbin.

Corbin still held the spindle in his hand.

"Princess Andaryn." He winced at the unfamiliar title, then shook his head. "Forgive me! Leaving you was all I knew to do." He half-smiled. "You told me you had six brothers, and when . . . my mother mentioned the six men you traveled with—I knew. I knew I had to hunt them to save them. I thought it was what you'd want." He shrugged, shoulders bending under his sadness. "Didn't I tell you I envied you the memory of your mother? That I knew what it was to have a heartless one?"

I nodded.

He looked down at the spindle, tossing and catching it in his hand. Finally, he held the spindle up. "Do you want it?"

It would be almost like a talisman. I'd hang it over the door to remind myself that the Queen had been thwarted, that I'd carried her undoing with me the entire time.

Then I looked back. Cadan lifted his hands as if asking why I was taking so long. I looked at my other brothers, at Carrick held in his father's arms.

I had all the reminders I needed.

I held my hand out, and Corbin gave me the spindle, his fingers brushing my palm. I strode to the shore and hurled the spindle as far as I could, watching it tumble and spin before it splashed into the lake.

I'd planned to tell him so many things! But all I could manage was, "I don't want to see it again."

I saw the rise of his chest when I finally spoke to him.

"What *do* you want, Princess?" He shook his head. "Ah! I say that word and I think I'm talking to another person. What is it you want, my Lady Ryn? For that's who you are to me. I know what *I* want."

Run. It was as clear as it had ever been, the command like thunder inside me.

With my last bit of strength, I ran. I didn't stop as I neared him, and he opened his arms the way a castle throws open its gates.

He caught me, half spinning me, his arms around my waist.

"Are you sure, my Lady Ryn?" he asked, then glanced at my brothers. "Are you certain, Princess?"

"Yes," I whispered, resting my palms against his chest. "Yes, Corbin."

I'd wanted to say his name for so long.

And perhaps he'd waited just as long to hear it, for he grew perfectly still.

And then the words came as thick as rain or tears, and I couldn't stop. "I wanted to tell you so many times, but I didn't know how. There was no way to draw my story. And what if I hurt you? What if she—?"

He rested his forehead against mine, his arms tight around my waist, as if I was his home, his castle. "She'd cut me long ago, my heart. Long ago."

For six years, I'd longed for speech, but now that I

could speak, I didn't know what to say. "She turned them to swans six years ago—and I agreed to it, six years of silence if she'd just set them free."

"Your brothers told me everything."

I nodded. "But *I* want to tell you. I want you to hear it from me. Besides, Cadan exaggerates."

Corbin peered over my shoulder. "Which one is he?"

"The loud one with the tunic made out of the cloak."

"Ahh." And he smiled down at me. "Tell me your story, Lady Ryn."

So I did.

⁎ ⁎ ⁎

I filled the next hour with speech, though I wished for silence all over again when I had to tell my brothers about Father.

The one small consolation was that he died as himself and not as the Queen's pawn.

By the end of the day, Corbin had arranged provisions so that the next day we could return with soldiers to Lacharra to set things right. Our country had made many enemies with the Queen's constant battling. We couldn't afford to leave it without a ruler for long.

After my brothers went to their beds, I lingered by the hall's fireplace, tracing pictures in the soot, grateful for the familiarity of it. Everything—almost everything—I'd longed for had come to pass. The old life I'd fought to reclaim had been won. Why did I feel like a stranger in it?

"Lady Ryn."

I turned to Corbin.

When the last of the fire's light flickered over his face, I saw the concern. "My lady Ryn, you've told me your story, but you've not yet told me how it ends."

"I must return to Lacharra," I said.

Corbin nodded slowly. "Of course."

"But first—" I stepped forward, suddenly uncertain.

"Yes?"

I stamped my foot, angry at my cowardice. "I told you what I wanted to do the day I could speak, but now that it's here, now that we're alone, I don't know if I can. I have to go back to Lacharra, you see."

The side of his mouth twitched and he stepped forward. "You already said that."

"Because it's true! And it'll take months, and—"

He grinned.

I kissed him. And when he kissed me back, every word flew from my mind. And he wasn't nearly close enough. I looped my arms around his neck and then I kissed him the way I'd wanted to for so long.

Because sometimes, words aren't enough.

ӿ ӿ ӿ

I returned with my brothers to Lacharra and remained there long enough to slip the shard of rock back into the Kingstone. It didn't fit perfectly. Six years had worn off the sharp edges so that anyone could see the violence that had happened, even after the Kingstone was whole again.

Before I returned to Corbin, I visited the library. The nobles told us that Father never visited the library after he'd banished his children, and I believed them. I found *The Annals of Lacharra* on the table where I'd left it years ago, buried under other books.

I sat one last time in Father's chair and opened it.

I smelled the faintest scent of cloves.

And I traced the figure of the Cynwrig crest at the top of the page.

I hadn't come here to mourn the time lost between Father and me. I came to celebrate his return to me, even if it had only been for a few moments.

I gathered six years of memories, moments as small as cloves, as common as nettles: my childhood in Lacharra, the Queen's curse, six years of hiding with my brothers.

They were all *my* Before: a story that could not be stolen or silenced.

I read aloud:

"The flight of swans, bearing swords . . ."

The library's silence fell away. I could hear Father's voice above and below mine, the way the rush of the ocean fills the empty spaces between words.

I heard Owain-the-hen's low, rolling clucks.

I heard Tanwen's voice, fire and laughter.

I heard Cadan saying he'd always call for me.

I heard Corbin calling me *Lady Wyn* when others had seen only a mad girl.

My voice filled the library, strong and sure. When I

reached the end of what Father had read, I marked the page with a strand of nettle yarn I'd cut from one of the tunics, and—

"Ryn?" Cadan poked his head in the library door. "I've been looking for ages! Carrick—"

He stopped when he saw me at Father's old place.

I motioned him to go on. "Carrick?"

Cadan raised an eyebrow. "Carrick walked into the kitchen and proceeded to eat every *single* sweet those soft-headed women fed him. He's crying fit to bring the walls down, and his new nursemaid doesn't know what to do. Aiden's in a meeting with his top lords, Mael is flirting with Landon's oldest daughter, who doesn't mind a black swan wing half as much as I predicted—" He drew a deep breath and hurried on: "Declan's trying to sing Carrick calm while Gavyn checks his books to see if anyone ever died from eating too many sweets, and Owain—"

Owain, sporting a beard that even Aiden would admire, joined Cadan at the door. "*I* was sent to discover what was taking Cadan so long!"

I laughed and didn't once think about holding it inside me. "I'm coming! Half a second and I'll be there."

I closed *The Annals of Lacharra,* leaving the nettle yarn pressed between its pages.

"Hurry, Ryn!" said Cadan. "Or Declan will be crying too."

"I'm ashamed to call you my brothers, every last one of you!" I called back. "I used to comfort that little man alone. *And* without being able to make a sound."

One last glance out the library window, past the forest, to where the island of Eyre lay beyond the horizon. In a week, I'd begin my journey back to Fianna. And Corbin.

My future lay ahead of me.

"I'm coming," I said.

Acknowledgments

I was told that sophomore novels were the hardest to write. I didn't believe it two years ago, but oh-my-word, I believe it now. Many times, *The Flight of Swans* felt like a marathon. Through the mountains. In the rain. Or relentless sun. (Whichever is worse.)

So I am deeply grateful for everyone who helped me reach the finish line:

My agent, Tracey Adams. I still can't quite believe I'm fortunate enough to be represented by such a rock star.

My editor, Alix Reid. Her unfailing patience and key insights helped me unravel some of the story's most tangled knots.

The entire team of people who take an author's words, turn them into a book, and then get that book onto bookshelves: designer Emily Harris, art director Danielle Carnito, production editor Erica Johnson, marketing manager Livy Traczyk, and marketing associate Libby Stille. Thanks also to copy editor Julie Harman (who I hope has forgiven my inability to distinguish between *further* and *farther*) and Junyi Wu for the amazing cover art.

All the teachers and librarians and bloggers who champion both books and their readers.

The women who helped me with the details of nettle-craft: Krista Rahm of Forrest Green Farm, who spent part of an afternoon teaching me about stinging nettles and sent me home with the nettles I harvested. Ann Vonnegut, who taught me how to use a drop spindle. (And Michelle, who introduced us.) Any mistakes are mine, not theirs.

The hen-whisperers, who helped me with Owain-the-hen: Maya, Lisa, Laura, Katy, and Martha.

Julie Dillard, who asked why nettles were so important and wouldn't accept "Because they were good enough for the Brothers Grimm and Hans Christian Anderson" as an answer. I wrote one of my favorite chapters after that conversation.

The Slushbusters, my critique group that still gives spot-on feedback.

My LYLP girls who read key portions and listened to the ups and downs of writing and selling books.

The amazing SCBWI community that has encouraged, taught, critiqued, and befriended me. What a joy it is to write with such talented, warm-hearted people!

Everyone at the 2015 Hood River Breakout Novel Intensive who helped me tackle this tale: Don, Lorin, Brenda, and Jason.

My family and friends. I am so, so grateful for you and wish I had another page to list all the ways that you are awesome.

Fred, who understands deadlines and celebrates hitting send, even though he wishes I wrote more explosions. I'm glad you asked me out for smoothies.

Topics for Discussion

1. How does Ryn's connection to the House of Cynwrig affect her actions? Why is the difference between "game of swans" and "flight of swans" so important?
2. Why is the Kingstone so important to Ryn and the Queen? Do you think Ryn does the right thing when her father demands she give part of it to the Queen?
3. List some of the things Ryn fears throughout the book. Which of those do you think she fears most, and why?
4. Ryn demonstrates her bravery many times over throughout the book. What do you think is her first brave decision? The hardest decision?
5. Where do you think Ryn's bravery comes from? Where does your bravery come from?
6. Does Ryn have a favorite brother? How does she recognize her brothers even when they are swans?
7. What are different ways that Ryn communicates? How would you communicate if you couldn't speak or write?
8. How does Ryn try to protect her brothers, and how do they try to protect her?

9. Why do you think Ryn's brothers don't always believe her? Do you think you would have believed her? Have there been times when you weren't believed?

10. Ionwyn talked about how a person could be the "turning point" in a story and cause everything to change. List characters that you think influenced Ryn during the six years of enchantment. Explain why you chose them.

11. How does Ryn change throughout her six years of silence? How does she stay the same?

12. What was Ryn's original opinion of the kingdoms of Eyre? How does her opinion change when she lives in the kingdom of Fianna?

13. What do the *Ri*, Tanwen, Finn, and the people of Fianna think of Ryn and Carrick when they first arrive at Castle Hill? How do their attitudes change, and what do you think causes that change?

14. Why doesn't Ryn want to face the Queen alone after her brothers are enchanted? Does she ever change her mind? Why or why not?

15. Now that the enchantment has ended and the Queen has returned to the Otherworld, what do you think the future holds for Lacharra and Fianna?

16. Compare and contrast *The Flight of Swans* with the original story, "Six Swans" (or Andersen's "Wild Swans"). What would you have changed or kept the same if you were retelling the story?

About the Author

Sarah McGuire is a nomadic math teacher who sailed around the world aboard a floating college campus. She writes fairy tale retellings and still hopes that one day she'll open a wardrobe and stumble into another world. Coffee and chocolate are her rocket fuel. She wishes Florida had mountains, but she lives there anyway with her husband (who wrote this bio in less than three minutes!) and their family.